What I Did for Love

ALSO BY SUSAN ELIZABETH PHILLIPS

What I Did for Love

Susan Elizabeth Phillips

HARPER LUXE

An Imprint of HarperCollinsPublishers

WHAT I DID FOR LOVE. Copyright © 2009 by Susan Elizabeth Phillips. All rights reserved. Printed in the United States of America. No part of this book may be used or reproduced in any manner whatsoever without written permission except in the case of brief quotations embodied in critical articles and reviews. For information address HarperCollins Publishers, 10 East 53rd Street, New York, NY 10022.

HarperCollins books may be purchased for educational, business, or sales promotional use. For information please write: Special Markets Department, HarperCollins Publishers, 10 East 53rd Street, New York, NY 10022.

FIRST HARPERLUXE EDITION

HarperLuxe™ is a trademark of HarperCollins Publishers

Library of Congress Cataloging-in-Publication Data is available upon request.

ISBN: 978-0-06-171984-4

09 10 11 12 13 ID/RRD 10 9 8 7 6 5 4 3 2 1

In memory of Kate Fleming/Anna Fields

There aren't enough words to fill
the silence you've left behind.
We grieve your loss and miss you
more than we can ever say.

Chapter 1

The jackals swarmed her as she stepped out into the late April afternoon. When Georgie had ducked into the perfume shop on Beverly Boulevard, only three of them had been stalking her, but now there were fifteen—twenty—maybe more—a howling, feral pack loose in L.A., cameras unsheathed, ready to rip the last bit of flesh from her bones.

Their strobes blinded her. She told herself she could handle whatever they threw at her. Hadn't she been doing exactly that for the past year? They began to shout their rude questions—too many questions, too fast, too loud, words running together until nothing made sense. One of them shoved something in her hands—a tabloid—and screamed into her ear. "This just hit the stands, Georgie. What do you have to say?"

Georgie automatically glanced down, and there on the front page of *Flash* was a sonogram of a baby. Lance and Jade's baby. The baby that should have been hers.

All the blood rushed from her head. The strobes fired, the cameras snapped, and the back of her hand flew to her mouth. After so many months of holding it together, she lost her way, and her eyes flooded with tears.

The cameras caught everything—the hand at her mouth, the tears in her eyes. She'd finally given the jackals what they'd spent the past year preying to capture—photographs of funny, thirty-one-year-old Georgie York with her life shattered around her.

She dropped the tabloid and turned to flee, but they'd trapped her. She tried to back up, but they were behind her, in front of her, surrounding her with their hot strobes and heartless shouts. Their smell clogged her nostrils—sweat, cigarettes, acrid cologne. Someone stepped on her foot. An elbow caught her in the side. They pressed closer, stealing her air, suffocating her. . . .

Bramwell Shepard watched the nasty scene unfold from the restaurant steps next door. He'd just emerged from lunch when the commotion broke out, and he paused at the top of the steps to take it in. He hadn't seen Georgie York in a couple of years, and then it had only been a glimpse. Now, as he watched the paparazzi attack, the old, bitter feelings returned.

His higher position on the steps gave him a vantage point to observe the chaos. Some of the paps held their cameras over their heads; others shoved their lenses in her face. She'd been dealing with the press since she was a kid, but nothing could have prepared her for the pandemonium of this past year. Too bad there were no heroes waiting around to rescue her.

Bram had spent eight miserable years rescuing Georgie from thorny situations, but his days of playing gallant Skip Scofield to Georgie's spunky Scooter Brown were long behind him. This time Scooter Brown could save her own ass—or, more likely, wait around for Daddy to do it.

The paparazzi hadn't spotted him. He wasn't on their radar screens these days, not that he wouldn't have been if they could ever catch him in the same frame with Georgie. *Skip and Scooter* had been one of the most successful sitcoms in television history. Eight years on the air, eight years off, but the public hadn't forgotten, especially when it came to America's favorite good girl, Scooter Brown, as played in real life by Georgie York.

A better man might have felt sorry for her current predicament, but he'd only worn the hero badge on-screen. His mouth twisted as he looked down at her. *How's your spunky, can-do attitude working for you these days, Scooter?*

Things suddenly took an uglier turn. Two of the paps got into a shoving match, and one of them bumped her hard. She lost her balance and started to fall, and as she fell her head came up, and that's when she spotted him. Through the madness, the wild jockeying and crazy shoving, through the clamor and chaos, she somehow spotted him standing there barely thirty feet away. Her face registered a jolt of shock, not from the fall—she'd somehow caught herself before both knees hit—but from the sight of him. Their eyes locked, the cameras pressed closer, and the plea for help written on her face made her look like a kid again. He stared at her—not moving—simply taking in those gumdrop-green eyes, still hopeful that one more present might be left for her beneath the Christmas tree. Then her eyes clouded, and he saw the exact moment when she realized he wasn't going to help her—that he was the same selfish bastard he'd always been.

What the hell did she expect? When had she ever been able to count on him for anything? Her funny girl's face twisted with contempt, and she turned her attention back to fighting off the cameras.

He belatedly realized he was missing a golden opportunity, and he started down the steps, but he'd waited too long. She'd already thrown the first punch. It wasn't a good punch, but it did the job, and a couple of the paps stepped in to form a wedge so she could get to her car. She flung herself inside and, moments later, peeled away from the curb. As she plunged erratically into the Friday-afternoon L.A. traffic, the paparazzi raced to their illegally parked black SUVs and took off after her.

If the restaurant's valet service hadn't chosen that moment to deliver his Audi, Bram would probably have dismissed the incident, but as he slid behind the wheel, his curiosity got the best of him. Where did a tabloid princess go to lick her wounds when she had no place left to hide?

The lunch he'd just sat through had been a bust, and he had nothing better to do with his time, so he decided to fall in behind the paparazzi cavalcade. Although he couldn't see her Prius, he could tell by the way the paps wove through the traffic that Georgie was driving erratically. She cut over toward Sunset. He flipped on the radio, flipped it back off, pondered his current situation. His mind began to toy with an intriguing scenario.

Eventually, the cavalcade hit the PCH heading north, and that's when it struck him. Her likely destination. He rubbed his thumb over the top of the steering wheel.

And wasn't life full of interesting coincidences . . .

Georgie wished she could peel off her skin and give it away. She didn't want to be Georgie York anymore. She wanted to be a person with dignity and self-respect.

Behind the tinted windows of her Prius, she swiped at her nose with the back of her hand. Once she'd made the world laugh. Now, despite all her efforts, she'd become the poster girl for heartbreak and humiliation. The only comfort she'd been able to take through the whole debacle of her divorce was knowing that the paparazzi's cameras had never, ever caught her without her head up. Even on the worst day of her life—the day her husband left her for Jade Gentry—Georgie had managed one of Scooter Brown's trademark grins and a goofy pinup pose for the jackals that stalked her. But today that final remnant of pride had been stolen away. And Bram Shepard had witnessed it.

Her stomach churned. She'd last seen him at a party a couple of years ago. He'd been surrounded by women—no surprise. She'd left right away.

A horn blared. She couldn't face her empty house or the public pity party that had become her life, and she found herself headed to her old friend Trevor Elliott's beach house in Malibu. Even though she'd been on the road for nearly an hour, her heart rate wouldn't slow. Little by little, she'd lost the two things that mattered the most—her husband and her pride. Three things, if she tossed in the gradual disintegration of her career. And now this. Jade Gentry was carrying the baby Georgie had yearned for.

Trevor answered the door. "Are you crazy?" He grabbed her wrist, jerked her into the cool foyer, then stuck his head back out, but his L-shaped entry offered enough privacy to shield her from the paps who'd be pulling over on the shoulder of the Pacific Coast Highway.

"It's safe," she said, an ironic statement, since nothing felt safe these days.

He rubbed his hand over his shaved head. "By tonight's *E! News,* they'll have us married and you pregnant."

If only, she thought as she followed him into the house.

She'd met Trevor fourteen years ago on the set of *Skip and Scooter* when he'd played Skip's dim-witted friend Harry, but he'd left his second-banana roles behind long ago to star in a series of successful gross-out comedies that were required viewing for eighteen-year-old males. Last Christmas she'd given him a T-shirt that read I BRAKE FOR FART JOKES.

Although he was barely five foot eight, he had a nicely proportioned body and pleasant, slightly cock-eyed features that made him perfect to play the goofy loser who still managed to come out on top. "I shouldn't have barged in," she said without meaning it.

He silenced the baseball game playing on his plasma TV, then frowned at her appearance. She knew she'd lost more weight than her naturally slender dancer's body could spare. It was heartache, not anorexia, that made her stomach rebel.

"Any reason you haven't returned my last two phone calls?" he said.

She started to take off her sunglasses, then thought better of it. Nobody wanted to see the tears of a clown, not even the clown's good friend. "Hey, I'm way too self-absorbed to care about anybody but myself."

"That's not true." His voice warmed with sympathy. "You look like you could use a drink."

"There's not enough alcohol in the world . . . But, yes."

"I don't hear any helicopters. Go sit on the deck. I'll make margaritas."

As he disappeared into the kitchen, she finally slipped off her sunglasses and forced herself across the speckled terrazzo floor to the powder room so she could repair the damage from the paps' attack.

With her weight loss, her round face had begun collapsing under her cheekbones, and her big eyes would have eaten up her face if her mouth weren't so wide. She shoved a lock of her stick-straight, cherry-cola hair behind her ear. In an attempt to lift her spirits and soften the new hard edges of her face, she'd adopted a choppy update of a bowl cut, with long, feathery bangs and sides that curved around her cheeks. In her *Skip and Scooter* days, she'd been forced to keep her dark hair tightly permed and dyed a clownish carrot-orange because the producers wanted to capitalize on her megasuccessful run in the Broadway revival of *Annie.* That humiliating hairstyle had also emphasized the contrast between her funny-girl appearance and Skip Scofield's dreamboat good looks.

She'd always had a conflicted relationship with her baby-doll cheeks, googly green eyes, and stretchy mouth. On the one hand, her unconventional features had brought her fame, but in a city like Hollywood, where even the supermarket checkout clerks were bombshells, it had been hard not being beautiful. Not that she cared anymore. But when she'd been the wife of Lance Marks, the town's biggest action-adventure superstar, she'd definitely cared.

Exhaustion crept through her. She hadn't taken a dance class in six months—she could barely get out of bed.

She repaired the damage to her eye makeup as best she could, then returned to the living room. Trevor had only recently moved into the house he'd decorated with amoeba-shaped midcentury furniture. He must have been taking a trip down memory lane because a book lay open on the coffee table, a history of the American television sitcom. The original *Skip and Scooter* cast photo stared back at her. She looked away.

On the deck, white stucco planters filled with tall greenery provided a measure of privacy from any gapers walking the beach. She kicked off her sandals and slumped into an aqua-and-brown-striped chaise. The ocean stretched beyond the white tubular railing. A few surfers had paddled just past the break line, but the sea was too calm today for a decent ride, and their surfboards bobbed on the water like fetuses floating in amniotic fluid.

A surge of pain stole her breath. She and Lance had been the fairy-tale couple. He was the macho prince who'd seen through her ugly-duckling exterior to the beautiful soul beneath. She was the adoring wife who'd given him the steadfast love he needed. During their two-year courtship and one-year marriage, the tabloids had followed them everywhere, but she still hadn't been prepared for the frenzy that had erupted when Lance had left her for Jade Gentry.

In private, she lay in bed, barely able to move. In public, she kept a smile plastered on her face. But no matter how high she held her head, the pity stories only grew worse.

The tabloids screamed:

Brave Georgie's Heartbreak
Valiant Georgie Suicidal as Lance Declares, "I never knew real love until I met Jade Gentry"
Georgie Wasting Away! Friends Fear for Her Life

Even though Lance had a much more successful film career, she was still Scooter Brown, America's sweetheart, and the tide of public sentiment turned against him for abandoning such a beloved television icon. Lance launched his own counterattack. *"Unnamed sources say that Lance desperately wanted children, but Georgie was too busy with her career to take time out for a family."*

She'd never forgive him for that lie.

Trevor came out on the deck balancing a white leather tray with margarita glasses and a matching pitcher. He gallantly ignored the tears trickling from beneath her sunglasses. "The bar is officially open."

"Thanks, pal." She took the frosty margarita from him and swiped at her cheeks as he turned away to set the tray on the white patio table. She couldn't talk to him about the sonogram. Even her best friends didn't realize how much having a baby meant to her. That pain had been a secret one. A secret today's photos would expose to the world.

"We wrapped *Cake Walk* last Friday," she said. "Another bomb." She couldn't afford three box-office flops in a row, and that's what she'd have once *Cake Walk* was released. She set her drink on the deck without tasting it. "Dad's really upset about this six-month vacation I'm taking."

He sank into a molded plastic tulip chair. "You've been working practically since you came out of the womb. Paul needs to cut you some slack."

"Yeah, that'll happen all right."

"You know the way I feel about how he pushes you. I'm not saying another word."

"Don't." She was already too familiar with Trev's generally accurate opinion of her difficult relationship with her father. She wrapped her arms around her knees and pulled them tight to her stomach. "Divert me with some good gossip."

"My costar gets crazier every day. If I even think about doing another film with that woman, kill me." He adjusted his chair so his shaved head was in the shade. "Did you know she and Bram used to date?"

Her stomach clenched. "Birds of a feather."

"He's house-sitting—"

She held up her hand. "Stop. I can't talk about Bramwell Shepard. Especially not today." Bram would have watched her get trampled to death this afternoon and never lost the smile on his face. God, she hated him, even after all these years.

Trev mercifully changed the subject without questioning her. "You saw last week's *USA Today* poll, right? Favorite sitcom heroines? Scooter Brown came in third after Lucy and Mary Tyler Moore. You even beat out Barbara Eden."

She'd seen the poll and couldn't bring herself to care. "I hate Scooter Brown."

"You're the only one who does. She's an icon. It's anti-American not to love her."

"The series has been off the air for eight years. Why can't everybody let it go?"

"Maybe those perpetual reruns blasting out all over the globe have something to do with it?"

She pushed her sunglasses on top of her head. "I was a kid when the show started, only fifteen. And barely twenty-three when it ended."

He took in her red eyes but didn't comment on them. "Scooter Brown is ageless. Every woman's best friend. Every man's favorite virgin."

"But I'm not Scooter Brown. I'm Georgie York. My life belongs to me, not to the world."

"Good luck with that."

She couldn't let herself do this any longer. Perpetually reacting to external forces. Unable to set her own counterforces in motion. Always acted upon. Never acting. She drew her knees closer and studied the rainbows she'd asked her manicurist to paint on her toenails in the vain hope of cheering herself up. If she didn't do this now, she never would. "Trev, what would you think about you and me having a little—a *big* romance?"

"Romance?"

"The two of us." She couldn't look at him, and she kept her eyes on the rainbows. "Falling very publicly in love. And . . . maybe—" She pushed out the words. "Trev, I've been thinking about this for a long time . . . I know you're going to think it's crazy. It *is* crazy. But . . . If you don't hate the idea, I was thinking . . . we should at least consider the possibility of . . . getting married."

"Married?" Trevor's feet hit the deck.

He was one of her dearest friends, but her cheeks burned. Still, what was one more monumentally humiliating moment in a year filled with them? She unlocked her arms from her knees. "I know I shouldn't be dumping this on you out of nowhere. And I know it's weird. Really weird. I felt that way when I first started thinking about it, but when I considered it objectively, I couldn't see a big downside."

"Georgie, I'm gay."

"You're *rumored* to be gay."

"I'm also really gay."

"But you're so deep in the closet hardly anybody knows." The fresh scrape on her ankle stung as she eased her legs over the side of the chaise. "This would finally put an end to the rumors. Face it, Trev. If the frat-boy crowd ever finds out you're playing for their team, your career is gone."

"Don't you think I know that?" He rubbed his hand over his shaved head. "Georgie, your life is a circus, and as much as I adore you, I don't want to be dragged into the center ring."

"That's the point. If you and I were together, the circus would stop." As he sat back down, she went to his side and knelt there. "Trev, just think about it. We've always gotten along. We'd be able to live our lives the way we want—without any interference from each other. Think about how much more freedom you'd have—we'd both have." She rested her cheek against his knee, just for a moment, then sat back on her heels. "You and I aren't an odd couple like Lance and I were. Trevor and Georgie are a boring match, and after the first couple of months, the press will leave us alone. We could live under the radar. You wouldn't need to keep going out with all those women you have to pretend to be interested in. You could see who you wanted. Our marriage would be the perfect cover for you." And for her, it would be a way to make the world stop its pity party. She'd have both her public dignity back and a kind of insurance policy to keep her from ever again throwing herself off an emotional cliff for a man.

"Think about it, Trev. Please." She needed to let him get used to the idea before she mentioned children. "Think how liberating it would be."

"I'm not marrying you."

"Me either." A horrifyingly familiar voice drifted across the deck. "I'd rather stop drinking."

Georgie shot to her feet and watched Bramwell Shepard saunter up the stairs from the beach. He stopped at the top, his mouth quirking with calculated amusement.

She sucked in her breath.

"Don't let me interrupt." He leaned against the rail. "This is the most interesting conversation I've eavesdropped on since Scooter and her friends debated dyeing their pubic hair. Trev, why didn't you tell me you're a fairy? Now we can't ever be seen in public together again."

Unlike Georgie, Trevor seemed relieved by the interruption, and he pointed his margarita glass in the general direction of Bram's sun-drenched head. "You fixed me up with my last boyfriend."

"I must have been wasted." Her former costar took her in. "Speaking of wasted . . . You look like crap."

She had to get out of here. She glanced toward the doors that led back into the house, but a frail ember of dignity still lingered in the ashes of her self-respect, and she couldn't let him see her run. "What are you doing here?" she said. "This isn't an accident."

He nodded toward the pitcher. "You two aren't really drinking that shit, are you?"

"I'm sure you remember where I keep the real liquor." Trev eyed her with concern.

"Later." Bram folded his long frame onto the chaise across from the one where Georgie had been sitting. The sand clinging to his calves sparkled like tiny diamonds. The breeze frolicked in his crisp golden-bronze hair. Her stomach twisted. A beautiful debauched angel.

The image had come from an essay written by a well-known television critic not long after the debacle that had ended one of the most successful television shows in history. She still remembered.

We can imagine Bram Shepard in heaven, his face so perfect the other angels can't bring themselves to cast him out even though he's drunk up all the sacred wine, seduced the pretty virgin angels, and stolen a harp to replace the one he gambled away in a celestial poker game. We watch him endanger the entire flock by flying too close to the sun, then plunging too recklessly toward the sea. But the angel community is mesmerized by the fields of lavender in his eyes, the rays of sun weaving through his hair, so they forgive him his transgressions . . . until his last dangerous plunge drives them all into the muck.

Bram rested his head on the back of the chaise, a position that outlined his still-flawless profile against the sky. At thirty-three, the softer edges of his pleasure-seeking youth had hardened, making his lazy, glittering beauty even more destructive. Bronze threaded his blond hair, cynicism tainted his choirboy's lavender eyes, and mockery lurked at the corners of his perfectly symmetrical mouth.

The fact that someone so utterly without scruples had overheard her conversation with Trevor made her ill. She couldn't flee, not yet, but her legs were giving out. "Why are you here?" She sank into one of the tulip chairs.

"I started to tell you," Trev said. "Bram sometimes uses my other house down the beach, the one I'm trying to sell. Since he's made himself unemployable, he doesn't have anything better to do than laze around and bother me."

"I'm not exactly unemployable." Bram crossed his sandy ankles. Even the arches of his feet were as gracefully curved as the blade of a scimitar. "Just last week I got an offer to humiliate myself on a new reality TV show. If I hadn't been stoned when the call came in, I'd probably have accepted. Just as well." He waved an elegant hand. "Too much work."

"Point made," Trev said.

She frantically scanned the sand for photographers. This was a private beach, but the press would do anything to get a photo of her with Bram again. Skip and Scooter publicly reunited after all this time. Her stomach churned at the thought of someone as predictably evil as Bram Shepard becoming part of her public nightmare.

He leaned back and closed his eyes again. He looked like a bored aristocrat taking in the sun—a deceptive image, since he was a high school dropout who'd been raised on Chicago's South Side by a deadbeat father. "I hope you hid your razor blades, Trev. Word is that our Scooter has a death wish now that life's dealt her such a cruel blow. Personally, I think she should celebrate finally getting rid of that moron she married. Jade Gentry must have lost her mind to let herself be taken in by Mr. All-American. Tell me the truth, Scoot. Lance Marks can't get it up, can he?"

"I see you're still a perfect gentleman. How reassuring." She had to escape without looking like she was running away. She made a play of slowly rising from the chair and sauntering over to fetch her sandals. Too late, she realized she couldn't remember where she'd left them.

He opened his eyes and gave her the lazy, mocking smile that had annihilated so many otherwise sensible women. "I read that the happy couple is back on foreign shores doing more of their well-publicized good work."

Lance and Jade had spent their honeymoon on a humanitarian trip to Thailand. She'd never forget their press release. "*We want to use our celebrity to spotlight Jade's pet cause, the exploitation of children in the sex industry.*"

Georgie didn't have a pet cause, at least nothing that went beyond writing some generous checks. She looked frantically around for her shoes.

Bram pointed the tip of a lean finger toward the base of the chaise where she'd been sitting earlier. "Their campaign to beef up laws against child-sex tourists is heartwarming. And while they're battling Congress, I hear you've been power shopping at Fred Segal."

Just like that, her self-control snapped. "I truly hate you."

"Impossible. Scooter could never hate her beloved Skip. Not after he spent eight years of his life getting her out of those crazy little jams."

She grabbed the sandals and shoved in one foot.

"Stop it, Bram," Trev said.

But Bram wasn't done with her. "Remember when you fell in the lake wearing Mother Scofield's fur coat? Or what about the time you released that cage of mice at her annual Christmas party?"

If she didn't react to his baiting, he'd stop.

But Bram had always loved slow torture. "Even on our wedding day, you got into trouble. A good thing we never actually shot that show. I heard I was going to knock you up on our honeymoon. If the network hadn't pulled the plug, I would have sired a little Skip."

Her fury erupted. "It wasn't a little Skip! It was twins! We were supposed to have *twins*—a girl and a boy. Obviously, you were too high to remember that small detail."

"Immaculate conception, I'm sure. Can you imagine Scooter naked and—"

She couldn't take any more, and she spun toward the house, one shoe on, one in her hand.

"I wouldn't go, if I were you," he said lazily. "Ten minutes ago, I spotted a photographer crawling into those shrubs across the road. Someone must have seen your car."

She was trapped.

He raked her with his eyes, one of his many unpleasant habits. "You haven't taken up smoking by any chance, have you, Scoot? I need a cigarette, and Trev refuses to keep a carton around for his guests. He's such a Boy Scout." Bram arched a flawless eyebrow. "Except for his filthy habits with members of his own sex."

Trevor tried to ease the tension. "You know I only put up with him because I secretly lust after his buff body. Such a pity he's straight."

"You're too fastidious to lust after him," she retorted.

"Look again," Trev said dryly.

It wasn't fair. Bram should be dead by now, killed by his own excesses, but the bony body she remembered from *Skip and Scooter* had grown tough, its wasted elegance transformed into hard muscle and long sinew. Beneath the sleeve of his white T-shirt a tribal tattoo banded a formidable bicep, and his navy swim trunks revealed legs with the taut, extended tendons of a distance runner. He wore his thick, bronzed hair rumpled, and the pale skin that had been as much a part of him as a hangover had disappeared. Except for the air of decadence that clung to him like a bad repu-tation, Bram Shepard looked shockingly healthy.

"He works out now," Trev interrupted with an ex-aggerated whisper, as if he were divulging a juicy bit of scandal.

"Bram never worked out a day in his life," she said. "He got those muscles by selling what was left of his soul."

Bram smiled and turned his badass angel's face to her. "Tell me more about this plan of yours to get your pride back by marrying Trev. Not quite as interesting as the pubic hair conversation, but still . . ."

She clenched her teeth. "I swear to God, if you breathe a word to anybody—"

"He won't," Trevor said. "Our Bramwell has never been interested in anybody but himself."

That was so true. But she still couldn't bear know-ing he'd overheard something so humiliating. She and Bram had worked together from the time he was sev-enteen until he was twenty-five. At seventeen, his selfishness had been thoughtless, but as his fame had spread, his behavior had become more deliberately reckless. It wasn't hard to see that he'd only grown more cynical and self-centered.

He drew up his knee. "Aren't you a little young to have given up on true love?"

She felt a hundred years old. Her fairy-tale marriage had failed, putting an end to her dreams of finally having a family of her own and a man who'd love her for herself instead of what she could do for his career. She flipped her sunglasses back over her eyes, weighing the danger of the jackals lurking outside against the danger of the beast in front of her. "I am not talking to you about this."

"Ease up, Bram," Trevor said. "She's had a tough year."

"The downside of being worshipped," Bram replied.

Trev sniffed. "Nothing you'll ever have to worry about."

Bram picked up her abandoned margarita, sipped, and shuddered at the taste. "I've never seen the public take a celebrity divorce so personally. I'm surprised none of your crazed fans set themselves on fire."

"People feel like Georgie's family," Trevor said. "They grew up with Scooter Brown."

Bram set the glass down. "They grew up with me, too."

"But Georgie and Scooter are basically the same person," Trevor pointed out. "You and Skip aren't."

"Thank God." Bram rose from the chaise. "I still hate that uptight little preppy prick."

But Georgie had loved Skip Scofield. She'd loved everything about him. His big heart, his loyalty, the way he'd tried to protect Scooter from the Scofield family. The way he'd eventually fallen in love with her silly round face and rubber-band mouth. She'd loved everything except the man Skip turned into when the cameras stopped rolling.

The three of them had fallen back into their old pattern—Bram on the attack and Trevor defending her. But she wasn't a kid any longer, and she needed to defend herself. "I don't think you hate Skip at all. I think you always wanted to be Skip, but you fell so far short of the mark that you had to pretend to despise him."

Bram yawned. "Maybe you're right. Trev, are you sure no one's left any weed lying around? Or even a cigarette?"

"I'm sure," Trevor said, just as the phone rang. "Don't kill each other while I answer that."

Trevor went inside.

She wanted to punish Bram for being exactly who he was. "I could have been trampled to death today. Thanks for nothing."

"You were handling it. And without Daddy. Now that was the real surprise."

She stared him down. "What do you want, Bram? We both know your showing up here isn't an accident."

He rose, wandered toward the railing, and peered down at the beach. "If Trev had been stupid enough to take you up on your bizarre offer, what would you have done for a sex life?"

"Right. That's something I'm going to talk to you about."

"Who better to confide in?" he said. "I was there at the beginning, remember?"

She couldn't bear another moment, and she spun toward the French doors.

"Just out of curiosity, Scoot . . . ," he said from behind her. "Now that Trev's rejected you, who's next in line to be Mr. Georgie York?"

She pasted on a smile full of mockery and turned back. "Aren't you sweet to tax that big evil head of yours worrying about my future when your own life is such a screwed-up mess." Her hand was trembling, but she gave what she hoped passed for a jaunty wave and went inside. Trev had just gotten off the phone, but she was too drained to do more than ask him to at least consider her idea.

By the time she reached Pacific Palisades, she was so tightly coiled she ached. She ignored the photographer parked at the end of her court and turned into a narrow driveway that curled down to an unassuming pseudo-Mediterranean ranch that could have fit into her former home's swimming pool. She hadn't been able to bear staying in the house where she and Lance had lived. This rental came furnished with bulky pieces that were too heavy for the small rooms, just as the ceilings were too low for the rough wooden beams, but she didn't care enough to look for another place.

She cranked open a bedroom window, then made herself check her voice mail.

"Georgie, I saw the stupid tabloid, and—"

Delete

"Georgie, I'm so sorry—"

Delete

"He's a bastard, kiddo, and you're—"

Delete

Her friends were well meaning—most of them, anyway—but their nonstop sympathy choked her. She wanted to be the one handing out sympathy for a change, not always having to receive it.

"Georgie, call me immediately." Her father's crisp voice filled the room. "There's a photo in the new *Flash* that's bound to upset you. I don't want you to be taken off guard."

Too late, Daddy.

"It's important that you rise to the occasion. I've e-mailed Aaron a statement to post on your Web site telling the world how happy you are for Lance. I'm sure you know—"

She jammed the delete button. Why couldn't her father just once behave like a father instead of a manager? He'd begun building her career when she was five, less than a year after her mother's death. He'd accompanied her to every cattle call, orchestrated her first television commercials, and forced her to take the singing and dancing lessons that had won her the starring role in the Broadway revival of *Annie,* the part that had led to her casting as Scooter Brown. Unlike so many other parents of child stars, her father had made sure her money was wisely invested. Thanks to him, she'd never have to work again, and while she was grateful he'd watched after her money so well, she'd give up every penny to have had a real father.

She stepped back from the phone as she heard Lance's voice. "Georgie, it's me," he said softly. "We arrived in the Philippines yesterday. I just heard about a story in *Flash* . . . I don't know if you've seen it yet.

I—I wanted to tell you myself before you read about it. Jade is pregnant . . ."

She listened to his message all the way to the end. She heard the guilt in his voice, the entreaty, the pride he wasn't a good enough actor to conceal. He still wanted her to forgive him for leaving, to forgive him for lying to the press about how she hadn't wanted a baby. Lance was an actor, with an actor's need for everyone to love him, even the woman whose heart he'd broken. He wanted her to hand him a free pass on guilt. But she couldn't. She'd given him everything. Not just her heart, not just her body, but everything she had, and look where it had taken her.

She sank down against the couch. It had been a year, and here she was. Crying again. When was she going to get over it? When was she going to stop acting exactly like the loser the world believed her to be? If she kept on like this, the bitterness eating away inside her would win, and she'd turn into a person she didn't want to be. She needed to do something—anything— that would make her look—that would make her *feel*— like a winner.

Chapter 2

What would Scooter Brown do? That was the question Georgie kept asking herself, and that was how she ended up crossing the outdoor patio at The Ivy to a table right by the restaurant's famous white picket fence. Scooter Brown, the spunky orphaned stowaway who'd hidden in the servants' quarters of the Scofield estate to keep herself out of foster care, would have taken charge of her own destiny, and it was long past time for Georgie to do exactly that.

She waved at a big-name rapper, acknowledged a talk-show host, and blew a kiss toward a former *Grey's Anatomy* star. Only Rory Keene, the new head of Vortex Studios, was too absorbed in her luncheon conversation with a C.A.A. honcho to notice Georgie's arrival.

Item number one on Georgie's new list: *Be seen with the perfect man.* With that humiliating photograph of her staring at the sonogram of Lance's baby plastered everywhere, she had to stop hiding and do what she should have done months ago. Today's lunch date needed to be big enough news for everyone to forget her stricken expression.

Unfortunately, the perfect man she'd chosen for her first date hadn't arrived, forcing her to sit at an empty table for two. Georgie tried to look as though she was happy to have a few extra minutes to herself. She couldn't get mad at Trevor. Maybe she hadn't been able to convince him to get married, but at least he'd agreed to step into her media circus for a few weeks.

The Ivy was an L.A. institution, the perfect place to see and be seen, with an army of paparazzi permanently camped out in front. Celebrities who dined at Ivy and pretended to be annoyed by the attention they received were the world's biggest hypocrites, especially those who sat outside on the patio where the weathered picket fence ran alongside the sidewalk and busy Robertson Boulevard.

Georgie settled under a white umbrella. Drinking wine at lunch could signal she was drowning her troubles in alcohol, so she ordered iced tea. Two women paused on the sidewalk beyond the picket fence to gawk at her. *Where was Trevor?*

Her plan was simple. Instead of avoiding publicity, she'd court it, but on her terms—as a single woman having the time of her life. She'd spend a few weeks with one perfect man, a few weeks with another. She wouldn't date any of them long enough to suggest a serious love affair. Just fun, fun, fun accompanied by lots of photos of her laughing and enjoying herself—photos that her publicist would make certain were well distributed. She knew a dozen great-looking actors who were anxious for publicity and understood the rules of the game. Trevor would kick off her campaign. If only he weren't so averse to being on time.

And if only the whole idea of voluntarily encouraging publicity weren't so repugnant.

Five minutes ticked by. She'd dressed exactly right for the occasion in the outfit her talented stylist had picked out for her—a black cotton sundress with wide scarlet piping at the bodice and a scatter of free-form tan and brown leaves tumbling down the short, narrow skirt. Matching ankle-wrapped brown wedges and amber earrings completed the look of casual, offbeat sophistication that suited her better than either frills or slut-clothes. She'd had the dress skillfully fit to camouflage her weight loss.

Eight minutes had passed. Rory Keene finally spotted her and gave a friendly wave. Georgie waved back. Fifteen years earlier, during the second season of *Skip and Scooter*, Rory had been a lowly production assistant, but now she was the head of Vortex Studios and one of the most powerful women in Hollywood. Since Georgie's last two films had been box-office flops and her newest one promised to do even worse, she hated having someone so influential see her sitting here looking like a loser. But then, what was new about that?

She never used to be a defeatist, and she had to stop thinking like one. Except ten minutes had elapsed . . .

Georgie pretended not to notice the stares she was receiving, but she'd started to perspire. Being alone at The Ivy was tantamount to a public shunning. She debated flipping open her cell, but she didn't want to look as though she had to track down her date.

Across the patio, a group of thin, painstakingly stylish young heiresses with beautiful, vacant faces had gathered for lunch. They included the vapid daughters of a fading rock star, a studio mogul, and an international soft drink tycoon. The girls were famous for being famous—icons of everything that was trendy and scrumptiously unaffordable for the ordinary women who poured over their photos. None of them wanted to admit they lived off Daddy's money, so they tended to list their occupation as "purse designer." But their real job was being photographed, and their leader, the soft drink heiress, rose from the table and glided like a sleek Ferrari toward Georgie.

"Hi, I'm Madison Merrill. We haven't met." She angled her hips for the long lenses of the paparazzi across the street, giving them a flattering view of her Stella McCartney trapeze dress. "I just loved you in *Summer in the City.* I don't understand why it wasn't a big hit. I love romantic comedies." A crease dented her perfect forehead, and she hastily added, "I mean, I love serious stuff, too, like, you know, Scorcese and everything."

"I understand." Georgie offered up her perky smile and imagined the paparazzi clicking away, getting great photos of the fabulously photogenic Madison Merrill standing by an emaciated Georgie York, who was seated *alone* at a table for two.

"*Skip and Scooter* was great, too." Madison moved a few steps back so the table umbrella didn't shadow her face. "It was my favorite TV show when I was like nine."

The girl was too stupid to be subtle. She'd have to work on that if she wanted to stay ahead in L.A.

Madison gazed at the empty chair. "I've got to get back to my friends. You could like sit with us if you don't have anybody to eat with?" She made the statement into a question.

Georgie tugged on one of her amber earrings. "Oh, no. He got held up in a meeting. I promised I'd wait for him. Men."

"I guess." Madison waved at the photographers and trotted back to her seat.

Georgie felt as if a flashing neon arrow was pointing at the empty chair across the table. Thousands of men all around the world—millions of them—would give anything to have lunch with Skipper Brown, but she'd had to pick her unreliable former best friend.

Georgie's server popped up for the third time. "Are you sure you wouldn't like to order now, Miss York?"

Georgie was trapped. She couldn't stay. She couldn't leave. "Another iced tea, please."

The server disappeared. Georgie lifted her wrist and gazed pointedly at her watch. She couldn't put it off. She had to pretend to be getting a call. It would be her date telling her he'd been in an automobile accident. First she'd pretend to be concerned, then she'd be relieved that no one was hurt, then she'd be totally understanding.

Stood Up! Mystery Man Ditches Date with Georgie
She could already see the photo of herself alone at a table for two. How could such a basic plan have

backfired so quickly? She should start traveling with an entourage like every other celebrity, but she'd always hated the idea of being surrounded by paid companionship.

As she reached for her cell, she grew aware of a subtle shift in the atmosphere, an invisible electric current zipping across the patio. She looked up and her blood froze. Bramwell Shepard had just walked in.

Heads ping-ponged all over the patio, bouncing from Bram to her and then back again. He was dressed like the aimless second son of an exiled European monarch: a designer blazer—probably Gucci—great jeans that emphasized all six feet two inches of his height; and a faded black T-shirt that signified he didn't give a damn. A pair of male models ogled him enviously. Madison Merrill half rose from her chair to intercept him. But Bram was heading right toward Georgie.

Car brakes squealed as the paparazzi dashed into the traffic from across the street to get the shot of the week, maybe the entire month, since they hadn't been seen together since the show ended. Bram reached her table, ducked under the umbrella, and brushed a kiss over her lips. "Trev couldn't make it." He kept his voice low against eavesdroppers. "Unavoidable last-minute circumstances."

"I can't believe you're doing this!" She could believe it. Bram wanted something from her—maybe a public scene? She forced her frozen lips into what she hoped the cameras would register as a smile. "What did you do to him?"

"So much suspicion. Poor guy wrenched his back getting out of the shower." Bram settled into the chair across from her, keeping his voice as quiet as hers and offering up his most seductive smile.

"Then why didn't he call me and cancel?" she said.

"He didn't want to bring up bad memories. Like the way Lance the Loser canceled your marriage. Trev's thoughtful that way."

Her smile broadened, but her whisper was venomous. "You're trying to set me up. I know it."

Bram faked amused laughter. "Talk about paranoid. And ungrateful. Even though Trev was writhing in pain, he didn't want to make you sit here by yourself. You might not know this, Scoot, but everybody in town already feels sorry for you, and Trev couldn't stand embarrassing you even more than you've embarrassed yourself. Which is why he called me."

She rested her cheek in her hand and gazed at him with counterfeit affection. "You're lying. He knows how I feel about you better than anyone."

"You should be thankful I was willing to help you out."

"Then why did you show up half an hour late?"

"You know I've always had trouble with time."

"Bull!" She grinned for the cameras until her cheeks ached. "You wanted to make a big entrance. At my expense."

He kept smiling, too, and she tilted her head and laughed, and he reached across the table and chucked her under the chin, and it was *Skip and Scooter* all over again.

By the time the server appeared, the crowd of photographers on the sidewalk had spilled into the street, and her stomach was a mass of knots. Within minutes these photos would be popping up on computer screens all around the world, and the circus would pick up steam.

"Crab cakes for Scooter here," Bram said with an elegant flick of his hand. "Scotch on the rocks for me. Laphroaig. And lobster ravioli." The waiter disappeared. "God, I need a cigarette."

He picked up her hand and rubbed his thumb over her knuckles. Her skin burned at his unwelcome touch. She felt a callus on the bottom of his finger and couldn't imagine how it had gotten there. Bram might have grown up in a rough neighborhood, but he'd never worked hard in his life. She came up with a merry laugh. "I hate you."

He took a drink from her iced tea glass and let the chiseled edges of his mouth curl into a smile. "The feeling's mutual."

Bram had no reason to hate her. She'd been the good soldier while he'd single-handedly ruined one of the best sitcoms in television history. During the first two years of *Skip and Scooter,* he'd only occasionally misbehaved, but as the years passed, he'd grown more uncontrollable, and by the time Skip and Scooter's on-screen relationship had begun to turn romantic, he cared about nothing but having a good time. He spent money as fast as he earned it on fancy cars, a designer wardrobe, and supporting an army of hangers-on from his childhood. The cast didn't know from one day to the next whether he'd show up on the set drunk or sober, whether he'd show up at all. He totaled cars, trashed dance clubs, and shrugged off any attempts to curb his recklessness. Nothing was safe from him, not women, reputations, or a crew member's drug stash.

If he'd been playing a darker character, the show might have survived the sex tape that had surfaced at the end of season eight, but Bram played buttoned-down, good guy Skip Scofield, youthful heir to the Scofield fortune, and even the most loyal fans were outraged by what they saw. *Skip and Scooter* was canceled a few weeks later, earning him the wrath of the public and the hatred of everyone connected with the show.

Their meal dragged on until Georgie couldn't bear it. She set down her fork next to her dismantled, uneaten crab cake, studied her watch, and tried to look as if Christmas Day had unfortunately come to an end. "Aw . . . Too bad. I have to go."

Bram speared the final bite of his ravioli and thrust his fork in her mouth. "Not so fast. You can't leave Ivy without having dessert."

"Don't you dare prolong this farce."

"Careful. You're losing your happy face."

She choked down the ravioli and pasted her smile back on. "You're broke, aren't you? My father invested my money, but you squandered yours. That's why you're doing this. No one will give you a job because you're unreliable, and you need publicity to get back on your feet." Although Bram still worked, he only got minor parts these days, playing morally weak characters—a cheating husband, a lecherous drunk—not even meaty villains. "You're so desperate you have to piggyback off my press coverage."

"You've got to admit it's working. *Skip and Scooter* together again." He lifted his hand for their server, who hurried over. "We'll have the pecan shortcake with hot fudge sauce. Two spoons."

When the server was gone, she leaned forward and dropped her voice even lower. "How do I hate thee? Let me count the ways. I hate thee for making my childhood miserable . . ."

"You were fifteen when the series started. Not exactly a kid."

"But Scooter was only fourteen, and I was naïve."

"I'll say."

"I hate you for embarrassing me in front of the cast, the crew, the press, in front of *everybody*—with your stupid practical jokes."

"Who knew you'd keep falling for them?"

"I hate you for all the hours I spent sitting around the set waiting for you."

"Unprofessional, I'll admit. But you kept your nose buried in books, so you should thank me for your superior education."

"And for your sleazeball behavior that got us canceled and cost me millions."

"You? What about the millions I cost myself?"

"At least I can feel good about that."

"Okay, my turn . . ." His smile had a silky edge. "You were a stuck-up little prude, sweetheart, and a big-time tattletale. Whenever you had the tiniest gripe, you made sure Daddy Paul ran to the producers and raised a stink. His little princess had to have everything her way."

Her mouth remained curled, but her eyes flashed outrage. "That is so not true."

"And you were a selfish actor. You always had to stick to the script, no room for improvisation. It was suffocating." He chucked her under the chin again.

She kicked him hard on the inside of his calf where no one could see. He winced, and she patted his hand. "You only wanted to improvise because you didn't have your lines memorized."

"Whenever I tried to push the show out of its comfort zone, you sabotaged me."

"Disagreement isn't sabotage."

"You trashed me in the press."

"Only *after* your sex tape!"

"Some sex tape. I had my clothes on."

"She didn't!" Georgie reinforced her own slipping smile. "Say what you really mean. You hated that I made more money than you and that I had more star power."

"Oh, yes. How could I forget your memorable turn on Broadway as *Annie*?"

"While you were ditching school and hanging out on street corners." She propped her chin on the back of her hand. "Did you ever get that high school diploma?"

"Well, well . . . Isn't this interesting?"

They'd been so absorbed in their argument, they hadn't noticed the tall, cool blonde approaching their table. Rory Keene, with her classic French twist and long, patrician features, looked more like an East Coast socialite than a powerful studio executive, but even during her single season as a lowly production assistant on *Skip and Scooter,* she'd been a little intimidating.

Bram shot to his feet and planted a cool kiss on her cheek. "Rory, it's great to see you. You look beautiful, as always. Did you enjoy your lunch?"

"Very much. I can't believe the two of you are sitting at the same table without a loaded weapon."

"Mine's in my purse," Georgie said with a Scooter grin.

Bram curled his hand around Georgie's shoulder. "Water under the bridge. We made peace a long time ago."

"Really?" Rory slipped her purse higher on her arm and gave Bram a long, hard stare. "Take care of Georgie. This town has a limited supply of nice people, and we can't afford to lose one of them." With a nod, she turned away and headed across the patio.

Bram's smooth smile faded. He glared down at Georgie. "When did you and Rory get to be such good buddies?"

"We're not."

Without excusing himself, he headed across the patio after Rory.

Being with Bram was as draining as ever, and Georgie welcomed having a few minutes to recharge. The dessert arrived. Her stomach rebelled. She averted her eyes and thought about the day her father had given her the pilot script for *Skip and Scooter.* She'd had no idea her life was about to change forever.

The show's silly premise had been perfect sitcom fare. Scooter Brown was a spunky fourteen-year-old orphan who showed up at the luxurious Scofield mansion on Chicago's posh North Shore. Scooter was trying to stay out of foster care by locating a stepsister who'd once worked there, but the stepsister had long since disappeared. With no place to go, Scooter had hidden out at the mansion only to be discovered by stuffy, fifteen-year-old Skip, the heir to the Scofield fortune. He, along with the servants, became unwillingly involved in a plot to hide her from the Scofield adults.

No one had expected the show to last more than a season, but the cast had exceptional chemistry, and the show's writing staff had come up with inventive plots.

More important, they'd managed to deepen the core characters beyond their initial stereotypes.

Georgie gave Bram a vicious smile. "Finished sucking up to Rory?"

"I went out to buy cigarettes."

"Sure you did."

"To buy cigarettes and suck up. I like to multitask. Is our lunch from hell finally over?"

"Before it even began."

Bram insisted on waiting inside with her until the valet brought her car. She braced herself, and, sure enough, as soon as they hit the sidewalk, the jackals surrounded them. Bram slipped a supposedly protective arm around her shoulders—she wanted to bite it off—held up his hand, and gave the cameras his dazzling smile. "Just a couple of old friends getting together for lunch," he said over their shouts. "Don't make anything more out of it."

"You guys are supposed to hate each other."

"Have you buried the hatchet?"

"Are you dating?"

"Georgie, have you talked to Lance? Does he know you're seeing Bram?"

Bram assumed an unhappy expression she knew was totally phony. "Give us a break, guys. It's only lunch. And don't pay any attention to those rumors about a *Skip and Scooter* reunion show. It's not going to happen."

Reunion show?

The paps went nuts.

"Is there a script?"

"Has the rest of the cast signed on?"

"When are you going to shoot?"

Bram muscled her through the crowd to her car. She tried to slam his fingers in the door, but he was too quick. As she pulled away, she made herself smile and wave to the cameras, but the moment she was out of sight, she let out a scream.

There was no reunion show, rumored or otherwise. Bram had made it up to punish her.

Chapter 3

On Saturday morning Georgie parked her car just off Temescal Canyon Road, sliding in behind a dusty blue Bentley and a red Benz Roadster. With the paparazzi still asleep from last night's club action, she didn't have any unwelcome escorts. "You're late!" Sasha said as Georgie got out. "Too busy smooching it up with Bramwell Shepard?"

"Yeah, that's what I was doing, all right." Georgie slammed the car door.

Sasha laughed. She looked incredible as always, tall and willowy in a white L.A.M.B. hoodie and gray pants. She'd pulled her straight brunette hair into a ponytail and shaded her face with a pink visor.

"Ignore Sasha." April, the oldest and only truly sane member of her inner friendship circle, wore a black

T-shirt from her husband's last tour. "She just drove up thirty seconds ago."

"I overslept," Sasha said. "*Young* people do that."

April was in her early fifties, with beautiful bold features, a dramatic square-jawed face, and a glow that spoke of well-earned contentment. She'd been Georgie's stylist for years, but even more important, she was a dear friend. April tossed her streaky blond hair and gave Sasha a sweet smile. "I slept like a dream. But then *I* had hot sex last night."

Sasha frowned. "Yeah, well, I'd have had hot sex, too, if I was married to Jack Patriot."

"But you're not, now are you?" April said smugly.

Three decades earlier, April had been a famous rock-and-roll groupie, but her notorious days were long behind her. She was now the wife of legendary rocker Jack Patriot as well as the mother of a famous NFL quarterback and a recent grandmother. She no longer worked as a stylist, except as a favor to Georgie.

Georgie tucked her hair behind her ears and slipped on a ball cap. She pulled a backpack heavy with water bottles from her car. She was the only one of them who didn't mind wearing a pack, so she carried all the water, a calorie-burner they'd been trying to talk her out of since she'd gotten so thin, but she refused to cave.

Sometimes she wondered how women who didn't have girlfriends coped with life. In her own life, these were the friends who never let her down, even though they were so frequently separated by geography, making these Saturday-morning hikes a rarity. Sasha lived in Chicago. April lived in L.A. but spent as much time as she could at the family farm in Tennessee. Meg Koranda, the baby of the group, was off on another of her journeys. None of them were exactly sure where.

Sasha led them toward the trailhead. She held back from her normal killer pace so Georgie, who used to be their leader, could keep up. "Tell us exactly what happened with Bram," she said.

"Honestly, Georgie, what were you thinking?" April frowned.

"It was an accident." Georgie yanked on her backpack. "On my part anyway. Totally premeditated on his." She told them about her plan to start serial dating, then explained what had happened at The Ivy. She avoided mentioning her marriage proposal to Trevor, not because she didn't trust them—unlike Lance, these women would never betray her—but because she didn't want her closest friends to know she was even more pathetic than they realized. By the time they reached the open ridge above the canyon, she was gasping for breath.

The last of the morning chill had burned off, and they could see the coastline from Santa Monica Bay to Malibu. They stopped for a moment to take off their jackets and tie the sleeves around their waists. Sasha pulled out two candy bars and offered one to Georgie, trying to be casual about it, but Georgie declined. "I ate this morning. Honest."

"A spoonful of yogurt," April said.

"A whole carton. It's getting better. Really."

They didn't believe her.

"Well, I'm starved," Sasha said.

As she bit into her candy bar, neither Georgie nor April pointed out that Sasha Holiday, the founder of Holiday Healthy Eating, might want to munch on a piece of fruit or a Holiday Power Bar instead of a Milky Way. Sasha was a secret junk-food junkie, something only they knew. Not that it showed on her body.

Sasha tucked the wrapper into the bodice of her white top where it made a lump under the stretchy fabric. "Let's think this through. Maybe seeing Bram isn't such a bad idea. For sure it'll distract everybody from talking about Lance and St. Jade." She took a bite. "Plus, Bram Shepard is still the hottest bad boy in town."

Georgie hated hearing anything even remotely complimentary about Bram. "He's not hot at the box office," she said. "And I'm lucky his drug dealer didn't show up while we were eating."

Sasha stuck the candy bar between her teeth and slipped behind Georgie so she could unzip the backpack and pull out their water bottles. "Trev told me Bram hasn't done drugs in years."

"Trev's gullible." Georgie twisted off the top of her bottle. "No more talk about Bram, okay? I'm not letting him spoil my morning." He'd spoiled enough, she thought.

They spent the next two miles hiking on a fire road that wound through the sycamore, live oak, and bay. Georgie relished the feeling of privacy. They reached a shallow creek bed. Sasha leaned over to stretch her legs. "I have the best idea. Let's all go to Vegas next weekend."

April knelt next to the water. "That town isn't good for me. And Jack and I have plans."

Sasha snorted. "Naked plans."

April grinned, and Georgie smiled with her, but inside she felt the familiar pain of betrayal. Once, she'd been as certain of Lance's love as April was of Jack Patriot's. Then Lance had met Jade Gentry, and everything had changed.

Lance and Jade had been filming a movie together in Ecuador. Lance had played a dashing soldier of fortune and Jade was a nerdy archaeologist, definitely a stretch, considering her exotic beauty. During Lance's early phone calls, he'd told Georgie how Jade was so absorbed in her work as a professional do-gooder that she seldom fraternized with the crew and that she spent so much time on the phone advocating for her pet causes, she didn't always have her lines memorized.

But gradually the stories had stopped. And Georgie hadn't noticed.

She turned to Sasha. "A trip to Vegas sounds just right. Count me in." She imagined photos of Georgie York and her glamorous friend whooping it up in Sin City. If she followed the trip with a few months of serial dating as she'd originally planned, maybe the stories of "Georgie's Unending Heartbreak" would finally give way to "Georgie's Wild Nights."

Sasha began to sing "Girls Just Want to Have Fun." Georgie made herself do a little dance. It was a good idea. A great idea. Exactly what she needed.

What do you mean you had to go back to Chicago?" Georgie hissed into her cell phone six days later. She was at a table in the Bellagio's Le Cirque restaurant where Sasha was supposed to be meeting her to kick off their Vegas weekend.

Sasha sounded harried instead of her normal sarcastic self. "I left three messages. Why didn't you call me back?"

Because Georgie had accidentally left her cell in her suitcase and only retrieved it on her way to the restaurant.

"We had a fire in the warehouse," Sasha went on. "I had to get back right away."

"Is everybody okay?"

"Yes, but there's a lot of damage. Georgie, I know the Vegas trip was my idea. I'd never have stood you up like this if—"

"Don't be silly. I'll be fine." Sasha was cool in a crisis, but she also wasn't the tough nut she pretended to be. "Take care of yourself, and call me when you know more. Promise."

"I will."

After Georgie hung up, she gazed around the hotel's jewel-like dining room with its silk-tented ceiling and view of Lake Bellagio. Several of the diners were openly staring at her, and she realized she was once again alone at a table for two. She left a hundred-dollar bill by her water goblet and slipped out into the casino through the restaurant's star-studded entry. She kept her head down as she walked past the Monopoly slot machines.

"I swear, you're stalking me."

She whipped around and saw Bram Shepard standing outside Circo, the sister restaurant to the one she'd just fled. He was predictably gorgeous in jeans and a pinstriped dress shirt with white French cuffs, a mix of casual and elegant that should have looked awful, but didn't. The casino lighting had turned his lavender eyes into mercury. He was like one of the Seven Wonders of the World—except he'd been tarnished by too much acid rain.

"This is *so* not an accident," she said.

"As a matter of fact, it is."

"Yeah, right." She moved quickly, trying to get away before anyone spotted them, but he fell into step next to her. "I had a benefit," he said.

"I don't care. Go away."

"It was a corporate shindig. I got twenty-five thousand dollars for spending two hours at the company cocktail party mingling with the guests."

"Not exactly a benefit."

"A benefit for *me*."

"It figures." She knew a dozen C-list celebrities who made a living like this, but not one of them admitted it.

She walked still faster, but it was too late. They were already attracting attention, no big surprise, since last week's lunch date was splashed all over this week's tabloids. She'd wanted positive stories she could control, and there was nothing controllable or positive about Bram Shepard.

They passed a circular bar with a rock band grinding out a Nickelback cover. She couldn't get away now, so she plastered on a smile. It was time she let him know her pushover days were behind her. "Let me guess," she said as they wound through the machines. "You're heading for the bedroom of an aging corporate mogul's third wife. She's paying you for extra services."

"Want to come along? Imagine how much she'd cough up to get it on with both of us."

"Thanks for thinking of me, but unlike you, I'm still filthy rich, so I haven't been reduced to selling myself."

"Who are you kidding? I saw you in *Pretty People*. You sold yourself to make that bomb."

She'd tried to convince her father the movie was a mistake, but he refused to listen. Failure was starting to cling to her like bad perfume.

"You should sue whoever did your costumes for that film." He winked at a cute Asian blackjack dealer. "They'd have done better to capitalize on your legs instead of your bust."

"While you're pointing out my flaws, don't forget my pop eyes and my rubber mouth and—"

"You don't have pop eyes. And a rubber mouth hasn't exactly hurt Julia Roberts."

But Georgie wasn't Julia Roberts.

His eyes slid over her. She was tall, but he was still half a head taller. "Nice look tonight, by the way. It almost hides how scrawny you are. April must still be styling you."

"She is." Although Georgie had chosen this V-neck sheath, which was printed in a black-and-white Jackson Pollock–splatter paint pattern. It hung straight from her shoulders, and the black leather belt slung low around the hips gave it a flapper feel. She'd arranged her hair in long, spiky pieces around her face and accessorized with a pair of chunky bangles.

He checked out a leggy blonde who was openly staring at him. "So tell me . . . Is the hunt still on, or have you found a guy stupid enough to marry you?"

"Dozens. Fortunately, I came to my senses in time. It's amazing what a little electric shock therapy will do for you. You should try it."

He thumped her once between the shoulder blades. "I'll say this for you, Scoot. You still know how to get yourself in those embarrassing little jams. Walking in on your tender scene with Trev was the best time I've had in months."

"Which only shows how sad your narrow little life really is."

They'd reached the crowded lobby. Its gorgeously gaudy ceiling of Dale Chihuly glass flowers didn't mesh well with the rest of the decor but was beautiful nonetheless. The buzz began immediately, and people stopped what they were doing to ogle them. Georgie plastered on her biggest smile. One woman lifted her cell phone to snap a picture. Great. This was just great.

"Let's get out of here." Bram grabbed her arm and pushed her through the crowd. The next thing she knew, they were in an elevator that smelled of Jo Malone's Tuberose. He slid a key card into a slot on the panel and punched in a floor. Their reflections stared back at her from the mirrored walls—Skip and Scooter all grown up. For the barest fraction of a second, she wondered who was watching the twins while Mom and Dad had a night on the town.

The elevator began to move. She reached around him and pressed the button for the thirtieth floor.

"It's not even eleven o'clock," he said. "Let's have some fun first."

"Good idea. I'll get my Tazer."

"Still as prickly as ever. You're all shiny package, Georgie, but there's no present inside. I'll bet you never even let Lance the Loser see you naked."

She pressed her hands to her cheeks. "I was supposed to take off my clothes? Why didn't somebody tell me?"

He rested his shoulder against the elevator wall, crossed his ankles, and gave her his expert bone-melting once-over. "You know what I wish. I wish I'd nailed Jade Gentry when I had the chance. That woman is pure sex."

His comment should have devastated her, but this was Bram, so her fighting instincts kicked in. "You never had a chance with St. Jade. She picks all her men from the A-list, and Lance's last film grossed eighty-seven million."

"Lucky bastard. Dude can't act for shit."

"As opposed to your incredible box-office record. I have to admit, though . . . you're looking good." She patted her purse. "Don't let me walk off without the name of your fabulous plastic surgeon."

He uncrossed his ankles. "Jade called me a few years back, but I was so out of it I never called her back. That's the real way drugs screw up your brain, but nobody ever warns kids about shit like that." The doors opened on the twenty-eighth floor. He grabbed her elbow. "Party time. Let's go."

"Let's not."

He dragged her out. "Come on. I'm bored."

"Not my problem." She tried to dig her heels into the thick carpet that ran down the middle of the opulent hallway.

His grip tightened. "You must have forgotten what I overheard at Trev's house, or you'd realize you're basically my slave."

She'd been the target of too many of Bram's cat-and-mouse games not to see where this was headed, and she didn't like it.

He steered her around a corner. "Do you have any idea how much money I could make selling the story of sad, desperate Georgie York begging a man to marry her?"

"Even you wouldn't do that." Except he might.

"I guess it depends on how good a slave you are. I hope you're wearing some sexy underwear because I'm in the mood for a lap dance."

"I'll make a phone call for you. There are a lot of desperate girls in Vegas."

He rapped on a door with the back of his knuckles. "I'm only admitting this to you, Scoot, but I'm pretty much shit-faced from all those martinis they were pouring down my throat. Since I want to be cold sober for your lap dance, I'm sticking to club soda for the rest of the night."

He didn't look shit-faced, but she'd learned from past experience that he could consume vast quantities of alcohol before he slurred a single syllable. He was probably messing with her mind about the lap dance, but that didn't mean he hadn't conjured up something just as evil to use as blackmail. She could have a big problem on her hands, and she needed to figure out fast how to cope with it.

The door opened, and he swept her into a spacious private suite filled with marble, gilt, fresh flowers, and some very young, very beautiful women only slightly outnumbered by men. Judging by their height, most of them seemed to be basketball players except for a couple of unctuous-looking agents wearing pricey suits, expensive watches, and anxious expressions hanging out in the corner.

"It's Scooter!" One of the basketball players rose to his feet and flashed a couple of gold teeth. "Damn, girl, you look good. Come on over here and have a drink."

"Your adoring public." Bram made a sweeping gesture, then headed for the bar where the women perched.

With only an empty hotel room waiting for her and plenty of women to claim Bram's attention, she decided she could safely stick around for a while. Besides, she wouldn't let Bram see her run. She soon discovered most of the men in the room played for the Knicks. The one who'd called her over turned out to be a goofball, but his teammate was a charmer. Kerry Cleveland had sexy dreadlocks, long dark eyelashes, and an infectious enthusiasm. Halfway through her first chocolate martini, she began to enjoy herself. She didn't have to worry about cameras snapping away, and Bram was too preoccupied with the pretty young things hanging all over him to bother her.

Sometime around two in the morning, the party moved to a private gaming room, where Kerry taught her to play craps. For the first time in months, she was having fun. She'd just made her initial bet when Bram appeared at her side. "You do realize those are five-hundred-dollar chips."

"I do, and I don't care. You're way too uptight."

"I don't think you're uptight, Bram." A lethal-looking redhead with a cigarette voice tried to drape herself around him, but he shrugged her off and announced he was playing, too.

When it was Georgie's turn to roll, Bram placed his chips on the Don't Pass Line. She threw the dice. A cheer went up as she rolled a winning six and five. Only Bram had bet against her.

"Too bad," she whispered. "I know money's tight for you, but I've heard male prostitutes can make a fortune if they find the right clients."

"Always looking out for me."

"That's what friends do."

The redhead kept trying to get Bram's attention, and he kept ignoring her. She finally disappeared, only to return with two fresh martinis. She pressed one in Bram's hand, but as she lifted the other to her lips, he took it away from her and handed it to Georgie. "Maybe this will loosen you up."

The redhead looked so undone by his rejection that Georgie would have felt sorry for her if she hadn't been so pushy. Bram rolled the dice and came up with a seven. So far, he'd broken even, while Georgie was down a few thousand. She didn't care. This was fun. She sipped her martini and cheered Kerry on when it was his turn.

Time slid by, and the world began to whirl into a kaleidoscope of color. The dice bounced against the table's edge. The stick swept across the green felt. The chips clicked. Suddenly, everything was beautiful, even Bram Shepard. They'd once created small-screen magic. Surely that counted for something. She rested her cheek against him. "I don't hate you anymore."

He draped his arm around her shoulder, sounding as happy as she felt. "I don't hate you, either."

Another beautiful minute ticked by, and then, for no reason at all, he pulled back. She wanted to protest as he walked away, but she felt too good.

Out of the corner of her eye, she saw him approach the redhead. He looked angry. How could he be mad on such a beautiful night?

The dice clicked and clicked again. Bram reappeared at her side. "We've got to get out of here."

That was the last thing she remembered until the next afternoon, when she made the mistake of waking up.

Chapter 4

Georgie groaned. Her head throbbed, her mouth tasted like battery acid, and she had a septic tank where her stomach should be. As she curled her knees to her belly, her bottom brushed against Lance's side. His skin was warm and—

Nooooooo!

She popped open the eye that wasn't buried in her pillow.

A cruel blade of afternoon sunlight seeped through the draperies and picked out her lacy white bra lying on the bedroom carpet of her suite at the Bellagio. One of last night's heels peeped out from beneath a pair of men's jeans.

Please, oh, please, let those jeans belong to that sweet basketball player.

She buried her face in the pillow. What if they didn't? What if they belonged to—

They couldn't. She and the basketball player . . . Kerry—his name was Kerry . . . They'd flirted up a storm over the craps table. It had felt so good to flirt. So what if he was a younger man?

Okay, she was naked, and this was awkward. But now Lance was no longer the last man she'd slept with, and that was a sign of progress, right? Her stomach rumbled unpleasantly. She peeled her eye open again. She'd suffered through a few hangovers, but nothing like this. Nothing that had ever wiped out her memory.

The thigh rubbed against her bottom. It felt exceptionally muscular, definitely an athlete's thigh. But no matter how hard she concentrated, the last thing she remembered was Bram dragging her away from the party.

Kerry must have come after her. Yes, she was sure she remembered him stealing her from Bram. They'd come back here where they'd talked till dawn. He'd made her laugh and told her she had more fortitude than any woman he knew. He'd said she was intelligent, talented, and a lot prettier than most people realized. He'd said that Lance had made himself look like an idiot walking out on a woman like her. They'd started talking about having children together—beautiful biracial babies, unlike Lance's future pasty-faced kid. They'd agreed to sell the photos of their beautiful baby to the highest bidder and donate the money to charity, which would be especially touching after the Drudge Report dug up news that Jade Gentry had used all the charity money she'd raised to buy herself a yacht. Then Georgie would win an Oscar, and Kerry would win the Super Bowl.

Okay, wrong sport, but her head was hammering, her stomach churning, and a hard knee was trying to wedge deeper into her bottom.

She had to put herself out of her misery, but that would involve turning over and dealing with the consequences of what she saw. She needed water. And Tylenol. An entire bottle.

It began to dawn on her that liquor didn't give a person total amnesia. This was no ordinary hangover. She'd been drugged. And she knew only one person corrupt enough to drug a woman.

She drove her elbow into his chest with as much force as she could muster.

He gave an *oof* of pain and rolled over, taking the sheet with him.

She buried her face in the pillow. Soon the mattress sagged as he got up. She heard the muffled sound of his footsteps dragging toward the bathroom. When the door shut, she fumbled for the sheet and made herself sit up. The room tilted. Her stomach roiled. She wrapped the sheet around her, wobbled to her feet, and staggered to the second bathroom, where she leaned against the sink and buried her face in her hands.

What would Scooter do if she'd been drugged and woke up naked in bed with a stranger? Or not a stranger. Scooter wouldn't do *anything* because nothing this horrible had ever happened to her. It was easy to be all feisty and optimistic when you had a full-time writing staff protecting you from the real crap life tossed out.

As she let her hands drop, a horrifying image greeted her in the mirror, like early Courtney Love. A witch's brew of tangled cherry-cola hair didn't hide the beard burn on her neck. Blotches of old mascara smudged her green eyes like mud around an algae pond. Her wide mouth sagged at the corners, and her complexion was the color of bad yogurt. She made herself drink a glass of water. All her toiletries were in the other bathroom, but she washed her face and swirled some hotel mouthwash.

She still didn't feel capable of coping with whatever lurked on the other side of that door, so she pushed her hair out of her face and sat on the marble tub deck.

She wanted to call someone, but she couldn't burden Sasha right now, Meg was unreachable, and she wasn't up to confessing her transgression to April, who would be so disappointed in her. A former rock-and-roll groupie had become her moral compass. As for her father . . . Never.

She made herself get up and tightened the sheet under her arms. The bedroom was empty, but her hopes that he'd left faded when she saw his clothes still on the floor. She shuffled across the carpet and out into the living room.

He stood at the windows with his back to her. He was tall. But he wasn't NBA tall. He was her worst nightmare.

"Don't say a word until the coffee gets here," he said without turning. "I mean it, Georgie. I can't deal with you right now. Unless you have a cigarette."

Rage swept through her. She snatched up a couch pillow and hurled it at Bramwell Shepard's rumpled tawny head. "You *drugged* me!"

He ducked, and the pillow hit the window.

She tried to go after him, but as he turned toward her, she tripped over the bedsheet, and it slipped to her waist.

"Put those away," he said. "They've already gotten us into enough trouble."

She had better luck connecting with one of his abandoned shoes.

"Ow!" He rubbed his chest and had the nerve to look outraged. "I didn't drug you! Believe me, if I was going to drug a woman, it wouldn't be you."

She tugged the sheet into her armpits and looked around for something else to throw. "You're lying. I was drugged."

"Yeah, you were. We both were. But not by me. By Meredith, Marilyn, Mary-somebody."

"Who are you talking about?"

"The redhead at the party last night. Remember those drinks she brought over? I took one and gave you the other—the one she made for herself."

"Why would she drug herself?"

"Because she likes the *feeling* she gets!"

Georgie had her first inkling that, for once in his life, Bramwell Shepard might be telling the truth. She also remembered the way he'd confronted the woman and how angry he'd looked. She jerked up the sheet and lurched toward him. "You knew those drinks were drugged? You knew, and you didn't put a stop to it?"

"I didn't know. Not until I finished mine, looked at you, and realized I wasn't totally *repulsed!*"

A rap sounded at the door, and a voice announced room service. "Get back in the bedroom," she hissed.

"And give me that robe! The tabloids have informants everywhere. Hurry up!"

"If you give me one more order . . ."

"*Please* hurry up, you *dickhead*!"

"I liked you better when you were drunk." He pulled off the robe, tossed it over her arm, and disappeared. She threw the sheet behind the couch and knotted the sash on her way to the door.

The waiter wheeled in the serving cart and arranged the dishes on the dining room table, which sat under a gilded chandelier. She heard the shower go on in the bathroom. Word would spread that she hadn't spent the night alone. Fortunately, no one knew whom she'd spent it with, so this might work to her advantage.

The waiter finally left. She made a dash for the coffee, then wobbled over to the windows and tried to pull herself together. Far below, tourists had gathered to watch the Bellagio's fountain show. What had taken place in that bedroom last night? She couldn't remember anything. Only the first time . . .

The day they'd met, she'd been fifteen, and he was seventeen. His beauty had left her dumbstruck, but he'd dismissed her with a bored grunt and a single sweep of those cocky lavender eyes. Naturally, she was smitten.

Her father's warnings about him only intensified her crush. Bram was arrogant, sulky, undisciplined,

and gorgeous—catnip for a fifteen-year-old romantic—
but he ignored her during those first two seasons unless
they were actually filming. She might have been on
the cover of a dozen teen magazines, but she was still
a skinny kid with gum ball green eyes, marshmallow
cheeks, and a Silly Putty mouth. Her skin was perpetually broken out from the makeup she had to wear,
and her curly orange Orphan Annie hair made her look
even younger. Going out with a few cute teen actors
didn't bolster her confidence, since her father had
arranged the dates for publicity. The rest of the time,
Paul York kept her locked up tight, safe from Hollywood's vices.

Bram's glittering good looks, cocky manner, and
street tough's attitude stirred all her fantasies. She'd
never known anyone so wild, so free of the need to
please. She laughed too loud trying to get his attention.
She bought him presents—a new CD he had to hear,
gourmet chocolates that were the best ever, funny T-
shirts he never wore. She saved up jokes to tell him,
agreed with all his opinions, and did everything she
could to make him like her, but unless the cameras
were rolling, she might as well have been invisible.

The contrast between his rough upbringing and
the polished preppy he played fascinated her, and she
pieced together his history from his hometown buddies, loudmouth jerks who hung around the set.

Bram had grown up on Chicago's South Side. From the time he was seven, when his mother died from a drug overdose, he'd had to look out for himself. His irresponsible father, a sometimes house-painter who relied on his girlfriends for beer money, had died when Bram was fifteen. Bram had dropped out of school not long after and started hustling. One day a wealthy forty-year-old divorcée spotted him while she was doing volunteer work and took him under her wing—maybe into her bed—Georgie had never been sure about that. The woman polished up his rough edges and talked him into modeling. After a high-end Chicago men's store snatched him up for an ad campaign, he'd dumped his benefactor, taken some acting lessons, and eventually landed a couple of parts with one of the local theater companies, which led to his audition for Skip.

The show's fourth season began. Georgie promised herself she'd make him see that she wasn't a nuisance but had grown into a desirable eighteen-year-old woman. They started work in July, shooting on location in Chicago. One of Bram's loser friends mentioned that Bram was chartering a yacht for a Saturday-night drinking cruise on Lake Michigan. Since her father was going to New York for the weekend, Georgie decided to crash the party.

She dressed carefully in a leopard-print halter dress and little platform sandals. As she stepped on the yacht, she noticed most of the women wore short shorts and bathing suit tops. R. Kelly blared from the boat's sound system. The women were all in their twenties with gleaming hair, long legs, and sexy bodies, but Georgie held the fame card, and as the boat left the dock, they detached themselves from Bram's homeboys to talk to her.

"Could I have your autograph for my niece?"

"Do you take acting classes and everything?"

"You're so lucky to be working with Bram. He's like the hottest guy on the planet."

Georgie smiled and autographed, all the while keeping an eye out for Bram.

He finally emerged from the cabin. He wore rumpled shorts and a tan polo shirt. He had a woman under each arm, a drink in his hand, and a cigarette dangling from his lips. She wanted him so badly she hurt.

The moon came up, and the party got rowdier— exactly the kind of party her father had always kept her away from. One of the girls took off her top. The men hooted. Two of the women started kissing. Georgie would have been okay with it if they'd been lesbians, but they weren't, and the idea of women making out just to put on a show for men disgusted her. When they started rubbing each other's breasts, she slipped inside to the salon, where half a dozen guests were hanging out around the bar and lounging on a horseshoe-shaped white leather couch.

An air-conditioning vent sent a chilly blast over her ankles. She'd nurtured so many hopes for tonight, but Bram hadn't even spoken to her. Above her head, the sound of catcalls grew louder. She didn't belong here. She didn't belong anywhere except mugging in front of a camera.

The door opened, and Bram ambled down the steps. This time he was alone. The hope that he might have followed her blossomed as he slouched into a bucket chair not far from where she was standing and looked her over. The combination of his preppy Skip haircut, golden beard stubble, and a brand-new tattoo circling his thin bicep just beneath the sleeve of his knit shirt thrilled her. He draped one leg over the chair arm and took a slug from his drink, his eyes still on her.

She tried to think of something clever to say. "Great party."

He gave her his familiar bored look, lit another cigarette, and squinted at her through the smoke. "You weren't invited."

"I showed up anyway."

"Meaning that Daddy's out of town."

"I don't do everything my father says."

"That's not the way it looks to me."

She shrugged and tried to look cool. He flicked an ash on the carpet. She'd never been able to figure out what she'd done to earn his dislike except get paid more, and that wasn't her fault.

He pointed his drink toward the deck. "Party getting a little too wild for you?"

She wanted to tell him that watching girls demean themselves depressed her, but he already thought she was a prude. "Not at all."

"I don't believe you."

"You don't know me. You only think you do." She'd tried to sound mysterious, and maybe it was working because his eyes slid over her in a way that made her finally feel as if he was really seeing her.

Her orange curls had gone wild with the humidity, but her makeup looked good. She'd used bronzy shadow on her eyes and nude-colored lipstick to downplay her mouth. The leopard-print halter dress wasn't anything Scooter Brown would wear, and she'd emphasized the difference by sticking cutlets in her bra, but as his gaze came to rest on her breasts, she had the feeling he knew they were fake.

He blew a thin ribbon of smoke. "I bet you're still a virgin."

She rolled her eyes. "I'm eighteen. I haven't been a virgin for a couple of years." Her heart began to pound at the lie.

"If you say so."

"He was an older man. You'd know who if I told you, but I'm not going to."

"You're lying."

"He had this hang-up about powerful women. That's why I finally had to break up with him." She loved how worldly she sounded, but his mocking smile wasn't reassuring.

"Daddy Paul wouldn't let an older man get near you. He never lets you out of his sight."

"I got here tonight, didn't I?"

"Yeah, I guess you did." He drained his glass, ground out his cigarette, and stood. "Let's go then."

She stared at him, her confidence slipping away. "Go?"

He jerked his head toward a door with an anchor etched into the wood. "In there."

She gazed at him uncertainly. "I don't . . ."

"Forget it then." He shrugged and started to turn away.

"No! I'll go."

And she did. Just like that. Without asking anything of him, she followed him into the first stateroom.

A half-dressed couple sprawled on the double berth. They lifted their heads to see who'd barged in.

"Beat it," Bram said.

They scrambled from the berth.

She should have gone with them, but she didn't. Instead, she stood there in her leopard-print dress and platform sandals with corkscrews tightening her carrot hair and watched the door close behind them. She didn't ask why he'd developed this sudden interest in her. She didn't ask what value she placed on herself to follow him like this. She simply stood there and let him press her to the door.

He splayed his hands on each side of her head. His thumbs slipped into her hair and snagged on a curl. She winced. He angled his head and kissed her with his mouth open. He tasted of liquor and smoke. She kissed him back with everything she had. The stubble on his jaw abraded her cheek. His teeth bumped against hers. This was what she'd wanted, for him to see her as a woman instead of as a kid he had to rescue from scripted jams.

He snagged the hem of her dress and pushed it up. She wore a frail pair of bikini panties, and the zipper on his jeans scraped her bare stomach. He was going too fast for her, and she wanted to ask him to slow down. If he'd been anyone else, she'd have pushed him away and told him to take her home. But this was Bram, her home was half a continent away, and she let him slip his fingers into her panties and touch her however he wanted.

Before she knew it, he'd gotten rid of her panties and pulled her to the berth. "Lie down," he said.

As she sat on the side of the bed and felt the boat's engines vibrating through the thin fabric of her dress, she told herself this was what she'd been dreaming about. He shoved his hand in his pocket and pulled out a condom. It was really going to happen.

Despite the cabin's air-conditioned chill, her skin was damp from nerves. She watched him kick off his jeans and tried not to stare at his penis, but it was fully erect, and she couldn't look away. He peeled his polo shirt over his head revealing a bony chest with threads of pale blond hair. She studied the ceiling as he pulled on the condom.

The bed was high, and he didn't have to reach far to slide her hips to the edge. She fell back on her elbows, and the skirt of her dress bunched beneath her. He hooked his hand under her knees, splayed her legs, and stepped between them. His expression was intent, his eyes smoky as he gazed down at her. She was helplessly open, and she'd never felt more vulnerable.

He slid his hands down the back of her thighs to her hips and angled them upward. More of her weight shifted onto her elbows. Her neck ached from the awkward position. She smelled latex from the rubber, she smelled him—the beer, the tobacco, a hint of another woman's perfume. His fingers dug into her bottom as he worked himself inside her. It hurt, and she winced. The boat lurched, pushing him deeper. Her head bumped against the wall as he began to thrust. She tilted her neck, but it didn't help. He ground into her. Again and again. She looked up at the perfectly symmetrical bones in his pale face, the diamond shadows cutting across his cheeks. Finally, he began to shudder.

Her elbows gave way, and she fell back. Moments later, he pulled out and dropped her legs to the carpet. They were so stiff she had a hard time drawing them together. He went into the tiny attached bathroom. She pushed her dress down and told herself this could still turn out all right. Now he'd have to see her in a new light. They'd talk. Spend time together.

She bit her lip and managed to stand up on her shaky legs. He came back out and lit a cigarette. "Later," he said. And the door closed behind him.

As the lock clicked, all her fantasies about him shattered, and she finally saw him for exactly who he was, a crude, self-centered, egotistical ass. She saw herself, too—needy and stupid. Shame took her to her knees, and self-hatred smoldered in her chest. She didn't know anything about people, about life. All she knew was how to make stupid faces into the camera.

She wanted vengeance. She wanted to stab him. To torture him and kill him and hurt him as he'd hurt her. How could she ever have imagined herself in love?

The following season was agonizing. Unless they were filming, she pretended he was invisible. Ironically, her awful tension led to a powerful on-screen chemistry, and their ratings grew. She surrounded herself with her friends in the cast and crew or studied in her trailer—anything to avoid him and whichever of his foul-mouthed cronies was hanging around the set on a particular day. Her hatred froze into a mass large and solid enough to protect her.

One season followed another, and by their sixth year on the air, Bram's antics had begun to chip away at the ratings. Drunken parties, reckless driving, rumors of drug abuse. The fans of good-guy Skip Scofield weren't happy, but he ignored the warnings from the show's producers. When the sex tape surfaced at the end of season eight, it all came crashing down.

As sex tapes went, it was fairly tame, but not tame enough to obscure what was happening. The press went wild, and no amount of spin control could repair the damage. The network brass decided they'd had enough of Bram Shepard's antics. *Skip and Scooter* was canceled.

"Damn it!"

She jumped as Bram appeared. It took her a moment to reconcile the oversexed youthful jerk she remembered with the healthy, full-grown jerk walking toward her. He wore a matching hotel robe, and his hair was wet from his shower. More than anything, she wanted to avenge her eighteen-year-old self.

He looked uncharacteristically grim as he gave the robe's sash an extra tug. The clock registered two, which meant this miserable day was already half over. "Did you happen to spot any condoms in the trash?"

Hot coffee splashed her hand, and her heart stopped. She rushed into the bedroom and began searching the trash basket, but she only found her panties. She dashed back out into the living room. He pointed his coffee cup at her head. "You better tell me you've been tested since the last time you slept with your scumbag ex-husband."

"*Me?*" She wanted to throw another shoe, but she couldn't find one. "You'll nail anything that walks. Hookers. Strippers. Pool boys!" *Eighteen-year-old virgins with misplaced fantasies.*

"I've never nailed a pool boy in my life."

Bram was notoriously heterosexual, but considering his hedonistic nature, she figured that was merely an oversight.

He went on the counteroffensive. "I keep my engine in top working order, and I happen to be clean as a whistle. But then, I never slept with Lance the Loser and whatever candy-ass boys you replaced him with."

She couldn't believe this. "*I'm* the tramp? You haven't seen single digits since you were fourteen."

"And I'll bet anything, you're still in them. Thirty-one years old. Have you been to a shrink?"

Thanks to her father's overprotection, she'd only slept with four men, but since Bram had been her first so-called lover, and, apparently her last, the overall total hadn't changed. "Ten lovers, so you can keep the tramp trophy. And I'm also 'clean as a whistle.' Now get out of here. This whole thing never happened."

But he'd been distracted by the food cart. "They forgot the Bloody Marys. Shit." He began taking the covers off the serving dishes. "You were an animal last night. Your claws in my back, your moans in my ear . . ." As he sat, his robe fell open over a muscular thigh. "The things you begged me to do to you." He speared a chunk of mango. "Even I was embarrassed."

"You don't remember any of it."

"Not much."

She wanted to beg him to tell her exactly what he did remember. For all she knew, he could have attacked her, but somehow that didn't seem as horrible as the notion that she'd willingly given herself to him. She felt woozy and sank down at the table.

"You called me your wild stallion," he said. "I'm sure I remember that."

"I'm sure you don't." She had to figure out what had happened, but how could she get him to tell her what he knew? He began eating an omelet. She tried to settle her stomach with a piece of hard roll.

He reached for a pepper shaker. "So . . . you're on the pill, right?"

She threw down her roll and jumped up. "Oh, God . . ."

He stopped chewing. "Georgie . . ."

"Maybe nothing happened." She pressed her fingers to her lips. "Maybe we were so out of it, we fell asleep."

He shot out of the chair. "Are you telling me—"

"It'll be okay. It has to be." She started to pace. "What are the odds, right? I couldn't possibly be pregnant."

He'd started to look wild around the eyes. "You could be if you aren't on the pill!"

"If it— If it happens, we'll—I'll—I'll give it away. I know it'll be hard to find a person desperate enough to take a baby with a forked tongue and a tail, but I'm sure I can find someone."

The color returned to his cheeks. He sat back down and picked up his coffee cup. "A stellar performance."

"Thanks." Her small retaliation might have been juvenile, but it lifted her spirits enough so she could eat a strawberry. But a second berry was beyond her as she imagined the warm, solid weight of the baby she'd never hold.

Bram poured another coffee. Antagonism clawed away at her, the first time in forever that she'd had strong feelings toward anything except the collapse of her marriage.

Bram tossed down his napkin. "I'm going to get dressed." His gaze drifted toward the open collar of her robe. "Unless you want to . . ."

"Not in this lifetime."

He shrugged. "It seems a shame, that's all. Now we'll never know if we were any good together."

"I was fabulous. You, on the other hand, were as selfish as ever." A momentary stab of pain reminded her of the girl she'd been.

"I doubt that." He pushed away from the table and headed into the bedroom. She studied the strawberries, trying to convince herself she could eat another one. A loud curse interrupted her thoughts.

Bram stormed back into the living room. His jeans were unzipped and his dress shirt hung open, the French cuffs flapping. She found it hard to relate those solid chest muscles with the bonier body of his youth.

He thrust a sheet of paper under her nose. She was used to his sneers and his mockery, but she couldn't remember ever seeing him look genuinely upset. "I found this under my clothes," he said.

"A note from your parole officer?"

"Go ahead and enjoy yourself while you can."

She examined the paper, but what she saw made no sense. "Why would someone leave their marriage license here? It's—" Her throat closed, and she started to choke. "No! This is a joke, right? Tell me this is one of your sick jokes."

"Even I'm not this sick."

His face was ashen. She jumped up out of the chair and snatched the paper from him. "We got—" She could barely say the word. "We got married?"

He winced.

"But why would we do that? I *hate* you!"

"Those cocktails we drank last night must have had enough happy pills in them to make both of us overcome our mutual loathing."

She was starting to hyperventilate. "This can't be. They changed the law in Vegas. I read about it. The marriage license bureau is closed at night so exactly this kind of thing can't happen."

His lips tightened into a sneer. "We're celebrities. Apparently we found someone willing to bend the rules just for us."

"But . . . Maybe it's not legal. Maybe this is a—a joke certificate."

"Run your fingers over the official seal of the state of Nevada and tell me that feels like a fucking *joke*."

The raised bumps scraped her fingertips. She rounded on him. "This was your idea. I know it."

"Mine? You're the one who's desperate for a husband." His eyes narrowed, and he shoved his index finger in her face. "You used me."

"I'm calling my lawyer."

"Not before I call mine."

They ran for the nearest phone, but his legs were longer, and he got there first. She made a dash for her purse and dug out her cell. He punched the buttons. "This should be the easiest annulment on record."

The word "record" sent a chill through her. "Wait!" She dropped her cell, rushed to him, and grabbed the hotel room phone out of his hands.

"What are you doing?"

"Let me think for a minute." She shoved the phone back on the cradle.

"You can think later."

He started to reach for the phone again, but she jammed her hand over it. "The marriage—the annulment—will be a matter of public record." She plowed her free hand through her tangled hair. "Within twenty-four hours, everyone will know. There'll be a media circus complete with helicopters and car chases."

"You're used to it."

Her fingers were icy, her stomach nauseated. "I'm not going through another scandal. If I even stumble on the sidewalk, somebody reports that I tried to kill myself. Imagine what they'll do with this."

"Not my problem. You brought it on yourself by marrying The Loser."

"Will you stop calling him that?"

"He dumped you. What do you care?"

"Why do you hate him so much?"

"I don't hate him for me," he said caustically. "I hate him for you, since you don't seem to be able to do it for yourself. The guy's a mama's boy." Instead of pushing her away from the phone, he bent down and snatched up his shoe, then started looking around for his socks. "I'm going to find that bitch who drugged us."

She followed him into the bedroom, still not quite believing that he wasn't on the phone with his lawyer. "You can't leave until we come up with a story."

He found his socks and sat on the side of the bed to pull them on. "I have my story." He yanked on the first sock. "You're a desperate, pathetic woman. I married you out of pity, and—"

"You will not say that."

He yanked on the other sock. "—and now that I'm sober, I realize I'm not cut out for a life of misery."

"I'll sue you. I swear."

"Get a sense of humor, will you?" Displaying not even a trace of humor himself, he shoved his foot into one shoe and went back into the living room to get the other. "We'll make a joke out of it. Say we had too many drinks and started watching *Skip and Scooter* reruns. We were swept away by nostalgia, and it seemed like a good idea at the time."

That would be fine for him, but not for her. No one would believe her if she told the truth about the drugged drinks. For the rest of her life, she'd be branded as both a loser and a loony. She was trapped, and she couldn't let her bitterest enemy see that she was at his mercy. She shoved her fists into the pockets of her robe. "We're going to retrace our steps from last night. There have to be some clues about where we were. Do you remember anything?"

"Does 'Give it to me, big boy' count?"

"At least pretend to be decent."

"I'm not that good an actor."

"You know all kinds of shady characters. Surely you know someone who can make the record of our marriage disappear?"

She expected him to brush her off. Instead, his fingers stalled on a shirt button. "There's this guy I met a couple of times. A former councilman. He loves hobnobbing with celebrities. It's a long shot, but we can pay him a call."

She didn't have a better idea, so she agreed.

He dug into his pocket. "Apparently this belongs to you." He opened his palm and held out a cheap metal ring with a plastic "diamond" solitaire. "You can't say I don't have taste."

As he tossed it at her, she thought of the two-carat engagement diamond locked in her safe-deposit box. Lance had told her to keep it, as if her engagement ring was something she'd still want to wear.

She shoved the plastic diamond in her pocket. "Nothing says 'I love you' like fake jewelry."

She'd hitched a flight to Vegas on a private jet, so they needed to use Bram's car. While she showered, he arranged a discreet exit from the hotel. She pulled on her gray cotton slacks and a wraparound white top, the least conspicuous clothes she'd brought with her. "They have my car waiting in the back," he said when she came out of the bedroom.

"We'll take the service elevator down." She rubbed her forehead. "This is like Ross and Rachel all over again. The exact same thing happened to them at the end of season—"

"Except Ross and Rachel *don't really exist!*"

Neither of them spoke while they rode the elevator to the first floor. She didn't even bother telling him that he'd buttoned his shirt wrong.

They entered a service hallway and headed for the exit. As Bram held the door open, a blast of afternoon heat swept over them. She squinted against the sun and stepped outside.

A camera snapped in her face.

Chapter 5

Mel Duffy, the Darth Vader of the paparazzi, trapped them in his lens. Georgie experienced the odd sensation of floating out of her body and taking in the whole disaster from a spot somewhere above her head.

"Congratulations," Duffy said, clicking away. "In the words of my Irish grandmother, 'May you be poor in misfortunes and rich in blessings.'"

Bram just stood there, his hand on the door, his shirt buttoned wrong, and his jaw wired shut. He was leaving it up to her. This time she wouldn't let the jackals get the best of her, and she plastered on her Scooter Brown smile. "It's nice to have your grandmother's blessing. But what for?"

Duffy was overweight, with ruddy skin and an unkempt beard. "I've seen a copy of your marriage license,

and I talked with the guy who performed the ceremony. He looks like a seedy Justin Timberlake." Duffy
continued to shoot as he spoke. "It'll be all over the
wires within an hour, so you might as well give me the
story. I promise I'll send you a great wedding present." He shifted his angle again. "How long have you
been—"

"There's no story." Bram whipped an arm around
Georgie's waist and yanked her back into the building.

Ignoring trespassing laws, Duffy caught the door before it closed and followed them in. "Have you talked
to Lance? Does he know about this?"

"Back off," Bram said.

"Come on, Shepard. You know the score as well as
I do. This is the biggest celebrity story of the year."

"I said *back off*." Bram lunged for Duffy's camera.

Georgie, with the ounce of sanity she had left,
grabbed his arm and held on. "Don't do it!"

Duffy quickly stepped back, took one final shot, and
ducked out the door. "No hard feelings."

Bram shook her off and started after him.

"Stop it!" Georgie blocked the door with her body.
"What good will smashing his camera do now?"

"It'll make me feel better."

"That's so *you*. Still trying to solve problems with
your fists."

"As opposed to smiling at any asshole who points a lens in your direction and pretending life's just peachy?" He narrowed his eyes at her. "The next time I decide to deck somebody, stay out of my way."

A busboy came into the hallway, forcing her to stifle a hot retort. They headed for the service elevator and rode up in furious silence. When they reached the suite, he kicked the door open, then whipped his cell from his pocket.

"No!" She snatched it from his hand and raced with it to the bathroom.

He rushed after her. "What the hell do you think you're doing?"

She tossed the cell in the toilet before he could grab it back. He pushed her aside and stared down into the tank. "I cannot *believe* you did that."

Scooter had once accidentally dropped Mother Scofield's ancestral photo album into the garden fountain, then spent the rest of the show trying to cover her tracks. In the end, Skip had saved her by taking the blame. That so wasn't going to happen this time. "You're not calling anybody until we figure this out together," she said.

"Is that right?"

Her chest heaved, and she focused all her anger on him. "Do *not* screw with me. I'm an American icon, remember. Lance barely got away with it, and he was Mr. Squeaky Clean. You're not, and you won't."

His clenched-jaw reflection in the mirror wasn't reassuring. "We're going with my original plan," he said. "In exactly one hour, your publicist and the one I'm about to hire are going to release a statement. Too much liquor, too much nostalgia, remain good friends, bullshit, bullshit." He stalked out of the bathroom.

She went after him as she'd never gone after Lance. "A bubbleheaded pop star might be able to get away with a Vegas marriage that lasts less than twenty-four hours, but I can't, and neither can you. Give me some time to think."

"No amount of thinking is going to make this little scrape go away." He headed for the phone next to the couch.

"Five minutes! That's all I need." She pointed toward the television. "You can watch porn while you're waiting."

"You watch porn. I'm finding a publicist."

She tore around the couch and once again slapped her hands over the phone. "Do *not* make me toss this one in the toilet, too."

"Do *not* make me tie you up, lock you in a closet, and toss in a *match*!"

Right now that didn't sound so horrible. And then—

An impossible idea came to her.

An idea so much worse than any murderous plot he could come up with . . .

An idea so unbearable, so revolting . . .

She backed away from the phone. "I need alcohol."

He jabbed the receiver in the general direction of her head. "Kerosene burns hotter and faster." She must have looked as sick as she felt because he didn't immediately start to dial. "What's wrong? You're not going to throw up, are you?"

If only it were that simple. She gulped. "J-just hear me out, okay?"

"Make it quick."

"Oh, God . . ." Her legs had begun to buckle, and she sank into the chair on the other side of the couch. "There's a . . ." The room started to spin around her. "There might be . . . a-a way out of this."

"You're right. And I promise, I'll have fresh flowers delivered to your grave once a month. Plus your birthday and Christmas."

She absolutely could not look at him, so she stared at the creases of her gray slacks. "We could . . ." She cleared her throat. Swallowed. "We could s-stay married."

Thick silence filled the room, followed by the piercing bleat of a telephone left too long off its cradle.

Her palms were sweating, and her cheeks burned. He set the phone back on its hook. "*What* did you say?"

She swallowed again and tried to pull herself together. "Just for—for a year. We stay married for a year." Her words sounded wheezy, as if she was squeezing them through a kazoo. "A—a year from today, we announce that—that we've decided we're better friends than lovers, and we're getting a divorce. But that we'll love each other forever. And— Here's the important part." Her thoughts tumbled over one another, then focused. "We—we make sure we're seen together in public after that. Always laughing and having a good time together so neither of us gets painted as a"—she caught herself just before she said "victim"—"so neither of us gets painted as a villain."

The bits and pieces came together in her mind like a sitcom episode on crack. "Slowly, we let the story leak that I've started fixing you up with some of my girlfriends and that you're fixing me up with a few of those cretins you hang out with. Everything incredibly friendly. All Bruce and Demi. No drama, no scandal."

And no pity. That was the important part, the only way she'd be able to keep it together. No more pity for pathetic, heartbroken Georgie York who couldn't hold on to love.

Bram was still stuck at the beginning. "We stay married? You and me?"

"Just for a year. It's—I know it's not a perfect plan"—a mind-numbing understatement—"but given the circumstances, I think it's the best we can do."

"We *hate* each other!"

She couldn't fold now. Everything was at stake. Her reputation, her career, and most of all, her battered pride . . .

Except it was more than pride. Pride was a surface emotion, and this went deeper—all the way to her sense of identity. She faced the painful truth that she'd lived her entire life without making a single important decision of her own. Her father had guided every step of her career and her personal life, from the jobs she took to how she looked. He'd even introduced her to Lance, who'd dictated when they'd get married, where they'd live, and a thousand other things. Lance had announced they'd have no children, and he was the one who'd delivered the verdict that had ended her marriage. For thirty-one years, she'd let other people chart her destiny, and she was sick of it. She could either continue to live by the dictates of others, or she could set her own path, however bizarre.

A frightening—almost exhilarating—sense of purpose came over her. "I'll pay you."

That got his attention. "Pay me?"

"Fifty thousand for every month we stay together. That's over half a million dollars, in case you can't add."

"I can add."

"A post prenup," she said.

Once again, he jabbed a finger toward her head. "You did this on purpose. You trapped me just like you tried to trap Trevor. This was what you had in mind all along."

She jumped up from the chair. "Even you can't believe that! Every minute I spend with you is misery. But I care more about my . . . career than about how much I hate you."

"Your career or your image?"

She wasn't discussing her self-worth issues with the enemy. "Image *is* career in this town," she said, giving him the easy answer. "You know that better than anyone. It's why you can't get a decent job. Because nobody trusts you. But the public does trust me—even through all this mess with Lance. My reputation will rub off on you. You have everything to gain and nothing to lose by going along with this. People will think you've reformed, and you might finally be able to get a decent job."

Something flickered in his eyes. She'd picked the wrong argument, and she quickly switched direction. "Half a million dollars, Bram."

He turned his back on her and wandered over to the balcony doors. "Six months."

Her boldness faded, and she gulped. "Really?"

"I'll go along with this for six months," he said. "And then we renegotiate. You also have to agree to every one of my conditions."

Alarm bells shrieked. She struggled to pull herself together. "Which are?"

"I'll let you know when the time comes."

"No deal."

He shrugged. "Okay. No deal. This was your idea, not mine."

"You're being completely unreasonable!"

"I'm not the one who wants this so badly. Either we do it by my rules or I don't play."

No way in the world was she doing it by his rules. She'd had her fill of that with her father and Lance. "Fine," she said. "Your rules. And I'm sure they'll be eminently fair."

"Oh, yeah, you can count on that, all right."

She pretended not to hear. "The first thing we should do—"

"The first thing we're doing is getting hold of Mel Duffy." Suddenly he was all-business, which was unnerving, since Bram never paid any attention to business. "We'll tell him he can take exclusive photos right here in the suite, but only if he turns over his shots from downstairs." He gazed at her along his sublimely shaped nose. "He didn't get my good side."

Bram was right. The photos Duffy had just taken would make them look more like fugitives than blissful newlyweds. "Let's get to work," she said. "You remember how to do that, right?"

"Don't push me."

She notified the switchboard to hold the calls that would soon flood in, and Bram set about locating Mel Duffy. Three hours later, she and her dearly detested bridegroom were both clad in white, courtesy of the Bellagio's excellent concierge service. Her dress had a bustier top, a handkerchief hem, and some strategically placed double-sided fashion tape to make it fit. Bram wore a white linen suit and an open-collared white shirt. All that white against his tanned skin, tawny hair, and rakish stubble made him look like a pirate who'd just stepped off a luxury yacht to plunder the Cannes Film Festival.

She phoned her people—all of them but her father—with the news. She did a halfway decent job of professing her joy and excitement at being married to the Playboy of the Western World, but it wouldn't be nearly as easy with her friends. She deliberately left messages on their home voice mail so she didn't have to speak to them directly. As for her father . . . One crisis at a time.

Bram came up behind her while she was in the bathroom. If she let him walk all over her now, there'd be no retakes. He needed to see a whole new Georgie York.

She picked up the lipstick wand she'd just set down. "I don't share my makeup," she said. "Use your own."

"Is this stuff really nonsmear? I don't want to get it all over me when I french you."

"You're not frenching me."

"Wanna bet?" He crossed his arms over his chest and planted a shoulder against the doorjamb. "You know what I think?"

"You actually *think*?"

"I think all that crap you were spouting off about protecting your career is bogus." The doorbell rang. "The real reason you want to go through with this farce is because you never got over me."

"Oh, gee, you found me out." She elbowed him hard as she passed through the doorway.

Bram caught her before she reached the living room, and he tousled her hair. "There. Now you look like you just tumbled out of bed." He headed for the door. "Smile for the nice photographer."

Mel Duffy lumbered in, bringing the smell of onion rings with him. "Georgie, you look gorgeous." He studied the room, then gestured toward the balcony. "Let's start out here."

A few minutes later, they were posing by the railing with the sun sinking and their arms entwined around each other's waists. Duffy took some close-ups of the bride and groom laughing over the plastic diamond, then suggested Bram pick her up.

Just what she didn't want . . . Bram Shepard dangling her thirty stories above the ground.

Her filmy white skirt swirled around them as he swept her into his arms. She dug her fingers in his bicep. He gazed down at her, his face all lovey-dovey. She slipped her palm inside his jacket and lovey-doveyed him right back. She wondered what it would be like not to fake emotions she wasn't even close to feeling. At least this time, she'd chosen her path, and that had to count for something.

Duffy shifted position. "How about a kiss?"

"Exactly what I had in mind." Bram's voice was liquid sex.

She manufactured a silky smile. "I was hoping you'd ask."

He dipped his head, and just like that, she was sucked back to the past—the day of their first on-screen kiss.

She'd stood by another railing then, one that looked down on the Chicago River near the Michigan Avenue Bridge. As usual, they were spending the first couple of weeks shooting exteriors before they returned to L.A.

to film the rest of what would be their fifth season. It was a Sunday morning in late July, and the police had temporarily closed off the area. Even with a breeze blowing in from the lake, it was already nearly ninety degrees.

"Is Bram here yet?" Jerry Clarke, their director, called out.

"Not yet," the A.D. replied.

Bram hated early-morning calls nearly as much as he'd come to hate playing Skip, and Georgie knew for a fact that Jerry had assigned a production assistant to get him out of bed. Her hands curled over the railing. She couldn't wait for today to be over. A year might have passed since the ugly night on the boat, but she still hadn't forgiven him for what he'd done or forgiven herself for letting him go so far. She coped by pretending he didn't exist. Only when the cameras began to roll and he turned into her Skip Scofield with his gentle, intelligent eyes and worried, caring expression did she let down her defenses.

They'd dressed her that day in a skinny, but not too skinny, T-shirt and a short, but not too short, cotton skirt. The producers had begun letting her have more auburn added to her hair, but she still hated the curls. Not only did the network own her hair, but they owned the rest of her, too. Her contract prohibited body piercing, tattoos, sexual scandal, and drug abuse. Apparently Bram's contract forbade nothing.

The director exploded in frustration. "Somebody go find the son of a bitch!"

"The son of a bitch is right here." Bram slithered forward, a cigarette dangling from the corner of his mouth, his bloodshot eyes at odds with his light blue knit shirt, pressed chinos, and preppy wristwatch.

"Did you have a chance to look over the script?" Jerry said with open sarcasm. "We're doing Skip and Scooter's first kiss."

"Yeah, I read it." He pitched a cigarette butt through the railing. "Let's get this bullshit over with."

As she stood there in her girl-next-door clothes, she hated him so fiercely she burned with it. Those first few years, she'd been so determined to see him as a moody romantic figure waiting for the right woman to redeem him, but he was really just a garden-variety snake, and she was a sucker not to have figured that out right away.

They ran their lines and found their marks. The cameras began to roll. She waited for the magic to begin as Bram transformed himself into Skip.

SKIP

(*Gazing tenderly at SCOOTER*)

Scooter, what am I going to do with you?

SCOOTER
You could kiss me. I know you don't want to. I know you're going to say that I'm—

SKIP
Trouble.

SCOOTER
I don't mean to be.

SKIP
I wouldn't have it any other way.
(SKIP looks searchingly into SCOOTER's eyes, then slowly kisses her.)

Georgie felt the hard touch of his lips, and this time the magic didn't work. Skip's lips should be soft. And Skip shouldn't taste of cigarettes and insolence. She pulled back.

"Cut," Jerry called out. "Is there a problem, Georgie?"

"There's a problem, all right." Bram scowled at the camera. "It's eight fucking o'clock in the morning."

"Let's do it again," the director said.

And they had. Again and again. It was only a simple stage kiss, but no matter how hard she tried, she couldn't make herself believe Skip was kissing her, and each time their lips met, she felt as though she was shaming herself all over again.

After the sixth take, Bram stormed off and told her to go take some "fucking acting lessons." She shouted back that he should swallow some "fucking mouthwash." The crew was used to temperament from Bram, but not from her, and she was ashamed. "I'm sorry, everybody," she murmured. "I don't mean to push my bad day off on you."

The director coaxed Bram back. Georgie reached inside herself and somehow managed to use her own churning emotions to show Scooter's confusion. They finally had their take.

And now here she was again, doing something she'd never thought she'd have to repeat. Kissing Bram Shepard.

Bram's mouth closed over hers, his lips soft as Skip's should have been. She began her mental retreat to the secret place she'd hidden in so many years ago. But something was wrong. Bram no longer tasted of late nights and seedy bars. He tasted clean. Not clean like Lance, who had an Altoids addiction, but clean like—

She couldn't put her finger on it, but she knew she didn't like it. She wanted Bram to be Bram. She wanted the sour taste of his condescension, the tainted bile of his disdain. Those were both things she knew how to handle.

She waited for him to try sticking his tongue down her throat. Not that she wanted him to—God, no—but at least it would be familiar.

He nibbled at her lower lip, then slowly set her back on her feet. "Welcome to married life, Mrs. Shepard," he said in a soft, tender voice even as his hand, hidden in the folds of her skirt, pinched her bottom.

She smiled with relief. Bram was finally acting like himself. "Welcome to my heart . . . ," she said just as tenderly, ". . . Mr. Georgie York." Beneath his jacket, she jabbed him in the ribs as hard as she could.

It was dark outside when Duffy left, and the management had slipped a message under the door. The switchboard was swamped with calls, and a horde of photographers had gathered outside. She turned on the television and saw that the news of their marriage was out. While Bram changed his clothes, she sat on the edge of the couch and watched.

Everyone was shocked.

No one had seen it coming.

Since only the bare-bones details were available, the cable news outlets were trying to fill out the story with comments from a string of so-called experts who knew absolutely nothing.

"After the devastating end to her first marriage, Georgie has returned to the comfort of the familiar."

"Perhaps Shepard's grown weary of his playboy lifestyle . . ."

"But has he really reformed? Georgie's a wealthy woman, and . . ."

Bram came out of the bedroom in a fresh pair of jeans and a black T-shirt. "We're leaving tonight."

She muted the remote. "I'm not exactly anxious to drive to L.A. with a herd of photographers chasing us. As Princess Diana would say, 'Been there. Done that.' "

"I've taken care of it."

"You can't even take care of yourself."

"Let me put it another way. I'm not staying here. You can either come with me or explain to the press why your new husband is leaving alone."

He was clearly going to win this skirmish, so she conjured up a sneer. "You'd better know what you're doing."

As it turned out, he did have the situation taken care of. A paneled plumbing van waited for them at the darkened loading dock. He tossed their suitcases inside and slipped the driver a couple of folded bills from his wallet. Afterward, he gave her an arm-up into the back, then climbed in himself and shut the door.

The interior smelled like rotten eggs. They wedged themselves into a space near the doors, drew up their knees, and set their backs against their luggage. "We'd better not be going all the way to L.A. in this," she said.

"Were you always so whiny?"

Pretty much, she thought. At least this past year. And that was going to change. "You worry about yourself."

The van lurched away from the loading dock, and she fell against his side. Her life had come to this. Sneaking out of Vegas in the back of a plumbing van. She rested her cheek on her bent knees and closed her eyes, trying not to think about what lay ahead.

SCOOTER
I never look up at the stars.

SKIP
Why's that?

SCOOTER
Because they make me feel too small. Less than a speck. I'd rather stick my hand in a lion's cage than look at stars.

SKIP
That's crazy. Stars are beautiful.

SCOOTER
Stars are depressing. I want to do big things with my life, but how can I when the stars only remind me of how small I really am?

Eventually the van pulled off the highway and came to a stop on a bumpy dirt road. Bram dropped to the ground. She poked her head out. It was pitch-black, and they were in the middle of nowhere. She climbed down and walked gingerly around to the front of the van. The headlights picked out a wooden sign reading JEAN DRY LAKE. Next to it, a tattered poster advertised some kind of rocket-launching festival. Bram was talking to the driver of a nondescript dark sedan. She didn't want to talk to anyone, so she stayed where she was.

The van driver passed her carrying their luggage. "I really liked you in *Skip and Scooter*," he said.

"Thanks." She wished more people would say they liked her in one of her movies.

The sedan's driver got out and put their suitcases in the trunk. Both men climbed into the van and pulled away. She and Bram stood alone, only his burnished hair shining in the moonlit darkness.

"They won't keep quiet about this," she said. "You know they won't. It's too juicy a story."

"By the time it gets out, we'll be long home."

Home. She couldn't imagine them trapped in her small rental house. She'd have to find another place quickly—something large enough so they'd never see each other. As she opened the car door, she checked her watch. It was two o'clock; only twelve hours since she'd awakened and found herself in this mess.

Bram slipped behind the wheel. He drove fast, but not recklessly. "A friend is driving my car back to L.A. in a couple of days. If we're lucky, it'll take that long before anybody figures out we've left."

"We need a place to live," she said. "I'll have my real estate agent find something fast."

"We're moving into my place."

"Your place? I thought you were house-sitting in Malibu."

"I only stay out there when I want to get away."

"From *what*?" She kicked off her sandals. "Wait. Didn't Trev tell me you live in an apartment?"

"Is there something wrong with apartments?"

"Yes. They're small."

"Have you always been such a snob?"

"I'm not a snob. This is about privacy. From each other."

"That's going to be a little tough with only one bedroom. Although it's a pretty big bedroom."

She glared at him. "We're not living in your one-bedroom apartment."

"You don't have to if you don't want to, but that's where I'm living."

Now she got it. This was how he intended to handle everything. It would be his way or the highway.

Her head ached, she had a stiff neck, and she saw no advantage to arguing about this until they got to L.A. She turned away and closed her eyes. Deciding to take control of her life was the easy part. Carrying it off would be a lot tougher.

She woke at dawn. She'd fallen asleep against the passenger door, and she rubbed her neck. They were driving up a winding residential street lined with houses hidden behind massive foliage. Bram glanced over at her. Other than heavier stubble, he didn't show any signs of his sleepless night. She scowled. "Where are we?"

"In the Hollywood Hills."

They passed a high ficus hedge, rounded another bend, then turned into a driveway set between stone pillars. A sprawling russet stucco and stone Spanish colonial house came into view. Bougainvillea twined around a Moorish bay made up of six arched windows, and trumpet vine climbed a round, two-story turret that angled off at one end. "I knew you were lying about the apartment."

"This is my girlfriend's house."

"Your *girlfriend*?"

He pulled up in front and turned off the engine. "You have to explain to her what happened. It'll go better if she hears the story from you."

"You want me to explain to your *girlfriend* why you're married?"

"Am I supposed to let her read it in the papers? Don't you think I should be a little more sensitive toward the woman I love?"

"You've never loved anyone in your life. And since when have you only had one girlfriend?"

"There's always a first time." He unsnapped his seat belt and got out of the car.

Georgie hurried after him toward a one-story arcaded entry porch paved in blue and white Spanish tiles. Assorted terra-cotta planters sat between three small twisted stone columns the same russet color as the stucco. "We're not telling anybody the truth about this," she whispered. "Especially a woman who's going to have an understandable need for revenge."

He stepped up onto the porch. "If she's as serious about me as I think she is, she'll keep her mouth shut and wait this out."

"And if she's not?"

He lifted one eyebrow. "Let's be honest, Scoot. When have you ever known a woman not to be serious about me?"

Chapter 6

Bram had his own key to his girlfriend's house, so he was either living with her, or he spent a lot of time here, which would explain why he only needed a one-bedroom apartment. Georgie followed him up the tiled steps into a foyer with bronze wall sconces and glazed, parchment-colored walls. "You should have told me about her earlier."

He tilted his head toward the back of the house. "The kitchen's that way. She's going to need coffee. I'll go prepare her while you make it."

"Bram, this isn't a good idea. I'm telling you as a woman that . . ."

He'd already disappeared up the stairs. She sank down on the bottom step and buried her face in her hands. A girlfriend. Bram had always been surrounded by beautiful women, but she'd never heard of him being involved in a serious relationship. Now she wished she hadn't cut Trevor off whenever he started gossiping about Bram's activities.

She rose from the step and began to look around. This girlfriend had exquisite taste in decorating, if not in men. Unlike so many older hacienda-style homes, this one had light hardwood floors that were either original or had been distressed to look warm and rustic. The furniture was comfortable—basic pieces upholstered in muted fabrics dressed up with embellished Indian pillows and Tibetan throws in ochre, olive, rust, pewter, and tarnished gold. A series of tall French doors opening to a rear veranda allowed the early-morning light to spill inside, which accounted for the lushness of the lemon and kumquat trees growing in decorative ceramic pots. An antique olive urn held a luxuriant vine that twined up the side of the fireplace and along the heavy stone mantel, which was carved in a Moorish design.

The well-equipped kitchen had roughly plastered walls, sleek appliances, and earth-toned tiles with deep blue accents. An iron chandelier with tin shades hung over the center island, and the bay with six arched windows she'd seen when they'd driven in made up the breakfast nook. She found the coffeemaker and made a pot. So far, she hadn't heard any screams coming from upstairs, but it was only a matter of time. She carried her mug out onto a roofed veranda with the same twisted russet columns and blue-and-white Spanish tile floor as the front entry porch. The filigreed metal lanterns, mosaic tables with curved iron legs, ornate wooden screen, and furniture upholstered in colorful Moroccan and Turkish fabrics made her feel as though she'd stepped into a casbah. Luxuriant vines, low palms, and stands of bamboo offered a sense of privacy.

She wrapped a cotton throw around her shoulders and settled in a comfortable lounge chair. The faint sound of brass wind-bells drifted through the chilly morning quiet. Bram obviously didn't know his girlfriend well because the kind of woman who owned a house like this wasn't going to accept having her boyfriend marry another woman, regardless of the circumstances. He was stupid to even imagine such a thing, which was odd because Bram was never—

She jolted upright. Coffee splashed on her hand. She sucked it off, then set her mug on a stack of newsmagazines and stomped inside. Within seconds, she'd climbed the steps and found the master bedroom where Bram lay facedown and sound asleep across the king-size bed. Alone.

Georgie had forgotten the most fundamental rule when dealing with Bram Shepard. Don't believe anything he says.

She was ready to dump a cold bucket of water over his head when she thought better of it. As long as he was asleep, she didn't have to deal with him. She went back downstairs and resettled on the veranda. At eight o'clock she called Trev, who, predictably, nearly blew out her eardrums. *"What the hell's going on?"*

"True love," she retorted.

"I can't believe he married you. I absolutely cannot believe you talked him into this."

"We were drunk."

"Believe me, he wasn't that drunk. Bram always knows exactly what he's doing. Where is he now?"

"Asleep upstairs in a magnificent house that, apparently, belongs to him."

"He bought it two years ago. God knows how he came up with the down payment. It's no secret that he hasn't been exactly fiscally responsible."

Which was why Bram had agreed to go along with this. The fifty thousand dollars a month she'd promised him.

But Trev didn't know about the blood money. "He's decided you're the ticket he needs to raise his profile.

This publicity could help him get some decent parts again. He pretends not to care that he's basically made himself unemployable, but, believe me, he does."

She moved restlessly from the veranda into the yard and gazed back at the house. A second set of twisted columns on top of the first held up the roof of the balcony that ran across much of the top story, and more vines climbed the russet stucco walls. "He can't be destitute," she said. "This place is amazing."

"And mortgaged to the hilt. He's done a lot of the work himself."

"No way. He's talked some lovesick woman into paying at least some of his bills."

"Always a possibility."

She needed to know more, but when she pressed, Trev shut her down. "You're both my friends, and I'm not getting involved in this, although I definitely want a dinner invitation so I can watch the fireworks."

She had a total of thirty-eight messages and texts on her cell, with her father accounting for ten of them. She could imagine how frantic he was, but she couldn't bear talking to him yet. April had left with her family for their Tennessee farm two days ago. Georgie dialed her number, and as she heard her friend's voice, some of her defenses fell away, and she bit her lip. "April, you have no way of knowing that just about everything

I'm getting ready to tell you is a pack of lies, so that means you can pass on the information with a clear conscience, okay?"

"Oh, sweetie..." April sounded like a worried mother.

"Bram and I met accidentally in Las Vegas. The sparks flew, and we realized how much we'd always loved each other. We decided we'd wasted too much time being apart, so we got married. You don't know for sure where we are, but you suspect we're still holed up at the Bellagio enjoying an impromptu honeymoon, and isn't everyone glad that Bram Shepard has finally reformed and the world has the happy ending they didn't get when *Skip and Scooter* was canceled?" Georgie's breath snagged in her throat. "Would you call Sasha and tell her the same thing? And if Meg resurfaces..."

"Of course I will, but, honey, I'm really worried about you. I'm going to fly back and—"

"No." The concern in April's voice made her want to burst into tears. "I'm fine. Really. Just shaken up. Love you."

As she hung up, she made herself face reality. She was trapped in this house for the immediate future. The public would expect Bram and her to be glued together while they were newlyweds. Weeks would pass before she could go anywhere without him. She leaned back on the veranda chaise, shut her eyes, and tried to think. But there were no easy answers, and eventually she dozed off to the sound of the brass wind-bells.

When she awakened two hours later, she felt no more refreshed than when she'd fallen asleep, and she reluctantly headed upstairs. Latin music reverberated from the far end of the hallway. On her way to investigate, she passed Bram's bedroom and spotted her suitcase sitting in the middle of the floor.

Yeah, right. Like that was going to happen.

If she'd had to guess what Bram Shepard's bedroom looked like, she'd have imagined a disco ball and a stripper's pole, but she'd have been wrong. The barrel vault ceiling and roughly plastered buckwheat-honey walls defined a space that was rich, elegant, and sensual without being sleazy. Rectangular leather panels set in a bronze metal grid made up the headboard of the king-size bed, and a comfortable lounging area occupied the turret she'd spotted from the front of the house.

As she went in to retrieve her suitcase, the music stopped. Moments later, Bram appeared at the bedroom door in a sweat-damp Lakers T-shirt and gray workout shorts. Just the sight of him looking so healthy made her temper erupt. "I met your *girlfriend* downstairs.

She fell on her knees and thanked me for getting you out of her life."

"I hope you were nice to her."

He didn't have the grace to apologize for his lie, but then he'd never told her he was sorry for anything he'd done. She moved in on him. "There's no girlfriend, and there's no apartment. This is your house, and I want you to stop lying to me."

"Couldn't help it. You were getting on my nerves." He walked right past her toward the bathroom.

"I mean it, Bram! We're in this together. No matter how much we hate it, we're officially a team. I know you don't understand what that means, but I do. A team only works if everybody cooperates."

"Okay. You've gotten on my nerves again. Try to entertain yourself while I clean up." He whipped off his damp T-shirt and disappeared into the bathroom. "Unless"—he stuck his head back out—"you want to hop in the shower with me and play some water games." He deliberately smoldered her with his eyes. "After last night . . . I'm not saying you're a nympho, but you sure are close."

Oh, no. He wasn't getting her that easily. She lifted her chin and smoldered him right back. "I'm afraid you have me confused with that Great Dane you used to own."

He laughed and shut the bathroom door.

She grabbed her suitcase and carried it out into the hallway. Once again, the sense of being trapped made her heart race, and once again she fought to steady herself. She needed someplace to sleep tonight. She'd glimpsed a guesthouse in the back, but he almost certainly had some kind of household staff, so she couldn't settle in that far away.

She explored the upstairs and discovered five bedrooms. Bram used one for storage, he'd converted another into a well-equipped exercise room, and a third was spacious but empty. Only the room next to the master had furniture, a double bed with an ornamental Moorish headboard and matching dresser. Light spilled in through a set of French doors that opened out onto the rear balcony. The cool lemony walls provided an appealing contrast to the dark wood and colorful Oriental rug.

Her assistant would bring over some clothes tomorrow, but until then, she had only one clean outfit left. She unpacked her suitcase and carried her toiletries into the adjoining glass block and cinnabar tile bathroom. She badly needed a shower, but when she returned to her room to undress, she found Bram stretched out on her bed in a clean T-shirt and cargo shorts with what looked like a tumbler of scotch balanced on his chest. It wasn't even two in the afternoon.

He swirled the liquid in the glass. "Your sleeping in here isn't going to work. My housekeeper lives over the garage. I have a feeling she'll notice if we have separate beds."

"I'll make the bed every morning before she sees it," she said with fake sweetness. "As for my things . . . Tell her I'm turning this into my dressing room."

He took a sip of scotch and uncrossed his ankles. "I meant what I said yesterday. We're doing this by my rules. A regular sex life is part of the deal."

She knew him too well to even pretend to be surprised. "This is the twenty-first century, Skipper. Men don't issue sexual ultimatums."

"This man does." He uncoiled from the bed like a tawny lion getting ready for the hunt. "I'm not giving up sex, which means I can either screw around on you, or we'll do what married couples do. And don't worry. I'm not nearly as much into S and M as I used to be. Not that I've given it up entirely . . ." His light mockery seemed more intimidating than the surly scorn she remembered. He took a lazy sip of scotch. "There's a new sheriff in town, Scooter. You and Daddy don't hold the power card any longer. We're playing with a fresh deck, and it's my deal." He lifted his glass in a mock toast and disappeared into the hallway.

She took a dozen deep breaths, then half a dozen more. She'd known turning herself into a woman of purpose wouldn't be easy. But she held the checkbook, didn't she? And that made her up to the challenge. Definitely, absolutely, positively up to the challenge.

She was almost sure of it.

At the bottom of the stairs, Bram's cell vibrated in his shorts' pocket. He moved into the farthest reaches of his living room before he answered. "Hello, Caitlin."

"Well, well . . . ," a familiar throaty female voice responded. "And aren't you just full of surprises?"

"I like to keep life interesting."

"Lucky I turned on the television last night, or I wouldn't have heard the news."

"Call me insensitive, but you weren't at the top of my contact list."

As she went off on him, he gazed out through the French doors onto the veranda. He loved this house. It was the first place he'd lived that felt like home, or at least the way he imagined home should feel, since he'd never before had one. The luxurious mansions he'd rented during *Skip and Scooter* had been more like frat houses than real homes, with at least four guys living with him at a time. Video games used to blare in half the rooms, porn in the others, beer cans and fast food everywhere. And women, lots of women—some of them smart, decent girls who'd deserved to be treated better.

As Caitlin ranted on, he wandered through the back hall and down a few steps into the small screening room he'd refurbished. Chaz must have watched a movie last night because it still smelled faintly of popcorn. He took a sip from his drink and sank into one of the reclining armchair seats. The empty screen reminded him of his current state. He'd blown the opportunity of a lifetime with *Skip and Scooter*, just like his old man had blown every opportunity that had come his way. A family inheritance.

"I've got another call, sweetheart," he said as his patience ran out. "I have to go."

"Six weeks," she retorted. "That's all you have left."

As if he'd forgotten.

He checked for messages, then turned off his phone. He couldn't blame Caitlin for being bitter, but he had a much bigger problem at the moment. When he'd heard that Georgie was going to spend the weekend in Vegas, he'd decided to follow her. But the game he'd set out to play had taken a lunatic twist he'd never anticipated. He sure as hell hadn't planned on getting married.

Now he had to figure out how to turn this farcical situation to his advantage. Georgie had a thousand excellent reasons to hate him, a thousand reasons to exploit every weakness she could find, which meant he could only let her see what she expected. Fortunately, she already thought the worst of him, and he wasn't likely to do anything to change her opinion.

He almost felt sorry for her. Georgie didn't have a ruthless bone in her body, so it was an uneven match. She put other people's interests before her own, then blamed herself if the same people screwed up. He, on the other hand, was a selfish, self-centered son of a bitch who'd grown up understanding he had to look out for himself, and he didn't have a single qualm about using her. Now that he finally knew what he wanted out of life, he was going after it with everything he had.

Georgie York didn't stand a chance.

Georgie showered and scrounged up a turkey sandwich. She ended up in his dining room searching for a book to read. A massive round, black, claw-footed table that looked Spanish or maybe Portuguese sat on an Oriental rug with a Moorish brass chandelier overhead, but the dining room was both a place to eat and a cozy library. Floor-to-ceiling bookcases lined every wall except the one that opened into the garden. In addition to books, the shelves held an eclectic mixture of artifacts: Balinese bells, chunks of quartz, Mediterranean ceramics, and small Mexican folk paintings.

Bram's decorator had created a cozy space that invited lingering, but the diverse collection showed his decorator either hadn't gotten to know him well or didn't care that her high school dropout client was unlikely to appreciate her finds. She carried a lushly illustrated volume of contemporary California artists over to a leather easy chair in the corner, but as evening approached, her concentration faded. It was time to get down to business. Maybe Bram didn't see the need for the two of them to have a cohesive plan for dealing with the press, but she understood it. They had to decide fairly quickly when and how to handle their reappearance. She put aside her book and set off to track him down. When she couldn't locate him anywhere, she followed a crushed-gravel path through a stand of bamboo and some tall shrubbery to the guesthouse.

It wasn't much larger than a two-car garage, with the same red barrel–tiled roof and stucco exterior as the main house. The two front windows were dark, but she heard a phone ringing from the back and followed a narrower path toward the sound. Light spilled through an open set of glass doors onto a small gravel patio that held a pair of lounges with chartreuse canvas cushions and some potted elephant-ear plants. Vines climbed the walls around the open doors. Inside, she saw a homey office with paprika-colored walls and a poured-concrete floor topped with a sea grass rug. A collection of framed movie posters hung on the walls, some predictable like Marlon Brando in *On the Waterfront* and Humphrey Bogart in *The African Queen,* but others less so: Johnny Depp in *Benny & Joon,* Don Cheadle in *Hotel Rwanda,* and Meg's dad, Jake Koranda, as Bird Dog Caliber.

Bram was on the phone as she entered. He sat behind an L-shaped wooden desk painted a dark apricot, an ever-present drink at his side. Built-in bookcases at one end of the office held a stack of the trades, as well as some highbrow film magazines like *Cineaste* and *Fade In.* Since she'd never known Bram to read anything more challenging than *Penthouse,* she tagged them as another of the decorator's touches.

He didn't look happy to see her. Tough.

"I've got to let you go, Jerry," he said into the receiver. "I need to get ready for a meeting tomorrow morning. Give my best to Dorie."

"You have an *office?*" she said as he hung up.

He hooked his hands behind his neck. "It belonged to the former owner. I haven't gotten around to converting it into an opium den."

She spotted something that looked like a copy of the *Hollywood Creative Directory* near the phone, but he flipped it shut when she tried to get a closer look. "What morning meeting do you have?" she said. "You don't do meetings. You don't even do mornings."

"You're my meeting." He nodded toward the phone. "The press discovered we're not still in Vegas, and the house is staked out. We have to put up a set of gates this week. I'll let you pay for them."

"There's a surprise."

"You're the one with the big bucks."

"Deduct it from the fifty-thousand a month I'm paying you." She gazed toward the poster of Don Cheadle. "We need to make plans. First thing tomorrow we should—"

"I'm on my honeymoon. No business talk."

"We have to talk. We need to decide—"

"Georgie! Are you out here?"

Her heart sank. One part of her wondered how he'd managed to find her so quickly. The other part was surprised it had taken him this long.

Shoes crunched on the gravel path outside the guesthouse, and then her father appeared. He was conservatively dressed as always in a white shirt, light gray trousers, and tasseled cordovan loafers. At fifty-two, Paul York was trim and fit, with rimless glasses and crisp, prematurely gray hair that caused him to be mistaken for Richard Gere.

He stepped inside and stood quietly, studying her. Except for the color of his green eyes, they looked nothing alike. She'd gotten her round face and stretchy mouth from her mother. "Georgie, what have you done?" he said in his quiet, detached voice.

Just like that, she was eight years old again, and those same cold green eyes were judging her for letting an expensive bulldog puppy get away during a pet food commercial or for spilling juice on her dress before an audition. If only he were one of those rumpled, over-weight, scratchy-cheeked fathers who didn't know anything about show business and only cared about her happiness. She pulled herself together.

"Hi, Dad."

He clasped his hands behind his back and patiently waited for her to explain.

"Surprise!" she said with a fake smile. "Not that it's really a surprise. I mean . . . You had to know we were dating. Everybody saw the photos of us at Ivy. Sure, it seems fast, but we practically grew up together, and . . . When it's right, it's right. Right, Bram? Isn't that right?"

But her bridegroom was too busy reveling in her discomfort to chime in with his support.

Her father studiously avoided looking in his direction. "Are you pregnant?" he asked in the same clinical voice.

"No! Of course not! This is a"—she tried not to choke—"love match."

"You hate each other."

Bram finally uncoiled from his chair and came to her side. "That's old history, Paul." He slipped his arm around her waist. "We're different people now."

Paul continued to ignore him. "Do you have any idea how many reporters are out front? They attacked my car when I drove in."

She briefly wondered how he'd found her back here, then realized her father wouldn't let a small thing like an unanswered doorbell stop him. She could see him now, tramping through the shrubbery and emerging without a single hair out of place. Unlike her, Paul York never got ruffled or confused. He never lost his sense of purpose, either, which was why he found it so difficult to understand her insistence on taking a six-month vacation.

"You need to get control of this publicity immediately," he said.

"Bram and I were just discussing our next step."

Paul finally turned his attention to Bram. From the beginning, they'd been enemies. Bram hated Paul's interference on the set, especially the way he made sure Georgie never lost her top billing. And Paul hated everything about Bram.

"I don't know how you talked Georgie into this charade," her father said, "but I know why. You want to ride on her coattails again, just like you used to. You want to use her to advance your own pathetic career."

Her father didn't know about the money, so he was uncharacteristically off the mark. "Don't say that." She needed to at least pretend to defend Bram. "This is exactly the reason I didn't call you. I knew you'd be upset."

"Upset?" Her father never raised his voice, which made his disgust all the more painful. "Are you deliberately trying to ruin your life?"

No, she was trying to save it.

Paul rocked on his heels just as he used to when she was a child and she didn't have her lines memorized. "And here I thought the worst of this mess was over."

She knew what he meant. He adored Lance, and he'd been furious when they split. Sometimes she wished he'd just come out and say what he really meant, that she should have been woman enough to hold on to her husband.

He shook his head. "I don't think I've ever been so disappointed in you."

His words bit to the quick, but she was working hard at being her own person, so she made herself manufacture another bright smile. "And just think, I'm only thirty-one. I have lots of years to improve my record."

"That's enough, Georgie," Bram said, almost pleasantly. He let his hand slip from her waist. "Paul, let me lay it out for you. Georgie is my wife now, and this is my house, so behave, or you'll lose your invitation to visit."

She sucked in her breath.

"Really?" Paul's lip curled.

"Really." Bram headed for the doors. But just before he got there, he turned back, performing the old false exit as flawlessly as he'd done it in a score of *Skip and Scooter* episodes. He even started off with the identical dialogue. "Oh, and one more thing . . ." That was when he went off script, and he did it with a smile. "I want to see Georgie's tax returns from the last five years. And her financial statements."

She couldn't believe it. Of all the— She took a step toward him.

An angry flush spread over her father's face. "Are you implying that I've mismanaged Georgie's money?"

"I don't know. Have you?"

Bram had gone too far. She might resent the way her father attempted to control her, and she definitely questioned his judgment in choosing her latest projects, but he was the only man in the world she trusted completely when it came to money. All kid actors should be lucky enough to have such a scrupulously honest parent guarding their incomes.

Her father grew more outwardly calm, never a good sign. "Now we get to the real reason for this marriage. Georgie's money."

Bram's lips curled with insolence. "First you say I married her to advance my career . . . Now you think I married her for her money . . . Dude, I married her for *sex*."

Georgie rushed forward. "Okay, I've had enough laughs for tonight. I'll call you tomorrow, Dad. I promise."

"That's it? That's all you have to say?"

"If you give me a couple of minutes, I can probably come up with a good punch line, but for now, I'm afraid that's the best I've got."

"Let me show you out," Bram said.

"No need." Her father strode toward the door. "I'll leave the same way I came in."

"No, Dad, really . . . Let me . . ."

But he was already crossing the gravel patio. She sank into a saggy brown couch right underneath Humphrey Bogart.

"That was fun," Bram said.

She clenched her fists in her lap. "I can't believe you questioned his integrity like that. You—the go-to guy for financial mismanagement. How my father handles my money is my business, not yours."

"If there's nothing to hide, he won't mind opening the books."

She shot up. "I mind! My finances are confidential, and I'm calling my lawyer first thing tomorrow to make sure they stay that way." She'd also have a private talk with her accountant about disguising the fifty thousand a month she was paying Bram from her father. "Household expenses" and "increased security" sounded a lot better than "blood money."

"Relax," he said. "Do you really think I'd know how to read a financial statement?"

"You were deliberately baiting him."

"Didn't you enjoy it just a little bit? Now your father knows he can't order me around the way he does you."

"I run my own life." At least she was trying to.

She expected him to debate the point, but he flicked off the desk lamp instead and nudged her toward the door. "Bedtime. I'll bet you'd like a back rub."

"I'll bet I wouldn't." She stepped outside as he pulled the doors closed behind them. "Why do you keep pushing this?" she said. "You don't even like me."

"Because I'm a guy, and you're available."

She let her silence speak for itself.

Chapter 7

The next morning Georgie carefully made the bed she'd slept in by herself and went downstairs. In the kitchen, she found a young woman standing at the counter, her back to the door, a colander of strawberries in front of her. She had dyed black hair clipped short on one side, but jaw-length and jagged on the other. Three small Japanese symbols tattooed on the back of her neck disappeared into a sleeveless gray T-shirt, and big safety pins secured a long hole in the side of her jeans. She looked like a 1990s punk rocker, and Georgie couldn't imagine what she was doing in Bram's kitchen.

"Uh . . . Good morning." Her greeting went unacknowledged. She wasn't used to people who didn't suck up to her, and she tried again. "I'm Georgie."

"Like I wouldn't know that." The girl still didn't turn. "This is Bram's special protein breakfast drink. You'll have to fix whatever you want for yourself." The blender roared to life.

Georgie waited until the motor went quiet. "And you are—?"

"Bram's housekeeper. Chaz."

"Short for?"

"Chaz."

Georgie got the message. Chaz hated her and didn't want to talk. Trust Bram to have a housekeeper who looked like she'd stepped out of a Tim Burton film. Georgie started opening cupboard doors, looking for a mug. When she found one, she carried it over to the coffeepot.

Chaz turned on her. "That's Bram's special blend. It's only for him." She had heavy dark eyebrows, one of which was pierced, and small, sharp, very hostile features. "The regular stuff is in that cupboard."

"I'm sure he won't mind if I have a cup of his." Georgie pulled the carafe from a high-end coffee-maker.

"I only made enough for one."

"Probably best to make a little more from now on." Ignoring the poison darts being shot at her, Georgie took an apple from a Mexican Talavera bowl and carried it, along with the coffee, out to the veranda.

She drank half a cup of his coffee—it was delicious—
and then checked her messages. Lance had called
again, this time from Thailand. "Georgie, this is crazy.
Call me right away."

She deleted the message, then phoned her publicist and lawyer. Her evasiveness about what had happened over the weekend was driving them nuts, but
she wasn't telling anyone the truth, not even the people
she was supposed to trust. She used the same script on
them that she'd tried out on her personal assistant yesterday when she'd made arrangements for him to start
packing up her things. "I can't believe that you of all
people didn't figure out Bram and I were dating. We
did our best to keep it quiet, but you can usually see
right through me."

She finally worked up the nerve to phone Sasha.
She asked about the fire, but Sasha brushed her off.
"I'm taking care of it. Now explain what's really going
on, not that cockamamie bull April told me about you
and Mr. Sexy getting nostalgic over *Skip and Scooter*
reruns."

"That's my story, and we're all sticking to it, okay?"

"But—"

"Please."

Sasha finally gave in. "I'll let it go for now, but on
my next trip to L.A., we're going to have a long talk.
Unfortunately, I need to stay in Chicago for a while."

Georgie always anticipated Sasha's L.A. visits, but she was more than happy to postpone what she knew would be a dogged interrogation.

She didn't bother calling her agent. Her father would handle Laura. Trying to earn his love was like being on a perpetual hamster wheel. No matter how fast she ran, she never got any closer to the goal. One of these days, she had to stop trying. As for telling him the truth . . . Not now. Not ever.

Bram came out onto the veranda, finishing the dregs of something pink, thick, and frothy. As she took in the way his T-shirt clung to those unfamiliar muscles, she decided she liked his old heroin-chic look better. At least she'd understood that. She watched a final strawberry morsel disappear into his mouth. She wanted a foamy pink breakfast shake, too. But then, she wanted a lot of things she couldn't have. A great marriage, kids, a healthy relationship with her father, and a career that would improve with age. Right now, she'd settle for a well-orchestrated plan to make the public believe she'd fallen in love.

"Vacation time's come to an end, Skipper." She rose from her chair. "The weekend's over, and the press is demanding answers. At the least, we have to plan for the next few days. The first thing we need to do is—"

"Don't upset Chaz." He wiped a pink foam bubble from the corner of his mouth.

"Me? That girl is a walking, talking rude machine."

"She's also the best housekeeper I've ever had."

"She looks like she's eighteen. Who has a house-keeper that young?"

"She's twenty, and I do. Leave her alone."

"That's going to be a little hard to do if I'm living here."

"Let me spell it out. If I have to make a choice between you and Chaz, Chaz wins hands down." He and his empty glass disappeared back inside.

They were sleeping together. That would explain Chaz's hostility. She hardly seemed like his usual sex bunny, but what did Georgie know about his current preferences? Not a thing, and she intended to keep it that way.

Aaron Wiggins, her personal assistant, arrived half an hour later. She held the front door open so he could wedge through with her biggest suitcase and some outfits on hangers. "It's a war zone out there," he said, with the relish of a twenty-six-year-old still obsessed with video games. "Paparazzi, a news crew. I think I saw that chick from *E!*"

"Excellent," she said glumly. Aaron had been her personal assistant since her previous P.A. had defected to Lance and Jade's camp. He was nearly as wide as he was tall—probably three hundred pounds and barely five feet nine. His wiry brown hair surrounded a roly-poly face decked out with nerd glasses, a long nose, and a small, sweet mouth.

"I'll have the rest of your clothes packed up by tomorrow," he said. "Where do you want these?"

"Upstairs. Bram's closet is full, so I'm turning the room next door into a dressing room."

Aaron was out of breath by the time they reached the top of the stairs, and his black man-purse had slipped down to the crook of his elbow. She wished he'd take better care of himself, but he ignored her hints. As they passed Bram's bedroom, he peeked in, then came to a stop. "Sweet."

The sound system had caught his attention, not the decor. "Mind if I set these down and take a look?" he said.

Knowing how much he loved gadgetry, she couldn't refuse. He deposited her clothes and suitcase in the next room, then returned to study the electronics. "Awesome."

"A party, babe?" a silky voice said from the doorway.

This produced a geek snort from Aaron. "I'm Aaron. Georgie's P.A."

Bram arched one of his perfect eyebrows at Georgie. Personal assistants tended to be cute young women or well-turned-out gay men. Aaron didn't fit either category. She almost hadn't hired him, even though her father had recommended him for the job. But during their interview, the smoke alarms in her house had shorted out, and he'd fixed the problem so effortlessly that she'd decided to give him a chance. He'd proved to be cheerful, smart, scarily well organized, and not particular about the tasks she assigned. He was also as low on self-esteem as he was on drama, and he never thought to ask her for favors, like getting him into a trendy club or hot restaurant, something her past P.A.s had taken for granted.

Lots of guys like Aaron had moved to L.A. from their midwestern hometowns with dreams of doing special effects in Hollywood only to discover those jobs weren't easy to come by. Now Aaron worked as her P.A. and ran her Web site. In his free time, he played video games and ate junk food.

Aaron shook Bram's hand, then gestured toward the sound system, which rested in a rough-hewn cabinet with doors that looked as though they'd come from a Spanish mission. "I've read about these. How long have you had it?"

"I put it in last year. Do you want a demo?"

While Aaron explored the gadgetry, Georgie investigated the empty room around the corner where she'd decided to set up her office. Eventually Aaron joined her, and they decided what pieces of furniture she needed from storage. After they'd made plans to close up her rental house and drafted a letter for her fan Web site, Georgie told Aaron to cancel the various meetings and appointments she'd intended to get out of the way before she left for her six-month vacation.

She'd planned to travel in Europe—staying away from big cities to drive around the countryside. She'd envisioned poking into small towns, hiking on ancient pathways, and maybe, just maybe, finding herself. But her journey of self-discovery had taken a far more treacherous path.

"I finally understand why you're taking six months off," Aaron said. "Good plan. With nothing on your schedule, you'll be able to enjoy a long honeymoon."

Some honeymoon.

She and Lance had stayed in a private villa in Tuscany that had looked out over an olive grove. Lance had gotten restless after a few days, but she'd loved the place.

She'd barely thought of her ex-husband all morning, which had to be a record. As Aaron got ready to leave, Chaz came through the foyer, and Georgie introduced them. "This is Aaron Wiggins, my personal assistant. Aaron, Chaz is Bram's housekeeper."

Chaz swept her black-rimmed eyes from Aaron's wiry hair to the straining buttons on his checked dress shirt to his pudding tummy and black, wedged-sole sneakers. She curled her lip. "Stay out of the refrigerator, okay? It's off-limits."

Aaron turned red, and Georgie wanted to slap her.

"If I have to make a choice between you and Chaz, Chaz wins hands down."

"As long as Aaron's working for me," Georgie said firmly, "he has free run of the house. I'll expect you to make him comfortable."

"Good luck with that." Chaz flounced away with the watering can.

"What's with her?" Aaron said.

"She's having a little problem adjusting to the fact that Bram's married. Don't take any crap from her." It was good advice, but Georgie had a hard time imagining mild-mannered Aaron holding his own against Bram's viper-tongued twenty-year-old housekeeper.

After Aaron left, Georgie went outside, looking for Bram. They had plans to make, and he'd put her off long enough. She followed the gurgle of water to a small, irregularly shaped swimming pool tucked away in a private nook behind swaying grasses and a live oak. A four-foot waterfall splashing over shiny black rocks at one end added to the sense of seclusion.

She moved on and found him locked in his office. He was talking on the phone again, and when she rattled the handle to get in, he turned his back on her.

She tried to eavesdrop through the glass but couldn't make out what he was saying. He hung up and started pecking away at his keyboard. She couldn't imagine what Bram was doing with a computer. Come to think of it, what was he doing out of bed before four in the afternoon?

"Let me in."

"Can't," he called out without breaking rhythm. "I'm too busy looking up ways to spend your money."

She didn't take the bait. Instead, she started singing "Your Body Is a Wonderland" and tapping out a bass line on the glass panes until he couldn't stand it any longer and finally ambled over to open one door. "This better not take long. Those hookers I hired will be here any minute."

"Good to know." She stepped inside and nodded toward his computer. "While you've been drooling over pictures of naked cheerleaders, I've been working on our reentry into the world. You might want to take notes." She sat on the saggy brown couch underneath Marlon Brando and crossed her legs. "You have a Web site, right? I wrote a letter from both of us to post for our fans." She lost her train of thought as Bram propped his elbows on his desk. Skip had a desk, not Bram. Skip also had a good education, a sense of purpose, and a strong moral fiber.

She pulled herself back together. "Aaron made dinner reservations for us tomorrow night at Mr. Chow. It'll be a zoo, but I think it's the fastest way for us to—"

"A letter to our fans and dinner at Mr. Chow? There's some powerful original thinking. What else've you got?"

"Lunch at the Chateau on Wednesday, then dinner at Il Sole on Thursday. There's a big Alzheimer's benefit in a couple of weeks. A charity ball is right after that. We eat, we smile, we pose."

"No balls. None."

"I'm sorry to hear that. Have you talked to a doctor?"

His smile curled like a snake's tail over shiny white teeth. "I'm going to have a great time spending that fifty thousand you're paying me every month to endure your company."

He had no shame. She watched him prop his feet on the edge of his desk. "That's it then?" he said. "Your plan for how we make a splash? We go out to eat."

"I suppose we could follow your example and pick up a couple of DUIs, but that seems a little extreme, don't you think?"

"Cute." He dropped his feet to the floor. "We're throwing a party."

She'd almost been enjoying herself, but now she regarded him suspiciously. "What kind of party?"

"A big, expensive party to celebrate getting married, what the hell do you think? Six weeks from now, maybe two months. Long enough to get out the invitations and build anticipation, but not long enough for the public to lose interest in our great love story. Why are you looking at me like that?"

"You thought this up on your own?"

"I'm pretty creative when I'm wasted."

"You hate anything formal. You used to show up barefoot for the network affiliate parties." And so gorgeously dissipated every woman in the room had wanted him.

"I promise I'll wear shoes. Get your guy to find a good party planner. The theme is obvious."

She uncrossed her legs. "What do you mean, the theme is obvious? It's not obvious to me."

"That's because you don't drink enough to think creatively."

"Enlighten me."

"*Skip and Scooter,* of course. What else?"

She came up off the couch. "A *Skip and Scooter* theme? Are you nuts?"

"We'll ask everybody to dress in costume. Either like the Scofields or the Scofield servants. Upstairs or downstairs."

"You're kidding."

"We'll have the cake designer put a set of those stupid-ass Skip and Scooter dolls on top."

"Dolls?"

"The florist should use whatever the blue flowers were in the opening credits. Maybe candy miniatures of the mansion for party favors. That kind of crap."

"Are you out of your mind?"

"Give the people what they want, Georgie. It's the first rule of business. I'm surprised a mogul like you doesn't know that."

She stared at him. He smiled back with an innocence that didn't fit his fallen angel's face. And that's when she understood. "Oh, my God . . . You were serious about a *Skip and Scooter* reunion show."

He grinned. "I think we should put the Scofield coat of arms on the table menus. And the family motto . . . What the hell was it? 'Greed Forever'?"

"You really *do* want a reunion show." She sank into the couch. "It's not just the money that made you agree to this marriage."

"I wouldn't bet on that."

"You want a reunion show, too."

His desk chair squeaked as he leaned back. "Our party will be a hell of a lot more fun than that pussy reception you had when you married the Loser. Tell me you didn't really leave the church in a carriage with six white horses."

The carriage had been Lance's idea, and she'd felt like a princess. But now her prince had run off with the wicked witch, and Georgie had accidentally married the big bad wolf. "I'm not doing a reunion show," she said. "I've spent eight years trying to get out from under Scooter's shadow, and I'm not walking back into it."

"If you'd really wanted to get out from under Scooter's shadow, you wouldn't have made all those lame romantic comedies."

"There's nothing wrong with romantic comedies."

"There's something wrong with bad romantic comedies. Those movies weren't exactly *Pretty Woman* or *Jerry Maguire,* babe."

"I hated *Pretty Woman.*"

"Audiences didn't. On the other hand, they did hate *Pretty People* and *Summer in the City.* And I'm not hearing anything good about the project you just wrapped."

"It's your career that's in the toilet, not mine." Only technically true, since *Cake Walk* wouldn't come out until next winter. "You aren't dragging me down with you."

His desk phone rang. He glanced at the caller ID and answered. "Yep? . . . Okay . . ." He hung up and came out from behind the desk, bringing his drink with him. "That was Chaz. Fix your makeup. It's time to start showing off for the press."

"Since when have you cared about showing off for anybody except trashy women?"

"Since I've become a respectable married man. I'll meet you by the front door in fifteen minutes. Don't forget to use that lipstick that doesn't smudge."

"Oh, I'll remember." She rose from the couch and swept ahead of him. "Gosh, all this talk you've been doing about holding the power card. Such a fascinating example of self-delusion . . ." With an airy wave, she headed back to the house.

By the time she'd finished touching up her makeup, finger combing her straight hair, and changing into a mint green Marc Jacobs cotton eyelet dress, the smell of fresh baked goods had drifted upstairs. Her stomach growled. She couldn't remember the last time she'd been so hungry. Bram was waiting in the foyer, along with Chaz, who was gazing up at him as if he hung the moon and the stars.

As Georgie reached his side, he slipped his arm around her shoulders. "Chaz, you'll make sure Georgie has whatever she needs."

Chaz responded with a friendliness that Bram might buy into but Georgie didn't believe for an instant. "Anything, Georgie. You just let me know."

"Thanks. As a matter of fact, I've hardly eaten all day, and I wouldn't mind—"

"Later, sweetheart. We have work to do." Bram kissed her forehead, then turned to pick up one of two trays piled with home-baked sugar cookies. "Chaz has made a goodwill offering for us to distribute to our friends in the press." He handed one tray to Georgie, then picked up the other for himself. "We're going to pass these out and pose for some photos."

The press liked nothing better than free food. It was a great idea, and she wished she'd thought of it. He opened the door for her. "I hired extra security until the gates go up," he said. "I'm sure you won't mind paying your portion of the bill."

"How big a portion is that?"

"All of it. Only fair, don't you agree, since I'm putting a roof over your head?"

"If you'd include some actual food with that roof—"

"Can't you think about anything but food?"

"Not at the moment." She grabbed one of the cookies from her tray and took a big bite. It was still warm . . . and delicious.

"No time for that." He snatched the cookie away and stuffed it in his mouth. "Damn, these are good. Chaz's cooking gets better all the time."

She watched the cookie disappear. For a year everyone had been trying to coax her to eat, and now that she had an appetite, he was taking food away. It made her even hungrier. "I wouldn't know."

The end of the driveway came into sight, along with the beefy security guards stationed there. Several dozen paps and a few members of the legitimate press clustered in a noisy pack in the street. Georgie gave them a gay wave. Bram took her free hand, and fingers linked, they carried the cookie trays forward. The paps began "hosing them down," a particularly distasteful term that described the aggressive shooting of celebrities.

"If you guys play nice, we'll pose for some pictures," Bram called out. "But if anybody comes too close to Georgie, we're going inside. I mean it. Nobody gets near her."

She was momentarily touched, and then she returned to Sanity Land as she remembered Bram was acting the role of the protective husband.

"We always play nice, Bram," one of the women reporters shouted over the din.

Even before Bram passed both trays over to the security guards to distribute, the questions began to fly. When had they hooked up? Where? Why, after all these years, had they gotten together? What about all the bad feelings between them? One question followed another.

"Georgie, is this a rebound from Lance?"

"Everybody's saying you're anorexic. Is that true?"

She and Bram were pros at handling the press, and they answered only the questions they wanted to.

"People think this whole thing is a big publicity stunt," Mel Duffy called out.

"You go on dates for publicity," Bram retorted. "You don't get married. But people can think what they like."

"Georgie, rumors are flying that you're pregnant."

"Really?" The wound ached, but Georgie played the clown and patted her waist. "Hello? Anything in there?"

"Georgie isn't pregnant," Bram said. "When it happens, we'll be sure to let you know."

"Are you taking a honeymoon?" The reporter had a British accent.

Bram rubbed her back between her shoulder blades. "When we get around to it."

"Do you know where?"

"Maui," he said.

"Haiti," Georgie said.

They looked at each other. Georgie went on tiptoe and kissed the corner of his jaw. "Bram and I intend to use this silly overexposure we're getting to call attention to the plight of people living in poverty." She didn't know a lot about Haiti, but she knew it had poverty, and Haiti was a lot closer than Thailand and the

Philippines, where Lance and Jade were doing their good works.

"As you can see, we're still discussing it," Bram said. Without warning, he drew her into his arms and gave her the lusty kiss the press had been waiting for. She went through all the proper motions in response, but she was tired, hungry, and trapped in the arms of her oldest enemy.

They finally separated. Bram addressed the crowd while he fixed her with a hungry lover's gaze. "You're all welcome to hang around, but I can guarantee we're not going anywhere tonight."

She tried to blush, but blushing was beyond her. Would she ever know what had happened in that Vegas hotel room? She hadn't seen any signs that they'd made love, except they'd both been naked, which she supposed was a fairly big sign.

As they walked back to the house, his hand strayed to her bottom for the benefit of the onlookers they'd left behind. "Nice," he said.

The sadness she'd been trying so hard to suppress oozed to the surface. "I've never forgiven you for what happened that night on the boat. I never will."

He drew back. "I'd been drinking. I know I wasn't exactly a dream lover, but—"

"What you did was a step away from a rape."

He snapped to a stop. "That's bullshit. I never forced a woman in my life, and I sure as hell didn't force you."

"No physical force, but—"

"You had a crush on me. Everybody knew it. You threw yourself at me from the beginning."

"You didn't even lie down with me," she said. "You shoved up my skirt and helped yourself."

"All you had to do was say no."

"Then you walked out. As soon as it was over."

"I was never going to fall in love with you, Georgie. I'd done everything I could to make that obvious, but you wouldn't take the hint. At least that night put an end to it."

"Don't you dare act as though you did me a favor! You wanted to get off and I was handy. You took advantage of a stupid kid who thought you were romantic and mysterious when you were really just an egotistical, self-centered ass. We're enemies. We were then, and we still are."

"Fine by me."

As he stormed off, she told herself she'd said exactly what she needed to. But nothing could change the past, and she didn't feel one bit better.

Chapter 8

Georgie swam for nearly an hour the next morning in the sheltered pool. Yesterday she'd let him see how much he'd hurt her, and displaying that kind of vulnerability was a luxury she couldn't repeat. Not anymore.

As she was getting out, she heard a voice coming from the path that ran behind the shrubbery. "Settle down, Caitlin . . . Yeah, I know. Have a little faith, sweetheart . . ."

Bram moved on before Georgie could hear any more. As she wrapped herself in a towel, she wondered who Caitlin was and how long it would be before Bram sought out one of his mystery women for extramarital sex.

She combed her wet hair with her fingers, tucked the towel under her arms, and went inside to rummage through the refrigerator. As she pulled out a carton of blueberry yogurt, Chaz came in and dropped a pile of mail on the center island. "I'd appreciate it if you'd stay out of the refrigerator. Everything's organized the way I like it."

"I won't move anything I don't eat." Chaz was a monumental pain in the ass, but Georgie still felt sorry for her. She didn't really believe Chaz was Bram's lover, but she did believe Chaz was in love with him. Remembering the pain of that particular disease, she took a fresh tack. "Tell me about yourself, Chaz. Did you grow up around here?"

"No." Chaz pulled a mixing bowl from the cupboard.

She tried again. "I can't cook much of anything. How did you learn?"

Chaz slapped the cupboard door closed. "I don't have time to talk. I need to get a head start on Bram's lunch."

"What's on the menu?"

"A special salad he likes."

"Fine by me."

Chaz grabbed the dishcloth. "I can't cook for both of you. I already have too much to do. If you don't want me to quit, you'll have to take care of yourself."

Georgie licked the inside of the yogurt lid. "Who said I don't want you to quit?"

Chaz's face flushed with anger. Georgie under-stood, but Chaz's hostility was making an already awful situation that much worse. She pulled a spoon from the drawer. "Make lunch for two, Chaz. That's an order."

"I take my orders from Bram. He said he'd never interfere with how I did my job."

"He wasn't married when he said that, but now he is, and your Godzilla act is getting old fast. You have two choices. You can play nice, or I'll hire my own staff, and you'll have to share your kitchen. Somehow I don't think you'd like that."

She and her yogurt headed back outside.

As Georgie's footsteps faded, Chaz pressed her fists to her belly, trying to hold in all the hatred that wanted to spill out. Georgie York had everything. She was rich and famous. She had great clothes and a big career. Now she had Bram, and only Chaz was supposed to take care of him.

Outside the kitchen windows a hummingbird flew onto the veranda. Chaz grabbed a paper towel and opened the refrigerator door. The milk wasn't where she'd left it, and a couple of the yogurt containers had fallen over. Even the eggs were on the wrong side of the shelf.

She straightened everything and wiped a smudge from the door. She couldn't stand the idea of another person in her kitchen. In her house. She pitched the paper towel into the trash. Georgie wasn't even that pretty, not like the women Bram went out with. She didn't deserve him. She didn't deserve anything she had. Everybody knew she was only famous because her old man had made her a star. Georgie had grown up with everybody kissing her ass and telling her she was hot shit. Nobody had ever kissed Chaz's ass. Not once.

Chaz gazed around her kitchen. The sunlight coming through the six narrow windows made the blue accents in the tiles sparkle. This was her favorite place in the world, even better than her apartment over the garage, and Georgie wanted to wedge her way in.

She still couldn't believe Bram hadn't told her he was getting married. That hurt the most of all. But something wasn't exactly right. He didn't treat Georgie the way Chaz had imagined he'd treat a woman he loved. Chaz made up her mind to figure out exactly why that was.

Georgie stayed out of sight while Aaron supervised the movers unloading her things. By late afternoon, he had her office set up, and she'd unpacked the wardrobe boxes that had taken over her bedroom but held only the clothes that weren't in storage. By the time Aaron left, the walls had closed around her. Even though her Prius sat outside in the driveway, she couldn't go anywhere by herself, not the fourth day of her marriage, when every photographer in town was staking out the house. She settled down to try to read.

Much later Bram found her standing by her bedroom balcony doors giving herself an internal pep talk about things like independence and self-identity. "Let's drive to the beach," he said. "I'm going stir-crazy."

"It'll be dark soon."

"Who cares?" He rubbed his knuckles over his golden beard stubble. "I've already smoked two packs of cigarettes. I need to get out."

So did she, even if she had to go with him. "Have you been drinking?"

"No, damn it! But I will be if I'm stuck here much longer. Now do you want to go or not?"

"Give me twenty minutes."

As soon as he left, she consulted the "Super Casual" section of the three-ring binder Aaron kept updated with Polaroid photos of all the pieces in Georgie's wardrobe, accompanied by April's instructions on how they fit together. Maybe one day Georgie would have the luxury of leaving the house without worrying about how she looked, but she couldn't do it now. She chose her Rock & Republic jeans, a corset top, and a simple Michael Kors kimono cardigan that April had noted would "pull the look together."

Georgie was capable of dressing herself, but April did a better job of it. The public had no idea how clueless most celebrity fashion icons were, and how much they depended on their stylists. Georgie was forever grateful that April continued to help her out.

The paps waited for them at the end of the driveway like a pack of hungry dogs. As Bram pulled out, they stormed his Audi. He maneuvered through, but half a dozen black SUVs quickly fell into place behind them. "I feel like we're leading a funeral cortege," she said. "Just once I'd like to be able to walk out of the house with bad hair and no makeup and go someplace without getting my picture taken."

He glanced in the rearview mirror. "There's nothing worse than a celebrity complaining about the hardships of fame."

"I've been dealing with this ever since Lance and I started to date. You've only had to put up with it for a few days."

"Hey, I get photographed."

"Sex videos don't count. And let's see how cheery you are after another couple months of this."

He braked for a stop sign, and they were nearly rear-ended, so she left him alone to concentrate on his driving.

The traffic was only moderately horrendous, and their entourage stayed with them all the way to Malibu. Several more SUVs joined the funeral procession, even though the paps had surely figured out Bram was headed for one of the semiprivate beaches.

First-time visitors to Malibu were always surprised to see long stretches of highway lined with private garages butting up to the road and forming a solid wall that restricted beach access to all but the privileged few who lived there. Just past Trevor's house, Bram pulled off the road in front of one of the sets of dun-colored garage doors. Moments later, they were walking through Trev's former beach house, the one he'd put up for sale.

Outside, the night was a romantic cliché. Moonlight frosted the tips of the waves. The surf lapped at the shore. Cool sand squished between her toes. The only thing missing was the right man. She thought about that scrap of conversation she'd overheard earlier with the mysterious Caitlin and wondered how long it would be before she found herself drawn into a second scandal involving another woman.

He slowed his steps as they neared the water. A ribbon of moonlight silvered the tips of his eyelashes. "You're right, Scooter," he said. "I was a jerk that night on the boat, and I apologize."

She'd never heard him apologize for anything, but too much hurt and shame lingered inside her for a few words to make a difference. "Apology not accepted."

"Okay."

She waited. "That's it?"

He stuffed his hands in his pockets. "I don't know what else to say. It happened, and I'm not proud of myself."

"You wanted to get off," she said bitterly, "and there I was, standing so conveniently in front of you."

"Hold on." Unlike her, he wasn't wearing a sweater, and the breeze pressed his T-shirt against his chest. "I could have *gotten off* with any of the women on the boat that night. And I'm not being arrogant. It's just the way it was."

A wave splashed her ankles. "But you didn't. You chose dumb-ass here instead."

"You weren't dumb. Just naïve."

She needed to ask him something, but she didn't want to look at him, so she leaned down to turn up the cuffs of her jeans. "Why did you do it?"

"Why do you think?" He picked up a beach stone and hurled it into the water. "I wanted to put you in your place. Knock you down a few pegs. Show you that even though Daddy made sure you got top billing and a bigger paycheck, I could get you to do what I wanted."

She stood up. "Nice guy."

"You asked."

The fact that he'd finally owned up to his bad behavior made her feel a little better. Not good enough to forgive him, but good enough to accept that she had to somehow coexist with him while they were trapped in this farce of a marriage. They began walking again. "It was years ago." She stepped around a sand turtle some kids had made earlier. "No lasting harm done."

"You were a virgin. I didn't believe that bull you handed out about being with an older man."

"Hugh Grant," she said.

"You wish."

She snagged a flyaway lock of hair and pushed it behind her ear. "Hugh told me I was sublime. No, wait. That was Colin Firth. I get those aging Brits I slept with mixed up."

"A common problem." He sent another stone flying into the water.

She gazed up at the single star that had begun to shine. At a beach party last year, someone had told her it wasn't a star at all, but the International Space Station. "Who was she?"

"Who?"

"The woman I heard you whispering to on your cell this morning."

"What big ears you have."

"All the better to catch you cheating."

"Isn't it a little early for me to cheat? Although you have to admit, the honeymoon's been a real bust-out so far."

She dug her heels deeper into the sand. "When it comes to vice, I never underestimate you."

"You've wised up."

"It wasn't just the sex, Bram. It was everything. You got handed the opportunity of a lifetime with *Skip and Scooter,* and you blew it. You didn't appreciate what you had."

"I appreciated what it got me. Cars, women, liquor, drugs. I had free designer clothes, a collection of Rolexes, big houses where I could hang out with my buddies. I had the time of my life."

"I noticed."

"The way I grew up—if you had money, you spent it. I loved every second."

But his pleasure had come at the expense of so many other people. She shoved up the sleeves of her sweater. "A lot of people paid a big price for your fun. The cast, the crew."

"Yeah, well, you've got me there."

"You paid a price, too."

"And you won't hear me complaining about it."

"No, you wouldn't."

His head came up. "Shit."

"What—?"

He pulled her hard against him and crushed her mouth in a fiery kiss. One hand slipped under her T-shirt at the small of her back, the other cradled her hip. A wave caught them, and the surf swirled around their ankles. Perfect moonlit passion.

"Cameras." He ground the word against her lips as if she hadn't already figured that out.

She wrapped her arms around his neck and tilted her head. Had they really thought they'd have privacy, even on a supposedly private beach? The jackals always found a way in. She wondered how much the pictures would bring. A lot.

Their kiss grew hotter. Deeper. Her breasts flattened against his chest, and the tips began to tingle. She felt him growing hard.

He settled his thumb into the soft flesh along her spine. Forced his thigh between her legs. "I'm going to feel you up now." His hand moved over her rib cage to her breast. The hand no photographer could see. He caressed her through her bra, and dirty little cesspools of illicit arousal swirled through her body. It had been a long time, and this was safe, because it was all so phony. And because it would only go as far as she let it.

His fingers traced the swells of her breasts above the cups, and he whispered against her lips, "When we stop playing games, I'm going to take you so hard and so deep you'll want it to last forever."

His crude words sent a surge of heat sizzling through her, and she didn't feel one bit guilty about it. They had no personal relationship. This was purely physical. Bram could be a stud she'd hired for the night.

But a stud went home when he'd done his job, and she reluctantly extracted herself from his arms. "Okay, I'm bored."

His fingers brushed her hardened nipple before he stepped away. "I can tell."

The breeze lifted her hair from the back of her neck and left a trail of goose bumps behind. She pulled her sweater tighter around her. "Well, you're no Hugh Grant, but your technique has definitely improved from the bad old days."

"Glad to hear it."

She didn't like that silky note in his voice. "Let's go back," she said. "I'm getting cold."

"I can fix that."

She'd just bet he could. "About that woman you were talking to on your cell today . . ." She walked faster.

"Are we back to that again?"

"You should know . . . If I die while we're married, all my money goes either to charity or to my father."

He came to a dead stop. "I don't exactly see the connection."

"You wouldn't get a penny." She picked up her pace. "I'm not making any accusations, just setting the record straight in case you and the *friend* you were talking to on the phone start thinking about how much fun you could have living off my money."

She was mainly being a smart-ass to irritate him. Still, Bram was broke and had no morals, so she felt marginally better for having made sure he understood there was no advantage in plotting her premature death.

His heels kicked up the sand as he closed the distance between them. "You're an idiot."

"Just covering my bases."

He grabbed her hand, more like a prison warden's than a lover's. "For your information, there was no camera. I just wanted to get my kicks."

"And for your information . . . I knew there wasn't a camera, and I wanted a few kicks myself." She hadn't known, but she should have suspected.

The breeze sighed, the waves lapped. She wasn't done antagonizing him, and she leaned against his arm. "Skip and Scooter, together in the moonlight. How romantic."

He retaliated by whistling "Tomorrow" from *Annie,* just the way he used to do whenever he wanted to piss her off.

Chapter 9

Georgie waited until the next morning when she heard Bram go into the workout room. She headed for the dining room, grabbed the key she'd seen him toss into a brass dish on the bookshelves, and made her way out to his office in the guesthouse. She still couldn't get used to Bram having an office instead of conducting his business from a bar stool.

As she moved along the gravel path, she thought about how different Bram's sexual aggression was from what she'd experienced with Lance. Her ex-husband had wanted her to be the seductress, and that's exactly what she'd tried to do. She'd read a dozen sex manuals and bought the most erotic lingerie she could find, no matter how much it pinched. She'd performed strip-teases that left her feeling stupid, whispered male fantasies in his ear that turned her off, and tried to find inventive lovemaking locales to keep things fresh. He'd seemed appreciative and always said he was satisfied, but obviously she'd come up short or he wouldn't have left her for Jade Gentry.

She'd worked too hard to have failed so miserably. Sex might be easy for some women, but it was complicated for her, and just thinking about the quandary she found herself in with Bram made her queasy. Bram wasn't going to give up sex. He'd either have it with her or with someone else. Maybe both.

She'd promised herself she'd face her problems head-on, but they'd only been married five days, and she needed some time to figure this one out.

She unlocked his office and turned on his computer. As she waited for it to boot up, she began searching his bookshelves. She had to know right now whether the reunion show was a figment of Bram's imagination or something more tangible.

She found a diverse book collection and an eclectic pile of scripts, but none of them for a *Skip and Scooter* reunion show. She spotted assorted DVDs ranging from *Raging Bull* to something called *Sex Trek: The Next Penetration.* His file cabinets were locked, but not his desk, and that's where she discovered a manuscript box under a bottle of scotch. It was taped shut. The label read SKIP AND SCOOTER: THE REUNION.

She was stunned. She'd hoped Bram had made this up to needle her. He knew doing a reunion movie would be a huge career setback for her, so why did he think he could convince her to go along with it?

She didn't like the only answer she could come up with. Blackmail. He might threaten to walk out on their marriage if she didn't go along with the project. But dumping her would put a stop to the money train, as well as making him look like an ass, although he might not care about that. Still . . . She remembered the way he'd behaved around Rory Keene. Maybe he cared more about his image than he'd led her to believe.

"What are you doing in here?"

Her head shot up, and she saw Chaz standing in the doorway looking like the love child of Martha Stewart and Joey Ramone. Her housekeeper's uniform for the day consisted of holey jeans, olive tank top, and black flip-flops. Georgie pushed the drawer closed with her foot. Since she couldn't conjure up a reasonable explanation, she decided to turn the tables. "Better question— what are you doing?"

Chaz's dark-rimmed eyes narrowed with hostility. "Bram doesn't like strangers in his office. You shouldn't be here."

"I'm not a stranger. I'm his wife." Words she'd never expected to hear coming out of her mouth.

"He doesn't even let the cleaning people in here." Chaz lifted her chin. "I'm the only one."

"You're very loyal. What's that about, anyway?"

She pulled a broom from a small closet. "It's my job."

Georgie couldn't snoop through his computer files now, so she began to leave, but as she got up, she spotted a video camera sitting on the corner of the desk. Chaz began to sweep the floor. Georgie examined the camera long enough to discover that Bram had erased whatever tawdry sexual encounter he'd last filmed.

Chaz stopped sweeping. "Don't mess with that."

Georgie impulsively turned the camera on Chaz and hit the record button. "Why do you care so much?"

Chaz pulled the broom handle to her chest. "What are you doing?"

"I'm curious about your loyalty."

"Turn that off."

Georgie brought her into sharper focus. Beneath the piercings and scowl, Chaz had delicate, almost fragile, features. She'd pulled one side of her chopped hair away from her eyes with a small silver barrette, and the other side stood out in a spiky tuft above her ear. Chaz's hostile independence fascinated Georgie. She couldn't imagine having that kind of freedom from caring what other people thought. "I guess you're the only person in L.A. who doesn't love a camera," Georgie said. "No ambitions to be an actress? That's why most girls come here."

"Me? No. And how do you know I haven't always lived here?"

"Just a feeling." Through the viewer, Georgie could see tension tightening the corners of Chaz's small mouth. "Most twenty-year-olds would be bored with a job like yours."

Chaz gripped the broom tighter, almost as if it were a weapon. "I like my job. You probably think housework isn't important."

Georgie quoted her father. "I think a job is what a person makes of it."

The camera had subtly altered the relationship between them, and for the first time since they'd met, Chaz looked uncertain. "People should do what they're good at," she finally said. "I'm good at this." She tried to return to sweeping, but the camera was clearly bothering her. "Turn that thing off."

"How did it happen?" Georgie edged around the corner of the desk to keep her in the frame. "How did you learn to run a house at such a young age?"

Chaz jabbed at a corner. "Just something I did." Georgie waited, and to her surprise, Chaz went on. "My stepmom worked at a motel outside Barstow. Twelve units with a diner. Are you going to turn that off?"

"In a minute." The camera made some people clam up and others talk. Apparently Chaz was one of the latter. Georgie took another step to the side. "You worked there?"

"Sometimes. She liked to party, and she didn't always get home in time to go to work the next day. When that happened, I skipped school and went in for her."

Georgie zoomed in on the girl's face, taking advantage of having the upper hand. "How old were you?"

"I don't know. Eleven or something." She went over the same place she'd just swept. "The guy who owned the place didn't care how old I was as long as the work got done, and I did a better job than her."

The camera recorded facts. It didn't offer an opinion about an eleven-year-old doing manual labor. "How did you feel about missing school?" The low-battery light came on.

Chaz shrugged. "We needed the money."

"The work must have been hard."

"There were good parts."

"Like what?"

Chaz continued poking at the same spot on the floor. "I don't know." She leaned the broom against the wall and picked up a dust rag.

Georgie gave her a gentle prod. "I can't imagine there were too many good parts."

Chaz slid the rag over a bookshelf. "Sometimes a family checked into a room with a couple of kids. Maybe they'd order pizza or bring burgers back from the diner, and the kids might spill something on the rug. The place would be a big mess." She concentrated on dusting the same book. "Trash and food everywhere. Sheets on the floor. All the towels used up. But by the time I left, everything would be neat again." Her shoulder blades slammed together and she threw down the rag. "This is bullshit. I've got work to do. I'll come back when you're out of here." She stalked away just as the camera ran out of power.

Georgie released the breath she'd been holding. Chaz would never have told her so much without the presence of the camera. As she pulled out the tape and slipped it in her pocket, she felt the same kind of rush she used to experience after she'd nailed a challenging acting scene.

That night, she found the world's most disgusting sandwich waiting for her: a towering monstrosity constructed with slabs of bread, thick wedges of meat, rivers of mayo, and half a dozen slices of cheese. She pulled it apart, fixed herself a simpler sandwich, and ate alone on the veranda. She didn't see Bram for the rest of the evening.

The next day Aaron handed over the new issue of *Flash*. One of Mel Duffy's balcony photos graced the cover along with blaring headlines:

The Marriage That Shocked the World!
Exclusive Photos of Skip and Scooter's Honey-moon Bliss

In the picture, Bram held her in his arms, her gauzy white skirt draping his sleeves, the two of them gazing deeply into each other's eyes. Her wedding photo with Lance had appeared on this same cover, but the genuine newlyweds hadn't looked nearly as love-dazzled as these phony ones.

She should have felt good. There were no pity headlines, only rapturous copy.

Georgie York's fans were stunned by her shocking Las Vegas elopement with former *Skip and Scooter* costar, bad boy Bramwell Shepard. "They've been secretly dating for months," Georgie's BFF April Robillard Patriot said. "They're delirious with happiness, and we're all overjoyed."

Georgie sent a silent thank-you April's way and skimmed the rest of the article.

. . . publicist dismisses stories of a bitter feud between the *Skip and Scooter* costars. "They were never enemies. Bram cleaned up his act a long time ago."

What a lie.

Friends say the couple has a lot in common . . .

Other than mutual hatred, Georgie couldn't think of a thing, and she tossed the magazine aside.

With nothing productive to do, she wandered into the living room and picked some dead leaves off the lemon tree. Out of the corner of her eye, she saw Bram go into the kitchen, probably for a refill. She didn't want him to think she was deliberately avoiding him, even though she was, so she pulled her cell from her pocket and called him. "You won this house in a poker game, didn't you? It explains so much."

"Like?"

"Great decorating, beautiful landscaping, books with words and not just pictures. But, never mind . . . Skip and Scooter need to make another public appearance today. How about a coffee run?"

"Okay with me." He wandered into the dining room, his phone cupped to his ear. He wore jeans and a vintage Nirvana T-shirt. "Why are you calling me as opposed to talking to me directly?"

She switched her own phone to the other ear. "I've decided we communicate better from a distance."

"Since when? Oh, I remember. Since two nights ago when I kissed you on the beach." He leaned against the doorframe and eye-smoldered her. "I can tell by the way you've been looking at me. I turn you on, and that scares the hell out of you."

"You're gorgeous, and I can be something of a slut, so how could I help myself?" She cradled the phone closer to her ear. "Fortunately, your personality totally cancels out the effect. The reason I'm calling you—"

"Instead of walking across the room and talking to me face-to-face . . ."

"—is because this is a business relationship, and—"

"Since when is a marriage a business relationship?"

That made her mad, and she flipped her phone shut. "Since you conned me into paying you fifty thousand dollars a month."

"Good point." He pocketed his own phone and wandered toward her. "I hear the Loser didn't give you a penny in the divorce."

Georgie could have gotten millions in guilt money from Lance, but for what? She hadn't wanted his money. She'd wanted him. "Who needs more money? Oops . . . You do."

"I have some calls to make," he said. "Give me half an hour." He reached into the pocket of his jeans. "One more thing . . ." He pitched a ring box toward her. "I bought it for a hundred bucks on eBay. You've got to admit, it looks like the real thing."

She flipped open the box and saw a three-carat cushion-cut diamond. "Wow. A fake diamond to go with a fake husband. Works for me." She slipped it on.

"That's a bigger stone than the ring you got from the Loser, the cheap bastard."

"Except his was real."

"Like his wedding vows?"

Some self-delusional part of her still wanted to believe the best of the man who'd left her, but she suppressed the urge to leap to Lance's defense. "I'll treasure it always," she drawled as she slipped past him and went upstairs.

She consulted April's three-ring binder and chose cotton poplin pants and a ruched, moss green top with small puffy sleeves. She added Tory Burch ballet flats but bypassed the three-thousand-dollar designer purse April recommended. Fans didn't realize those obscenely expensive purses their favorite celebrities carted around so carelessly were freebies, and Georgie had gotten fed up with being part of the conspiracy to make ordinary women overspend on an "it" bag that would be replaced by another "it" bag before their credit cards came due. Instead, she dug out a funky fabric purse Sasha had given her last year.

She did her hair, fixed her makeup, and had to choke back her resentment when she went downstairs and saw Bram standing in the foyer wearing exactly the same jeans and Nirvana T-shirt he'd had on earlier. As far as she could see, he hadn't done one thing to get ready for the photographers, and even more aggravating, he hadn't *needed* to do anything. His beard stubble was as photo worthy as his crisp, rumpled hair. Another sign of Hollywood's conspiracy against its female celebrities.

He fingered the card tucked into an extravagant flower arrangement sitting on the credenza. "How did you and Rory Keene get to be such buddies?"

"Is that from her?"

"She wishes us the best. Correct me if I'm wrong, but she seems to take a special interest in you."

"I barely know her." That was true, although Rory had once phoned Georgie to suggest she avoid signing onto a certain project. Georgie had taken her advice, and sure enough, the film had run into money problems and shut down halfway through. Since Vortex hadn't been involved, and Rory didn't have anything to gain from the tip, Georgie had been puzzled by her interest. "I guess she feels some kind of connection with me because of the year she spent working as a P.A. on *Skip and Scooter.*"

Bram flicked the card back down on the credenza. "She doesn't feel any connection with me."

"*I* was nice to her." Georgie barely remembered Rory from those days, but she did remember Bram's habit of making life hard for the crew.

"Lowly P.A. to the head of Vortex Studios in fourteen years," he said. "Who'd have guessed?"

"Apparently, not you." She gave him her most annoying smile. "Payback's a bitch."

"I guess." He slipped on a pair of devastatingly sexy aviators. "Let's go show off your ring to the American public."

They posed for the paps outside the Coffee Bean and Tea Leaf on Beverly Boulevard. Bram kissed her hair and smiled at the photographers. "Isn't she beautiful? I'm the luckiest guy in the world."

After her hellish year of public humiliation, his words of phony adoration felt like balm to her bruised soul. How pathetic was that? She stepped on his foot to retaliate.

Chaz was coming back to the house from cleaning Bram's office when she saw Georgie's lardo assistant standing by the swimming pool, gazing down into the water. She marched over to him. "You're not supposed to be out here."

He blinked behind his glasses. The guy was a mess. Wiry brown hair exploded from his head, and whoever had picked out those big nerd glasses must have been blind. He dressed like a fat sixty-year-old man with his stomach hanging out over his belt and a checked sports shirt that pulled at the buttons.

"Okay." He stepped around her to go back to the house.

She brushed off her hands. "What were you doing anyway?"

He shoved his fists in his pockets, adding to the bulk at his hips. "Taking a break."

"From what? You've got an easy job."

"Sometimes. It's a little busy now."

"Yeah, it looks like you're real busy."

He didn't tell her to fuck off, which she deserved for being so rude, but she hated having all these people running around her house. And that whole thing yesterday in Bram's office with Georgie and the camera had thrown her off. She should have walked right out, but . . .

She tried to make up for being a bitch. "Bram probably wouldn't mind if you used the pool once in a while, as long as you don't do it too much."

"I don't have time to swim." He pulled his hands from his pockets and walked away from her toward the house.

She didn't swim anymore, either, but she'd loved the water when she was a kid. He was probably embarrassed about the way he looked in a suit. Or maybe only women felt that way.

"It's private back here," she called out. "Nobody would see you."

He went into the house without answering her.

She retrieved the net from behind the waterfall rocks and began to skim for leaves. Bram had a pool service, but she liked making the water all clean and smooth. Bram told her she could swim whenever she wanted, but she never did.

She tossed down the net. Until Monday, she'd been so happy here, but now, with all these strangers invading her space, the bad feelings were coming back.

Half an hour later, she entered Georgie's upstairs office. A big, kidney-shaped desk, matching wall unit, and a couple of streamlined chairs upholstered in spice-colored fabric printed with a tree branch design made up the new furnishings. Everything was too modern for the house, and she didn't like it.

Aaron had his back to her, talking on the phone. "Ms. York isn't giving interviews yet, but I'm sure she'd be more than happy to contribute to your charity auction . . . No, she's already donated her *Skip and Scooter* scripts to the Museum of Broadcast Communications, but every year she designs some Christmas ornaments for groups like yours, and each one is personally autographed . . ."

He sounded like a different person on the phone, sure of himself and not so geeky. She set a turkey wrap on the desk. She'd made it with a fat-free tortilla, lean meat, sliced tomato, a few spinach leaves, a sliver of avocado, and carrot sticks on the side. Dude needed to get a clue.

He took in the wrap as he finished his conversation. When he hung up, she said, "Don't count on this every day." She picked up the new issue of *Flash* with Bram and Georgie on the cover and sat on the corner of his desk to thumb through it. "Go ahead and eat."

He picked up the turkey wrap and took a bite. "You got any mayo?"

"No." She carried a perfume sample to her nose and sniffed. "How old are you?"

He had good manners and he swallowed before he answered. "Twenty-six."

Six years older than her, but he seemed younger. "Did you go to college?"

"University of Kansas."

"A lot of people who go to college don't know shit." She studied his face and decided somebody had to tell him. "Your glasses are lame. No offense."

"What's wrong with them?"

"They're ugly. You should get contacts or something."

"Contacts are too much trouble."

"You have nice eyes. You should show them off. At least get decent frames." His eyes were bright blue and thick-lashed, the only decent thing about him.

He frowned, which made his cheeks look as though they were swallowing the rest of his face. "I don't think a person with holes in her eyebrows has room to criticize anybody else."

She loved her pierced eyebrows. They made her feel tough, like a rebel who didn't give a damn about society. "I really care what you think."

He turned back to his computer and pulled up some kind of graph-thing. She rose to leave, but on her way out, she spotted his big ugly briefcase lying open on the floor with a bag of chips inside. She went over and pulled it out.

"Hey! What are you doing?"

"You don't need these. I'll bring you some fruit later."

He pushed himself up from his chair. "Give those back. I don't want your fruit."

"You want this junk instead?"

"Yeah, I want it."

"Too bad." She dropped the chips to the floor and brought her foot down hard on the bag. It split open with a loud pop. "There you are."

He stared at her. "What's your problem, anyway?"

"I'm a bitch." As she left the office and went back downstairs, she could almost see him reaching for those smashed chips.

Bram kept disappearing into his office, as if he had a real job, leaving Georgie no way to work off her frustration. She eventually wandered up to his exercise room and began going through the ballet warm-up routine she used to do every day. Her muscles were stiff and uncooperative, but she kept at it. Maybe she'd have a barre installed. She'd always loved to dance, and she knew she shouldn't have let herself set it aside. The same with singing. She wasn't a great singer. The big, belting Broadway voice that had made her so winning as a kid hadn't matured with age, but she could carry a tune, and her energy made up for what she lacked in vocal nuance.

After her workout, she talked to Sasha and April on the phone and did some online shopping. Her daily routine had been whittled down to bothering her busy friends and making sure she looked good enough to be photographed. She cheered herself up by following Chaz around with the video camera and asking intrusive questions.

Chaz complained bitterly, but that didn't stop her from talking, and Georgie learned a little more. Her growing fascination with Bram's housekeeper was all that kept her from bringing in her own cook.

On Friday morning, day seven of her marriage, she and Bram met with a party planner, the stridently officious, very expensive, and highly recommended Poppy Patterson. Everything about the woman grated, but she loved the idea of a *Skip and Scooter* theme, so they hired her and told her to work out the details with Aaron.

That afternoon, her father decided he'd punished her long enough and finally took her phone call. "Georgie, I understand you want me to put my stamp of approval on your marriage, but I can't do it when I know how wrong it is."

She wouldn't tell him the truth, but she also wouldn't lie more than she already had. "I just thought we could have a nice conversation. Is that too much to ask?"

"Right now? Yes. I don't like Shepard, I don't trust him, and I'm worried about you."

"There's nothing to worry about. Bram isn't . . . He isn't exactly like you remember." She struggled to conjure up a convincing example of Bram's greater maturity, at the same time trying not to think about his drinking. "He's . . . older now."

Her father wasn't impressed. "Remember this, Georgie. If he ever tries to hurt you in any way, promise you'll come to me for help."

"You make it sound like he's going to beat me."

"There are different kinds of hurt. You've never been rational about him."

"That was a long time ago. We're not the same people."

"I have to go. We'll talk later." Just like that, he hung up.

She bit her lip, and her eyes stung. Her father loved her—surely he did—but it wasn't the cozy kind of dad love she wanted. A love that didn't have any strings attached to it. A love she didn't have to work so hard to deserve.

Chapter 10

Georgie awakened around three on Saturday morning and couldn't fall back to sleep. One week ago just about now, she'd been standing next to Bram saying her wedding vows. She wondered exactly what she'd vowed.

The bedroom was stuffy. She kicked off the sheet, slipped into an old pair of yellow Crocs, and padded across the rug to step out onto the balcony. Palm fronds clicked in the breeze, and the gentle splash of the waterfall drifted up from the pool. Lance had left another phone message this afternoon. He was *worried* about her. She wished he'd leave her alone or that she could hate him. Except frequently she did, and it didn't make her feel any better.

The clink of ice cubes interrupted her thoughts, and a voice drifted through the dark. "If you're going to jump, wait until morning. I'm too drunk to deal with a dead body tonight."

Bram sat by his open bedroom doors, just off to her left. He'd stuffed his feet into an ancient pair of sneakers and propped them on the railing. With a drink in his hand and a sickle-shaped shadow slicing across his profile, he looked exactly like a man contemplating which of the seven deadly sins to take on next.

She knew all the back bedrooms opened onto this same second-floor balcony, but until now she hadn't seen Bram out there. "No jumping necessary," she said. "I'm on top of the world." She curled her hand over the railing. "Why aren't you asleep?"

"Because this is the first chance I've had all week to drink in peace." He took in her sleepwear, which was a far cry from the tiny teddies and flyaway baby-dolls she'd worn for Lance. Still, he didn't seem overly critical of her comfy boxers printed with pink and yellow pop art lips.

As she observed the slouch to his spine, the lazy droop to his wrist, she had the feeling she was missing something, but she couldn't put her finger on what it was. "Has anybody told you that you drink too much?"

"I'll think about quitting after our divorce." He took another sip. "What were you doing poking your nose in my office on Wednesday morning?"

She'd wondered when Chaz would get around to ratting her out. "Snooping. What else?"

"I want my video camera back."

She ran her thumb over a rough place on the railing. "You'll get it back. Aaron's buying me one of my own."

"Why do you want it?"

"Mess around."

He set his glass on the tile floor. "Other than walking off with my stuff, what else were you doing out there?"

She debated how much to say, then decided to come right out with it. "I needed to know whether the reunion show was real or a figment of your imagination. I found the script, but the box was taped up nice and tight. Not that I would have read it anyway."

He rose from his chair and wandered toward her. "You should have asked me. Trust is the foundation of a good marriage, Georgie. I'm hurt."

"No, you're not. And I won't do a reunion show. Ever. I'm sick of being typecast. I want parts I can sink my teeth into. Playing Scooter again would be the worst career decision I could make. And you hate Skip, so I don't get why you're so set on this. Well, I do get it, and I'm sorry you're broke, but I'm not sabotaging my career to help you solve your cash flow problems."

He slipped past her and poked his head in her bedroom. "I guess that's it, then?"

"Definitely."

"Okay." He ran his hand along the doorframe, as if he were examining it for dry rot, but she wasn't buying his easy surrender.

"I mean it," she said.

"I get that." He turned to her. "And here I thought you were trying to snoop into my love life."

"You're married to me, remember? You have no love life." As soon as the words came out of her mouth, she wanted to snatch them back. She'd given him a mile-wide opening to delve into the subject she most wanted to avoid. "I'm going to bed."

"Not so fast." He touched her arm before she could make it inside, and that's when it hit her. The nagging feeling that she'd been missing something . . . "You don't smoke anymore!"

"Where did you get that idea?" He released her and walked over to retrieve his drink.

She'd noticed the way he smelled, like soap and citrus, but until this precise moment, she hadn't jumped to the logical conclusion. They'd only been together for seven days, but still, how could she have missed something so obvious? "You're always talking about cigarettes, but I haven't once seen you light up."

"Sure you have." He flopped down in his chair. "I smoke all the time. I just finished a cigarette before you came out."

"No, you didn't. You don't smell like smoke, and I've never tasted tobacco when I've had to endure one of your pathetic kisses. In our *Skip and Scooter* days, kissing you was like licking an ashtray. But now . . . You really have stopped smoking."

He shrugged. "Okay, you've got me. I stopped, but only because my drinking has gotten out of hand, and I can't deal with more than one addiction at a time." He tipped the tumbler to his lips.

At least he was aware of it. Even in the morning, she'd see him with a glass in his hand, and last night he'd had wine with dinner. So had she, but that had been her only drink of the day. "When did you stop smoking?"

He muttered something she couldn't make out.

"What?"

"Five years ago, I said."

"Five years!" That made her furious. "Why couldn't you have just said you'd stopped smoking? Why do you have to play all these mind games?"

"Because I like to."

She knew him, and she didn't know him, and she was worn out from keeping her guard up. "I'm tired. We can talk in the morning."

"You know we can't go on like this much longer, right?"

She pretended not to understand. "Neither of us has killed the other one yet, so I think we're doing pretty well."

"Now you're the one playing games." His glass clinked as he set it on the tiles and uncoiled from the chair. "You have to admit I've been patient."

"We've only been married a week."

"Exactly. An entire week without sex."

"You're a maniac." She turned toward the door, but once again he stopped her.

"I'm not bragging, just offering up information. I don't expect sex on a first date, but it usually seems to happen that way. Second date max."

"Fascinating. Unfortunately for you, I believe in establishing a relationship first, but, hey, marriage is all about compromise, so I'm willing to compromise."

"What kind of compromise?"

She made a play out of thinking it over. "I'll have sex with you . . . after our fourth date."

"And exactly how do you define 'date'?"

She waved her hand breezily. "Oh, I'll know it when I see it."

"I'll just bet you will." He ran his thumb down her bare arm. "Frankly, I'm not too worried. We both know you won't last much longer."

"Because of your overwhelming sexiness?"

"That, but also because—let's be honest—you're ripe for the picking."

"You think so?"

"Baby, you're an orgasm waiting to happen."

Her skin prickled. "Oh, really?"

"You've been divorced for a year. And the Loser is half girl, so nothing will make me believe he was any kind of lover."

She predictably—pitifully—jumped to Lance's defense. "He was a great lover. Gentle and considerate."

"That's a bummer."

"Naturally, you'd say something sarcastic."

"Fortunately for you, I'm neither gentle nor considerate." He slid his thumb into the crook of her arm. "I like my sex rough and dirty. Or does the idea of getting it on with a full-grown man scare our little Scooter?"

She pulled away. "What man? All I see is an overgrown pretty boy."

"Cut the crap, Georgie. I've given up a lot for you, but I'm not giving up sex, too."

She'd known she could only ignore this for so long. If she didn't give him what he wanted, he'd have no qualms about dialing up someone who would. She hated feeling trapped. "You cut the crap," she retorted. "We both know the odds of you staying faithful are smaller than your bank account."

"I'm not Lance Marks."

"That's right. Lance only cheated with one woman. With you, there'll be legions." She pointed her finger at his perfect face. "I've been publicly humiliated once. Call me overly sensitive, but I don't want it to happen again."

"I can stick with one woman for six months." His eyes drifted to her breasts. "If she's good enough in bed to hold my interest."

He was deliberately baiting her, but his words stung just enough so her sarcastic comeback didn't sound sarcastic at all. "Then obviously we have a problem."

He frowned. "Hey, I'm the only one who gets to put you down. It takes all the fun out of our relationship if you do it to yourself."

She hated having him witness even a moment of self-doubt. "I'll make sure it doesn't happen again."

He looked annoyed. "I can't believe you let that jerk-off do such a number on you. It's his problem. Not yours."

"I know that."

"I don't think you do. Your marriage fell apart because of his character, not yours. Guys like Lance will always gravitate toward the woman they think is the strongest, and the Loser decided that was Jade."

Georgie's control snapped. "Of course it was Jade! She does everything! She's beautiful, she's a great actress, and when it comes to giving back, she walks the walk. Jade is out there saving lives. Thanks to her, little Asian girls are going to school right now instead of being forced to sell their bodies to sexual perverts. She's probably going to win the Nobel Peace Prize one of these days. And she deserves it. It's a little hard to compete."

"I'm sure Lance is starting to figure that out."

All the emotions she tried so hard to control boiled to the surface. *"I care about people, too!"*

He blinked. "Okay."

"I do care! I know there's suffering in the world. I know, and I'm going to do something about it." She told herself to shut up, but the words kept tumbling out. "I'm going to Haiti. As soon as I can arrange it. I'm getting medical supplies, and I'm taking them to Haiti."

He cocked his head. There was a long pause. When he finally spoke, he displayed an unusual degree of gentleness. "Don't you think that's a little . . . cold? Using a country's misery for a press op?"

She buried her face in her hands. He was right, and she hated herself. "Oh, God, I'm horrible."

He turned her by the shoulders and drew her to his chest. "I finally get married, and I pick the biggest nutcase in L.A."

She was mortified, and she didn't trust his sympathy. "You've always had lousy taste in women."

"And a one-track mind." He tipped up her chin with his finger. "As sympathetic as I am toward that embarrassing nervous breakdown you just had, let's return to more pressing matters."

"Let's not."

"As long as you're wearing my fake diamond, I promise there'll be no cheating."

"Your promises are worthless. The minute the challenge is gone, you'll be on the prowl, and we both know it."

"Wrong. Come on, Georgie. Put out."

"I need a little more time to adjust to the idea of being a slut."

"Let me speed things along." He crushed his mouth to hers.

This kiss was real, with no photographers watching or directors ready to call "cut." She began to pull away only to realize she didn't feel the need. This was Bram. She understood exactly how duplicitous he was, exactly how little his kisses meant, and that kept her expectations comfortably low.

He slid his tongue into her mouth in a sensuous exploration. He'd turned into a great kisser, and she'd missed this intimacy more than she wanted to admit.

She slipped her arms around his shoulders. He tasted of dark nights and treacherous winds. Of youthful betrayal and heartless abandonment. But because she knew him so well, because she was beginning to trust herself, she wasn't in any emotional peril. Bram wanted to use her. Fine. She'd use him, too. Just for a moment. Just for the lifetime of one kiss.

He splayed a hand across the small of her back, bringing their hips together. He was hard, and she was going to say no, and possessing that power freed her to indulge. His hand curled over her hip. If only the man who smelled so good, and felt so good, and kissed so well weren't Bram Shepard.

Night and the dim light from her bedroom turned his eyes from lavender to jet. "I want you so damned much," he said.

A dark, erotic thrill swept through her punctuated by a flash of blue-white light.

Bram's head shot up. "Fuck!"

It took a moment for her brain to function. By the time she processed the fact that the sudden light had come from a strobe, he'd already sprung into action. He swung his legs over the balcony railing and dropped to the roof of the veranda below. She gasped and leaned over the rail. "Stop! What do you think you're doing?"

Ignoring her, he scrambled over the roof tiles, just like either Lance or his stunt double had done in a dozen films. The flash seemed to have come from the big tree that draped the property between Bram's house and his neighbor's. "You're going to break your neck!" she cried.

He lowered himself over the edge of the veranda roof, hung by his fingers for a moment, then dropped to the ground.

All the security lights in the rear of the house came on. He clambered to his feet, shot off across the yard, and disappeared behind a thicket of bamboo. Seconds later, his head and shoulders emerged as he climbed the high stone wall that divided his property from next door.

Of all the stupid . . . She rushed downstairs and ran out into the backyard, which was lit up like midday. The idea of having such a private moment exposed to the world made her sick. She hurried along the path to the wall, her Crocs slapping her heels. The wall rose a good two feet above her head, but she found some footholds in the stones and began pulling herself up. A sharp edge scraped her calf. Finally, she climbed high enough to brace her arms across the top and see what was happening on the other side.

The neighbor's yard was bigger and more open than Bram's, with formally clipped shrubbery, a rectangular swimming pool, and a tennis court. Here, too, the security lights had come on, and she could see Bram racing across the lawn, chasing a man who was gripping what could only be a camera. He must have climbed the tree to spy on them, but he had to be using some kind of high-speed film, so the flash must have gone off accidentally. Who knew how many pictures he'd taken before he'd given himself away?

The photographer had a long head start, but Bram wasn't conceding. He jumped over a row of shrubs. The man hit an open space of lawn. He was small and wiry, no one she recognized. He disappeared around a cabana.

A woman flew out of the neighboring house. In the light flooding the yard, Georgie saw long, light hair and a silky peach robe. The woman rushed down a set of semicircular stone steps into the yard, which didn't seem like the brightest thing to do with an unknown intruder on the prowl. As she stepped into a pool of bright light, Georgie realized two things at once.

The woman was Rory Keene . . . and she had a gun.

Chapter 11

George called out softly . . . ever so softly . . . and in her friendliest, most soothing voice. "Uhm . . . Rory? Please don't shoot."

Rory spun toward the wall, her blond hair flying. "Who is that?"

"It's Georgie. York. And that man you just saw running across your yard was Bram. My . . . uh . . . husband. You probably shouldn't shoot him either."

"Georgie?"

Her toes were going numb inside her Crocs, and she was starting to slip. "A photographer climbed your tree to take pictures of us. Bram went after him." She tried to cling tighter to the top of the wall, but her arms were getting tired. "I'm . . . losing my grip. I have to get down."

"I think there's a gate at the end of the wall."

Georgie made it to the ground, but not before she'd scraped her other shin.

"It's here somewhere," Rory called from the other side as Georgie picked her way along the stones. "The studio owns the house, and I haven't lived here long, so I haven't really looked for it."

Georgie located the wooden gate, partially hidden behind some shrubs. "I found it, but it's stuck."

"I'll push from my side."

The gate dragged but eventually gave way enough for Georgie to slip through. Rory stood on the other side with the gun resting in the folds of her nightgown. Despite her long, sleep-rumpled blond hair, she looked cool and calm, as if confronting nighttime intruders was all in a day's work. "What's going on?"

Georgie looked around for Bram, but he was nowhere in sight. "I'm really sorry about this. Bram and I were out on our balcony when a flash went off. A photographer was hiding in that big tree of yours. Bram went after him. It happened so fast."

"A photographer sneaked on my property to watch your house?"

"It looks that way."

"Do you want me to call the police?"

If Georgie were an ordinary citizen, that's exactly what she'd do, but she wasn't, and the police weren't an option. Rory arrived at the same conclusion. "Stupid question."

"I need to . . . I'd better make sure Bram hasn't killed anybody." She took off in the direction he'd disappeared. Just as she reached the pool, she spotted him coming around the side of the house. Other than a slight limp and a murderous expression, he seemed unharmed. "The son of a bitch got away from me."

"You could have killed yourself jumping off the roof like that."

"I don't care. That cockroach stepped way over the line."

Just then he spotted Rory coming toward him, the gun dangling at her side like a Prada purse. Georgie couldn't help but envy her. A woman as coolheaded as Rory Keene would never wake up in a Las Vegas hotel room married to her oldest enemy. But then a woman like Rory Keene controlled her life, not the other way around.

Bram froze. Rory ignored him. "I'll call my security company first thing tomorrow, Georgie. Obviously, the lights aren't enough to discourage unwelcome visitors."

Bram stared at the handgun. "Is that thing loaded?"

"Of course."

Georgie bit back a wisecrack about the dangers of being armed and blond. Even in jest, it didn't seem smart to crack a joke at the expense of such a powerful woman, especially one they'd awakened at three in the morning.

"It looks like a Glock," Bram said.

"A thirty-one."

His interest in the gun gave Georgie a chill, and she quickly intervened. "You can't have one. You're way too hotheaded to be armed."

Bram chucked her under the chin in a way that made her itch to slap him. He gave her a quick, businesslike kiss that couldn't have been more different from the intimate one they'd exchanged a few minutes earlier. "I can't get used to the way you worry about me, sweetheart," he said. "How did you get over here?"

"There's a gate."

Bram nodded. "I'd almost forgotten. Apparently the original families were good friends."

Georgie wondered why Rory was in a house leased by the studio instead of in a place of her own. "Bram forgot to mention that you lived next door." She slipped her hand behind his back, an affectionate gesture except for the sharp pinch she gave him to retaliate for the way he'd chin-chucked her.

He winced. "Sure I mentioned it, sweetheart. I guess there's been so much going on that it slipped your mind. Besides, this isn't exactly a get-to-know-your-neighbors kind of neighborhood."

It was true. Pricey estates separated by high walls and locked gates didn't make for a block party atmosphere. In the Brentwood neighborhood where she and Lance had lived, they'd never met the nineties pop star in the house next door.

Georgie's gaze wandered to Rory's Glock. "We'd better let you go back to bed."

Rory slipped her nightgown strap up on her shoulder. "I doubt if any of us will get much sleep after this."

"Good point," Bram said. "Why don't you come over to the house? I'll put on a pot of coffee and heat up some of my housekeeper's cinnamon rolls. You'll be our first official company."

Georgie stared at him. It was the middle of the night. Had he lost his mind?

"Another time. I need to catch up on some reading." Rory gave him her coolest look, then shocked Georgie by offering a quick hug. "I'll call you as soon as I talk to the security company." She turned back to Bram. "Be good to her. And, Georgie, if you need any help, let me know."

Bram's fake good humor slipped. "If she needs any help, I'll take care of it."

"I'm sure you will," Rory replied in a manner that suggested she wasn't sure at all. She walked away, the folds of her nightgown concealing her gun.

Bram waited until they were on their own side of the wall before he spoke. "If the tabs run any of those shots, we're going after them."

"They probably won't," she said. "Not here. But there's a big market in Europe, and then they'll hit the Web. We won't be able to do anything about it."

"We're suing."

"Our marriage will be long over before a lawsuit reaches the courts."

"What do you suggest? We just forget the whole thing? This doesn't bother you?"

The truth was that she'd gotten numb. "I hate it," she said.

They walked silently across the yard. She shouldn't be so upset. The photos of the two of them would lend legitimacy to her sham marriage. But she felt almost as violated as the day the paps had caught her looking at the sonogram. "I'm going to bed," she said, when they reached the house. "Alone."

"Your loss."

She was heading up the steps when an interesting piece of the puzzle that made up Bram Shepard fell into place. "Rory has something to do with your re-union show project, doesn't she? That's why you were sucking up to her at The Ivy two weeks ago. And that embarrassing invitation to heat up cinnamon rolls . . ."

"Babe, I suck up to anybody who might be able to get me a decent acting job."

"That's pathetic. But I'll admit it's enormously gratifying to watch you grovel."

"Whatever it takes to get ahead," he said lightly.

Sleep was beyond him, so Bram went to the pool. Life had become way too complicated, he thought as he stripped and dove in. He'd hoped this idiotic marriage would make things run smoother for him, but he hadn't factored in how protective Rory was of Georgie.

He flipped to his back and let himself drift. Every time he tried to dig his way out of the tunnel he'd fallen into, another cave-in threatened to bury him. Georgie thought it was all about money. She didn't know that he needed respectability more. And he didn't want her to know. He intended to make sure Georgie continued to see him as the bastard he'd always been. His life was his own, and he wasn't letting her into any part of it that mattered.

He hadn't always been a loner. Growing up without a real family had made him quick to create an artificial one from the guys who'd eventually bitten him in the ass. He'd thought they were his friends, but they'd been users—spending his money, exploiting his connections, and eventually setting him up for that damned sex tape. Lesson well learned. Looking out for number one meant going it alone.

Georgie wasn't a user, but that didn't mean he wanted her rooting around in his psyche, figuring out how much he needed to create a new life for himself. She'd known him too long, she saw too much, and she was dangerously easy to talk to. But he couldn't stomach the idea of having her watch him fail, a possibility that grew more likely every day.

Georgie was useful for polishing his reputation and for sex. As much as he wanted to rush that last part, his ugly behavior that night on the boat meant he had to give her as much time as she needed . . . and then draw her in.

Four days passed. Just as Georgie began to hope the balcony photos would never appear, they showed up in a U.K. tabloid. After that, they were everywhere. But instead of revealing a lovers' tryst, the blurry nighttime images the photographer had caught seemed to show Georgie and Bram having a nasty argument. In the first frame, Georgie looked combative with her hand splayed on her hip. Next came Georgie with her face buried in her palms, remorseful over her self-serving plan to go to Haiti, except even the most casual observer would believe she was crying from their fight. Another picture showed Bram holding her by the shoulders. It had been a comforting gesture, but the shadowy image made his posture look menacing. The final shot, the blurriest of them all, showed their private kiss. Unfortunately, it was impossible to tell whether he was kissing her or shaking her.

All hell broke loose.

"I can't believe these bastards get away with this kind of crap." Bram took a vicious swipe at a fly that had the temerity to land on the table next to his coffee mug. He'd once made an art out of shrugging off bad publicity, but now he wanted blood—the photographer's and everyone who'd printed the photos, from the original tabloid to the online gossip sites. "If I could just get my hands on one of them . . ."

"Don't look at me if you're going to turn violent," she said. "I'm on your side for once."

They were sitting outside at Urth Caffé on Melrose sipping cups of organic coffee. Seven days had elapsed since the photos had appeared. Photographers and gawkers lined the sidewalk, and the Caffé's other customers were openly staring at the city's most famous newlyweds.

Everything she'd hoped to achieve with this marriage was backfiring. All her friends had called except Meg, who was still M.I.A. She'd had to keep both April and Sasha from flying back to L.A. As for her father . . . He'd stormed over to the house and threatened to kill Bram. She still wasn't sure he believed her account of what had really happened, and his resistance to their marriage had only intensified. So much for taking charge of her life. Her self-confidence was shakier than ever.

"Will you smile at me, for chrissake?" His clenched jaw made his own smile suspect, but she played the good soldier and leaned forward to kiss the tight corner of his mouth.

There'd been no more private kisses since the night on the balcony eleven days ago, although she'd thought about that kiss more than she wanted to. She might dislike Bram as a person, but apparently his body was another matter, because the only pleasure she'd managed to conjure up all week had been watching him walk around with his shirt off, or even with his shirt on, like now.

"And this is a date, damn it. Our *fifth* this week."

"Bull," she said, keeping her smile. "This is business, damage control like all the rest. I told you—it's not a date until we're both having a good time, and in case you haven't noticed, we're miserable."

He clenched his teeth. "Maybe you could try a little harder."

She dunked her second biscotti in her coffee and took a desultory nibble. At least she'd gained a few pounds, but that was small compensation for being trapped in an impossible situation with the press dogging them . . . and with a man who trailed testosterone.

He set down his own cup. "People think pictures don't lie."

"These do."

The headlines read:

Marriage Over! Next Stop Splitsville
More Heartbreak for Georgie
Georgie's Ultimatum! Get to Rehab!

Even Bram's old sex tape had resurfaced.

They'd been trying to repair the damage by hitting all the paparazzi hot spots daily. They'd bought muffins at City Bakery in Brentwood, lunched at the Chateau, visited The Ivy again, as well as Nobu, the Polo Lounge, and Mr. Chow. They spent two nights club hopping, which left Georgie feeling old and even more depressed. Today, they'd shopped at Armani's home store on Robertson, Fred Segal on Melrose, then stopped at a trendy boutique where they'd bought a set of obnoxious matching T-shirts they'd never wear anyplace but in public.

They'd only been able to risk a few separate outings. Bram slipped away for a couple of mysterious meetings. She took a few dance classes, went for an early-morning hike, and sent a huge anonymous check to Food for the Poor's Haitian relief program. Generally, however, they had to stick together. At his suggestion, she was pulling the publicity-hungry celeb's favorite trick of changing her clothes several times a day, since every new outfit meant the tabs bought a fresh photo. After having spent the past year trying to stay out of the public eye, she didn't miss the irony.

The other coffee-shop customers had been content merely to stare, but now a young guy with a scraggly goatee and a fake Rolex came up to their table. "Can I get your autographs?"

She didn't mind signing autographs for genuine fans, but something told her these would be up for sale on eBay by the end of the day.

"Just your signature is okay," he said, confirming her suspicions as she took the felt pen and pristine piece of paper he handed her.

"Let me personalize it," she said.

"You don't have to do that."

"I insist."

Personalizing a signature devalued it, and his loser's mouth grew sullen as he realized she had his number. He muttered the name Harry. She signed, "To Harry, with all my love." On the next line, she deliberately misspelled her last name, adding an *e* to York, so the autograph looked bogus. Bram, in the meantime, scrawled "Miley Cyrus" across the other piece of paper.

The kid balled up both signatures and stalked away. "Thanks for nothing."

Bram slumped back in the chair and muttered, "What the hell kind of life is this?"

"Right now it's our life, and we need to make the best of it."

"Do me a favor and spare me the *Annie* sound track."

"You're a very negative person." She made her point by launching into the chorus of "Tomorrow."

"That's it." He shot to his feet. "Let's get out of here."

They set off down the sidewalk, their hands linked, his bronze hair glistening in the sun, hers desperately in need of a cut, and the paps trailing close behind. The trip took a while. "Do you have to stop and talk to every little kid you see?" Bram grumbled.

"Good photo op." She didn't reveal how much she loved talking to children. "And who are you to complain? How many times have I had to stand around while you flirted with other women?"

"That last one was sixty if she was a day."

She'd also had a big mole on her face and bad makeup, but Bram had admired her earrings and even given her an eye-smolder. He did that a lot, she'd noticed, bypassing the beauty queens to stop and chat with their homelier sisters. For the space of a few moments, he made them feel beautiful.

She hated it when he did nice things.

Still, his generally foul mood had lifted her own, and when she spotted a pretty flower shop, she pulled him inside. The interior was fragrant, the flowers beautifully arranged, and the clerk left them alone. Georgie took her time studying the arrangements and finally chose a mixed bouquet of iris, roses, and lilies. "Your treat."

"I've always been a generous guy."

"You're going to bill me, aren't you?"

"Sad, but true."

Before they got to the register, his cell rang. He glanced at the display and flipped the phone shut without answering. He was on the phone a lot, she'd noticed, but seldom where she could overhear. She held out her hand before he could pocket the phone. "Lend it to me, will you? I need to make a call, and I forgot mine."

He passed it over, but instead of punching in a number, she flicked through the display to the most recent entry. "Caitlin Carter. Now I know your lover's last name."

He snatched the phone back. "Stop snooping. And she's not my lover."

"Then why won't you talk to her in front of me?"

"Because I don't want to." He headed for the counter with the bouquet. As he stopped near a florist's cart filled with frilly pastel blooms, she was struck by the contrast between his confident masculinity and those lacy flowers. Once again, she felt that distracting sexual stirring. This morning she'd even made an excuse to work out with him just so she could watch the show.

It was pathetic, but understandable. She was even a little proud of herself. Despite the current chaos stirred up by the photos, she was experiencing lust at its most elemental, separate from even a minimal amount of affection. Basically, she'd turned into a guy.

Bram gave her the flowers to carry from the shop. They'd been lucky enough to find a rare parking space close by, but they still had to get through the crowd of noisy paps stalking the sidewalk in front.

"Bram! Georgie! Over here!"

"Have you two patched up your fight?"

"Make-up flowers, Bram?"

"Georgie! Right here!"

Bram pulled her against him. "Stand back, guys. Give us some room."

"Georgie, I heard you saw a lawyer."

Bram shoved the burly photographer who'd gotten too close. "I said to stay back!"

Out of nowhere, Mel Duffy emerged from the swarm and lifted his camera toward them. "Hey, Georgie. Any comment about Jade Gentry's miscarriage?"

His shutter clicked away.

Georgie felt sick. Her envy had somehow poisoned that defenseless fetus. Duffy had told them the miscarriage had happened in Thailand nearly two weeks ago, only a few days after her Vegas wedding, when Lance and Jade had been about to join up with a U.N. task force. Their publicist had just released the news, saying the couple was devastated but that doctors had assured them there was no reason they couldn't have another child. All those phone messages Lance had left her . . .

Bram didn't say anything until they were nearly home. Then he turned down the radio and gazed over at her. "Tell me you're not taking this to heart."

What kind of woman resented an innocent, unborn child? She was nauseated by guilt. "Me? Of course not. It's sad, that's all. Of course, I'm sorry for them."

His knowing expression made her look away. She needed a gigolo, not a shrink. She adjusted her sunglasses. "Nobody wants something like this to happen. Maybe I wish I hadn't been quite so upset when I heard she was pregnant. That's only natural."

"This had nothing to do with you."

"I know that."

"Your brain knows it, but the rest of you is seriously screwed up when it comes to anything associated with the Loser."

Her self-control snapped. "He just lost his baby! A baby I didn't want to see born."

"I knew it! I knew you'd decide you were somehow responsible. Toughen up, Georgie."

"You think I'm not tough? I'm surviving this marriage, aren't I?"

"This isn't a marriage. It's a chess game."

He was right, and she was sick of the whole thing.

They drove the rest of the way to the house in silence, but after he'd parked the car in the garage, he didn't immediately get out. Instead, he sat there, pulling off his sunglasses and messing with the stems. "Caitlin is the daughter of Sarah Carter."

"The novelist?" She let go of the door handle.

"She died three years ago."

"I remember." Considering Bram's past history, she'd been certain Caitlin was a bimbo, but that was unlikely, with an author of Sarah Carter's caliber as her mother. Carter had written a number of literary thrillers, none of them successful. Several years after her death, a small press had brought out *Tree House*, a previously unpublished work. The novel had gradually caught fire with the public, and eventually became the darling of book clubs. Like everyone else, Georgie had loved it.

"Caitlin and I were dating when the book first came out," Bram said. "Before it hit the best-seller lists. She mentioned that the last thing her mother had written before she died was a screenplay for *Tree House*, and she let me read it."

"Sarah Carter turned the book into a screenplay herself?"

"A damn good one. I optioned it two hours after I finished it."

Georgie nearly choked. "You hold the film option on *Tree House*? *You*?"

"I was drunk and didn't think about what I was getting into." He climbed out of the car looking as gorgeous and worthless as ever.

She hurried across the garage after him. "Wait a minute. Are you telling me you optioned it *before* the book became a best seller?"

He headed into the house. "I was drunk *and* lucky."

"I'll say. How lucky?"

"Very. Caitlin could sell a new option on that screenplay for twenty times what I paid her, something she never stops reminding me about."

Georgie pressed her palm to her chest. "Give me a minute. I don't know which is harder for me to visualize. You as a producer or the fact that you actually read an entire screenplay start to finish."

He made his way to the kitchen. "I've matured since our *Skip and Scooter* days."

"In your opinion."

"I hardly had to look up any of the big words." She didn't expect him to say more and was surprised when he went on. "Unfortunately, I'm having a little trouble getting it financed."

She stopped. "You're actually trying to get the project made?"

"Nothing better to do."

That explained all the mysterious phone calls, but it didn't explain why Bram had kept this such a big secret. He tossed his car keys on the kitchen counter. "The bad news is that my option runs out in less than three weeks, and if I can't get a package put together by then, Caitlin will have her rights back."

"And be considerably richer."

"She doesn't give a damn about anything except the money. She hated her mother. She'd sell *Tree House* to a cartoon factory if they made the best offer."

Georgie had never optioned a book or screenplay, but she knew how the process worked. The option holder—in this case Bram—had only a specific amount of time to get solid backing for his project before his option expired and the rights reverted to the original owner. Since all he'd have left when that happened would be a hole in his bank account, his suck-up attitude toward Rory Keene finally made sense.

"How close are you to getting someone to green-light *Tree House*?" she asked, even though she already had an inkling of the answer.

He grabbed a water bottle from the refrigerator. "Pretty close. Hank Peters loves the screenplay, and he's interested in directing, so that's caught a lot of attention. With the right casting, we can make the movie on a shoestring, another plus."

Peters was a great director, but Georgie couldn't imagine him being willing to work with unreliable Bram Shepard. "Is Hank interested or committed?"

"Interested in committing. And I have a leading man to play Danny Grimes. That's part of the deal."

Grimes was a fabulously multidimensional character, and it didn't surprise her that lots of actors would be interested. "Who did you get?"

He twisted off the bottle cap. "Who do you think?"

She stared at him, then groaned. "Oh, no . . . You're not."

"A couple of acting lessons . . . I'll be able to handle it."

"You can't play a part like that. Grimes is a complex character. He's conflicted, tortured . . . You'd be laughed out of town. No wonder you can't get financing."

"Thanks for the vote of confidence." He took a slug of water.

"Have you really thought this through? Successful producers need a reputation for something other than gross unreliability. And the way you're insisting on playing the lead . . . Not smart."

"I can do it."

His intensity unsettled her. The Bram she knew only cared about pleasure. She considered the possibility that she didn't understand him as well as she thought, and not just because of his interest in Tree House . . . She hadn't seen any signs of drug abuse, and he spent hours every day in his office. He'd even gotten rid of his old, disreputable friends, which was odd for a guy who'd hated being alone. Alcohol and pathological arrogance seemed to be his last vices.

"I'm going for a swim." He disappeared toward the pool.

She went to her room to change into shorts and a tank. If the screenplay was as good as he said, everyone in town had to be waiting for his option to expire so they could pounce on the project themselves. The leading role would go to the male Flavor of the Month instead of the actor best equipped to handle the part, which in any case wouldn't be Bram. He'd handled Skip Scofield brilliantly, but he didn't have the skills or the depth to tackle anything more emotionally intricate, witness the lightweight roles he'd taken on since then.

As she was slipping into her most comfortable pair of sandals, her head shot up. "Bastard!"

She charged downstairs and across the veranda to the pool, where he was swimming laps. "You jerk! There isn't any *Skip and Scooter* reunion movie! That was a smoke screen you threw up to hide what you were really doing."

"I told you there was no reunion movie." He dove under.

"But you made me think there was," she said the instant he resurfaced. "This stupid fake marriage . . . My money was just a bonus, wasn't it? *Tree House* is the real reason you agreed to cooperate. You couldn't afford to be the second man in recent history to break sweet Georgie York's heart. Not when you need the honchos to believe you've turned into a solid citizen so they'll take you seriously."

"Do you have a problem with that?"

"I have a problem being misled," she said.

"It's me you're dealing with. What did you expect?"

She stalked across the pool deck as he swam toward the waterfall. "If people believe my respectability has rubbed off on you, you've gone a long way toward improving your chances of getting your movie made, now haven't you?"

"You shouldn't call the sacred bonds of holy matrimony 'stupid.'"

"What sacred bonds? The only reason you're finally telling me the truth is because you want to get in my panties."

"I'm a guy, so sue me."

"Don't speak to me ever again. For the rest of your life." She stalked away.

"Fine by me," he called after her. "Unless you're planning to say dirty words, I don't like a woman who talks too much in bed."

The phone he'd left by the side of the pool rang. He swam to the edge and grabbed it. She stopped to listen in.

"Scott . . . How's it going? Yeah, it's been crazy . . ." He switched to the other ear and climbed the ladder. "I don't want to say too much on the phone, but I have something I know you'll be interested in. Let's meet at the Mandarin tomorrow afternoon for a drink so we can talk about it." He frowned. "Friday morning? Okay, I'll shift a couple of things around. Hey, I need to let you go. I'm late for a meeting."

He flipped his phone shut and grabbed a towel. She tapped her toe. "Late for a meeting?"

"It's L.A. Always be first to end the call."

"I'll remember that. And you're not getting another penny from me."

Instead of returning to the house, she stomped out to his office. The idea of Bram being willing to work at anything unsettled her. But at least his disclosure about the screenplay had given her something to think about other than whatever metaphysical part she'd played in the loss of Lance's baby.

She ripped open the manuscript box that was supposed to contain the *Skip and Scooter* reunion script and tilted out a neat stack of porno magazines with a blue Post-it note on top.

THE REAL THING IS SO MUCH BETTER.

As Bram headed up to his workout room, he wondered what stupid-ass weakness had made him tell Georgie about *Tree House*. But she'd looked so frickin' tragic when she'd heard about Lance and Jade's baby— that overdeveloped sense of responsibility popping up again—and somehow he'd let the truth slip out only to immediately regret it. Failure already hung over him like a mushroom cloud. With the odds stacked so high against him, the fewer people who knew how much *Tree House* meant to him, the better. That especially applied to Georgie, who couldn't wait for him to fail.

He didn't bother changing out of his wet trunks but went right to his workout room. A ballet barre had appeared a couple of days ago. One more invasion of his private space. What would he do with his life if *Tree House* slipped away from him? Go back to guest roles as vapid playboys? The idea turned his stomach.

He put on an Usher CD and eyed the elliptical machine with distaste. He wanted to be outside, free to run for miles in the hills like he used to, but thanks to his Vegas misadventure, he was trapped.

At least he had the room to himself. Watching Georgie go through her stretching routine had become torturous. She tied up her hair before she worked out, so that even the nape of her neck became an erogenous zone. Then there was the sexy extension of those long legs. It said something about his life that getting down and dirty with Little Orphan Annie had gone to the top of his thrill list.

But he couldn't dismiss her as easily as she dismissed herself. She had an unconscious sex appeal that trumped big tits and phony posturing. Nobody was going to catch Georgie York flashing her goody bits in public.

Or in private . . . Something he was growing increasingly intent on changing. She might hate his guts, but she definitely liked the packaging they came in. Georgie didn't know it yet, but her days of wasting away over the Loser were coming to an end.

Who said he only cared about himself? Liberating Georgie York had become his civic duty.

Chapter 12

Two more days passed. Georgie was in the kitchen, trying to figure out how to make one of Chaz's delicious smoothies, when she heard a noise coming from the front of the house. Seconds later, Meg Koranda exploded into the room like a frisky young greyhound who'd been kicked out of obedience school so many times her owners had given up trying to train her. In this case, her owners were her adoring parents, screen legend Jake Koranda and Fleur Savagar Koranda, the Glitter Baby, a woman who'd once been America's most famous cover girl and who was now the powerful head of the country's most exclusive talent agency.

Meg hurled herself at Georgie, bringing the smell of incense with her. "Ohmygod, Georgie! I only heard the news when I called home two days ago, and I took the first plane out. I was at this fabulous ashram—totally isolated from the world—I even got head lice! But it was so worth it. Mom says you've lost your mind."

As Georgie returned Meg's fierce hug, she hoped the head lice were one of her twenty-six-year-old friend's exaggerations, but Meg's dark brown crew cut didn't bode well. Still Meg's hairstyles changed with the weather, and the addition of a red *bindi* between her eyebrows and dangling earrings that looked as though they were made from yak bone, led Georgie to suspect her friend might be going for a monastic-chic fashion statement. Meg's chunky leather sandals and a gauzy brown top confirmed the impression. Only her jeans were 100 percent L.A.

Meg was a tall, slender reed who'd inherited her mother's large hands and feet, but not her mother's extravagant beauty. Instead, Meg had her father's more irregular features, along with his brown hair and darker coloring. Depending on the light, Meg's eyes were either blue, green, or brown, as changeable as her personality. Meg was the little sister Georgie had always wanted, and Georgie loved her dearly, but that didn't make her blind to Meg's faults. Her friend was spoiled and impulsive, five feet ten inches of good times, good intentions, good heart, and almost total irresponsibility in her quest to outrun her famous parents' legacies.

Georgie squeezed her shoulders. "How could you disappear for so long without calling one of us? We've missed you."

"I was cut off from civilization. Time got away from me." Meg pulled back far enough to spot the blender with its messy, unprocessed pink contents. "If that has alcohol in it, I want some."

"It's ten o'clock in the morning."

"Not in Punjab. Start at the beginning and tell me everything."

Bram, who must have let her in the house, appeared in the doorway. "How's the grand reunion going?"

Meg ran to him. They'd dated a few times, over the protests of Georgie, Sasha, April, and both of Meg's parents. Meg swore they'd never had sex, but Georgie didn't entirely believe her. Now Meg snaked her arm around his waist. "Sorry to ignore you when I came in." She gazed back at Georgie. "We never hooked up. I swear. Tell her, Bram."

"If we never hooked up," Bram said in his huskiest, sexiest drawl, "how do I know you have a dragon tattooed on your ass?"

"Because I told you. Don't believe him, Georgie. Really. You know I only went out with him because my parents gave me such a hard time about it." She looked up at Bram, which, with her considerable height, only required lifting her eyes a few inches. "I have oppositional disorder. The minute somebody tells me not to do something, I'm all over it. It's a character flaw."

He ran his hand up her spine and dropped his voice to a sexy purr. "If I'd known about that when we went out, I'd have demanded you keep your clothes on."

Meg's eyes flashed from sea green to a stormy blue. "Are you hitting on me?"

"Make sure you tell Georgie."

Meg pointed her finger. "She's standing right there."

"How do you know she's paying attention? If you're her friend, you won't let her ignore what's going on right under her nose."

Georgie lifted an eyebrow at him, then drowned them both out by switching on the blender. Unfortunately, she'd forgotten to tighten the lid.

"Watch it!"

"Jeez, Georgie . . ."

She lunged for the blender controls, but the buttons were slippery, and the machine spewed its contents everywhere. Strawberries, banana, flaxseed, wheatgrass, and carrot juice flew across the pristine counter, down the cabinets, spattered the floor and Georgie's exorbitantly expensive wheat-colored tunic top. Bram pushed her aside and found the right button, but not before he decorated himself and his white T-shirt with colorful glop. "Chaz is going to kill you," he said, the sexy drawl forgotten. "Seriously."

Meg had been far enough away to escape unscathed, except for a bit of banana that she licked from her arm. "Who's Chaz?"

Georgie snatched up a dish towel and started dabbing at her tunic. "Do you remember Mrs. Danvers, the scary housekeeper in *Rebecca*?"

Meg's yak bone earrings bobbed. "I read the book in college."

"Imagine her as a surly, twenty-year-old punk rocker who runs the place like Nurse Ratched in *Cuckoo's Nest,* and you have Bram's charming housekeeper, Chaz."

Meg watched Bram pull his T-shirt over his head. "I'm not picking up a real strong love vibe between you two."

Bram grabbed a dishcloth. "Then I guess you're not as perceptive as you think. Why else would we have gotten married?"

"Because Georgie's not accountable for her actions these days, and you're after her money. Mom says you're the kind of guy who never grows up."

Georgie couldn't hold back a smirk. "That might explain why Mommy Fleur refused to represent you."

Bram's expression of displeasure would have been more effective if his cheek hadn't been smeared with gooey flaxseeds. "She wouldn't represent you, either."

"Only because I'm so close to Meg. It would have been a conflict of interest."

"Not really," Meg pointed out. "Mom loves you as a person, Georgie, but she wouldn't be caught dead having to deal with your father. Do you guys mind if I crash here for a couple of days?"

"Yes!" Bram said.

"No, of course not." Georgie regarded her with concern. "What's up?"

"I want to spend some time with you, that's all."

Georgie didn't entirely believe her, but who knew exactly what Meg was thinking? "You can stay in the guesthouse."

Bram bristled. "No, she can't. My office is in the guesthouse."

"Only in half of it. You never go into the bedroom."

Bram turned on Meg. "We haven't even been married for three weeks. What kind of loser barges in on people who are practically on their honeymoon?"

Scatterbrained Meg Koranda disappeared, and in her place stood Jake Koranda's daughter, her expression as steely as her father's when he played the gunslinger Bird Dog Caliber. "The kind of loser who wants to make sure her friend's best interests are being protected when she suspects that same friend might not be looking out for herself."

"I'm fine," Georgie said quickly. "Bram and I are passionately in love. We just have a weird way of showing it."

Bram abandoned his clean-up efforts. "Have you told your parents you want to stay here? Because I swear to God, Meg, I don't need Jake on my ass right now. Or your mother."

"I'll deal with Dad. And Mom already dislikes you, so she's no problem."

Chaz chose that moment to enter her kitchen. Today two tiny rubber bands made miniature devil horns out of the now fluorescent red hair on top of her head. She looked fourteen, but she cussed like a veteran sailor when she saw the condition of her kitchen. Until Bram stepped forward . . .

"I'm sorry, Chaz. The blender got away from me."

Chaz immediately softened. "Wait for me next time, okay?"

"I sure will," he said contritely.

She began ripping off squares of paper towel and handing them out. "Wipe your feet so you don't track this shit all over the house."

She refused any offers of help and began attacking the mess with single-minded focus. As they left the kitchen, Georgie remembered Chaz's enthusiasm for cleaning up messes and wished she had her video camera handy.

She decided to settle for Meg instead, and later that afternoon as they sat around the pool, she turned the camera on her and began asking about her experiences in India. But unlike Chaz, Meg had grown up around cameras, and she answered only the questions she chose to. When Georgie tried to press her, she said she was bored talking about herself and wanted to swim.

Bram appeared not long after. He closed up his phone, sprawled on the chaise next to Georgie, and gazed at Meg in the pool. "Having your pal around isn't a good idea. I still have the hots for her."

"No, you don't. You just want to annoy me." He hadn't put a shirt on, and lust shot right through her slutty little body. Bram thought she was playing games by holding him off, but it was more complicated. She'd never viewed sex as meaningless entertainment. She'd always needed for it to be important. Until now.

Was she finally clear-eyed and self-assertive enough to indulge in a mindless fling? A few steamy romps and then, "Arrivederci, babe, and don't let the door hit you on your way out." But that scenario had a major flaw. How could she have a mindless fling with a man she couldn't send home afterward? No matter which way she looked at it, living under the same roof was a complication she couldn't get around.

"You haven't mentioned your meeting at the Mandarin this morning," she said to distract herself.

"Nothing to say. The guy mainly wanted the dirt on our marriage." Bram shrugged. "Who cares? It's a beautiful afternoon, and neither of us is miserable. You have to admit this is a great third date."

"Nice try."

"Give it up, Georgie. I've noticed the way you look at me. You do everything but lick your lips."

"Unfortunately, I'm human, and you're a lot hotter than you used to be. If only you were a real person instead of a male blow-up doll . . ."

He swung his legs over the lounge and stood above her like a golden Apollo who'd sauntered down from Mount Olympus to remind female mortals about the consequences of messing with the gods. "One more week, Georgie. That's all you've got."

"Or what?"

"You'll see."

Somehow it didn't sound like an idle threat.

Laura Moody finished her salad and tossed the container into the trash basket by her desk, which was located in a glass-walled office on the third floor of Starlight Artists Management. She was forty-nine years old, single, and perpetually dieting in an attempt to lose the extra ten pounds that made her grossly obese by Hollywood standards. She had flyaway brown hair, still without a speck of gray; brandy-colored eyes; and a long nose balanced by a strong chin. She was neither pretty nor plain, which made her invisible in L.A. The designer suits and jackets that were a Hollywood agent's required uniform never looked quite right on her short frame, and even when she was dressed in Armani, someone invariably asked her to get coffee.

"Hello, Laura."

She nearly knocked over her Diet Pepsi at the sound of Paul York's voice. A week of dodging his phone calls had finally caught up with her. Paul was a great-looking guy with his thick, steel-gray hair and even features, but he had the personality of a prison warden. Today he wore his customary uniform: gray slacks and a powder-blue dress shirt with a pair of Ray-Bans hooked in the breast pocket. His easy, loose-jointed walk didn't fool her. Paul York was as laid-back as a cobra. "You seem to be having trouble returning phone calls lately," he said.

"It's been crazy." She felt around under her desk with her bare foot for the stilettos she'd kicked off earlier. "I was just getting ready to call you."

"Five days too late."

"Stomach flu." As she located one shoe, she forced herself to remember everything she admired about him. He might be the stereotypical overbearing stage father, but he'd done a decent job raising Georgie. Unlike so many other child stars, Georgie had never needed a stint in rehab. She hadn't changed boyfriends every week or "forgotten" she wasn't wearing panties when she got out of a car. Paul had also been scrupulous about handling her money, taking only a modest management fee for himself so that he lived comfortably, but not ostentatiously. What he hadn't done was protect her from his own ambition.

He wandered over to the wall behind her office couch and took his time studying the plaques and photos on display—civic commendations, professional certificates, shots of her with various celebrities, none of whom she actually represented. Georgie was her only high-profile client and the major source of her income.

"I want Georgie in the Greenberg project," he said.

Somehow she kept her smile even. "The bimbo vampire story? An interesting idea." *A horrible idea.*

"It's a great script," he said. "I was shocked at how clever it is."

"Genuinely funny," she agreed. "Everyone's talking about it."

"Georgie will bring a new dimension to the story."

Once again, Paul was ignoring his daughter's wishes. *Revenge of the Bimbo Vampire,* despite its funny premise and witty dialogue, represented exactly the kind of role Georgie wanted to get away from.

Laura tapped her fingernails on her desk. "The part could have been written for her. I just wish Greenberg weren't so determined to have a dramatic actress play the lead."

"He only thinks he knows what he wants."

"You're probably right." She rolled her eyes. "He believes bringing in a serious dramatic actress will give the project more credibility."

"I didn't say this was going to be easy. Earn your fifteen percent and make him see her. Tell him she loves the script and wants to do it more than anything."

"Absolutely. I'll talk to him right away." How the hell was she going to convince Greenberg to meet with Georgie? She had much more confidence in Paul's ability to steamroll his daughter into going after a part she didn't want.

"You know . . ." She'd only found one shoe, so she couldn't stand, which gave Paul the advantage of being able to tower over her desk. "They start shooting next month, and Georgie's demanded six months off."

"I'll take care of Georgie."

"She's basically on her honeymoon, and—"

"I said I'd take care of her. When you talk to Greenberg, don't let him forget how perfect her comic timing is and how much female audiences identify with her. You know the drill. And remind him about all the press she's getting. That's going to sell tickets."

Not necessarily. Georgie's success as a tabloid darling had never translated into big box office. She nudged the legal pad on her desk. "Yes, well . . . You know I'll do my best, but we have to remember this is Hollywood."

"No excuses. Make it happen, Laura. And make it happen quick." He gave her a curt nod and walked out.

Her head ached. She'd been so thrilled six years ago when Paul had chosen her instead of one of the other agents at Starlight to represent Georgie. She'd viewed it as her big break, belated recognition for a decade of hard work during which she'd been passed over by a dozen young Ivy League hotshots with half her experience. She hadn't understood that she'd made a deal with the devil, a devil named Paul York.

Her dreams of becoming a Hollywood power player seemed laughable now. She didn't have the cockiness of the other agents, or their flash. The only reason Paul had hired her was because he wanted a mouthpiece he could control, and the top Starlight agents wouldn't play his game. Her livelihood, which now included a luxury condo, depended on her ability to carry out Paul's wishes.

She used to pride herself on her integrity. Now she barely remembered what the word meant.

Over the next four days, Bram met with another potential investor, who was no more willing to gamble on him than the rest had been. Georgie took two more dance classes, got an inch snipped off her hair, and worried about her future. When that became too depressing, she tried persuading Meg to go shopping. But Meg was wise to the ways of Hollywood.

"If I wanted my face plastered all over the pages of *US Weekly*, I'd go out with my parents. You guys chose this life. I didn't."

Meg went horseback riding instead, and Georgie endured a difficult lunch with her father at L.A.'s newest luncheon hot spot, where they sat in a leather booth beneath a sheet metal chandelier.

"*Revenge of the Bimbo Vampire* is brilliantly written and really funny," he said, digging into his grilled steak salad. "You know how rare that is."

He pushed the bread basket at her, but she didn't have much appetite. For the past two weeks, Chaz had been feeding her mountains of mac and cheese, slabs of lasagna. True, the edges of her bones had begun to lose their sharpness, and her cheeks had stopped looking like fatal cave-ins, but she was fairly certain that wasn't Chaz's intent.

"I'm sure it'll do amazingly well. But . . ." She poked at a bowl of lemon risotto and fought to hold on to her resolve. It was her life, her career, and she had to carve her own path. "I need a break from playing emotional lightweights. I've paid my dues, Dad, and I don't want to sign on for another comedy. I want something that'll challenge me, something I can get excited about."

She didn't bother bringing up the six-month vacation she'd fought for so fiercely. She needed to get back to work as soon as possible just to avoid spending so much time around Bram.

He leaned back in the booth. "Don't be a cliché, Georgie—another comic actress who wants to play Lady Macbeth. Do what you're good at."

She couldn't let herself cave. "How do I know I won't be good at other kinds of parts when I've never had a chance?"

"Do you have any idea how hard Laura is working to get you a meeting with Greenberg?"

"She should have talked to me first." As if Laura would even think about consulting her.

He took off his glasses and rubbed his eyes. He looked tired, which made her feel guilty. It hadn't been easy for him, widowed at twenty-five with a four-year-old to raise. He'd dedicated his life to her, and all she had to give him in return these days was resentment. He slipped his glasses back on and picked up his fork only to set it back down. "I'm guessing this laziness of yours—"

"That's not fair."

"This lack of focus, then, is Bram's influence, and frankly, it scares me that he's passing his unprofessional attitude on to you."

"Bram doesn't have anything to do with it."

As she pushed around her risotto, she waited for him to point out how much more cooperative she'd been during her marriage to Lance. Her father and Lance had seen eye to eye about everything, so much so that she'd often thought Lance should have been his kid instead of her.

But Paul was picking his battles. "They're planning to release *Bimbo Vampire* over the Fourth of July weekend next year. A perfect summer movie. It has blockbuster written all over it."

"Not if I'm in it."

"Don't do that, Georgie. Negative thoughts bring negative results."

"*Cake Walk* is going to tank. We both know it."

"I agree they made some bad decisions, and that's why you need to have your name linked with *Bimbo Vampire* as soon as possible. All this publicity has given you a window of opportunity that won't come again. If you pass on this, you'll regret it the rest of your life."

She suppressed her anger by reminding herself that her father always looked out for her best interests. From the beginning, he'd been her staunchest champion. If she lost out on a part, he'd tell her the casting agents were the losers. That was the thing about him. He'd always done his best to protect her. He'd even refused to let her take the starring role of a child prostitute when she was twelve. If only his protectiveness had been rooted in love instead of ambition.

Once again, she considered how things might have been different if she hadn't lost her mother. "Dad . . . If Mom hadn't died, do you think you'd have gone on with your own acting career?"

"Who knows? It's useless to speculate."

"I know, but . . ." The risotto was too salty, and she pushed it aside. "Tell me again how you met."

He sighed. "We met in college our senior year. I was playing Becket in *Murder in the Cathedral,* and she interviewed me for the college newspaper. Attraction of opposites. She was a complete scatterbrain."

"Did you love her?"

"Georgie, it was a long time ago. We need to focus on now."

"Did you?"

"Very much." The impatient way he bit out the words told Georgie he was only saying what he knew she wanted to hear.

As she gazed down at her uneaten risotto, she found it ironic that she'd grown more comfortable with her disreputable husband than with her own father. But then she didn't care about Bram's opinion.

Maybe one of these days she'd stop caring about her father's.

Before the end of their lunch, Georgie's guilt got the better of her, and she invited him to dinner that weekend. She'd ask Trev, too, and make Meg stick around. Maybe she'd even call Laura. Her puppet agent was good at keeping conversations going, and with Bram and her father tossing darts at each other, she'd need a mediator.

Chaz threw a fit when Georgie told her she intended to hire a caterer. "My meals have always been good enough for Bram and his friends," she declared, "but I guess you're too high class."

"Fine!" Georgie retorted. "If you want to cook, then cook. I was only trying to make it easy on you."

"Then tell Aaron he has to help me serve."

"I'll do that." She had to ask: "What friends of Bram's did you cook for? He doesn't seem to have a lot of people hanging around."

"Sure he does. I cooked for his *girl*friends. For Trevor. And he had that big director guy, that Mr. Peters, over a couple of months ago."

Hank Peters really had met with him. Interesting.

The bad publicity from the balcony photos finally began to die down, but she and Bram needed to make another public appearance before it started up again. On Thursday, two days before the dinner party, they visited Pinkberry in West Hollywood. Bram hadn't commented on their lack of a sex life in days. It was disconcerting. He behaved as if sex weren't even an issue, except he couldn't seem to keep his shirt on, and he touched her arm whenever he went by. Georgie had started to feel as if she were burning up.

He was playing her.

The West Hollywood Pinkberry had become a celebrity favorite, which meant the paps always hung around. Georgie chose navy slacks and a scooped-neck white blouse with a row of six retro red plastic buttons down the front. It had taken her an hour to get ready. Bram was still in the jeans and T-shirt he'd pulled on that morning.

Georgie ordered her frozen yogurt topped with fresh blueberries and mango. Bram grumbled about wanting a damned Dairy Queen and didn't get anything. As they came out of the shop, the half a dozen photographers who'd gathered sprang to attention.

"Georgie! Bram! We haven't seen you guys in a few days. Where have you been?"

"We're newlyweds," Bram shot back. "Where do you think?"

"Georgie, anything you want to say about Jade Gentry's miscarriage?"

"Have you talked to Lance?"

"Are you two planning a family?"

The questions kept coming until a photographer with a pronounced Brooklyn accent called out, "Bram, are you still having trouble landing a decent job? I guess Georgie and her money came along just in time."

Bram tensed, and Georgie snaked her arm through his. "I don't know who you are"—she maintained her smile—"but Bram's days of slugging photographers who act like worms aren't all that far behind him. Or maybe that's what you want?"

A few of the other paps regarded the man with disgust, but that didn't prevent them from keeping their cameras ready in case Bram lost his temper. A shot of him throwing a punch would bring thousands of dollars, along with the possibility of a lucrative legal settlement for the photographer who'd provoked the attack.

"I wasn't going to hit him," Bram said as they finally broke clear. "I'm not stupid enough to fall for that crap."

"Only because you fell for it so many times in the past."

He cocked his head toward the paps, who were on their heels. "Let's give them their money shot."

"Which is . . .?"

"You'll see." He took her hand and pulled her down the sidewalk, the paps trailing close behind.

Chapter 13

The small shop with its rich, mustard yellow exterior reminded Georgie of an old-fashioned British haberdashery. Above the door, an art nouveau figure of a woman curled around the glossy black letters that spelled out the shop's name. PROVOCATIVE. The two os formed her breasts.

Georgie had heard about the upscale sex shop from April, but she'd never visited. "Excellent idea," she said.

"And here I expected you to go all prudish on me." Bram's hand settled in the small of her back.

"I haven't done prudish in years."

"You could have fooled me." He held the door open for her, and they stepped inside the store's perfumed interior accompanied by the shouts of the photographers and the deafening click of shutters. Trespassing laws would keep the paps outside, and they scrambled for position, trying to get a shot through the window.

The Edwardian interior featured subtle mustard yellow walls and warm wooden moldings. A painted spray of peacock feathers encircled the chandelier, and erotic Aubrey Beardsley drawings mounted in gold frames decorated the walls. She and Bram were the only customers, although she suspected that would change as word of their presence spread.

The shop was a buffet of sexual fantasy. Bram zeroed in on the erotic lingerie collection, while Georgie couldn't pull her eyes away from an artistically arranged display of dildos in front of an antique mirror. She knew she'd stared too long when Bram's lips brushed her ear. "I'll be happy to lend you mine."

Georgie's stomach took a tiny dip.

The clerk, a middle-aged woman with long brunette hair, a tastefully shrink-wrapped top, and a gauzy skirt, snapped to attention as she recognized them. Her peep-toe stilettos sank into the carpet. "Welcome to Provocative."

"Thanks," Bram replied. "Interesting place."

Breathless from the excitement of having two such notorious celebrities in her store, the clerk began listing the shop's special features. "We have a fabulous bondage center through that archway. Lovely whips,

paddles, nipple clamps, and some really luxurious re-
straints. You'll be surprised how comfortable they are.
All our toys are high quality. As you can see, we have a
wide variety of dildos, vibrators, some jade cock rings,
and"—she gestured toward a glass case—"a really
beautiful set of pearl anal beads."

Georgie winced. She'd heard of anal beads, but she'd
never quite figured out how or why anyone would use
them.

As the clerk turned away to survey the shelves,
Bram whispered, "Been there, done that. Although not
with you."

Her stomach took another dip.

The clerk addressed Georgie. "I just finished un-
packing a new shipment of jeweled merkins. Have you
ever worn a merkin?"

"Give me a hint."

With a prim smile, the saleswoman clasped her
hands at her waist like an art museum docent. "Merkins
were originally pubic wigs worn by prostitutes to conceal either thinning pubic hair or syphilis. The modern
versions are much sexier, and with so many women
going bare, they've become quite popular."

Georgie was both erotically and philosophically opposed to ripping out all her pubic hair. The idea of
completely giving up something so womanly to look

like a prepubescent girl smacked too much of kiddie porn. But the salesclerk had already opened a display case and taken out a jeweled, triangular piece set with sparkling purple, blue, and crimson crystals. Georgie examined the object and saw a small V-shaped indenture at the bottom point of the triangle, obviously put there to showcase the cleft beyond. "Naturally, all our merkins come with adhesive."

Bram picked up the merkin to examine it, then returned it to the clerk. "I think we'll pass. Some things don't need extra decoration."

"I understand," the woman said, "although this one does have matching jeweled nipple covers."

"They'd just get in my way."

Georgie's flush told her she was in big trouble.

"We have amazing lingerie," the clerk said to him. "Our three-petal bras are very popular. Your wife can wear them with all of the petals up, or just the side ones fastened. Or she can peel them all down."

Georgie's breasts tingled.

"Very efficient." Bram slipped his hand under her hair and touched the back of her neck. Her skin pebbled.

"Have you heard about our VIP dressing room?"

It all came back to her from a conversation with April. She tried to look thoughtful. "I, uh, think a friend might have mentioned something."

"It has a peephole in the back wall," the clerk said. "You can open it if you like. There's a smaller dressing room behind for your husband."

Bram laughed, one of his few genuine laughs since the balcony photos had appeared. "If more men knew about this place, they'd stop saying they hate to shop."

The salesclerk gave Georgie a knowing smile. "We have an exotic collection of men's briefs, and the peephole works two ways." She couldn't hold back any longer. "I just have to say that I loved you both in *Skip and Scooter*. Everybody's so excited about you getting married, and don't let all those stupid stories bother you." She had to break off as more customers entered the store. "I'll be right back if you need anything."

Georgie gazed after her. "A list of whatever we buy is going to be all over the Internet by dinnertime. Massage oil would be safe."

"Oh, I think we can be a little more exciting than that."

"No whips and paddles. I'm so over S and M. At first it was fun, but making all those grown men cry got boring after a while."

He smiled. "No dildos, either, even though I know how much you want one. Which is no surprise, since—"

"Will you get over it?"

"Over it . . . Under it . . ." He touched the bow of her top lip. "Inside it . . ."

A bolt of heat zipped through her body. She was going to melt.

He nudged her toward the lingerie collection, where softly lit shadow boxes displayed kinky bra-and-panty sets, garter belts, and skimpy teddies with front ties and see-through panels. All the lingerie was beautifully made and ultraexpensive. Bram held up a bra with a silky drawstring across the top of each cup. "You're what? About a—?"

"Thirty-four double D," she said.

He lifted a dark eyebrow and snagged a 34 B, which was exactly right, not surprising considering his knowledge of female anatomy. Several more customers entered the store, but for now, everybody was giving them space.

"Just so you know," she whispered, as much to herself as him. "This isn't a date, and the peephole door is staying shut."

"This is definitely a date." He examined a one-piece bondage body wrap made of black mesh. "Great workmanship." He fingered the satin ties. "A lot softer than leather."

"I love leather." She snatched up a pair of low-cut leather briefs constructed with a man-pouch in front.

"Not in a million years," he retorted.

She stole the bondage wrap from him. "Too bad."

They had a stare-down. He broke first. "Okay, you win. I'll trade you."

"Deal."

They exchanged garments, as if this were for real instead of two actors playing a skillful game of pretend. Bram added several cupless bras to her pile and some panties missing their crotches. She picked up a few more items for him in leather, but when she found an interesting pair of chaps, he looked so pained she put them back. He returned the favor by abandoning a torturous-looking corset. Finally, they exchanged garments, and the clerk led them to the back corner of the shop and the VIP dressing room. She unlocked a paneled wooden door with an old-fashioned skeleton key and hung Georgie's garments on a curly brass hook before taking Bram away to his dressing room.

Georgie stood surrounded by antique rose walls; a full-length, gilded mirror; a tufted footstool; and wall sconces with fringed, rose-colored shades that gave the space a soft, flattering glow. The room's most intriguing feature sat at eye level in the back wall, a door about one foot by one foot with a tiny knob shaped, not so subtly, like a partially opened clamshell with a pearl at its tip.

Enough was enough. Game over. Definitely over. Except . . .

No. Absolutely not.

A tap sounded on the wall. "Open up."

She tugged on the "clamshell" and opened the door. Bram's face peered back at her through the black iron grillwork. Hardly a peephole. The antique rose walls framing his face should have feminized his face but only made him appear more masculine. He rubbed his jaw. "I'm embarrassed to admit it, but this place has seriously turned me on."

He wasn't one bit embarrassed, and the store's over-the-top atmosphere had seriously turned her on, too. She twisted her fake wedding ring. Melrose Avenue might be only a few blocks away, but this erotic emporium made her feel as though they'd stepped into another world. An oddly safe world where an untrust-worthy man could look but not touch. A world where everything was about sex and where heartache wasn't a possibility.

"I wish we'd taken a look at that bondage equip-ment," he said.

She couldn't resist playing with fire. "Just out of curiosity . . . Which one of us did you want tied up?"

"Starting off? You." His voice took on a low, husky note. "But once you demonstrated proper submission, we could trade off. Now what do you say you try on that black mesh thing for me?"

The lure of romping with the devil in this sexual playground was nearly irresistible. "What do I get in return?"

"What do you want?"

She thought for a moment. "Step back." When he did, she put her face to the grille and saw that his smaller dressing room had dark gold walls and oversize iron bolts to hold the garments she'd chosen for him. "Those black leather briefs."

"No way."

"Too bad." She shut the door.

"Hey!"

She took her time opening it again. "Have you reconsidered?"

"If you go first."

"Right. Like I'm going to fall for that."

They had another stare-down. She kept her eyes steady even though her heart was beating like crazy.

"Come on, Georgie. I've had a bad week. Trying on some clothes for me is the least you can do."

"I've had a bad week, too, and these aren't clothes. They're sex aids. If you want this so badly, you go first."

"How about we do it together?"

"Deal." She shut the door again. Her hands were shaking. She stepped out of her navy and white polka-dot ballet flats.

Several minutes passed before he knocked from the other side. "Are you ready yet?"

"No. I feel stupid."

"*You* feel stupid. This thing has a frickin' codpiece."

"I know. I chose it, remember? And I'm the one who should be complaining. These corset straps are arranged so they don't hide anything."

"Open the door. *Now.*"

"I've changed my mind."

"On the count of three," he said.

"You have to step back so I can see."

"All right. I'm stepping back. One . . . two . . . *three.*"

She opened the door and looked through.

Bram looked back.

Both of them were fully clothed.

Bram shook his head. "You have serious trust issues."

She narrowed her eyes at him. "At least I took off my shoes. You didn't even do that."

"New deal," he said. "The door stays open. You take off one thing. I'll take off one thing. I'll even go first." He pulled his shirt over his head.

She already knew he had a great chest. She'd spent enough time sneaking peeks at it. The muscles were defined but not so overdeveloped that he lost I.Q. points, because, really, how sexy could a man be who had nothing better to do all day than work out?

"I'm waiting," he said.

A quick calculation told her she was wearing more clothes. Was she really going to do this? Having sex with Bram offered no guarantee that he still wouldn't cheat, but he also wasn't stupid. He knew the kind of microscope they were under and how difficult it would be for him to get away with anything. Besides, Bram always took the easy way out, and in this case, that would be her.

She slipped her hand behind her neck and removed her silver necklace.

"No fair."

Her trip to the devil's playground demanded at least a few swings from the monkey bars. "Drop your jeans. You have a codpiece waiting."

"I still have my shoes on, remember?" He stepped back so she could watch him kick off a single sneaker.

"That's cheating." She pulled away and slipped a small diamond stud from her earlobe.

"Talk about cheats." Another sneaker came off.

"I've never cheated in my life." She removed the remaining diamond stud.

"I don't believe you." One sock.

"Maybe at Pictionary." Her wedding ring.

As they removed each new item, they took turns stepping back from the grille so the other could see. Up and back . . . up and back . . . a sensual dance of reveal and conceal.

His second sock hit the carpet. "Did a man ever dribble honey down your belly and lick it off?"

"Dozens of times." She toyed with the top button on her blouse, playing for time, still not certain how far she'd go with this private peep show. "How long since your last lover?"

"Too long." He slipped his thumb inside the snap at the top of his waistband.

"When?" She squeezed the red plastic button between her fingers.

"Could we talk about this another time?" He popped the snap.

"I don't think so." Bringing up past lovers should be diminishing her desire, but that wasn't happening.

"Later. I promise."

"I don't believe you."

"If I welsh, you can walk across my bare back in stilettos."

"If you welsh"—her top button seemed to open of its own accord—"you'll never see these again." She unfastened her blouse button by button, then let it slide off her arms. She wore a lacy white La Perla bra with matching panties he didn't yet know about.

His hand went to his wrist. Slowly, he slipped off his watch—she'd forgotten about his stupid watch—

leaving him only in jeans with—what?—beneath. She couldn't catch a deep breath. She moved back and unfastened her navy slacks. Looking him squarely in the eye, she tugged them down.

Her legs had always been her best feature—long, slender, and strong—a dancer's legs, and his gaze lingered. Endless seconds ticked by before he stepped back and pulled off his slacks. He wore a pair of gray knit End Zone boxer briefs that molded to a sizable erection. She stared at it.

"Now your panties," he said, approaching the grille again.

She'd never been so aroused, and they hadn't exchanged a single touch. She unfastened her bra. The straps slipped down her shoulders, but she curled her hands over the lacy cups to keep them in place and moved back to the grille. "Work for it," she whispered.

His voice grew husky. "I'm going to have to trust you on this one."

He tucked his thumbs into the waistband of his End Zones, worked them down, and stood in front of her magnificently naked. She grazed him with her eyes, the wide tanned shoulders, the muscular chest, the narrow hips a few shades paler than the rest of him. She barely felt her bra drifting through her fingers.

"Step back," he said on a gruff whisper.

He was using her, and she was using him, and she didn't care. She moved into the center of the dressing room and drew off her fragile nylon panties. He gazed at her with such intensity her skin prickled. He'd been with women far more beautiful, but she experienced none of the grinding insecurity she'd suffered with Lance. This was Bram. She didn't care about his opinion. She only cared about his body. She tilted her head. "Stand back so I can look at you again."

But his patience had ended. "The game's over. We're getting out of here. Now."

She didn't want to leave. She wanted to stay in this sensual fantasy world forever. She pulled the ice-blue petal bra from its hook. "I wonder how this will look."

"You're putting clothes *on?*"

"I need to check the fit." She turned her naked bottom to him and donned the bra. Each cup was made up of three silky petals. She faced him again and, without a word, unfastened each petal, the sides first, and then the center. Taking forever.

His eyes glittered through the grille. "You're killing me."

"I know." She snagged the matching panties from their hook and stood back so he could watch her slip them on. They were open at the crotch. "These fit well, don't you think?"

"I can't think. Come here."

She took her time approaching the peephole. When she got there, he whispered, "Closer."

They pressed their faces to the grille, and their mouths met through the whirls of black metal. Only their mouths.

And then the earth moved.

Really moved.

Or at least the wall. Her eyes flew open. She gave a startled gasp as the last obstruction between them swung inward. She should have known a shop as inventive as Provocative wouldn't overlook something like this. Her feeling of safety dissolved.

Bram ducked and came through. "Not everyone gets told about the door."

She'd never had sex without love, and Bram offered only dirty thrills. She knew exactly how duplicitous he was, how undependable. She had no illusions. Her eyes were wide open. Exactly the way she wanted it. "This is only our first date."

"One hell of a date."

He secured the door behind him and looked down at her naked breasts, showcased by the open-cup bra. "Lady, I do love your underwear." The back of his knuckles brushed her nipple. He took one of the gauzy petals, drew it up, and fastened it. Then he suckled her through the frail barrier.

Her legs grew weak. He pulled her down on the big tufted ottoman so that she straddled his thighs. They kissed. He suckled. She sank her fingers into his hair and bit her lips to keep from crying out. His thighs had pushed her own far apart. She still wore the panties that had no crotch. He separated the nylon fabric, reached into her silk, and played until she was trembling with desire.

When she couldn't tolerate it any longer, she braced her knees on the ottoman, lifted herself upon him, and slowly took him into her body.

His breath came in ragged gasps, but he didn't try to push himself into her. Instead, he gave her all the time she needed to accept him. And she took advantage. Wicked advantage. As soon as she gained a hard-earned inch, she gave it up and started all over again. His shoulders grew slick with sweat. She didn't care about his need—about whether she was pleasing him. She didn't care about his feelings, his fantasies, his ego. All she cared about was what he could do for her. And if he didn't satisfy her—if, at the end, he turned out to be a dud—she wouldn't make up excuses for him as she had with Lance. Instead, she'd complain loud and long until he got it right. Although it didn't seem as though that would be necessary.

"You're going to pay for this," he said through gritted teeth. But still he let her do as she wanted until she became so mindless that she had to give up the game. Only then did he dig his fingers into her bottom and pull her down hard upon him.

They couldn't make any noise. Only a thin wall shielded them from exposure. He buried his face in her breasts and rubbed her where their bodies joined. She arched against his hand, threw back her head, clutched his shoulders, and joined him on a wild, silent ride.

Not loving him. Only using him.

He shuddered. She flung back her head.

Release . . .

The practicalities didn't hit her until afterward. The mess. The used lingerie they hadn't paid for. The inconvenient husband. As they disengaged, her sanity returned. She had to make sure he understood this hadn't changed anything. "Well done, Skipper." She stretched out the kinks in her legs. "You're no George Clooney, but you definitely show promise."

He moved toward the hidden door, then surveyed her body, as if he were marking his territory. "At least this answers one question."

"What's that?"

He gave her a lazy smile. "I finally remember what happened that night in Vegas."

Chapter 14

Through the window Chaz saw Aaron's dark blue Honda pull to a stop in the motor court. A few minutes later, the front door opened. He was such a mess. She stomped out into the hallway to meet him, but he carried only his nerdy black bag instead of the sack of doughnuts she'd expected. He didn't look happy to see her, and he tried to get past her with only a nod, but she blocked the bottom of the stairs. "What did you have for breakfast?"

"Leave me alone, Chaz. You're not my mother."

She braced one arm on the wall and the other on the handrail. He'd already started to sweat, and it wasn't even hot out. "I'll bet she used to fix her little boy eggs and sausage every morning with a big side of pancakes."

"I had a bowl of cereal, okay."

"I told you I'd make you breakfast."

"I'm not falling for that again. Last time I got two scrambled egg whites."

"And toast and an orange. Stop being such a baby. You need to face your problems instead of trying to eat them away."

"So now you're a shrink." He pulled her arm from the wall and wedged past her. "You're only twenty years old. What the hell do you know about anything?"

He never cussed, and she liked that she'd gotten under his skin enough to make him do it. She followed him upstairs. "So did you see Becky this weekend?"

He was out of breath by the time they reached the top. "I never should have told you about her."

Becky lived in the apartment next to his. Aaron had a crush on her, but Becky barely knew he existed, like that was some big surprise. Apparently Becky was a brain like Aaron, and she was okay-looking, but not beautiful, which meant Aaron might stand a chance with her if he lost some weight, got a good haircut, bought some decent clothes, and stopped acting like such a geek. "Did you try to talk to her like I said?"

"I have work to do."

"Did you?" She'd told him to be friendly, but not too friendly, which meant he shouldn't do that stupid pig snort laugh. And he couldn't talk about video games. Ever.

"I didn't see her, okay?"

"Yes, you did." She followed him into Georgie's office. "You saw her, but you didn't have the balls to talk to her. How hard is it to say hi and ask her how things are going?"

"I think I could be a little more original than that."

"When you try to be original, you only sound weird. Be cool for once. Just 'Hi' and 'How's it going?' Did you bring your swim trunks like I told you?"

He dropped his black bag on the chair. "You're not my personal trainer, either."

"Did you?"

"I don't know. Maybe."

She thought she was making progress. He let her fix him lunch now, and he'd stopped bringing junk food with him because he knew she'd find it and toss it out. It had only been three weeks, but she was pretty sure his gut was starting to shrink. "Laps for half an hour before you can go home tonight. I mean it."

"You might think about working on yourself for a while instead of other people." He heaved himself into his chair at the computer. "Taking care of your personality disorder for one thing."

"I like my personality disorder. It keeps the creeps away." She smirked. "Although right now that doesn't seem to be working too well." Aaron wasn't really a creep. He was a decent guy, and she secretly admired how smart he was. But he was totally clueless. And lonely. If he'd only do what she said, she thought she could fix him up enough so he could get a girl. Not anybody hot, but somebody smart like he was.

"Lunch is at twelve-thirty," she said. "Be on time." As she turned to go back downstairs, she saw Georgie standing in the office doorway, filming the whole thing with her video camera.

Chaz slammed her hands on her hips. "That's illegal, you know. Filming people without their permission."

Georgie kept her eye glued to the camera. "Get a lawyer."

Chaz stomped into the hallway and headed for the back stairs. Georgie was the last person she wanted to talk to right now. Yesterday, when Georgie got home with Bram, they'd both been acting weird. Georgie had beard-burn on her neck, and she wouldn't look at Bram, who kept smiling at her in this kind of smart-ass way. Chaz didn't know what was going on with them. They thought she hadn't figured out they'd been sleeping in separate rooms—like Georgie knew how to make a bed so it looked halfway decent. So what had happened yesterday?

Chaz thought about how much money she could make if she went to the tabloids and told them about the famous newlyweds and their separate beds. Maybe she'd do it, too, if it would only hurt Georgie. But she wouldn't hurt Bram.

Georgie trailed her down the back stairs. "Why do you give Aaron such a hard time?"

Chaz could have asked a few questions of her own, like why Georgie gave Bram such a hard time, and what had happened yesterday, and why Georgie had still slept in her own bed last night? But she'd learned to keep what she knew to herself until she had a reason to use it.

"I've got a better question," Chaz said. "Why haven't you tried to help Aaron? He's a mess. He can hardly walk upstairs without practically having a heart attack."

"And you like to clean up messes."

"So what?" This whole camera thing was weird. She didn't know why Georgie kept filming her or why Chaz didn't just refuse to talk. But every time Georgie came after her with that camera, Chaz found herself blabbing away. It was like . . . like talking about herself to the camera somehow made her important. Like her life was special, and she had something worth saying.

They reached the bottom of the stairs, and Georgie followed her into the kitchen. "Tell me what happened after you left Barstow."

"I told you. I came to L.A. and found a place to stay off Sunset."

"You hardly had any money. How did you make rent?"

"I got a job. What do you think?"

"What kind of job?"

"I have to pee." She headed toward the small bathroom off the kitchen. "Are you going to follow me in here, too?" She shut the door and locked it. Nobody would ever make her talk about what happened when she got to L.A. Nobody.

When she came out, Georgie had disappeared and Bram was finishing a phone call. She picked up a dishcloth and wiped the counter. "Tell Georgie to stop following me around with that camera," she said as he hung up.

"It's hard to tell Georgie anything." He pulled the iced tea pitcher from the refrigerator.

"What's with her anyway? Why does she keep doing it?"

"Who knows? A couple of days ago I saw her filming the women who clean the house. She was talking to them in Spanish."

Chaz wouldn't admit it, but she didn't like the idea of Georgie filming anybody but her. "Good. Maybe she won't bother me so much."

Bram fingered his cell phone. "Have you done it yet?"

She opened the dishwasher and stuck in the glasses from breakfast. "I'm thinking about it."

"Chaz, there's a big world out there. You can't hide here forever."

"I'm not hiding! Now do you mind? People are coming to dinner tomorrow night, and I have a lot of things to do."

He shook his head. "Sometimes I don't think I did you a favor by giving you a job."

He was wrong. He'd done her the biggest favor of her life, and she'd never forget it.

That afternoon, as Georgie got dressed for the paps, she kept asking herself why sex with a bad boy was so much more thrilling than getting it on with a decent guy. Even if that decent guy had left her for another woman. So why had she made herself sleep alone last night? Because yesterday had been too good. Too much fun. Too deliciously debauched. So mindless and uncomplicated she wasn't ready to spoil it with real life. She'd also wanted Bram to understand she hadn't turned into a pushover just because that had been the most thrilling sexual escapade of her life. But shutting him out had taken all her willpower, and she didn't like the knowing look he'd given her when she'd said she was sleeping alone.

They left the house for a midmorning coffee run and photo op. She decided the best way to restore a sense of normalcy was to pick a fight. "Stop humming." She scowled at him across the passenger seat. "You only think you can carry a tune."

"What's eating you? Not me, unfortunately."

"You're disgusting."

"Hey, what happened to your famous sense of humor?"

"You."

"I guess that'd do it." He started humming a few bars of "It's the Hard-knock Life" just to provoke her. "You were a lot friendlier yesterday afternoon. A *lot*."

"That was lust, pal. I was using you."

"And doing a damn fine job of it."

She didn't like the way he refused to join her in the fight she needed to have with him. "You shouldn't have said you remembered what happened that night in Vegas when you really didn't."

"Process of elimination. I guarantee that one of us passed out before the deed was done, because if we'd finished up, I'd have remembered."

For once, she was inclined to believe him.

The paps surrounded them when they emerged from The Coffee Bean & Tea Leaf. Georgie thought about the zillions of photos she'd seen of celebs carrying either coffee cups or water bottles. Since when had dehydration become an occupational hazard of fame?

"Right here! Look here!"

"Any plans for the weekend?"

"Are you guys still solid?"

"Like a rock." Bram tightened his arm around her waist and whispered, "If you were really as tough as you pretend to be, you wouldn't have run off to your nice safe bed last night."

She beamed up at him. "I told you. I got my period."

He beamed down at her. "And I told you I didn't give a damn."

Lance had given a damn. He'd been nice about it, but sex with a menstruating woman wasn't his thing. Not that she'd really gotten her period.

"Obviously I haven't made myself clear," she whispered, playing the role of the female sexual predator as shutters clicked around them. "You passed your audition yesterday at Provocative. From now on, your only function is to service me. When and where I want it. And I don't want it right now."

Liar. She wanted it all right, and she wanted it with him. Yesterday's experience had been so incredible specifically because she'd been with gorgeous, useless, depraved Bram Shepard. Sex didn't mean anything more to him than a handshake, and knowing that gave her an exciting new freedom. Her fake—and possibly alcoholic—husband could never have the hold over her Lance had possessed. With Bram, she wouldn't stew over whether a negligee was alluring enough to attract him or feel as if she needed to read the latest sex manual to keep him interested. Who cared? She might not even shave her legs.

He kissed the top of her ear. "Just so we're straight, Scoot. You didn't get your period. You chickened out because you're afraid you can't handle me."

"Not true."

He gave a final wave to the photographers and began steering her toward the street, still speaking so only she could hear. "The thing about these restrictions you keep trying to set up . . ." He brushed his knuckles down her spine. "I'm not going to pay attention to any of them."

Bram loved messing with Georgie—mentally and physically. She'd shocked the hell out of him yesterday. In his mind, Georgie and Scooter had always been pretty much the same person, but no way in hell would Scooter have put on a show like that. What had happened at Provocative proved the Loser hadn't managed to whip all the self-confidence out of her, something that had become increasingly evident in the past few weeks. The fact that Lance had traded Georgie in for a cold fish like Jade gave Bram a lot more pleasure than it should.

As they returned from their coffee run, he toyed with the idea of getting her naked right away—it wouldn't take much effort—but Aaron ruined his plans by meeting them at the door.

"Rory Keene's secretary called. You're invited to her house for a glass of wine at five."

Bram did a mental high jump. He'd been hoping Rory's affection for Georgie would translate into an opportunity for a face-to-face meeting so he could state his case personally, instead of through her people. He grinned and jiggled his car keys. "Call her back and tell her we'll be there."

Aaron pushed his glasses higher on his nose. "She didn't mention anything about you, Bram. Just Georgie."

Bram tightened his hand around his keys. "She meant both of us."

"I don't think so. She said to tell Georgie not to get dressed up because it would be just the two of them." Aaron beat a hasty retreat.

Bram let loose with a string of obscenities. Rory was still stonewalling him. She loved the *Tree House* script, but according to her V.P. in development, she wouldn't consider backing the film unless he stepped aside as producer and lead actor, which would defeat the goal of restarting his career. Sometimes he thought he should buy an ad in *Variety* and announce to the world that he wasn't the same feral kid who didn't have enough character to survive his success. Or maybe a simpler message . . . *How about a fucking second chance?*

If only Rory would meet with him personally, but the closest he'd been able to get was during the nighttime incident in her backyard. He'd even slipped through the rear gate with a bottle of Cristal a few days later as an apology for having woken her up, but one of her lackeys had taken the champagne from him and shut the door.

He glared down at Georgie. Thanks to Chaz's cooking, she'd gained enough weight so those big green eyes peeping at him through a fringe of bangs had lost their sunken appearance, and her shiny brown hair curved around fuller cheeks. "I want you in my office in ten minutes."

She opened her mouth to tell him to go to hell, but he was ready for her. "Unless you aren't interested in seeing the script for *Tree House* . . ."

He knew he had her, and he walked away without looking back.

She kept him waiting ten minutes longer than he expected. She hadn't used the time to change her clothes, and she still wore the outfit from their paparazzi coffee run: a bright lemon knit top with a modestly curved round neck, a tiny cropped cardigan as insubstantial as a spiderweb, and wide-cut green-and-cream mattress-ticking slacks only someone so slender could carry off. The outfit concealed far more than it revealed, which made it sexy as hell.

She made the first move in this new game they were playing by tilting her head toward the poster of Jake Koranda playing Bird Dog Caliber. "Now there's a real man."

"I'll be sure to tell him you said so." He squeezed a rubber exercise ball in his fist, channeling Humphrey Bogart in *The Caine Mutiny.* "I need a little cooperation for a change."

She looked wounded. "What do you mean, 'for a change.' I'm always cooperative." She plopped down on his couch. "Okay, mainly cooperative with other people, but still . . ."

"Stop screwing around and listen." He curled the ball in his palm and pointed his index finger at her nose. "Don't sabotage me with Rory Keene."

"I wouldn't do that."

"Wouldn't you? Rory loves everything about the *Tree House* project except . . ."

"You?" She widened those gum ball green eyes. "It's because you have a bad reputation."

"Thanks for pointing that out." He set the ball on his desk. "I have to make this film, Georgie. Me and nobody else. You need to convince her I've turned into Husband of the Year."

"You haven't."

"Pretend."

"You're asking me for help?" Again the big-eyed Orphan Annie thing, but Georgie had always been a team player, and he figured she'd help him . . . after she gave him a hard time.

She put a finger to her cheek. "If I suck up to Rory for you, what do I get in return?"

"Hot sex and my undying gratitude."

She pretended to think it over. "Nope. Not good enough."

"I'll let Meg stay in the guesthouse."

"Meg's already staying in the guesthouse."

"Let me put it another way. I won't hit on her while she's staying in the guesthouse."

"You won't hit on her anyway. You treat her like she's twelve." She finally got down to business. "I want to read the script before I meet Rory this afternoon. Hand it over."

"I told you I'd let you see it."

"Yes, but you didn't tell me you'd let me *read* it."

"You noticed that."

She held out her hand.

He hesitated. "You don't exactly have the best judgment when it comes to scripts. You're the one who made *Summer in the City.*"

"*Pretty People,* too, another stinker. And *Cake Walk,* which you haven't seen yet, and which I recommend you don't." She wiggled her hand at him. "That's all in the past. You're looking at a whole new Georgie York. Give it up."

She was no longer the pushover she'd once been, so he didn't have much choice. He pulled the bound script from his middle desk drawer, the one she'd searched three weeks ago only to find a broken telephone. She snatched it from him before he could change his mind, gave him a cheery wave, and left.

He hated asking anybody for help, especially Georgie, and he slumped in his chair to brood. When that got him nowhere, he turned back to his computer. As good as the script had been, it still needed work, and he'd been tinkering with one scene or another from the beginning. He could imagine what Georgie would say if she learned that a high school dropout was monkeying around with Sarah Carter's words. Or . . . even worse, how she'd laugh if she discovered he'd finished a script of his own.

Except she wouldn't laugh. Unlike him, she didn't have a cruel bone in her body, and he could even imagine her mustering up a few well-intentioned words of encouragement.

The idea stuck in his craw. He didn't need phony encouragement from anybody, especially Georgie. He'd raised himself, screwed up his life by himself, and now he was digging out the same way. By himself.

Georgie couldn't read fast enough, and she finished the script in two hours. It was just as amazing as the book. An incredible opportunity . . . and not only for Bram.

Tree House told the story of Danny Grimes, a man who'd been falsely imprisoned for sexually abusing a child. Released on a technicality, he's forced by his father's terminal illness to return home and face both the town and the ruthless female prosecutor, now a state senator, who hid DNA evidence to ensure his conviction. Danny's self-imposed isolation is threatened by his suspicions that the child next door is being abused by her father. The script was powerful and heart wrenching, filled with fascinating and complex characters, none of whom were exactly what they seemed to be.

She found Bram swimming laps in the pool. She stood on the edge near the waterfall and shifted impatiently from one leg to the other, waiting for him to stop. He saw her, but he continued cutting through the water. She picked up the leaf skimmer and whapped him on the head.

"Hey!" Water flew as he spun around.

She took a deep breath. "I want to play Helene."

"Good luck with that." He dove under and swam for the ladder on the opposite side of the pool.

She dropped the leaf skimmer, her heart thumping with excitement. By the time she'd finished the first scene, she'd known she had to play the coldly ambitious prosecutor. This was exactly the opportunity she'd been waiting for. Playing Helene would cut through years of typecasting and give her the challenge she so desperately wanted. She strode toward the ladder. "The script is brilliant. Bone chilling, intricate, thoughtful. Everything you said it was. I have to play Helene. I mean it."

Water sluiced down his body as he climbed out of the pool. "In case you haven't been paying attention, I'm having a small problem getting the movie financed, so casting Helene is the last thing on my mind."

She grabbed his towel and handed it over. "But if you do get a green light . . . The only reason no one ever thinks of me as a dramatic actress is because I've never gotten a chance to show what I can do. And don't tell me audiences wouldn't be able to get past the two of us in *Skip and Scooter*. The love story is between Danny and the home nurse, not with Helene. I know exactly how to do that part. And I'll work for scale."

"Bottom line, Georgie, if I can get this film made, you still won't be playing Helene." He rubbed the towel over his head, then draped it around his neck. "Considering my own recent lackluster career, this film needs an actress with a proven record at the box office, and let's face it, your face sells a lot more tabloids than movie tickets."

She refused to concede his point. "Think of the publicity value of the two of us doing a film together. Audiences will line up to see if we can pull it off."

"We can't." He dropped the towel on the chair. "Georgie, this whole discussion is beyond premature."

"You think I can't play a complicated character? You can do it, but I can't? You're so wrong. I have the discipline and focus to pull it off."

"Meaning you think I don't."

She didn't want to flat out insult him, but truth was truth. "You can't rely on tricks to play Danny. He's bitter and tortured. He's endured something no one should ever have to go through."

"I've lived with this material for over a year," he shot back. "I know exactly what makes him tick. Now instead of arguing, why don't you use your brain to figure out how you're going to convince Rory Keene that I'm a solid Hollywood citizen and that she needs to meet with me?"

Georgie used the rear gate. Rory's white brick French Normandy mansion was grander than Bram's home, but not nearly as welcoming. From the back, sweeping terraces overlooked the pool and formal gardens. Rory sat in the shade of the side terrace on a black wrought-iron couch covered with bright tangerine cushions. With her long blond hair pulled into a ponytail and her legs curled beneath her, Rory should have looked like a soccer mom, but she didn't. Even in such an informal setting she projected the cool, intimidating confidence of a formidable studio executive.

She pushed aside the script she'd been reading and offered Georgie a glass of champagne. Now that Bram wasn't the only person with something at stake, Georgie fought to keep her nervousness under control as she accepted the drink and settled into an adjacent chair.

They discussed last weekend's box-office receipts and the success of a new Jack Black film. Finally, Rory got down to the reason for her invitation.

"Georgie, this is a bit awkward . . ." Her steady gaze indicated awkwardness didn't bother her much. "Ever since those awful photos came out, I've been telling myself to mind my own business, but I can't do it. If anything happened to you, I'd never forgive myself."

Georgie hadn't expected this, and she was embarrassed. The worst of the tabloid gossip might be fading, but obviously Rory wasn't so easily convinced. "Don't give it another thought. Really. Everything's fine. Now tell me about the house. I was surprised to hear you're leasing."

Rory took a sip of champagne, then set her flute on the table next to her. "The studio leases it. It's our version of the White House. I have my private quarters, but we keep a separate wing for special guests—corporate VIPs, directors, producers, whomever we want to court. Right now we're hosting some incredibly talented international filmmakers—part of a project I'm spearheading."

"I'm sure they're flattered to be invited to stay here."

"A special staff takes care of them. I don't have to entertain anyone I don't want to." Rory uncrossed her legs and once again turned the full force of her iceberg eyes on Georgie. "If you ever feel . . . uncomfortable, as if you need to get away quickly, you can come over here anytime, night or day."

Georgie didn't know which she hated more—the idea that Rory thought Bram was a wife batterer or her belief that Georgie had so little self-regard she'd allow herself to be abused. "Those photos were deceptive, Rory. I know it looked like we were having a fight, but we weren't. Honestly. Bram would never hurt me. Drive me crazy, yes. But physically hurt me, never."

"Women don't always think straight where men like Bram Shepard are concerned," Rory said. "And after what you went through with Lance . . ."

"I'm touched by your concern. Truly. But it's unnecessary." Georgie couldn't let this go. "You've . . . tried to look out for me before. I'm grateful, but I can't help wondering why."

"You don't remember what you did for me, do you?"

"I'm hoping I loaned you a gorgeous pair of diamond earrings you're about to return?"

Rory smiled her snow-goddess smile. "No such luck." She picked up her champagne flute and twisted the stem. "When I worked on *Skip and Scooter,* you were always good to the crew."

Georgie had never understood the logic of stars who made life miserable for the people whose job it was to make them look good. Besides, her father wouldn't have tolerated diva behavior. Still, being courteous to the crew didn't seem like a good enough reason for Rory to keep extending herself.

"I also like seeing decent people succeed." Rory took another sip.

Georgie didn't feel like much of a success right now. "You were the best production assistant the show ever had. I was sorry you only stayed one season."

"It was a hard show to work. A lot of testosterone."

Georgie remembered the way she'd teased Bram about having given Rory a hard time, but now it didn't seem so amusing. "Bram hit on you, didn't he?"

"Daily." She tugged absentmindedly on a diamond stud earring. "But his friends were the real problem."

"They were such losers. A bunch of parasites living off him. I'm happy to report he's shaken them off." He'd shaken everyone off, which seemed odd for someone who'd once kept himself surrounded.

"They'd slip pornographic pictures on my clipboard," Rory said coolly. "Snap my bra when I walked by. Sometimes worse."

"And Bram didn't stop it?"

"I don't think he knew about the worst of it. But they were his friends, and he was the one who insisted they be allowed on the set. When I tried to talk to him about it, he told me to lighten up." She draped her wrist over her thigh. "Then one afternoon, two of them cornered me."

Georgie sat up straight in her chair. "Now I remember. We'd finished shooting for the day, but I'd left a book or something on the set. I went back to get it and saw them pinning you against the wall. I'd forgotten that was you."

"It was me. You started yelling at them, and you even threw a couple of punches. You might only have been a teenager, but you had a lot more power than a lowly P.A., and they backed off. Afterward you went to the producers. They were banned from the set, and Bram couldn't do a thing about it." She tilted her head almost imperceptibly. "I've never forgotten the way you went to bat for me."

"I'm sure anyone would have done the same thing."

"Who knows? The point is, I don't forget my friends."

Georgie thought about Bram. "I'm guessing you don't forget your enemies either."

Rory cocked an eyebrow. "Not unless my memory loss will make the studio a lot of money."

Georgie smiled, then sobered. "If you and Bram didn't have that old history, would it change the way you feel about *Tree House*?"

"A studio invests in more than a screenplay. It's the whole package."

"And in this case, Bram's the centerpiece."

"He doesn't have any experience with a project like this."

Bram had been around the business since he was a teenager. It was his character, not his lack of experience, that put Rory off, and she didn't pull her punches. "He earned his bad reputation, Georgie. He's let a lot of people down."

"I know. But . . . people do change. I've never seen him so passionate about anything."

Rory offered a distant Hollywood smile that meant she'd already made up her mind. With Paul as a father, Georgie had never needed to be pushy, but no one else could fight this particular battle. She desperately wanted a shot at playing Helene, and Bram's success was her ticket. "I think passion counts for a lot when it comes to making a great film. All the experience in the world doesn't mean anything if the filmmaker isn't in love with the project."

Bram's genuine passion for *Tree House* forced her to confront how long it had been since she'd felt that kind of passion for herself. Playing Helene would give it back.

Rory leaned forward and gazed at Georgie with a steady intensity. "If you really want to help Bram, convince him to step aside and let me have the project."

"Meaning he wouldn't be the producer . . . or the leading man."

"Bram's a good actor, but this film needs a great actor. He's too limited."

Limited. Just as Georgie was supposed to be.

"Enough shop talk." Rory had made her point, and she deliberately changed the subject. "I hear Jake and Fleur's daughter is back in L.A."

Georgie couldn't push any more, and she let the subject drift to girlfriends.

"Good female friendships require a time investment I've never had," Rory said in her cool way. "But everything has its price, and I love my work, so I'm not complaining."

Maybe she wasn't, but Georgie thought she heard regret in her voice. She couldn't imagine life without the support of her friends, and just before she left, she heard herself invite Rory to tomorrow night's dinner party.

To her surprise, Rory accepted.

Bram was waiting for her on the other side of the gate. "How did it go?"

"Fine." Tomorrow would be soon enough to break the news that she'd invited Rory. If she told him now, he'd fly in a French chef and book an orchestra. With her money.

"How fine?"

"I said I wouldn't sabotage you, and I didn't."

"You mean you meant it?"

"I told her you'd matured, and that you have real passion for the project."

"With a straight face?"

"*Yes*, with a straight face. Jeez."

He pulled her into his arms and gave her a long kiss, which was sexy, because he was a sexy kisser, but mainly exuberant, like a killer Doberman confronted with a juicy bone that had been unexpectedly tossed his way. Just like that, she began to melt. And why not? After everything she'd been through, she deserved as much mindless pleasure as she could get.

He curled both hands around her bottom. "Where's Meg?"

"At a concert. You want a threesome?"

"Not tonight." He kissed her again. And again. Before long, their hands were all over each other.

He let her go so abruptly she nearly fell. "Chaz! Aaron!" He shot toward the veranda. "Come out here!"

He had to call them twice before they appeared. Aaron had been putting in overtime redesigning her Web site, and a set of Bose headphones hung around his neck. Chaz appeared carrying a brutal-looking chef's knife. Bram extended a pair of fifty-dollar bills he'd just pulled from his wallet. "You're both done for the night. Here's a little bonus for being such loyal employees. Now get out. We'll see you in the morning."

Aaron looked at the bills as if he'd never seen money. Chaz unlocked her semipermanent scowl. "I'm in the middle of making dinner."

"And I know it'll be delicious for lunch tomorrow." He took each of them by one arm and nudged them toward the door that opened into the garage, with Chaz protesting the entire time. "At least let me turn off the frickin' stove before you burn down the house!"

"I'll handle it." When Chaz and Aaron were gone, he came after Georgie. Within seconds, he'd locked them in the house. After a quick detour to turn off the stove, they reached the bedroom. His urgency thrilled her, so she frowned at him.

"Don't you think that was a little . . . rash?"

"No." He locked the bedroom door. "Take off your clothes."

Chapter 15

D on't make me ask twice," Bram said when she didn't react quickly enough.

His air of sexy menace sent a new frenzy of desire rushing through her. This was so blissfully uncomplicated. All he cared about was getting laid, and that was all she cared about, too. Her head was finally screwed on straight enough to enjoy every illicit moment.

"You're on." She pulled her top over her head. "Knock yourself out."

He gazed at her breasts cupped in pale yellow lace, and the way he looked at her filled her with pleasure. She loved feeling desired, never mind that she was merely a convenience.

He snared her wrist. "This time I want a bed. So I can see every inch of you."

She nearly dissolved, right there in the middle of his bedroom. As she gazed into his smoky lavender eyes, she reminded herself she didn't care enough about him to ever be hurt. Then he kissed her, and she stopped thinking at all.

This time there was no slow striptease. They threw aside their clothes and fell on each other. Until yesterday, she'd never given herself without love, but now she offered up her body with abandon. He explored every inch, opening her legs, propping one of her ankles on his shoulder. She teased and tormented him in return, not to turn him on, but because she wanted to, because this affair was about her pleasure and not about trying to hold on to a man who didn't love her.

He was earthy. Thorough. Demanding. Using his fingers, his mouth, his sex. She experienced a blissful, soaring freedom. The final explosion was cataclysmic.

Afterward, she lay limp beneath him, so drained she could barely muster the words. "Oh, well . . . I'm sure the next time will be better."

He rolled over on his back, his skin as damp as hers, his mouth curling in a lazy smile. "Let's face it, you're a lot of woman for one man to handle."

She grinned. The air-conditioning kicked on, blowing a cool breeze across their hot bodies. She felt . . .

She struggled to put a name to her emotions and finally came up with one.

She felt happy.

Bram was the only guy who'd ever been in Chaz's apartment, but now Aaron was sitting on her couch, his headphones still around his neck, the jack dangling by his knee. He wore farmer jeans and a wrinkled green T-shirt that said ALL YOUR BASE ARE BELONG TO US, which made no frickin' sense. His curly hair exploded around his round face, and his glasses were crooked. "You can't stay here," Chaz said. "You have to leave."

"I told you. My car keys are in Georgie's office."

"Take my car." Bram had bought her a shiny new Honda Odyssey, but she didn't like leaving the house unless she had to, so she didn't use it for much except household errands. Otherwise, she stayed mostly in her apartment. Bram had let her furnish it the way she wanted. She'd chosen modern pieces in chocolate and light brown along with a basic black shelving unit, an angular reading chair, and a couple of simple black-and-white abstract prints. No clutter. No mess. Everything neat and peaceful. Everything except Aaron.

He rubbed his chest through his T-shirt. "My driver's license is in my wallet, and that's in Georgie's office, too."

"So what? I drove without a license for years." She'd taught herself to drive at thirteen, figuring she posed less of a danger on the road than her drunken step-mother.

She and Aaron both had door keys, but neither of them was anxious to go back in the house right now. At least her garage apartment was on the opposite side of the house from the master bedroom. She couldn't imagine having to listen to Bram and Georgie getting it on. She hated Georgie. Hated watching Bram laugh at some stupid thing she said, hated listening to them talk about movies Chaz had never seen. Chaz wanted to be the one who came first with him. Which was stupid.

He'd better have remembered to turn off the stove.

"You're not sleeping here," she said.

"Who said I was? I'll give them some time, then go back in and get my stuff." He got up and wandered over to her bookcase, which held a TV, cookbooks, and some other books Bram had given her, including some by this important food writer named Ruth Reichl, who talked about how she got interested in food and everything. They were the best books Chaz had ever read.

"You should stop acting like such a bitch around Georgie." Aaron took one of the Reichl books off the shelf and flipped it over to read what was on the back.

"You might as well hang a sign around your neck saying that you're in love with Bram."

"I'm not in love with him!" Chaz shot up, grabbed the book from Aaron, and shoved it back on the shelf. "I care about him, and I don't like the way she treats him."

"Just because she doesn't kiss his ass like you do."

"I don't kiss his ass! I always tell him exactly what I think."

"Yeah, and while you're cussing at him, you're running around making him special meals and ironing his T-shirts. Yesterday, I saw you jump up to brush some crumbs off a chair before he sat on it."

"I take care of him because it's my job, not because I'm in love with him."

"It seems like more than a job. It seems like your whole life."

"That's bullshit. I just . . . owe him, that's all."

"For what?"

For everything.

She turned away from Aaron and went into her tiny galley kitchen. He was too stupid to know the difference between loving someone and being in love. Chaz loved Bram with all her heart, but it wasn't sex-love. It was like he was the best brother in the universe, one she'd do anything for.

She rooted around in her refrigerator for a Mountain Dew. Aaron had told her he'd gotten addicted to Mountain Dew when he was in college, but she only poured a glass for herself. Chaz had wanted to go to culinary school, not college. After her stepmother died, she'd saved up enough money to come to L.A., but jobs were harder to find than she'd imagined for someone without a high school diploma, and her plan to earn tuition money by working at an expensive restaurant quickly disappeared. She ended up washing dishes and busing tables at a couple of cheap Mexican places, but L.A. was expensive, and even working sixteen-hour days, she still had to dip into her savings to get by.

One day she came home from work and discovered somebody had broken into her crappy rented room and stolen everything she had, including her savings. She told herself not to panic. She might have to cut out a meal here and there, and she wouldn't be able to buy a car for a while, but she could still make the rent if she worked some extra hours.

She might have done it, too, if she hadn't gotten struck by a hit-and-run driver as she was crossing the street to the Laundromat. She didn't suffer anything more serious than some cracked ribs and a broken hand, but she lost both jobs because she couldn't wash dishes with a cast on. Within a month she was living on the streets.

Aaron came into the kitchen behind her. "Do you have anything to eat? I haven't had anything since lunch."

She had a cabinet full of junk food she wasn't going to tell him about. "Only cereal and some fruit." She nudged her glass of Mountain Dew behind her toaster where he couldn't see it, not because she was being mean, but because it wasn't diet.

"I guess it's better than nothing," he said.

She pulled out the cereal box and shoved some fresh strawberries at him, but he started tossing them in the bowl without slicing them, so she pushed him out of the way and did the job herself. She wished she had Special K to give him instead of Frosted Flakes.

The kitchen had a tiny, built-in eating counter. She wiped out her silverware drawer while he ate. She'd already noticed he had good table manners, and she thought his neighbor Becky might like that if she ever noticed him. As he finished his last bite, she pulled the cereal bowl out from under him. "I'm going to cut your hair."

"You are not. My hair's fine."

"It looks like a shrub. Do you want Becky to notice you or not?"

"If she's so shallow that all she cares about is looks, then I'm not interested in her." He took in her jeans and black T-shirt. "You're not exactly an expert on fashion?"

"I have my own style."

"Well, I have my own style, too."

"Geek style." She studied the slogan on his green T-shirt. all your base are belong to us. "What's that about anyway?"

He rolled his eyes, as if she should know. "Zero Wing. A 1989 Japanese video game. It's historic. Look it up."

"Whatever." She grabbed a pair of scissors from a drawer. "Let's go in the bathroom. I don't want your hair all over the place."

"If you want to cut hair so bad, cut your own." He snorted and gestured toward her choppy bob. "No, wait. You already did that."

She liked her hair, and she slammed the scissors on the counter. "You might as well forget about Becky. Or any other woman . . . because they won't look at you twice."

"Why should I take advice from somebody who doesn't have a life?"

"You think I don't have a life?"

"I haven't seen any guys hanging around."

"That doesn't mean I don't have a life." She didn't tell him she couldn't stand the idea of being with a man. It hadn't always been that way. In high school, she'd had two serious boyfriends, and she'd had sex with one of them. He'd turned out to be a jerk, but she'd liked the sex. Not now, though.

Aaron was looking at her like he thought he was her shrink, and that made her so mad, she charged toward him. "Take off those stupid headphones. You look stupid."

"I'll wait in my car." He headed out her apartment door, then clomped down the stairs to the back entrance.

She rushed over and called down after him. "Fine! But I have potato chips *and* Mountain Dew!"

"Good for you." The door slammed, and everything was quiet.

She went back to the couch and picked up the cookbook she'd been studying. She was glad he'd left. She hadn't wanted him to stay anyway.

She reached for the notebook she kept on the end table so she could make a list of everything she needed to do before the party tomorrow. Screw him. Now her apartment was just the way she liked it. All hers.

But the notebook slipped from her fingers, and the cookbook dropped to the carpet. She began to cry.

304 · SUSAN ELIZABETH PHILLIPS

All morning Bram couldn't seem to keep his clothes on, and by lunchtime, Georgie wanted to hit him in his delectable bare chest. He was either wandering around the backyard in nothing but his swim trunks sipping from one of his bottomless tumblers of scotch or—and this was the kicker—climbing an extension ladder half naked to clean out some gutters he said were clogged, as if anyone in Hollywood cleaned out their own gutters.

He was punishing her for slipping out of bed to spend the rest of the night in her own room. Tough. Their relationship was about debauchery, not the intimacy of nighttime cuddling.

She tried to escape to the kitchen, but Chaz was a total pain, refusing help and ignoring all of Georgie's suggestions. And Meg was no better. When she saw Georgie carrying around her video camera, she draped a scarf over her head and pretended to be one of Michael Jackson's kids, which was funny but not exactly what Georgie had in mind to record. She finally shut herself in her room to reread *Tree House* and think about Helene.

In the afternoon she set the table. Despite the possibility of rain, they were eating on the veranda, which managed to stay dry during all but the biggest storms.

She arranged a centerpiece of artichokes, lemons, and eucalyptus leaves in a blue pottery bowl. It was a little lopsided, but she liked the way it accented the bright yellow place mats and cobalt plates. Once she added a couple of chunky candles, it would be perfect.

She sensed Bram coming up behind her just before his hand curled around her bottom. "Why's the table set for seven?"

"Seven?" The time had come to deliver the news, but she acted as though she'd never heard the number before. "Let's see. You, me, Dad, RoryandTrev, Laura, Meg . . . Yes, that's right."

His hand, which had been exploring her bottom, came to a dead stop. "Did you say . . . Rory?"

"Uhm . . ."

"Rory Keene is coming to dinner tonight?"

"You never listen when I tell you things. I swear, my voice is just white noise to you. It's like we've been married forever."

"*Rory?*" He abandoned her bottom.

"I'm positive I mentioned it."

"I'm positive you didn't! Are you crazy? Your father hates my guts. I only have two and a half weeks left until that option expires, and I don't want him anyplace near Rory."

"I'll take care of him."

"Like you've done such a good job taking care of him so far."

"I thought you'd be happy." She attempted a pout and wasn't surprised when she couldn't pull it off.

"Rory loves that script," he said more to himself than to her. "If I could just get her to trust me."

"From what she told me, that's probably a lost cause." As he paced the veranda, she replayed her conversation with Rory. When she finished, she said, "Why did you bring those cretins out to L.A. with you?"

The bitterness he kept tucked away escaped. "Because I was a stupid kid. I didn't have a family, and I thought— I don't know what I thought."

Georgie had a fairly good idea.

He hunched his shoulders and looked away. "The guys told me Rory made the whole thing up. I wanted to believe them, so I did, and when I finally wised up, she was long gone. By the time I found her, my career was in the tank, and let's just say she doubted the sincerity of my apology."

"And now she has her revenge."

"It's not over till it's over. She wants that script, and she can get it a lot cheaper working with me than trying to snatch it up after my option expires." The same guy who'd once blown off three days' shooting to go deep-sea fishing was suddenly all-business. "We need to be on top of our game tonight. She likes you, and I'm fully prepared to take advantage of that. Lots of touching. Affection. Not a single wisecrack."

"Everybody will think we're sick."

"I'm counting on you to help make sure I get some time alone with her." He took in her lemon and artichoke centerpiece. "See if you can find a florist. I'll hire a bartender and someone to wait tables. And we need to get a real chef in here."

She held up her hand. "Stop right there. No florist, no bartender, and Chaz is making do-it-yourself kebabs. Chicken, beef, and scallops."

"Are you crazy? We can't serve Rory Keene kebabs."

"You'll have to trust me. Remember, I have a purely selfish interest in convincing Rory to back your project. If you screw this up for me . . ."

"Georgie, I told you. Helene has to be cast—"

"Leave me alone. I have things to do." Mainly she had to help him convince Rory that he was the person to make the film. If Rory saw how well he could behave these days, she might forget his past idiocy.

Unlike Georgie, who couldn't forget a thing.

After he left, she busied herself setting candles around the veranda, but eventually she couldn't resist grabbing her video camera. Today of all days, she should leave Chaz alone, but what had begun as a whim was turning into an obsession. In addition to her fascination with Chaz, she was also falling in love with the whole process of recording other people's lives. She'd never imagined how absorbing standing behind a camera instead of in front of one could be.

She found Chaz in the kitchen making a ginger-garlic marinade. When she spotted Georgie, she slammed her chef's knife down on some garlic cloves. "Get that camera out of here."

"You won't let me help. I'm bored." She panned around the kitchen, taking in the well-organized chaos.

"Go film the cleaning people. You seem to have all kinds of fun doing that."

Did Georgie hear a note of jealousy? "I like talking to them. Soledad—she's the tall, pretty one—sends most of her money back to her mother in Mexico, so she has to live with her sister. There are six of them in a one-bedroom apartment. Can you imagine?"

Chaz rocked the blade over the garlic. "Big deal. At least she's not sleeping on the streets."

Georgie's skin prickled. "Like you did?"

Chaz dipped her head. "I never told you that."

"You told me about the accident and that you got fired after you broke your hand." Georgie zoomed in. "I know your money was stolen. It's a fairly obvious conclusion."

"There are a lot of kids on the streets. It wasn't a big deal."

"Still . . . It had to be especially hard for you. All that mess and no way to clean it up."

"I handled it. Now get out. I mean it, Georgie. I have to concentrate."

Georgie should leave, but the turbulent emotions bubbling behind Chaz's tough facade had drawn her in from the beginning, and somehow the camera demanded she record it. She shifted her questioning. "Does fixing dinner for more than one person make you nervous?"

"I fix dinner for more than one person practically every night." She tossed the chopped garlic in a bowl with some peeled ginger. "I feed you, don't I?"

"But you don't put your heart into it. I swear, Chaz, even your desserts taste bitter."

Chaz's head shot up. "That's a crappy thing to say."

"Just a personal observation. Bram loves your cooking, and so does Meg. But then you seem to like Meg."

Chaz pressed her lips tight. Her blade moved faster.

Georgie stepped to the end of the counter. "You'd better watch yourself. Great cooks know that extraordinary food is about more than mixing ingredients. Who you are as a person—how you feel about other people—shows up in what you create."

The rhythm of Chaz's chopping slowed. "I don't believe that."

Georgie told herself to let it go, but she couldn't, not with the camera in her hands, not when this seemed so right. A wave of compassion overcame her, along with an odd sense of understanding. She and Chaz had each found her own way of coping with a world over which they seemed to have little control. "Then why do your desserts taste so bitter?" she said softly. "Is it really me you hate . . . or is it yourself?"

Chaz dropped her knife and stared into the camera, her black-rimmed eyes wide.

"Leave her alone, Georgie." Bram spoke sharply from the doorway. "Take your camera and leave her alone."

Chaz turned on him. "You told her!"

Bram came into the room. "I haven't told her anything."

"She knows! You told her!"

Chaz's anger and self-hatred were visceral, and Georgie wanted to understand it. She wanted to film it as a testament to all the young girls consumed by their own pain. Except she had no right to invade her privacy like this, and she made herself—forced herself—to lower the camera.

"She doesn't know anything you haven't told her with your big mouth," Bram said.

Once again Georgie ordered herself to leave, but her feet weren't moving. Instead, she said, "I know you're not the only girl who's come to L.A. and done what she had to so she could survive."

Chaz's hands curled into fists. "I wasn't a whore. That's what you're thinking, isn't it? I was some kind of crack whore!"

Bram shot Georgie a death glare and moved to Chaz's side. "Let it go. You don't have to defend yourself to anyone."

But something seemed to have broken open inside her. She focused only on Georgie. Her lips pulled tight over her teeth and her voice became a snarl. "I wasn't doing drugs! Never! I just wanted a place to live and some decent food."

Georgie turned off the camera.

"No!" Chaz cried. "Turn it back on. You wanted to hear this so bad . . . Turn it on."

"It's all right. I don't—"

"Turn it on!" Chaz said fiercely. "This is important. Make it important."

Georgie's hands had begun to shake, but she understood, and she did as Chaz asked.

"I was dirty and living out of a backpack." Through the lens Georgie watched tears spill over the inky dam of Chaz's bottom lashes. "I went a day without eating and then another day. I heard about this soup kitchen, but I couldn't make myself go in. I was feeling crazy from not eating and it seemed better to sell my body than take charity."

Bram tried to rub her back, but she pushed him away. "I told myself it would be just once, and I'd charge enough so I could get by until the cast came off my hand." Her words pummeled the camera. "He was an old guy. He was going to pay me two hundred bucks. But after it was over, he pushed me out of his car instead and drove away without giving me anything. I threw up in the gutter." Her mouth tightened with bitterness. "After that I learned to get my money first. Mostly twenty bucks, but I wasn't using—I never used drugs—and I made them wear condoms, so I wasn't like the other girls who were using and didn't care about anything. I cared, and I wasn't a whore!"

Once again, Georgie tried to shut off the camera, but Chaz was having none of it. "This is what you wanted. Don't you dare stop now."

"All right," Georgie said softly.

"I hated sleeping on the street." Muddy tears dripped down her cheeks. "And I hated trying to keep clean in public bathrooms most of all. I hated it so much I wanted to die, but killing yourself is a lot harder than you think." She grabbed a tissue from a box on the counter. "I met this guy not too long before Christmas, and I got some pills from him. Not to get high. Pills so I could . . . stop everything." She blew her nose. "I was going to save them for Christmas Eve, like this present to myself where I would take the pills, then just curl up in somebody's doorway and fall asleep forever."

"Oh, Chaz . . ." Georgie's heart ached. Bram drew Chaz's spine against his chest and rubbed her shoulders.

"All I had to do was wait until Christmas Eve, but I got too hungry." She balled the tissue in her hand. "One night I saw this guy coming out of a club. He was by himself, and he looked really clean. When I went up to talk to him, he asked me how old I was. A lot of them asked that, and I would answer depending on what they wanted to hear, like sometimes I'd say fourteen or even twelve. But he didn't seem like one of those creeps, so I told him the truth. He pulled out some money, gave it to me, and walked away. It was a hundred dollars, and I should have just said thank you, but I was sort of crazy from not eating, and I yelled that I didn't need his charity. And when he turned to look at me, I sort of threw it at him."

She pulled away from Bram and dropped the tissue in the trash. "He came back and picked up the money and asked how long since I'd had anything to eat. I told him I didn't remember, and he took me into the bar and ordered hamburgers and stuff. He wouldn't let me go wash my hands because he said I'd try to duck out the back, but I wouldn't have. I was too hungry. I wrapped a paper napkin around the food and ate it that way, so my hands didn't touch anything."

She went to the sink and turned on the water. Keeping her back to them, she washed her hands. "He waited until I was done, and then he said he'd take me to this place, like this homeless shelter where they had social workers, and I told him I didn't need any social workers, what I needed was a job in a restaurant, but even though my cast was off, I couldn't get a job because I didn't have an address, and I couldn't keep myself clean."

Georgie lowered the camera and licked her lips. "So he gave you a job himself. He invited a street kid he didn't know into his house and gave her a job."

Chaz spun back to face her—proud, defiant, sneering. "And he thinks he's so smart about everything. I could have stuck a knife in him. He doesn't understand how bad people can be. Do you see why I have to watch him so close?"

"I do," Georgie said. "I didn't before, but now I do."

"I'm sure I could have held my own against a runt like you," Bram said.

Chaz grabbed a paper towel and stalked toward Georgie, as if he hadn't spoken. "Now that you've got all that in your camera, maybe you'll leave me alone."

"Maybe," Georgie said. "Probably not."

Chaz whipped around to confront Bram. "Do you see how weird she is? Now do you see?"

He slipped his hand in his pocket. "What do you want me to do about it?"

"Just— I don't know. Just tell her she's fucking weird."

"You're weird," he said to Georgie. "Chaz is right."

"I know. I appreciate the two of you putting up with me."

Feeling as though she'd done something good, she left them alone.

Chapter 16

Georgie locked herself in Bram's bathroom and soaked in his tub. She and Chaz had both been betrayed by men—Chaz, much more horribly, on the streets; Georgie on a boat in the middle of Lake Michigan, and later by the husband she'd promised to love forever. Now they were each trying to figure out how to move on. She wondered if Chaz would have told her heart-wrenching story if the camera hadn't been there? *This is important,*" Chaz had said when Georgie tried to stop filming. *"Make it important."*

Did the camera simply record reality or did it alter it? Could it change the future? Georgie wondered if having her story documented might help Chaz begin putting her past behind her so she could live a fuller life. Wouldn't that be amazing? And wouldn't it be even more amazing if recording Chaz's story helped Georgie put her own life in perspective.

She sank deeper into the water and considered the only part of Chaz's story that had truly shocked her. Bram's role. He'd been Georgie's destroyer, but he'd been Chaz's rescuer. She kept learning new things about him, and none of it fit with what she thought she already knew. He proudly proclaimed that he cared about no one but himself, but that wasn't entirely true.

She washed her hair and blew it dry so that it fell straight and shiny around her fuller face. She applied smoky eye makeup and one of her many nude lipsticks, then dressed in cayenne red stretch chinos and a shiny gray cami accompanied by silver ballet flats. With the addition of a pair of abstract silver earrings, she was done.

At the bottom of the stairs, she found Bram pacing the foyer in white pants and shirt. "I thought you were wearing jeans," she said.

"I changed my mind."

He took her in, doing his eye-smolder thing, which made her nervous. "You look like Robert Redford in *Gatsby*," she said. "Except hunkier. A statement of fact, not a compliment, so no need to thank me."

"I won't." He kept smoldering her, his gaze moving from her silver ballet flats, up over her legs and hips, lingering on her breasts, and ending up at her face. "You look pretty good yourself. Those big green eyes . . ."

"Bug eyes."

His smoldering gave way to exasperation. "You don't have bug eyes, and you should have gotten over your insecurities a long time ago."

"I'm a realist. Moon face, bug eyes, and rubber mouth, but I'm starting to like my body again, and I'm not getting implants."

He sighed. "Nobody wants you to get implants, especially me. You don't have a moon face. And when are you going to stop trying to camouflage your mouth and splash it with some red lipstick? I happen to have an intimate acquaintance with that mouth, and I'm here to tell you it's spectacular." He slid the palm of his hand along her hip. "A statement of fact, not a compliment."

This was getting way too hot for her, so she broke the mood with a friendly suggestion. "If you want Rory to think you're reformed, maybe you should lay off the booze."

"Iced tea."

"Yeah, right."

She headed for the kitchen to check up on Chaz. Cobalt pottery bowls with red pepper chunks, figs and mangoes, curls of sweet onion, and wedges of fresh pineapple covered the counter. "Make sure you turn the chicken on the grill after four minutes," Chaz told Aaron, who was arranging glasses on a tray. "No more. Understand?"

"I understood the first two times you told me."

"Those rosemary sprigs go on top of the beef while it's cooking." Ignoring Georgie, she pitched a tomato she'd dropped into the sink. "And baste the scallops with the sweet chili sauce. Remember they dry out fast, so don't keep them on the heat too long."

"You should be grilling instead of me," he said.

"Like I don't have enough to do?"

Chaz seemed as bad-tempered as ever, which was reassuring. Georgie gave her a break and spoke only to Aaron. "What happened to your hair?"

"I got it cut this afternoon." Chaz snorted, and he glared at her. "It was taking too long to dry in the morning, that's all."

Another snort.

"It looks great." Georgie observed him more closely. The buttons lined up in a neat row down the front of his dark green shirt with no sign of strain, and his khakis no longer stretched so tightly across his stomach. Aaron was losing weight, and she had a feeling she knew who was responsible.

"Thanks for helping Chaz tonight," she said as she stole a mushroom from a bowl on the counter. "If she gets too dangerous, use some pepper spray on her."

"He'd squirt himself in the eye," Chaz retorted. She was all attitude, but she knew Georgie had witnessed her pain, and she wouldn't look at her.

Georgie squeezed Aaron's arm. "Remind me to give you hazardous-duty pay when this is over."

Meg stuck her head in. She wore a very short chartreuse tunic with blue leopard-pattern leggings and orange ankle boots. A narrow, braided jute headband had replaced the *bindi* on her forehead. She grinned and spread her arms. "I look fabulous! Admit it."

She did, although Georgie knew her well enough to understand that Meg didn't really believe it. She could wear even the most outrageous outfits with the same authority as her former supermodel mother, but she still insisted on seeing herself as an ugly duckling. Even so, Georgie envied Meg's relationship with her famous parents. Despite the messy complexities between them, they loved each other unconditionally.

The doorbell rang, and by the time Georgie reached the foyer, Bram had let in Trevor. "Mrs. Shepard, I presume." He handed over a gift basket piled with expensive spa products. "I didn't want to add to his drinking problem by bringing alcohol."

"Thank you."

Bram took a slug of scotch. "I don't have a drinking problem."

Laura arrived immediately afterward, slightly breathless, her pale, flyaway hair disheveled, not exactly the portrait of a high-powered Hollywood agent, but that was why Paul had hired her. She tripped coming into the house and blanched as Bram caught her arm. "Sorry," she said. "I haven't used these feet all day, and I've forgotten how they work."

Bram smiled. "A common problem."

"Great news." Laura pecked Georgie on the cheek. "You have a meeting with Greenberg on Tuesday." Georgie's hackles went up, but Laura had already turned to Bram. "This is a beautiful house. Who decorated it for you?"

"I did it myself. Trev Elliott helped."

He and Laura disappeared toward the veranda leaving Georgie staring after him. Bram had picked out the Oriental rugs and Tibetan throws? The Mexican folk paintings and Balinese bells? And what about all those well-thumbed books lining the dining room shelves?

Her father showed up before she could process this new information. His lips felt frosty on her cheek. "Dad, I need you to be decent to Bram tonight," she said as she led him through the foyer. "Rory Keene's invited, and Bram needs her support on a project. No put-downs. I mean it."

"Maybe I should come back sometime when you don't feel like you have to lecture me as soon as I walk in the door."

"Let's just have fun tonight. Please. It's important to me for the two of you to get along."

"You're talking to the wrong person."

As he walked away, a wisp of memory tugged at her . . . Her mother sitting cross-legged on a blanket and laughing at her father, who was running across a patch of grass with Georgie on his back. Had it really happened, or was it something she'd dreamed?

When she reached the veranda, she saw that Bram and her father had taken up posts as far away from each other as possible. Bram was charming Laura while her father listened to Trev's description of the comedy he was currently shooting. Meg appointed herself bartender, and eventually Paul drifted her way. He'd always liked Meg, something Georgie had never understood, since he should have hated her undisciplined lifestyle. But unlike Georgie, Meg made him laugh.

Georgie was suppressing a pang of jealousy when Rory came up the path from the back. Laura tipped over her wineglass, and her father stopped talking in midsentence. Only Meg and Trev weren't thrown off by the new addition to the party. Bram would have jumped to his feet if Georgie hadn't clamped her fingers around his wrist to slow him down. Fortunately, he took her cue and greeted Rory in a more leisurely fashion. "The roses could use a little pruning while you're out there."

"Sorry. Plants die if I even look at them."

"Then let me get you a drink instead."

Meg began entertaining them with stories of her recent travels. Before long, she had everyone laughing as she described an ill-advised kayaking trip on the Mangde Chhu River. Aaron brought out trays with the ingredients for the do-it-yourself kebabs, and they all gathered around to assemble their own. Rory surprised everyone by kicking off her shoes and volunteering to help with the grilling. By the time they were seated at the table with their wineglasses refilled and plates piled with food, everyone except Bram and Georgie had relaxed.

Bram made the first move in his campaign to earn Rory's good opinion. He raised his glass and locked eyes with Georgie at the opposite end of the table. "I'd like to propose a toast to my funny, smart, wonderful wife." His words were soft and filled with emotion. "A woman with a loving heart, an ability to see beneath the surface"—his voice caught oh-so-touchingly—"and a willingness to forgive."

Her father frowned. Meg looked bemused, Laura a bit dreamy-eyed. Trev seemed confused, but Rory was impossible to read. Bram smiled at Georgie with a heart full of love.

A heart full of bullshit.

Georgie choked herself up. "Stop it, you big idiot. You'll make me cry."

They drank their toast. Laura smiled. "I know I speak for all of us when I say how great it is to see the two of you so happy."

"We both had some growing up to do," Bram said with all kinds of sincerity. "Especially me. We'll be nice and ignore Georgie's marriage to Mr. Stupid. But we're finally where we want to be. Not that we still don't have a few things to work out . . ."

Georgie braced herself for whatever was coming.

"Georgie only wants two kids," he said, "but I want more. We've had some fairly big arguments about it."

The man had no shame.

Paul set down his fork and addressed Bram for the first time. "With Georgie barefoot and pregnant, it'll be tough to support your current lifestyle." He gave a short laugh, an unconvincing attempt to pass off his comment as a joke.

This was exactly what Bram had warned her would happen, but he merely kicked back in his chair and offered up a lazy grin. "Georgie's healthy as a horse. They can shoot her from the chest up. Hell, I'll bet she could have a baby and be back on the job the next day. What do you think, sweetheart?"

"Or I could just squat in the middle of the set and give birth right there."

Bram winked. "That's the spirit."

"The unions wouldn't put up with it," Trevor said. "A violation of their labor contract."

Meg groaned.

Bram had won that round, and her father looked sulky as he turned his attention to his plate. Trev told a funny story about his current costar. They all laughed, but a shadow had crept across Georgie's heart. She wished Bram hadn't brought up children. She either had to give up the idea of having a baby or find the courage to go it alone. And why not? Fathers were vastly overrated. She could go to a sperm bank, or . . .

No. *Absolutely not!*

For dessert they indulged in a rich lemon cake garnished with a few fresh raspberries and a chocolate curl. Afterward, Bram dragged Chaz out from the kitchen. Everybody complimented her, and she blushed furiously. "I'm glad you . . . like enjoyed it." She shot Georgie a glare.

"A great dessert, Chaz," Georgie said. "A perfect balance between tart and sweet."

Chaz regarded her suspiciously.

Trev had a 6 A.M. call and left, but the others were in no hurry to end the evening even though the wind had picked up and the air smelled like rain. Bram put on some jazz and engaged Rory in a quiet conversation about Italian cinema. Georgie mentally congratulated him for displaying so much restraint. When Rory excused herself to go to the powder room, Georgie slipped to his side. "You're doing great. Give her plenty of space when she comes back, so you don't look desperate."

"I am desperate. At least—" He stared at her hand as she tucked a strand of hair behind her ear. "Where's your wedding ring?"

She glanced at her bare finger. "I accidentally knocked it down the drain while I was getting dressed. You're just noticing?"

"You *what?*"

"It's cheaper to order another one than pay for a plumber."

"Since when are you worried about *cheap?*" He spun toward the guests, speaking calmly, but with an underlying tension. "Excuse me for a few minutes. One of my fans is on his deathbed, poor guy. I promised his wife I'd call him tonight." And just like that, he disappeared.

She smiled sadly and acted as if deathbed phone calls were all in a day's work.

Rain began to fall in a gentle spatter that made the candlelit veranda seem even cozier. With all her guests engaged in conversation, Georgie slipped away unnoticed.

She found Bram on his knees, his head stuck under her sink, a plastic bucket and a pipe wrench by his knees. "What are you doing?"

"Trying to rescue your ring," he said from inside the vanity.

"Why?"

"Because it's your wedding ring," he said tightly. "Every woman has a sentimental attachment to her wedding ring."

"I don't. You bought mine on eBay for a hundred bucks."

He pulled his head out. "Who told you that?"

"You did."

He muttered something, grabbed the monkey wrench, and stuffed his head back inside the vanity.

She was getting a creepy feeling. "You did buy it on eBay, right?"

"Not exactly," came his muffled reply.

"Then where did you get it?"

"At . . . this store."

"*What* store?"

He poked his head out. "How am I supposed to remember?"

"It was only a month ago!"

"Whatever." His head disappeared.

"You told me the ring was a fake. It's a fake, right?"

"Define 'fake.'" The wrench clanged against a pipe.

"As in, 'Not genuine.'"

"Oh."

"Bram?"

Another clang. "It's not a fake."

"It's the *real thing*?"

"That's what I said, isn't it?"

"Why didn't you tell me that from the beginning?"

"Because we have a relationship based on deceit." He stretched out his hand. "Give me the bucket."

"I don't believe this!"

He fumbled for the bucket, his head still inside.

"I would have been more careful!" She thought of all the places she'd left the ring lying around, and she wanted to kick him. "I set it on the diving board when I went swimming yesterday!"

"That's just stupid." Water sloshed into the bucket. "Got it!" he said a moment later.

She sank down on the toilet lid and dropped her forehead into her hands. "I'm sick of having a marriage based on deceit."

He emerged, bringing the bucket with him. "If you think about it, having a marriage based on deceit is all you know anything about. That should be a comfort."

She leaped up. "I want a fake ring. I liked having a fake ring. Why don't you ever do what you're supposed to?"

"Because I can never figure out what that is." He dropped the sink stopper and began washing off her not-fake ring. "When we get back downstairs, I'm going to pull Rory away. Don't let anybody interrupt us, okay?"

"Georgie!" Meg called from the bottom of the stairs. "Georgie, you need to come down here. You have a guest."

How could she have a guest with a guard stationed at the gate?

Bram grabbed her hand and slipped the ring back on. "Let's be a little more careful this time."

She stared down at the big stone. "I paid for this, didn't I?"

"Everybody should have a rich wife."

She jerked past him and hurried along the hall. Halfway down she stopped.

Her ex-husband stood at the bottom of the stairs.

Chapter 17

Meg tugged nervously on an amber earring. "I told him he couldn't come in."

Lance looked as bad as someone so buff could possibly look. He was apparently growing both a beard and long hair for his next action film because he had an inch of unkempt black scrub sprouting from his jaw, and his dark hair hung unevenly around his square face, not an attractive look, although one that was certain to improve after his hair and makeup people got done with him. His coffee-stained T-shirt stretched over the bulging muscles he spent several hours a day maintaining. Narrow braided bracelets, similar to Meg's headband, but more frayed, hung at his wrist, and he wore sandals made of rope and canvas. Skillful dentistry had shaped his strong white teeth, but he'd never let anyone touch his slightly crooked nose. His press kit said he'd broken it in a teenage street fight, but he'd really tripped on the front steps of his college frat house and been too frightened of surgery to have it fixed.

"Georgie, I've left half a dozen messages. When you didn't call me back, I was afraid— Why wouldn't you call me back?"

Her fingers curled around the railing. "I didn't want to."

Like most of Hollywood's leading men, he wasn't exceptionally tall, barely five feet nine, but his granite jaw, manly chin-cleft, soulful dark eyes, and pronounced musculature compensated for his lack of height. "I needed to talk to you. I needed to hear your voice, to make sure you're all right."

More than anything, she wanted him to grovel. She wanted to hear him say he'd made the biggest mistake of his life, and he'd do anything to get her back, but that didn't seem to be happening. She came down one step. "You look awful."

"I drove here right from the airport. We just got in from the Philippines."

She forced herself the rest of the way into the foyer. "You were in a private jet. How tough could the trip have been?"

"Two of our people got sick. It was—" He glanced over his shoulder at Meg standing guard behind him. She'd kicked off her orange boots, and the way her bare ankles emerged from her blue leopard-print leggings made her look as though she'd been dipped upside down into a tub of melted crayons. "Could we talk? Privately?"

"No. But Meg has always liked you. You can talk to her."

"Not anymore," Meg said. "I think you're a creep."

Lance hated not being adored, and distress flickered in his eyes. Good. "Send me an e-mail," Georgie said. "I have guests, and I need to go back to the party."

"Five minutes. That's all."

An alarming thought struck her. "Photographers are all over the place. If they spotted you driving in—"

"I'm not that stupid. I was driving my trainer's car, and the windows are dark, so no one could see in. Somebody buzzed me through the gate."

Georgie didn't have any trouble figuring out whom. The kitchen had an intercom, and Chaz had to know how much Georgie would hate having Lance show up. Georgie slipped her thumb into the pocket of her chinos. "Does Jade know you're here?"

"Of course. We tell each other everything, and she understands why I need to do this. She knows how I feel about you."

"And exactly how is that?" Bram sauntered down the stairs. With his rumpled bronze hair, world-weary tanzanite eyes, and Gatsby whites, he looked like the jaded, overindulged, but potentially dangerous heir to a lost New England liquor fortune.

Lance moved closer to Georgie, as if he needed to protect her. "This is between Georgie and me."

"Sorry, sport." Bram ambled into the foyer. "You lost your opportunity for a private chat when you traded her in for Jade. You poor bastard."

Lance took a menacing step forward. "Stop right there, Shepard. Don't say another word about Jade."

"Relax." Bram rested an elbow on the newel post. "I have nothing but admiration for your wife, but that doesn't mean I'd ever want to be married to her. Very high maintenance."

"Nothing you need to worry about," Lance said tightly.

Even though Bram was considerably taller than her ex-husband, Lance's perfect physique should have made him a stronger presence. But somehow Bram's lethal elegance gave him an edge in the macho wars. She couldn't help wondering how a woman like herself had ended up married to two such impressive men.

She moved closer to Bram. "Say what you need to, Lance, and then leave me alone."

"Could you . . . step outside for a minute?"

"Georgie and I don't have secrets from each other." Bram let his voice slip into an Eastwood whisper, circa 1973. "I don't like secrets. I don't like them at all."

She considered rising above her baser instincts, but only for a moment. "He's very possessive. *Mostly* in a good way."

Bram curled his fingers around the back of her neck. "And let's keep it like that."

Her flash of amusement proved she'd spent too much time living with the devil. Still, this was her fight, not Bram's, and as much as she appreciated the support, she needed to handle it on her own. "Lance doesn't seem like he's leaving, so I might as well get this over with."

"You don't have to talk to him." Bram dropped his hand from her neck. "I'd like nothing better than a good excuse to throw the son of a bitch out on his ass."

"I know you would, sweetie, and I'm sorry to spoil your fun, but leave us alone for a few minutes, will you? I promise I'll tell you everything. I know how much you love a good laugh."

Meg shot Lance a glare and looped her arm through Bram's. "Come on, pal. I'll fix you another drink."

Exactly what he didn't need, but Meg's intentions were good.

Bram gazed at Georgie, and she could see him trying to decide how long and how hard to kiss her. But he wisely underplayed the scene by merely touching her hand. "I'll be nearby if you need me."

She'd intended to stay in the foyer, but Lance had other ideas, and he walked ahead of her into the living room. His passion for clean surfaces and hard modern lines would make him contemptuous of this lovely room with its kumquat trees, Tibetan throws, and mirrored Indian pillows. And while Bram's house was spacious, it could have fit inside one corner of the massive property she and Lance had shared.

She remembered something she should have thought of earlier. "I'm sorry about the baby. Truly."

He stopped in front of the fireplace, so that the vine curling over the mantel looked as though it was growing from his head. "It's been hard, but it was early, and Jade got pregnant so easy that we're not letting ourselves get too upset. Everything happens for a reason."

Georgie didn't believe that. She believed things sometimes happened just because life could really suck. "Still, I'm sorry."

His shrug made her suspect he was secretly relieved. She heard a distant rumble of thunder and wondered how she could ever have loved this man with his shallow emotions and flexible passions. She'd given him tears and entreaties, but she'd never once unleashed her anger. No time like the present to fix that.

She moved toward him. "I'll never forgive you for the lie you spread about me not wanting children. How could you do something so cowardly?"

He was taken aback by her attack, and he picked at the frayed bracelet on his wrist. "It . . . was an over-zealous publicist."

"That's a lie." Her anger erupted along with a flash of lightning. "You're a liar and a cheat. You had dozens of chances to correct that story, and you never did."

"Why are you being so hostile? What was I supposed to say?"

"The truth." She closed the distance between them. They were nearly the same height, and she looked him squarely in the eye. "Except being honest would have made you look like even more of a jerk to the public, and you couldn't stand that."

He started to sputter. "Don't talk to me about jerks? How could you marry that ass?"

"Easy. He's hot and he worships me." Truth and lie rolled up together.

"You've always hated him. I don't understand how this could happen."

"There's a thin line between hating someone and finding the grand passion of your life."

"Is that what this is about? Sex?"

"Definitely a big part of it. And I do mean big."

That was just plain mean. The fact that Lance wasn't super-endowed had never bothered her, but it bothered him, and she should be ashamed of herself. She wasn't. "Bram's insatiable. I've spent so much time naked lately, it's a wonder I still remember how to wear clothes."

He'd always refused to acknowledge any problems with their sex life, and he turned his back to examine the Moorish carving on the mantel. "I don't want to fight with you, Georgie. We're not enemies."

"Think again."

"If you'd just called me back . . . I have enough guilt. I don't know how he did it, but I know he coerced you, and I want to help. I have to help you get out of this."

"Fascinating. Except I don't need help."

"The fact that you married him . . ." He turned to face her again. "Don't you see? Not only is it bad for you, but it cheapens what we had together."

At first she was too stunned to respond, and then she laughed.

He puffed up, all injured dignity. "It's not funny. If he'd been someone decent . . . Our relationship was true and honest. Just because it didn't last doesn't mean it wasn't right at the time." He stepped away from the fireplace. "If you married Bram of your own free will—and I'm having a hard time believing that—but if you did, you've tainted our relationship and demeaned yourself."

"Okay, you have officially overstayed your welcome."

Lance plowed on. "He's a player. He's lazy, aimless. The guy's a drunk and a drug addict, for god's sake. He's nothing but a bum."

"Get out of here."

"You're not going to tell me the truth, are you? You're still too angry. Then tell me this . . . What would you have done if you were me? What if you'd met the love of your life while you were married to someone else? What would you have done?"

"Easy. I'd never have married someone who wasn't the love of my life in the first place."

He flinched. "I know you think what I did was unforgivable, but I'm asking you to look at it a different way. Try to see that what happened with Jade and me could never have happened if you hadn't shown me what it means to really love someone—with your whole heart."

His audacity made her want to laugh—scream—she didn't know which. He pulled at his scruffy beard. "It's hard to understand, I realize that, but without you, I wouldn't have known what the heart is capable of." He started to reach out for her, then must have seen something in her eyes that made him think better of it. "Georgie, you gave me the courage to love Jade the way she deserves to be loved. The way I deserve to love someone."

A weird sort of fascination had taken hold of her. "Are you for real?"

"I've told you how sorry I am for hurting you. I never wanted to cause you so much pain." She'd witnessed that same haunted expression when he watched television news, read a particularly moving book, or even visited an animal shelter. Lance had always felt things deeply. Once she'd seen him tear up at a beer commercial.

"You can't imagine how much courage it took for me to leave you," he said. "But my feelings for Jade . . . Jade's feelings for me—they were bigger than both of us."

"Did you just say 'bigger than both of us'?"

"I don't know how else to explain it. You showed me the way to love, and I owe you everything. You won't tell me how you got trapped in this situation with Bram. That's your choice. But I'll help you anyway. Let me do that for you. Please, Georgie. Let me help you get out."

"I don't want out." Another crash of lightning, closer this time, rattled the windows.

"Jade and I have talked about it. She has a house on Lanai. It's completely private. Leave him, Georgie. Go there for a couple of weeks to relax and then . . ." He held up his hand, even though she hadn't said a word. "Hear me out, will you? I know it's going to seem strange at first, but promise you'll listen."

She stared at him. "I wouldn't miss this for the world."

"I think we've found a way to turn what happened between the three of us into something good. Something really extraordinary that will put the polish back on your reputation."

"I didn't know my reputation needed polishing."

"Let's just say that it'll make people forget you ever married Bram Shepard." He tugged on the bracelet again. "You and Jade and I . . . We have a chance to do something good. Something that will . . . set an example for the whole world. Promise that you won't say no until you've given it serious thought. That's all I'm asking."

"The suspense is killing me."

"We—Jade and I—want you to come with us when we go back to Thailand."

Thunder shook the house. "Come with you?"

"I know it sounds crazy. At first I thought so, too. But the more we talked about it, the more we both understood that we've been given a golden opportunity. We have the chance to show the world in a big way how people who are supposed to be enemies can live together in peace and harmony."

Georgie didn't know whether to throw up or grab a Coke.

Rain slashed at the windows. "The press will go crazy," he said. "You'll look like a saint—everyone will forget about your crazy marriage. The causes that Jade and I are fighting for—good causes—will get more attention. But best of all, people all over the world will be forced to examine their own personal feuds and religious vendettas. Maybe we can't change the world, but we can make a start."

"I'm . . . speechless."

The doors flew open and everyone on the veranda spilled inside. Obviously Bram and Meg hadn't shared the news of Lance's appearance because, one by one, they all stopped talking and stared. Finally Rory broke the silence. "You guys throw one hell of an interesting party."

"I'll say." Laura couldn't take her eyes off Lance, who'd broken into a smile at the sight of Paul.

"Paul, it's great to see you again." He strode across the room, hand outstretched. "I've missed you."

"Lance."

Georgie found it shocking that Paul merely shook her ex's hand instead of falling on his knees and begging Lance to take her back. But then, he'd probably already done that.

A flush-faced Chaz came in from the kitchen carrying a tray of mugs and a plate of what looked like homemade chocolate truffles. Aaron followed with a coffeepot. Chaz couldn't take her eyes off Lance and nearly tripped on the rug before she set the tray down. "Th-there's somebody in the car outside," she said.

"It's Jade," Lance said. "I'd better go."

"You brought Jade here?" A swarm of bees buzzed through Georgie's head.

"I told you," Lance said. "I came right from the plane. And the car windows are dark. No one can see inside."

A thick silence fell over the room until Bram ambled forward. "Shame on you, Lancelot, for making your wife stay in the car." His eyes narrowed dangerously. "Grab an umbrella for me, Chaz, so I can invite her in."

Georgie froze. Surely she'd misheard. But she hadn't. Bram was angry and reacting in his typical bullheaded, impulsive way.

Paul leapt forward. "Stop right there."

Bram's jaw set in a stubborn line. "It's a party. The more the merrier."

She hated him, but she was supposed to love him, and with so many witnesses, she couldn't let them see how she really felt. Instead, she had to show how a happily remarried funny girl would react to meeting the woman who'd stolen her idiotic ex-husband. "Chaz, while you're getting Bram's umbrella, grab a gun so I can kill myself."

It was the right thing to say because Rory grinned. "This is the best party I've been to in years."

"Ever!" Laura exclaimed.

"Fluff your hair," Meg said to Georgie as Bram and Chaz disappeared, with Lance trailing behind. "And put on more lipstick. Quick."

"Don't you dare." Rory's hand shot out. "You're fine just the way you are."

"Rory's right," her kiss-up agent said. "Jade Gentry doesn't have a thing on you."

Meg rolled her eyes. "Except the most beautiful face in the universe, a body to die for, and Georgie's ex-husband."

"No, really," Georgie retorted as she sank down on the couch. "All I need is a gun."

Paul hurried forward. "Come with me, Georgie. You're not doing this."

Her father's ill-timed order made her determined to do exactly the opposite. "Sure I am. Jade's not important to me." A lie. Just because Georgie had stopped loving Lance didn't mean she'd ever forgive either him or Jade. She wanted revenge.

Moments later, Jade entered her living room while an invisible klieg light seemed to illuminate her stunning presence. Why did Jade have to be so exquisite? It was ironic . . . Most male movie stars looked better in person, but female stars tended to look vaguely encephalitic with heads too big for their sticklike bodies. Not Jade. She was even more breathtaking in person, an exquisite throwback to old Hollywood with Audrey Hepburn's doe eyes, Katharine Hepburn's cheekbones, and creamy Grace Kelly skin. A shiny sweep of straight dark hair framed a perfect valentine face without even a dab of makeup. Her breasts were generous but not vulgar. Her waist small and legs long. She wasn't as tall as Georgie, but she carried herself with such commanding confidence that Georgie had to talk herself out of feeling as though she'd started to shrink.

Lance stood on Jade's left and Bram on her right. As Paul stepped forward to greet Jade, he blocked her view of Georgie. Who knew whether it was deliberate or accidental? "I'm Paul York. I understand you just got off a plane."

"It seems like we've been traveling forever." Like Lance, she was rumpled, but her straight-legged black slacks and sleeveless black top still looked chic. Nothing about her signaled a woman who'd lost a baby less than a month ago. She shifted her weight, trying to see around Paul. She undoubtedly wanted to find Georgie so she could give her a big freaking hug. Fortunately, her cell rang before that could happen. "I need to take this. A couple of our people were deathly ill on the plane."

She slid her hobo bag off her shoulder, pulled out her phone, and stepped away from them. Laura filled a coffee mug, and Meg swiped a chocolate truffle. Bram drifted toward Georgie. She hoped he didn't get too close because she'd never be able to resist the temptation to kick him.

Rory did her best to ease the tension. "Laura, I hear you've been pushing Georgie for the lead in Rich Greenberg's project? It's a cute script. I wish we'd had a shot at it."

"The movie about the bimbo vampire?" Meg wrinkled her nose. "Mom was talking about it."

"Georgie's perfect for the part," Paul said.

"Georgie's not interested," Bram said. "She's tired of doing comedy."

He was right, but Georgie was angry and not the only immature person in this marriage. "Laura's set up a meeting for me with Greenberg."

Jade was growing agitated, although none of them could make out more than a few words. Finally, she snapped her phone shut and returned to Lance's side, her perfect brow knit in distress. "Bad news about Dari and Ellen. Remember that outbreak of SARS in the Philippines? The doctors are afraid they both might have it."

"SARS? My God . . ." Lance took her hand, the two of them against the world. "Are they going to be okay?"

"I don't know. They're in isolation right now, being shot full of antibiotics."

"We'd better get over to the hospital right away."

"That's not possible."

"Sure it is. We'll go in through the back."

"That's not the problem." She shoved the phone back in her purse and flipped her hair over her shoulder. "We can't go anywhere."

Lance stroked her fingers. "What do you mean?"

"That was the head of the county public health department on the phone. The hospital alerted him. Ellen's and Dari's test results won't be back for forty-eight hours, and until they know for sure whether or not it's SARS, everybody who was on the plane is under quarantine." She looked around the room. "Along with anyone we've come into contact with since."

Dead silence fell. Georgie felt dizzy, and Bram went still at her side.

"You don't mean us," Paul finally said.

"I'm afraid so."

Bram didn't move. "Are you saying we're all supposed to stay here—in my house—for the next two days? We've barely had any contact with either of you."

"Until Tuesday morning," she said tightly. "Ironic, isn't it?" Her gaze drifted to Georgie.

"Impossible," Laura said. "I have back-to-back meetings on Monday."

Meg frowned. "Mom and I are going riding tomorrow."

"If I have to be quarantined, I'm doing it in my own house." Rory glanced around for her purse. "I'll go out through the back gate."

"You'd better clear it with Public Health first," Jade said. "These guys mean business. I'm sure you'd have to send your staff away first."

Rory paused in her search for her purse, apparently remembering the filmmakers she was housing.

Chaz had taken the coffeepot from Aaron and turned to Bram. "What's SARS? I don't know what that is."

Aaron answered for him. "Severe acute respiratory syndrome. It's a serious disease. Very contagious. There was a pandemic a few years ago that killed hundreds of people and made thousands sick. A pandemic is like an epidemic, except a lot bigger."

"I know what a pandemic is," Chaz retorted so defensively Georgie knew she was lying.

"This is bullshit," Bram said. "Lance hasn't even been in the house fifteen minutes. And, god knows, nobody kissed him."

Jade flipped her hair over her shoulder. "I explained that to Public Health, but they won't budge."

Laura whipped out her cell. "Give me the number. I'll make them budge."

But she wasn't the only alpha dog in the room, and the others—Bram, Paul, and Rory—already had their hands on their own phones. Aaron took one look at Georgie and grabbed his, too. Lance glanced around. "Everybody can't call."

"I'll do it," Rory said. "I have contacts."

For the next half hour while Georgie sat silently, the rest of them listened in on Rory's conversations as she spoke to officials in the county's Public Health Department and then the mayor himself. Finally, she conceded defeat. "Pulling strings isn't going to work. This is political. Because celebrities are involved, nobody wants to be held responsible if this thing gets out of hand. It's definitely overkill, but it seems as though we're trapped."

People began looking in Georgie's direction, judging her reaction to being cooped up with her ex and his new wife. Scooter Brown would have known how to handle this. Scooter always came through in tough situations. *Fine.* Let that perky little bitch deal with it.

She pushed Scooter up from the couch. "We'll make the best of it. Like a big house party. It'll be fun."

Chaz plunged into the mess. "I have a ton of food in the freezer, so that's not a problem."

"I need a drink," Bram said.

"Of course you do," Georgie snapped before she could stop herself, which meant Scooter had to jump in and rescue her. "A great idea, sweetie. Open a couple of bottles."

Chaz turned to Bram. "Where's everybody going to sleep?"

Georgie should suggest Paul share a room with Lance. He'd love cozying up to his favorite person.

Gradually they sorted it out. Meg insisted on taking the couch in Bram's office, leaving the guesthouse bed to Rory and Laura. Paul would sleep in Georgie's office. The guest room where Georgie had been sleeping went to Lance and Jade, which forced Georgie to explain that she'd been using it as her dressing room and would need to get some of her things out first. In a whispered argument, Chaz begrudgingly agreed to let Aaron sleep in her living room. That left Georgie cuddled up in her husband's bed. It was such an unsettling prospect that Scooter once again had to come to Georgie's aid. "I think the wind is calming down," she chirped. "Let's light a fire on the veranda. We could even make s'mores."

"Or not," Skip drawled.

Rory phoned her housekeeper and arranged for some personal items to be placed in a rainproof bag by the back gate. Meg lent Laura a roomy sleeping shirt. Jade announced that she slept nude so Georgie didn't need to bother finding her anything. Chaz and Aaron distributed towels, washcloths, extra bedding, and toothbrushes. All the while Georgie struggled with a sense of unreality.

After the worst of the storm passed, Meg led Rory and Laura to the guesthouse while Bram made his way through the remaining sprinkles to retrieve Rory's things. Her father poured a brandy and went out to sit on the veranda. Lance and Jade wanted to clean up after their long trip, and Aaron led them upstairs.

Georgie began helping an unappreciative Chaz pick up. Before long, she heard the shower go on in her bathroom and—twenty minutes later—turn off.

One shower. How cozy.

Her stomach churned. Having Lance here was horrible enough, but Jade's presence made the situation unbearable. And it was all Bram's fault.

She closed herself in his bedroom. She'd make the turret that occupied the far end of the room her sanctuary. An inlaid wooden table sat between a pair of easy chairs, and a lamp with a heavy bronze base rested near a chaise upholstered in a nappy chocolate brown chenille that complemented the buckwheat-honey walls. The chaise could only hold one person, and that's where she'd sleep. Bram's bed was for sex, not all-night intimacy.

She walked over to the window and gazed down along the rain-slicked driveway toward the gates. Even though it was after midnight, she could see at least two cars still parked on the street, the paps keeping their eternal vigil and praying for the magic shot that would bring them their fortune.

Public Health now had the names of everyone who'd been quarantined, so the story would leak quickly. They'd all have to release statements. *Old problems forgotten. One big happy family.* Lance would finally get what he wanted—the appearance of her forgiveness and final absolution in the public eye.

She rested her cheek against the window frame and wondered what it would be like to go through life always speaking the truth. But she lived in the wrong town for that. This was a city built on illusion, on false fronts and streets that led nowhere.

The door opened behind her. She heard the inevitable clink of ice cubes and caught the scent of rain as he came nearer. "I didn't mean it to turn out like this when I invited her inside. I'm sorry."

His unsolicited apology took some of the wind out of her sails. "Exactly how did you expect it to turn out?"

"Look, I was pissed." He kept his voice down in deference to the single wall separating them from their unwelcome visitors in the next room. "Where does that guy get off showing up here? Then the whole idea of Jade sitting in the car feeling sorry for you because she figures you're so destroyed by their great love affair that you don't have enough backbone to look her in the fucking eye. It got to me."

Put like that . . . Still, his high-handedness felt too much like her father's. "It wasn't your decision to make."

"You weren't going to make it." He tugged at the buttons on his damp white shirt. "I'm sick of watching you wimp out whenever her name comes up. Where's your pride? Stop believing she's better than you."

"I don't—"

"Yes, you do. Jade may be better at some things. She sure as hell is better at going after another woman's husband. But what Jade is or isn't has nothing to do with you. Grow up and start being happy living in your own skin."

"You're talking to me about growing up?"

He wasn't done ripping on her. "Jade and Lance were made for each other. He was no more the right man for you than . . ."

"Than you are?"

"Exactly." He took a long swig from his glass.

"Thanks for your insightful input." She snatched the robe and nightgown she'd fetched earlier and stomped into the bathroom to change. But as she washed her face, she had to admit Bram's heart had been in the right place. Inviting Jade into the house had been his twisted version of being protective. He couldn't have predicted the consequences.

When she came out, she found him propped against the pillows, wearing only a pair of knit boxer briefs that gleamed white against his skin. He'd kicked the covers back, and he had a book propped open on his chest. Seeing Bram Shepard reading a book looked weird enough, but not as weird as the pair of steel-rimmed glasses anchored to the bridge of his nose. She stopped dead. "What are those?"

"What?"

"You're wearing glasses?"

"Just for reading."

"You have *reading* glasses?"

"What's wrong with that?"

"People with tattoos shouldn't have reading glasses."

"I didn't have them when I got the tattoo." He slipped off the glasses and took in her T-shirt and blue pajama bottoms. "I was kind of hoping you'd be wearing one of those numbers from Provocative."

"Even if I were in the mood, which I'm definitely not, I wouldn't do it with them on the other side of this wall."

"I see your point." He got out of bed and pulled her across the carpet to the bathroom, where he shut the door and sealed them inside. "No more problem."

"I'm still furious with you."

"I understand. It's only because I haven't made a sincere-enough apology." And he started to kiss her.

Chapter 18

George hated movies where all the hero had to do to make the heroine forget she was mad at him was to kiss her senseless. She had no intention of putting her grievances aside that easily, just as she had no intention of giving up this welcome diversion. Instead, she poured her frustration into the kiss. She dug her fingernails into his bare shoulders and sank her teeth into his lip. She pushed her knee against . . .

"Hey, watch it," he muttered.

"Shut up and earn your keep."

He didn't like that, and the next thing she knew, her pajama bottoms were around her ankles. She lifted her knee again, but he caught it, and in one motion, pushed that same knee far apart from its mate and set her hips on the long granite counter.

This was all he was good for. She snagged the waistband of his boxer briefs, but she couldn't pull them off by herself. He released her to complete the job, and she dropped down off the counter. He kicked aside his briefs and set her back up. She squirmed away and headed for the glass block shower with its copper granite walls and multiple jets. Turning lovemaking into a power struggle was hardly the most mature way to handle a difficult relationship, but it was all she had right now.

"On second thought . . ." He stepped in with her.

She whipped her top over her head. "Turn the water on hard."

He didn't have to be asked twice, and within moments, the hot spray pounded their bodies.

Two people. One shower. She wanted Lance to hear.

And then Bram began rubbing her with soap, and she forgot all about Lance. Breasts, hips, thighs. Bram attended to everything. She took the soap from him and left her own slick swirls on his body.

"You're killing me." He groaned.

"If only." She moved her hand to the place where it would have the most effect.

The water streamed over their bodies. He went to his knees and loved her with his mouth. Just as she was ready to fall apart, he set her against the hard wet walls and lifted her upon him. She clung to his shoulders and buried her face in his neck. They gasped and moved together, riding the flood to its crest.

"Don't talk to me," she said afterward. "I paid good money for that, and I don't want it spoiled."

He bit the side of her neck. "Mum's the word."

Despite her earlier resolution, she ended up in his bed, tossing and turning while he slept peacefully—except during a second bout of lovemaking that she might possibly have initiated, but only to cure her insomnia. Afterward, he had no trouble falling back to sleep, but she wasn't so lucky. She crept out of bed and carried his unfinished tumbler of scotch to the turret, where she sat in one of the deep, comfortable chairs and gazed at the shadowy patterns on the walls. She didn't like hard liquor, but the ice had long since watered it down, so she took a big swallow and braced herself for the hit to her stomach.

Something hit . . . but it wasn't scotch.

She sniffed the glass and flicked on a table lamp. The remaining liquid had the faint brownish tinge of diluted alcohol, but not the taste. Slowly, it dawned on her . . . Bram and his bottomless tumblers of scotch . . . No wonder he never seemed drunk. All this time he'd been swilling iced tea! He'd told her that's what he was drinking, but it had never occurred to her to believe him.

She rested her chin in her hands. One more vice down the drain. She didn't like it. Bram was supposed to be a creature of excesses. Without his vices, who was he? The answer wasn't long in coming. A more subtly dangerous version of the man he'd always been. A man who continued to prove that nothing he said, nothing he did, could be trusted.

Chaz couldn't sleep. So much to do. So many people to take care of. The cleaning staff couldn't come in because of the quarantine so she'd have to take care of everything. Meals to prepare, beds to make, towels to wash. Georgie would try to help, but Chaz doubted she knew what a washing machine looked like, let alone how to use one.

Chaz got up to pee. Usually she slept in a T-shirt and panties, but tonight she'd added sweatpants. When she was done in the bathroom, she looked in on Aaron. Having a guy in her apartment should have freaked her out, but not when it was Aaron. She liked that he was a little bit scared of her, especially because he was older and so smart. Life would have been a lot easier if she'd had a brother like Aaron. She used to want a big brother more than anything, someone who'd always look out for her.

She'd been too busy to obsess over how much she'd told Georgie, but as she stood in the doorway with everything quiet around her, she realized she didn't feel as panicked as maybe she should. Georgie was like her worst enemy, but even Georgie hadn't said Chaz was a horrible person. And if her worst enemy hadn't looked at her like she was dirt, maybe Chaz shouldn't look at herself that way. One thing was for sure. She couldn't lie about her past anymore or pretend it hadn't happened, not after she'd blabbed the truth into the camera. For all Chaz knew, Georgie would put that video up on YouTube.

So what if she did?

Chaz stood there for a long time, thinking about everything she'd gone through. She'd survived, hadn't she? She was still alive and she had this great job. If anybody turned their nose up, that was their problem, not hers. All this time, she'd tried to pretend the past hadn't happened, but it had happened, and she must have been ready to stop hiding it or she wouldn't have kept talking to Georgie.

She glanced toward the bookcase where she'd stashed the unopened GED workbooks Bram had gotten her. He'd told her lots of people went on to college with only a GED. He'd done it himself, although hardly anybody knew about the classes he'd taken over the years. Chaz didn't care about going to college, but she did care about culinary school, and she needed a GED to get in.

She must have been making more noise than she thought because Aaron began to stir. She wished he'd stop being so stubborn. If he'd just listen to her, she was sure she could get Becky to like him.

"What do you want?" he grumbled.

She headed for the bookcase. "I couldn't sleep. I need something to read."

"Get it and go away."

She liked that he'd started talking like a real person instead of a geek. "It's my place."

"Just go to sleep, will you?"

Instead of getting a book, she settled in the chair across from him and pulled her bare feet up on the edge of the seat. "What if we get SARS?"

"That's highly unlikely." He sat up, yawned, and rubbed one eye. Other than kicking off his shoes, he was still wearing all his clothes. "I guess it wouldn't hurt to sterilize the dishes Lance and Jade use."

She wrapped her arms around her knees. "I can't believe Lance Marks and Jade Gentry are in the house." Aaron put on his glasses and made his way toward her kitchen. She rose and followed him. "The only celebrity Bram ever invites over is Trevor. He's great and everything, but I want to meet more famous people than just him. I wish Meg's dad would show up sometime."

He got a glass of water. "What about Georgie?"

"Like I care about her."

"You're so damned jealous."

"I'm not jealous!" She turned toward the doorway. "I just think she should be nicer to Bram."

"He's the one who needs to be nicer to her. She's great, and he doesn't appreciate her."

"I'm going to bed. Don't eat my food."

"You think I can sleep after you woke me up?"

"That's your problem."

They ended up watching one of Trevor's movies. She'd already seen it three times, so she fell asleep against one arm of the couch.

In the morning when she woke up, she discovered Aaron asleep at the other end. For a moment she just lay there and thought about how nice it was to feel safe.

Georgie couldn't cope with facing the morning, so when Bram, her nonalcoholic husband, got up, she kept her face buried in the pillow. He cracked open one of the balcony doors to let in the morning air, but even when he patted her butt, she didn't stir. Why rush a day that promised to be memorable in its awfulness?

He left the bedroom, and she dozed off, but hardly any time seemed to have elapsed before he came back. "Do you need to make so much noise?" she grumbled into her pillow. "I like my men sexy and silent, re-member?"

"Georgie?"

That tentative voice didn't belong to Bram. It didn't belong to a man at all. Georgie's eyes flew open. She twisted and saw Jade Gentry standing just inside the open balcony door. She wore yesterday's sleeveless black top and slacks, but somehow she still looked refreshed, even elegant. She'd gathered her smooth, straight hair into a casual knot at the nape of her neck and applied dusky eye makeup and pale mocha lip gloss. Her understated jewelry consisted of silver hoops and a simple silver wedding band. "It's eight-thirty," Jade said. "I assumed you'd be awake by now."

Georgie blinked against the sun and slipped her left hand with its impressive diamond out from under the sheet. "Not to be impolite, Jade, but get the hell out of here."

"You need to have this conversation."

"Wrong." Georgie yanked the sheet free and wrapped it around her naked body. "I don't want a conversation with either one of you."

Jade's eyes fastened on Georgie's neck. "We're stuck together for the next two days. It'll make things less awkward if you and I clear the air privately before we go downstairs."

"Awkwardness doesn't bother me at all." She bunched the sheet between her breasts just as Lance came in through the balcony door.

"Jade? What are you doing?" he said.

"I was hoping to talk to Georgie alone," Jade replied calmly. "She has other ideas."

"Like throwing both your asses over that balcony!"

Lance slipped his arm through his wife's. "Georgie, give Jade a chance."

Georgie grabbed another fistful of sheet and stalked toward them, doing her best not to trip. "I already gave Jade a husband. And my apologies for that, by the way."

"Kinky," Bram said from the doorway that opened into the hall. "Do I get to play, too?"

"Throw them out of here," Georgie ordered, gripping the sheet tighter. "I'd do it, but I only have one free hand."

Bram shrugged. "Okay."

"Stop." Jade held out her arm. "You and I need to be the reasonable people here, Bram. All I wanted to do was talk to Georgie without everybody listening in. She's a good person. I want to apologize for hurting her. I know that will help her let go of her animosity so she can heal."

"How generous," he said. "I'm sure Georgie's healing would make you both feel a lot better."

"Don't attack Jade." Lance flexed some muscle. "Georgie, you've always been sensible. Jade needs to do this—I need to do it—so everyone can move on." His gaze went to her neck.

Bram lifted an eyebrow. "I have to admit you two clowns have raised my curiosity. Georgie, aren't you the least bit interested in hearing what they have to say?"

"I already heard what one of those clowns had to say last night, but it turns out I don't want to end our marriage and set off to Thailand for a gigantic photo op with the two of them."

"You're kidding."

"It's not the way she's making it sound," Jade said quickly. "Lance and I are talking about a humanitarian trip. Georgie, we all need to start thinking globally instead of personally."

"I'm not that spiritually advanced."

"Me either," Bram said. "Besides, Georgie and I already have a trip planned. To Haiti. We're delivering medical supplies."

Jade looked genuinely excited. "Really? That's great. Anything I can do to help, just let me know."

"Start by getting out of my bedroom," Georgie said.

Jade looked gorgeous and hurt. "I think you're a wonderful person, Georgie, and I'm sorry you've been so badly hurt."

"I'm not hurt, you bozos. I'm furious."

"I recognize your right to be angry, Georgie. I know what Lance and I are suggesting is crazy, but let's do it anyway. Just for the hell of it. Let's show the world that women are more sensible than men."

"I'm not more sensible! You and my ex-husband had an affair behind my back, he lied to the press about me, and now you want me to go off on some kind of altruistic ménage à trois? I don't think so."

Jade's doe eyes melted into bottomless pools of sadness. "I told Lance you were too self-focused to consider it."

"Well, I think that does it." Bram shoved the balcony doors open. "It's been a great visit, but Georgie has to go throw up now."

This time Lance and Jade didn't argue.

"Fun couple," Bram said as he flipped the lock on the doors behind them. "A little intense, but still a barrel of laughs."

Georgie headed for the bathroom. "And here I am, naked under this sheet, my hair sticking out all over my head. I haven't even brushed my teeth. Jade can get the best of me without even trying."

"I should have been more sensitive toward your pathetic self-esteem issues," Bram said, following her. "I'm going to punish myself by taking you back to bed and working extra hard to be the man of your sexual fantasies."

"Or not." She caught sight of her reflection in the mirror. No wonder they were staring at her neck. She had a giant sucker bite. She touched it with the tip of her finger. "Thanks a lot."

He slid his own finger over the slope of her shoulder. "I wanted to make sure Lance didn't forget who you belong to."

She grabbed her toothbrush. Women weren't property, especially this woman. Still, it was nice of him to have thought ahead. What she didn't find so nice was her discovery that he had one fewer vice than he'd led her to believe, something she'd have to confront him about very soon.

He handed her the toothpaste. "Last night when I went outside to get Jade, she was already walking toward the front door, talking on her cell. I can't prove it, but I think she was discussing the quarantine with someone."

"Before she came in?" Georgie said around a mouthful of toothpaste. "But that doesn't make sense. If she already knew about the quarantine, why would she let herself get stuck here?"

"Maybe because she didn't trust her husband to be holed up with his still-sexy ex-wife for two days?"

"Really?" She smiled and spit. "Cool."

"You'll tell me, won't you, when you're ready to stop obsessing over the two of them and start living your real life."

She rinsed out her mouth. "This is L.A., so real life is an illusion."

"Bram!" Chaz yelled from the bottom of the stairs. "Bram, come quick! There's a snake in the swimming pool. You have to get it out!"

Bram shuddered. "I'm going to pretend I didn't hear that."

"You should make Lance and Jade do it." Georgie docked her toothbrush. "It's probably one of their relatives."

"Bram!" Chaz called out. "Hurry!"

Georgie ended up pulling a robe around herself and following him out to the pool, where a rattlesnake had climbed up on a kickboard floating in the water. It wasn't a big rattler, maybe two feet long, but it was still a poisonous snake and one that didn't like the water.

Chaz's yelling had alerted the other houseguests. As Lance and Jade appeared, Bram picked up the leaf skimmer and held it out. "Here you go, Lancelot. Impress the women."

"I'll pass."

"Don't look at me," Jade said. "I'm phobic."

"I hate snakes." Chaz made a face.

Georgie extended her hand toward Bram. "Oh, give it here. I'll do it."

"Good girl." Bram passed over the leaf skimmer.

As Georgie took it, Laura appeared, followed by Rory, who flipped her cell closed and dashed to the rim of the pool, the heels of her very expensive Gucci sandals clicking on the deck. "It that a rattler?"

"It sure is." Bram glanced at Rory, then held out his hand to Georgie. "Honey, what are you doing? Give me that. No way am I letting you go after a dangerous rattlesnake."

She suppressed a smile and handed back the swimmer. Bram gritted his teeth and gingerly extended it across the pool. Meg and Paul appeared and watched the process, with Meg occasionally throwing out advice. The snake hissed and coiled but Bram eventually managed to knock it off the kickboard into the skimmer. A patch of flop sweat had formed between his shoulder blades as he carted the extended skimmer to the very back of his property and flipped the snake over the stone wall.

"Great," Rory said. "Now it can crawl back into my yard as soon as it's full grown."

"You let me know if it does," Bram said. "I'll come right over and take care of it for you."

"You should have killed it," Lance said.

"Why?" Meg retorted. "Because it acted like a snake?"

Georgie realized she needed to clarify something, and with Rory standing there, she might as well do it now, however awkward it might be. "You know, Rory . . . Those drinks Bram's always carrying around. It's iced tea."

Bram looked at her as though she'd lost her mind, as did the others. "Just so everyone understands you're not a drunk anymore," she said lamely. "You stopped smoking cigarettes five years ago, and the oregano in the kitchen is really oregano. As for drugs . . . I've found some Flintstone vitamins and Tylenol, but—"

"I don't take Flintstone vitamins!"

"One A Day. Whatever. If people know you're not such a badass anymore, they might stop treating me like I was crazy for marrying you." And, she thought, Rory might be more willing to get behind *Tree House*. Her newly calculating brain ticked away.

Bram finally climbed on board. "You *were* crazy to marry me, but I'm glad."

They did a little marital cuddle, although she could tell from the tight furrow between his brows that he wasn't happy with her. "My hero." She patted his chest.

"You're too good to me, sweetheart."

Laura asked Lance and Jade the question that should have been at the forefront of all their minds. "How are you two? Any symptoms?"

"Jet-lagged, but otherwise healthy," Jade said.

Rory flicked open her cell. "Give me a list of whatever any of you need. One of my assistants will get it all together and put it by the back gate."

Lance clapped Paul on the shoulder. "It's great to see you again. We finally have a chance to catch up."

Georgie didn't have the stomach for this reunion, and she began to move away, only to be stopped by her father's reply. "I'm afraid I don't have much to say to you these days, Lance."

Lance didn't seem to know how to respond. "Paul . . . This has been hard on everyone, but . . ."

"Has it?" her father said. "The way I see it, it's mainly been hard on Georgie. You seem to be doing just fine."

Lance looked stricken, and Jade's forehead crinkled. Georgie was touched. "Go ahead, Dad. I don't mind."

"I mind," he said and walked away.

The corner of Bram's mouth curled. "I don't understand it. Dad was in such a good mood last night when the two of us made plans to go fishing."

Georgie studied him. Since when had Bram Shepard become a person she could count on? As for her father . . . Had he snubbed Lance out of respect for her or only to salve his own pride?

She took extra time with her hair and makeup, but dressed in jeans and a plain white T-shirt so she didn't look as though she were trying too hard. When she came downstairs, she found her houseguests on their cells nibbling an assortment of cereals and muffins. Chaz stood at the stove, making eggs by request, and Lance mouthed that he'd like two scrambled egg whites. Next to him, Jade interrupted her phone conversation to order up hot water for herbal tea. A helicopter buzzed overhead. Georgie saw Paul through the French doors talking to someone on his cell. Laura sat in the dining room with a notepad, her phone to her ear. At the kitchen table, Rory furiously scribbled a note to herself in the margin of the *Los Angeles Times* front page, while Meg, perched on a counter stool, was doing her best to reassure her mother that she was all right.

Bram carried a case of bottled water in from the garage. He looked up at the ceiling as the sound of a second helicopter joined the first and began to circle. "There's no business like show business."

Word had leaked out even more quickly than she'd expected. Georgie imagined a photographer hanging off the skids, his telephoto lens pointed at their house, willing to risk his life to get that first picture of her with Lance and Jade. What would a photo like that bring? Six figures for sure.

She filled a coffee mug and slipped outside into the shelter of the veranda. The whirl of helicopter blades was louder here. Her father, leaning against one of the twisted columns, saw her approach and ended his phone conversation. They studied each other. His eyes looked tired behind his rimless glasses. Maybe things had been easier between them when she was little, but she didn't remember it that way. Still, he'd been a twenty-five-year-old widower left to raise a daughter alone. She cradled her coffee mug. "Are you still signing autographs for Richard Gere?"

"I signed one just yesterday."

He'd started getting requests when his hair had gone silver. At first, he'd tried to explain that he wasn't Gere, but people hadn't always believed him, and some had even made comments about stuck-up movie stars. Paul eventually decided he wasn't doing Gere any favors by pissing off his fans, so he'd started signing. "I'll bet it was a woman," Georgie said, "and I'll bet she loved you in *An Officer and a Gentleman*. People need to get over that. It wasn't your best film."

"True. They conveniently forget about *Unfaithful* and *The Hoax*."

"What about *Chicago?*"

"Or *Primal Fear.*"

"Nope. Ed Norton stole that one from you."

He smiled, and they both fell silent, neutral territory exhausted. She set her coffee on one of the tile tables and made herself act like a grown-up. "I appreciate what you said to Lance earlier, but the two of you had your own relationship. It wouldn't be right for me to spoil that."

"Do you really think I'm going to pal around with him after what he did to you?"

Of course not. Her father cared too much about her image to be seen with Lance Marks.

A jagged ray of sunlight cut a silver blaze across his hair. "You delivered a moving defense of Bram earlier," he said, "but I doubt anyone believed it. What are you doing with him, Georgie? Explain it to me so I can understand. Explain how you could instantly fall in love with a man you detested. A man who's—"

"He's my husband. I don't want to hear any more."

But the gloves were off, and he came closer. "I hoped by now you'd have finally figured out the kind of man you belong with."

"What do you mean, 'finally.' I already figured it out, remember? And that marriage wasn't exactly a rousing success."

"Lance was never the right man for you."

It was the helicopters. They were making so much noise they'd distorted his words. "Excuse me?"

He turned away from her. "I supported you with Lance, even though I knew he'd never make you happy, but I'm not doing it again. I'll say the right things in public, but privately I'm going to speak my mind. I don't have the stomach to start up the pretend game with you again."

"Wait a minute! What are you talking about? You introduced me to Lance. You loved him."

"Not as your husband. But you wouldn't hear a word of criticism."

"You never said you didn't like him, just that he didn't have as many dimensions as I did, once again implying that I need to be more focused."

"That's not what I meant at all. Georgie, Lance is a decent actor—he's found his niche, and he's smart enough to stick to it. But he's never had a personal identity of his own. He relies on the people around him to define who he is. Until he met you, he'd hardly read at all. You're the one who got him interested in music, dance, art—even current events. The way he absorbs other people's personalities helps make him a good actor, but it doesn't make him a good husband."

This was virtually the same thing Bram had said.

"I could never stomach the way you acted around him," he went on, "as though you were grateful he'd chosen you when it should have been the other way around. He fed off that. He fed off you—your sense of humor, your curiosity, how easy you are with people. Those things don't come naturally to him."

"I can't believe . . . Why didn't you say something? Why didn't you tell me how you felt about him?"

"Because every time I tried, your back went up. You worshipped him, and nothing I said was going to change that. We had enough tension over your career. What would criticizing him have accomplished except to make you resent me even more?"

"You should have been honest. I always believed you cared more about him than you did about me."

"You like to think the worst of me."

"You blamed me for the divorce!"

"I never blamed you. But I do blame you for marrying Bramwell Shepard. Of all the stupid—"

"Stop. Don't say any more." She pressed her fingers to her temples. She felt upended. Was her father telling her the truth, or was he trying to rewrite history so he could preserve the illusion of his own omnipotence?

Phones were ringing inside, and she could hear the gate intercom buzzing. A third helicopter dropped down, lower than the other two. "This is crazy." She made a dismissive gesture with her hand. "We can . . . talk about it later."

Laura waited until Georgie disappeared to emerge from the back of the veranda. Paul looked as vulnerable as an invincible man of steel could look. He was such a mystery to her. So tightly controlled. She couldn't imagine him laughing at a great dirty joke, let alone being caught up in a colossal orgasm. She couldn't imagine him doing anything to excess.

He lived modestly by Hollywood standards. He drove a Lexus instead of a Bentley and owned a three-bedroom town house instead of a mansion. He had no personal staff, and he dated women his own age. What other fifty-two-year-old Hollywood male did that?

Over the years, she'd spent so much energy resenting him that she'd stopped thinking of him as anything more than a symbol of her ineffectiveness, but she'd just witnessed his Achilles' heel, and something inside her shifted. "Georgie's a terrific person, Paul."

"You think I don't know that?" He quickly reverted to his starchy self. "Is this how you've built your career? By eavesdropping?"

"It wasn't intentional," she said. "I came out here to see if I could get better cell reception, and I heard the two of you talking. I didn't want to interrupt."

"Or go back inside and leave us alone?"

"I got sucked in by your cluelessness. It temporarily paralyzed me." She caught her breath, unable to believe those words had come from her mouth. She wanted to chalk up her unguarded tongue to a sleepless night, but what if it was something more dangerous? What if all these years of self-disgust had finally eaten away at the last threads of her restraint?

He wasn't used to anything but her obsequiousness, and his eyebrows lifted. Her entire career depended on representing Georgie York, and she had to apologize quickly. "I just meant . . . You always seem so together. You're sure of your opinions, and you don't second-guess yourself." She took in his navy slacks and expensive polo shirt, and her apology began to go awry. "Just look at you. Those are the same clothes you had on last night, but you don't muss. You don't wrinkle. You're very intimidating."

If only he hadn't reared back on his heels and looked down his nose at her sadly wrinkled kimono top and wilted ivory slacks, she might have been able to stop herself. Instead, she said, much too loudly, "That was your daughter you were talking to. Your only child."

His fingers curled around the coffee cup Georgie had left behind. "I know who she is."

"I always thought my father was screwed up. He was lousy with money, and he couldn't hold a job, but a day never went by that he didn't give all us kids a hug and say how much he loved us."

"If you're suggesting I don't love my daughter, you're wrong. You're not a parent. You can't understand what it's like."

She had four wonderful nieces, so she had a fairly good idea what parental love involved, but she had to stop herself right now. Except her tongue seemed to have disconnected from her brain. "I don't get how you can be so distant with her. Can't you just act like a father?"

"Apparently you weren't eavesdropping hard enough or you'd know that's exactly what I was doing."

"By lecturing and criticizing? You don't approve of what she wants to do with her career. You don't like her taste in men. Exactly what do you like about her? Other than her earning power."

His face flushed with fury. She didn't know which of them was more shocked. She was ruining everything she'd taken so many years to build. She had to beg his forgiveness, but she was too sick of herself to find the right words.

"You just stepped way over the line," he said.

"I know. I'm— I shouldn't have said that."

"You're damned right you shouldn't have."

But instead of rushing away from him before she could do any more damage, her feet remained stubbornly in place. "I've never understood why you seem so disapproving of her. She's a terrific woman. She might not have the best taste in men, although I have to say Bram has been a pleasant surprise, but . . . She's warm and generous. How many actors do you know who try to make life easier for the people around them? She's smart as a whip, and interested in everything. If she were my daughter, I'd want to enjoy her instead of always behaving as though she needs to be made over."

"I have no idea what you're talking about." But she could see he understood exactly what she meant.

"Why don't you just have fun with her sometimes? Goof off. Do something that doesn't involve business. Play a card game, splash around in the pool."

"How about a trip to Disneyland?" he said caustically.

"How about it?" she tossed back.

"Georgie's thirty-one, not five."

"Did you do those things with her when she was five?"

"Her mother had just died, so I was a little preoccupied," he snapped.

"That must have been horrible."

"I was the best father I knew how to be."

She saw real pain in his eyes, but it didn't stir her compassion. "Here's what bothers me, Paul . . . If I don't understand how much you love her, how's she supposed to?"

"That's enough. More than enough. If this is all the respect you have for our professional relationship, then maybe we need to reassess where we are."

Her stomach twisted. She could still salvage this. She could plead illness, insanity, SARS . . . But she didn't do any of it. Instead, she squared her shoulders and stepped off the veranda.

Her heart pounded as she made her way back to the guesthouse. She thought about her killer mortgage, about what would happen to her reputation if she lost her star client, about how badly, how *catastrophically*, she'd screwed up. So why didn't she run back and apologize?

Because a good agent—a great agent—served her client well, and for the first time, Laura felt as though she'd done exactly that.

Chapter 19

All day Bram watched the human chess game being played out in front of him as helicopters circled overhead. He observed Georgie doing her best to stay away from Lance, Jade, and her father, while Paul barely spoke to anyone. He saw Chaz pandering to Lance and Jade but remaining her customary pain in the ass to Georgie and Aaron. Meg helped out in the kitchen, sneered at Lance whenever he passed by, and acted as if Jade were invisible. Laura assumed the role of a nervous Switzerland, trying to move neutrally among all warring nations. And everybody sucked up to Rory, including himself.

With the possible exception of Chaz, Bram decided, he was the only one happy about the quarantine. He'd planned to pitch to Rory last night only to have Lance show up, but now he had the rest of the weekend to get her alone, and she couldn't keep avoiding him forever.

Between the helicopters and the snake incident, no one wanted to go in the pool. A few of them congregated in the kitchen, and he noticed Georgie beginning to mess around again with the video camera. Chaz started to bristle, and he quickly stepped in. "Georgie, why don't you practice your interviewing techniques on Laura? A female agent in the Hollywood shark pool and all that."

"I don't want to talk to Laura. I want to talk to Chaz again."

"Only because the housecleaners aren't here," Chaz sneered. "She *loves* talking to them."

It was unusual for him to feel like the only adult in the room. "How about interviewing Aaron then," he said with what seemed to him great reasonableness.

"I'm not interested in talking to men," Georgie snapped. "Fine. I'll interview you."

"Make him take off his clothes," Meg piped up from the kitchen table. "It'll spice things up."

"Great idea," he said. "Let's do it in the bedroom."

Georgie finally recalled her role of loving wife. "Don't tantalize me like that when we have company."

A series of semipornographic images flashed through his head. Who'd have figured Georgie would turn out to be such a firecracker? From the beginning, her sexual bossiness had turned him on. Unlike other women, she didn't give a damn about arousing him, and somehow that only aroused him more. The sex part of this phony marriage had turned out to be a lot more fun than he could have imagined. So much fun that he'd started to feel a little uneasy. He only had room for one person in his life, and that was himself. Chaz had been an accident.

By late afternoon, everyone's cell phones and PDAs were running out of power. Only Rory, who'd had a charger and a spare phone included in the package left by the gate, continued to work. Laura announced that being without a phone was making her hyperventilate, and she asked Georgie to sing, but there was no piano in the house, and Georgie declined. As much as he teased her about her Annie past, she was fun to listen to with her big voice and inexhaustible energy. Maybe he'd get a piano in here to surprise her.

Jade settled in his library with a book on international economics, Georgie disappeared with Aaron, and the others drifted off to the screening room. Bram headed out to his office with a glass of extra-strong iced tea, a less harmful addiction than his earlier ones.

He picked up the script his agent had sent over. With all the publicity from his marriage, he was seeing a few more scripts than he used to, but the parts hadn't changed: playboys, gigolos, an occasional drug dealer.

He couldn't remember the last time he'd seen something that wasn't a piece of crap, and after reading only a few pages, he realized this was no different. He wanted a cigarette, but he took a slug of iced tea instead, checked his e-mail, then headed back to the house so he could get down to the real work of the day.

Rory had moved her center of operations to a corner of the veranda. Even though it was Sunday, she'd been on her phone all afternoon, making and destroying careers, but now she was hunkered over her laptop. He wandered to the table where she was working and, without waiting for an invitation that wouldn't come, took the chair across from her.

"As much as I appreciate your hospitality," she said without looking up, "unless you want to talk about the weather, you're wasting your time."

"I guess that's better than wasting Vortex's money."

She looked up.

He extended his legs and settled back in the chair, playing it cool, even though his guts were in a knot. "You're one of the smartest women in town. But right now you're being stupid."

"It's usually best to begin a pitch with flattery."

"You don't need flattery. You know exactly how good you are. But your personal grudge against me is getting in the way of your normally excellent judgment."

"In your opinion."

"Caitlin Carter has gotten greedy. If you wait until my option expires, you're going to spend a lot more money for *Tree House* than you will now. How are you going to explain that to your board of directors?"

"I'll risk it. And you're the one who's being stupid. If you turn over *Tree House* now, without any restrictions, you're guaranteed a credit as associate producer—"

"Meaningless."

"—and you'll actually make money on your initial investment. But if you stay stubborn, you'll end up with nothing. I can get that picture made. What more do you want?"

"I want the picture that's in my head to get made." He fought to stay cool, but this meant too much, and he could feel himself losing it. "I want to play Danny Grimes. I want a guarantee Hank Peters will direct." He came out of his chair. "I want to be on the set every day making sure the script I'm delivering is the one that gets shot instead of some studio asshole stepping in and deciding he wants to add a fucking *car chase*."

"I wouldn't let that happen."

"You have a studio to run. You wouldn't even notice."

She rubbed her eyes. "Bram, you're asking too much. To put it bluntly, you're only known for three things: *Skip and Scooter,* a sex tape, and being an undependable party boy. I'm starting to believe Georgie when she says you've outgrown that last one, but you haven't scored big with anything since the show ended. Can you really imagine me going to my board and telling them I've entrusted a project like *Tree House* to you?"

"I have a fucking vision! Can't you understand that?" The veins in his neck throbbed. "I know exactly how this film should be made. What it should look like. How it should feel. I'm the *only* one who can deliver the movie you want. Is that so hard to understand?"

She gave him a long, steady gaze. "I'm sorry," she said softly. "I can't do it."

The genuine regret in her voice told him he'd finally reached the end of the road. He'd done everything he could to convince her, and he'd lost. He was shocked to realize his hands were shaking, but somehow he managed a shrug. He wasn't going to beg.

His office offered the only refuge in this overcrowded house, but as he turned away, a movement near the door caught his attention. It was Georgie. Even from fifteen feet away, he could see the concern in her furrowed brow and the pity in those green eyes.

She'd overheard every word. He hated that nearly as much as he hated losing his dream.

Dinner was torture. Lance kept trying to charm his way back into Paul's good graces, but Paul remained unresponsive. Jade launched into a powerful lecture about the child sex industry that left all of them depressed and guilty. Georgie barely spoke, Rory seemed preoccupied, and Laura kept darting anxious glances at Paul and Georgie. Bram'd be damned if he'd let Rory see she'd beaten him, so he forced himself to tease Meg, the only person at the table who didn't look as though she'd rather be anywhere else.

The helicopters finally flew away for the day. Chaz served a gooey caramel dessert so rich that only Georgie ate her entire portion, forking it down with a dogged determination Bram didn't entirely understand. Jade, who didn't seem to care much about food, left hers untouched and, when Chaz reappeared, ordered a quarter of an apple. Her demand must really have pissed off Georgie because she hopped up from the table and slipped into her Scooter Brown act. "It's barely eight o'clock. Let's all go into the living room. I have a special entertainment planned."

That was news to him. Bad news. All he wanted to do was escape.

"I'm not playing charades," Meg said. "Or any other game you actors like to play."

Laura and Rory looked pained, but Georgie wasn't giving up. "I have something a little more interesting in mind."

"Hold it right there," Bram said, determined to make sure Rory understood she hadn't gotten to him. "You promised you'd never let anybody see you dance naked except me."

"No dances," she replied, without missing a beat. "The last time I worked the pole I pulled a tendon."

Even Paul cracked a smile, and all the women laughed except Jade, but Bram had the feeling life weighed too heavily on her to take anything lightly. Lance immediately grew solemn in support of his wife. What a dick.

As everyone else cleared the table, Jade demanded Chaz make a second pot of mint tea because the first wasn't hot enough. He was getting the idea that Jade preferred directing her humanitarian instincts to the world at large while ignoring the people waiting on her. Eventually Georgie, still doing the chipper act, herded them into the living room and assigned seats, giving Bram the armchair by the fireplace. She pointed Rory toward the couch next to him and arranged the others in a fashion that might have made sense to her but not to anyone else. He wished like hell she'd consulted him before she began playing her little parlor games.

And then Aaron came in with a pile of scripts, and it all became clear.

Georgie handed the first script to him. "Surprise, honey."

He gazed down at the cover. It was *Tree House.* What did she think she was doing?

"Some of you may have heard by now that Bram has optioned Sarah Carter's *Tree House.*"

That caused more than a few heads to shoot up.

Georgie's hand dropped to his shoulder. "But as far as I know, he's never heard it read, so this afternoon I had Aaron make copies for us. With all this amazing talent in one place, I think we should give our host a treat, don't you?"

All this amazing talent in one place . . . And Rory Keene sitting next to him. Georgie had thrown the dice. She didn't want him to give up, even after the conversation she'd overheard. She'd arranged the ultimate audition for him.

And then he woke up.

She wasn't doing this for him. She was doing it for herself.

He saw exactly how she hoped this would play out. She knew Rory would snap up his option the moment it expired, and she intended to use tonight as a private audition to get the inside track on Helene.

A ballsy plan, he thought bitterly, even though it wouldn't work. Georgie didn't have it in her to play that part. She dug her fingers into his shoulder. "Honey, if you don't mind, I'll play casting director."

He had to hand it to her. She was doing exactly what he'd have done under the circumstances. So why did he feel so disappointed?

Because he was the selfish jerk, not her.

She began passing out scripts. "Bram, you'll read Danny Grimes, of course. Dad, why don't you take Frank, Danny's dying father? Lance, you're Ken, the abusive next-door neighbor. Playing the bad guy will be such a nice change for you. Jade, you read Marcie, Ken's doormat wife."

The most thankless role.

She held a script out to Laura. "Call on your inner child and read Izzy, their five-year-old. And Meg, you read Natalie, the home care nurse who's Danny's love interest, but don't get any ideas."

"I'm not an actress."

"Pretend."

He couldn't blame Georgie for wanting a shot at Helene. It was the kind of role that turned careers around. But Helene needed an actress like Jade, who'd cut her teeth on strong characters. Even in a cold read, Jade would be fantastic, something Georgie knew as well as he did, which was why she'd assigned Marcie to her.

Georgie took a straight chair at the opposite end of the living room. "Aaron's agreed to pick up the slack with the leftover male characters. I'll read the action and handle the female leftovers."

Helene was hardly a leftover. His confusion turned to shock as Georgie handed Rory a script. "You never get to have any fun. You read Helene."

"Me?"

"Try out your acting chops," she said with a bright smile.

"I don't think I have any."

"Who cares? This is just for fun."

He didn't get it. Why had she chickened out? He could come up with only one explanation, and something like panic tripped through him. She was giving him the audition instead of taking it for herself.

Damn it! He hadn't asked for this. She must have decided Rory would be more invested in the project if she read such a key part. Or, even more disturbing, maybe she wanted to keep the spotlight focused on him, instead of herself. Whatever her logic, Little Miss Scooter Brown was once again flying around sprinkling her goddamned fairy dust.

He started to sweat. She was so fucking stupid. When was she going to realize she needed to look out for herself? If she wanted to change the course of her career, she should be going after what she wanted and to hell with everybody else. He'd never have made this kind of sacrifice for her. But she didn't care. Because Georgie York was a fucking team player.

She crossed her legs. "Bram, talk a little bit about the script before we start, will you? Give everyone an idea of what you want from them."

He hadn't prepped, and he was shaken. If he blew it, he wouldn't get another chance, but he couldn't pull his thoughts together. "A few of you . . . Some of you have . . . uh . . . probably read the book. Most of you, probably. You know it's a—" He forced himself to get a grip. "It's a beautiful story. A beautiful script— maybe better than the book." The words began to come more easily. "Since this is a cold read for everyone, let it be what it is. Don't try to push your character beyond what you see on the page. Strip it down and read it naked. First . . ."

Georgie watched Bram from the other end of the living room. He'd gotten off to a bumpy start, but slowly his passion began to shine through. She stole a glance at Rory, but it was hard to decipher anything from her expression.

The idea for the script reading had come to her right after she'd overheard their conversation and seen the desperation Bram was working so hard to conceal. Two big obstacles lay in his way—his reputation for unreliability and his insistence on playing Danny Grimes. She couldn't do anything more about the first, but it occurred to her that she could give him a shot at the second. He'd either be able to pull off the character or he wouldn't, but at least he'd have a chance.

Everyone listened intently as he briefly described each character. Asking Rory to read Helene instead of taking the part herself had been wrenching, but this was Bram's project, and this needed to be his audition. Besides, on the remote chance her plan worked, Bram would owe her big-time, and she intended to make sure he paid up.

Still, she'd once again put the needs of a man ahead of her own, but witnessing Bram's passion for this project had given her a peephole into his soul. Right or wrong, this felt like the only path to take. She'd wait for another day to be ruthless.

They began to read, and it quickly became obvious that her ulterior motives had led to some serious miscasting. Jade couldn't resist adding a repressed anger to Marcie that wasn't on the page, turning her into a more formidable character than either Rory's stilted Helene or Meg's Natalie. Lance practically twirled a villain's mustache in the role of Ken, and Laura was an unconvincing five-year-old. Her father, on the other hand, was shockingly good as Danny's father. But not as good as Bram, who peeled his character down to its bones so that everyone in the room felt the mute suffering of a man wrongly convicted of one of society's most heinous crimes. A man who was doggedly trying not to see the same crime unfolding in the house next door.

They reached the last page. Danny Grimes stood over his father's grave with Natalie at his side.

NATALIE
The rain's stopped. It's going to be a nice day after all.

DANNY
(*Takes Natalie's hand*)
A good day to build a tree house. Let's get started.

Silence fell over the living room. One by one, they began closing their scripts.

Bram's eyes found hers, and she felt her mouth curve in a slow smile. His performance had been brilliant— quiet, desperate, inspired—completely unexpected. Once again, she'd sold him short.

Meg finally broke the silence. "Damn, Bram . . . Does anybody else know you can act?"

Laura blew her nose. "Son of a bitch." She gazed toward Paul, who was staring off into space.

"Good job, Bram," Lance said. "A little flat, but not bad for a first reading . . ."

"I thought it was brilliant," Jade said bluntly. "You've been wasting your talent on bullshit parts."

"Right." Lance jumped back in. "A really interesting performance."

Georgie gazed at her ex-husband. Bram and her father were right. Lance was like a . . . a giant block of tofu. He had no flavor of his own. Instead, he assumed the flavors of the people closest to him.

Laura still had her eyes on Paul, who abruptly left the room. Georgie was afraid to look at Rory until she heard a long, weary sigh. "All right, Bram . . . This is against my better judgment, but let's go someplace and talk."

Georgie gave a strangled yelp, but other than a small twitch at the corner of his mouth, Bram didn't exhibit anything except lazy confidence. "Sure. We can talk in my office."

"Well . . . well . . . ," Jade remarked as Rory and Bram disappeared.

"I'll say." Meg uncrossed her legs and rose from her perch on the floor. "I can't wait to tell Mom about this."

Lance drummed his fingers on his thigh, something he did when he was unhappy. Chaz came in from the kitchen, where she'd undoubtedly been eavesdropping, and asked if anyone wanted more coffee. What Georgie wanted to do was leap up and dance.

Her guests drifted off to their various beds. Georgie finally went upstairs. She was dying to hear about Rory's conversation with Bram, and she tried to read while she waited but finally gave it up. Her thoughts drifted to her ex-husband. From the time they'd started dating until the end of their marriage, she'd let her love for him define who she was—first Lance Marks's girl-friend, then Lance Marks's wife, and finally Lance's tragically victimized ex-wife. She'd let herself become the emotional slave of a famous, talented, unfaithful, but not really rotten . . . slab of tofu.

Bram shot through the door and dive-bombed the bed. Yanking the covers away, he kissed her until she was delirious.

"I take it . . . ," she said breathlessly, ". . . that you're demonstrating your gratitude."

"I am." He grinned and brushed her temples with his thumbs. "Thank you, Georgina. I mean it." He slipped his hand under her tank top and pinched her nipple. "But don't ever do anything like that again without warning me. I nearly had a heart attack."

She decided she could wait to hear the details of his meeting and arched her breast into his hand. "You're welcome. Now show me how grateful you really are."

He did exactly that.

The next morning Bram was as happy as Georgie had ever seen him. His eyes sparkled, and the razor edges of his mouth had softened. Rory had agreed to produce *Tree House* through Siracca Productions, a subsidiary of Vortex that made low-budget, so-called independent, films. He finally had exactly what he wanted. Georgie experienced a brief pang of envy. She felt more creative excitement filming Chaz than she'd felt for her real work. And then she remembered Helene.

That afternoon the health department lifted the quarantine after blood tests determined that Jade's assistants were suffering from a virus, not from SARS. Both women were still weak, but improving. By the time everyone was ready to leave, three helicopters buzzed overhead, and a media maelstrom waited at the gates. Rory slipped out the back, but the rest of them waited for the police to arrive and clear the way.

Now that Bram's dreams were coming true, Georgie had to take the next step toward realizing her own. She went outside to find Laura. As her agent came back up the path from the guesthouse, Georgie walked down the steps to meet her. Laura's baby-fine hair bounced this way and that around the soft prettiness of her face. She didn't look tough enough to be an agent, and maybe she wasn't. Georgie licked her lips. "I want you to cancel my meeting with Rich Greenberg tomorrow."

Laura stopped in her tracks, her brown eyes widening with alarm. "Georgie, I can't do that. You have no idea how hard I worked to get that meeting. You weren't even on Rich's radar screen until I talked to him, but now he's thinking seriously about you."

"I understand, but you didn't talk to me about it first. I'm not doing that film."

"Rich has some great ideas. You should at least hear him out."

"It's a waste of his time. I'll call him myself and apologize."

Laura tugged on her necklace. The deep shadows under her eyes indicated she hadn't been sleeping well. "Your father is . . . He strongly believes this is the best project for you."

"I'll make sure he understands this was my decision."

Laura looked unconvinced.

"I can't do it," Georgie said. "That last film I made . . . All I did was go through the motions."

"Don't say that. You're a brilliant performer."

"Spoken like a true agent." She knew what she had to do. Bram, of all people, had shown her. "I don't think people should live their lives just going through the motions. I want more from myself."

"I understand that, but—"

"I want to play Helene in *Tree House*."

Laura blinked. "Wow. I didn't see that coming. That's . . . quite a different part for you. Bram has . . . agreed to this?"

"He owes me an audition. I know I can do it. It's a role that excites me, and I'm going to put everything I have into landing it."

"Of course you have my support, but . . ."

"We'd better get inside." She squeezed Laura's wrist, a gesture of regret, and led her across the veranda.

The police were at the gate, and Bram met Georgie in the foyer to see everyone off. Aaron appeared with a notepad and asked Lance and Jade for their autographs. "Would you sign these to Chaz?" He passed the notepad and a pen to Jade. "Maybe something about liking her food. She's too embarrassed to ask for herself."

Jade looked blank.

"Our housekeeper," Georgie said. "The girl who's been making our meals all weekend."

"Oh, yes . . ."

Bram snorted.

Jade signed, then tapped her foot, impatient to go. Lance hung back, still waiting for Georgie's forgiveness. The wounds he'd inflicted on her began ticking through her head. But she'd played the filmstrip too many times, and watching it had grown boring. She thought of all the things she could say to hurt him, but that proved to be boring, too.

She narrowed her eyes at him. "You're absolved, Lancelot. Go and sin no more."

Bram's hand settled in the small of her back and rubbed.

"Do you mean it?" Lance said. "You've forgiven me?"

"Why not? It's hard to hold on to a grudge when you don't care anymore. Besides, you have enough trouble on your hands."

"What do you mean by that?"

She meant that Jade never looked at Lance the way Lance looked at Jade, with such single-minded adoration. Jade probably loved him in her own way, but not as much as he loved her, and that didn't bode well for a man with such massive insecurities.

Revenge came in strange forms, but she only said, "Changing the world isn't easy, and the two of you have your work cut out for you."

She'd given him what he wanted, but she saw that it didn't make him entirely happy. Some part of him had liked her suffering—just a little bit—and he wasn't quite ready to let it go. She smiled and looped her arm through Bram's. Lance scowled, and Jade glanced at her watch, oblivious to it all.

As they finally left, Bram chuckled softly in her ear, "Impressive. Since when did you grow up?"

"Your influence, I'm sure," she said dryly. But in a way it was true. Life was moving too fast for her to waste time gnawing over wounds that had healed when she wasn't paying attention.

Meg announced that she was moving back home for a while. "Now that I know Bram's not beating you, I'll leave you alone." She shot Bram her version of her father's Bird Dog Caliber squint. "But don't think I won't be checking up on you."

Finally, only Paul remained. "I've drafted a statement to the media that I suggest you release as soon as possible."

Georgie automatically bristled, but Bram stepped in. "What do we have to say in this statement?"

"Exactly what you'd expect." Paul passed over the paper he was holding. "How grateful you both are that the two women in the hospital are feeling better . . . The past is the past . . . You both couldn't be more supportive of the good work Jade and Lance are doing. Et cetera. Et cetera."

"Who knew we were so civilized?" Georgie said.

Bram nodded. "Sounds good to me. Aaron can take care of it." He handed the paper off to Georgie, then headed for his office with the jaunty step of a man who'd just won the lottery.

"What are you doing this afternoon?" Paul asked.

She dreaded telling him she'd canceled the Greenberg meeting. "I have a ton of paperwork to catch up on."

"Do it later. The helicopters have flown off. What do you say the two of us go for a swim?"

"A swim?"

"I saw some extra trunks in the guesthouse. I'll meet you at the pool." He set off without waiting for her agreement, which was so typical. She stomped upstairs and took her time pulling on a lemon-yellow bikini, then wrapping a beach towel around her waist. She'd been through enough these past few days, and she wasn't ready to plunge into what was guaranteed to be an ugly scene.

He waited for her in the pool, standing awkwardly in the middle of the water. He swam for exercise, not for enjoyment, and he looked odd just standing there. She dropped the towel, sat on the edge of the pool near the steps, and took her time dipping her toes in the water. "I need to talk to you about the meeting tomorrow. I spoke to Laura, and—"

"Let's swim."

He loved career talks, especially when they involved upcoming meetings with producers and directors. He could go on forever about the attitude she should project and what she should say. She looked at him curiously, trying to figure out why he was being so weird.

"The water's perfect," he said.

"O-kay." She slipped in.

He immediately began swimming toward the deep end. As he turned back toward her, she kicked off.

It went on that way for a while, the two of them swimming back and forth in opposite directions, neither one speaking. When she couldn't stand it any longer, she finally put her feet down. "Dad, I know how much this Greenberg meeting means to you, but—"

He stopped swimming. "We don't always have to talk about business. Why don't we just . . . relax a little?"

She regarded him quizzically. "Is something wrong?"

"No, no. Nothing's wrong." But he wasn't meeting her eyes, and he seemed uncomfortable. Maybe she'd watched too many movies, because she started wondering if he might have some kind of terminal disease, or maybe he'd decided to marry one of the women he dated, none of whom Georgie could warm up to, although she was grateful her father dated age-appropriately instead of going out with the twenty-somethings he could still attract.

"Dad, are you—"

An enormous splash of water hit her full in the face. She put up her hands, but not before he drew back his arm and sent another splash flying directly at her. Water shot up her nose and stung her eyes. She sputtered and choked. *"What are you doing?"*

His arm dropped to his side. His face flushed with what, if she didn't know him better, would have been embarrassment. "I was just . . . having a little fun."

She coughed and finally caught her breath. "Well, stop it!"

He took a step back. "I'm sorry. I thought . . ."

"Are you sick? What's wrong?"

He lunged for the ladder. "I'm not sick. We'll talk later."

He grabbed his towel and hurried off toward the house. She gazed after him, trying to figure out what had just happened.

Chapter 20

After Georgie had dressed and showered, she went into her office. Aaron sat at the computer, working away to the invisible beat coming through his headphones. He started to remove them, but she gestured for him to leave them on. Her father's things were gone. Good. That meant she could take the coward's way out and text him this evening to tell him she'd refused the meeting instead of delivering the news face-to-face.

She glanced at the guest list for their wedding party, which was less than three weeks away, and saw that nearly everyone had accepted—no surprise. A stack of invitations to benefits, fashion shows, and the debut of her hairdresser's new product line waited for her, but she didn't want to do any of it. She only wanted to look at the film she'd shot of Chaz.

Aaron had helped her set up her new editing equipment in the far corner of the room. She loaded the footage and quickly became absorbed in what she saw. As much as Chaz's story fascinated her, she was also intrigued by Soledad, the housecleaner. And there were so many others she wanted to talk to. Waitresses and shopgirls. Meter maids and nursing-home aides. She wanted to record the stories of everyday women doing everyday work in the glamour capital of the world.

When she finally looked up from the monitor, she discovered Aaron had left for the day. Laura should have canceled her meeting by now, but just in case she hadn't, Georgie would wait until tomorrow morning to call Rich Greenberg with her apologies.

She went downstairs and was unpleasantly surprised to find her father coming out of the screening room. "Catching up on an old Almodóvar film," he said.

"I thought you'd left."

"My cleaning service discovered a mold problem in the town house. I'm having it treated, but I need to move out for a few days while that's going on. I hope you don't mind if I stay here a little longer."

She did mind, especially now that she had to deliver the news about the canceled meeting to his face. "That's fine."

Bram emerged from the kitchen. "Stay as long as you want, Dad," he drawled. "You know you're always welcome here."

"Like the plague," her father shot back.

"Not as long as you follow the rules."

"Which means?"

Bram was clearly enjoying himself, but then the world was his oyster, so why not? "First, leave Georgie alone. She's my headache now, not yours."

"Hey!" Georgie planted her hand on her hip.

"Second . . . Actually, that's it. Ease up on your daughter. But I'd also like to hear your thoughts on *Tree House*."

Her father glowered. "Don't you ever get tired of being sarcastic, Shepard?"

Georgie stared at Bram. "I don't think he's being sarcastic, Dad. He really wants your opinion. And, believe me, I'm as surprised as you."

Her fake husband looked down his nose at her. "Just because Paul's a controlling pain in the ass who drives you crazy doesn't mean he's not smart. He gave a hell of a reading last night, and I'd like to hear what he has to say about the script."

Her father, who was never at a loss for words, didn't seem to know how to respond. Finally, he slipped a hand in his pocket and said, "All right."

Their dinner conversation got off to an awkward start, but no one came to blows, and before long, they were brainstorming ways to solve a credibility problem in Helene and Danny's first scene. Later, Paul argued that Ken's character should be more nuanced, insisting that adding more layers to the abusive father's personality would make him additionally menacing. Georgie agreed with her father, and Bram listened attentively.

Gradually, she realized that the original script hadn't been as flawless as Bram had led her to believe, and that Bram was the person who'd polished it, sometimes making only minor tweaks, but also adding new scenes while still remaining faithful to the original book. Knowing Bram could write so well added another crack in the foundation of her old convictions about him.

Bram downed the last of his coffee. "You've given me some good ideas. I need to make a few notes."

It was long past time for her to get down to the gruesome business of being honest with her father, and she reluctantly waved Bram off.

As a predictably uncomfortable silence fell between them, another fragment of memory slipped through her. She'd only been four when her mother died, so she didn't have a lot of memories, but she remembered a shabby apartment that seemed perpetually filled with laughter, sunshine, and what her mother called freebie plants. She'd lop off part of a sweet potato or the top of a pineapple and stick it in a pot of dirt, or suspend an avocado pit with toothpicks over a glass of water. Her father hardly ever talked about her mother, but when he did, he described her as a well-meaning but disorganized scatterbrain. But they'd looked happy in their photos.

She curled her fingers around the napkin in her lap. "Dad, it's about tomorrow . . ."

"I know you're not entirely enthusiastic, but don't let Greenberg see that. Describe how you'll put your own spin on the character. Get him to offer you that part. It's going to take your career to the next level, I promise."

"But I don't want the part."

She could see his frustration, and she braced herself for a pointed lecture on her stubbornness, lack of vision, naïveté, and ingratitude. But then he did the oddest thing. He said, "Why don't we play some cards?"

"Cards?"

"Why not?"

"Because you hate cards. Dad, what is *wrong* with you?"

"There's nothing wrong with me. Just because I'd like to play cards with my daughter doesn't mean anything's wrong. We can do more than talk about business, you know."

She wasn't buying it, not for a minute. Laura had spilled the beans about the canceled meeting, and instead of confronting Georgie directly about it, her father had decided to change his strategy. The fact that he believed he could manipulate her with these clumsy attempts at being a "pal" devastated her. He was dangling what she most wanted in front of her to make her do his bidding. This was his newest tactic to keep her from slipping away.

Her pain morphed into anger. It was time she let him know she was no longer letting him control her life in the futile hope that he'd throw a few crumbs of genuine affection her way. This past month had changed her. She'd made mistakes, but they'd been her mistakes, and she intended to keep it that way. "You're not going to talk me into rescheduling the meeting," she said flatly. "I canceled it."

Her heart started to pound. Did she have the guts to hold her ground, or was she going to give in to him once again?

"What are you talking about?"

A lump formed in her throat. She spoke quickly, working around it. "Even if Greenberg offered me the part with my name over the title, I wouldn't take it. I'm only doing projects that excite me, and if you're not okay with that, I'm sorry." She swallowed hard.

"I don't want to hurt you, but I can't keep going on like this, with you and Laura making decisions behind my back."

"Georgie, this is crazy."

"I'm grateful for everything you've done for me. I know you only want what's best for my career, but what's best for my career isn't always best for me." Oh, God, she couldn't cry. She needed to be as businesslike with him as he was with her. She dug deeper into her growing reservoir of resolve. "I need you to step aside now, Dad. I'm taking over."

"Step aside?"

She gave a jerky nod.

"I see." His handsome features didn't show even a hint of emotion. "Yes, well . . . I see."

She waited for the coldness, the condescension, the scathing arguments. Without her career holding them together, they had nothing, and if she didn't back down, they'd have no relationship at all. It was so ironic. Half an hour earlier, she'd been enjoying her father's company for the first time in longer than she could remember, and now she was about to lose him forever. Still, she wouldn't retreat. She'd emancipated herself from Lance. Now it was time to free herself from her father. "Please, Dad . . . Try to understand."

He didn't even blink. "I'm sorry, too, Georgie. I'm sorry that it's come to this."

And that was all. He walked away. Without another word. Out to the guesthouse to get his things. Out of her life.

She resisted a nearly overwhelming urge to go after him. Instead, she dragged herself upstairs. Bram must have been too lazy to go to his office because he was sitting on the couch in hers, an ankle resting on his knee, one of Aaron's legal pads propped on his thigh. She stopped in the doorway. "I think I . . . fired my father."

He looked up. "You're not sure?"

"I—" She sagged against the doorjamb. "What have I done?"

"Grown up?"

"He'll never talk to me again. And it's not like I have any other family."

Poor, pitiful Georgie York.

She straightened. She was sick of this. "I'm firing Laura, too. I'm doing it right now."

"Wow. A Georgie York bloodbath."

"You think I'm wrong?"

He uncrossed his leg and set down the legal pad. "I think you don't need anyone else telling you how to run your career when you're perfectly capable of doing it yourself."

She appreciated that. At the same time, she wished he'd either argue with her or agree.

He watched her reach for the phone. She felt like throwing up. She'd never fired anyone in her life. Her father had always taken care of it.

Laura picked up on the first ring. "Hi, Georgie. I was getting ready to call you. I'm not happy about it, but I canceled the meeting. I think you should call Rich yourself tomorrow and—"

"Yes, I'll do that." She sank into Aaron's desk chair. "Laura, I have something to tell you."

"Are you all right? You sound funny."

"I'm all right, but . . ." She studied the neat stack of papers without really seeing them. "Laura, I know we've been together for a long time, and I appreciate all your hard work, everything you've done for me, but . . ." She rubbed her forehead. "I need to let you go."

"Let me go?"

"I—I have to make some changes." She hadn't heard Bram come up behind her, but his hand settled between her shoulder blades. "I know how difficult my father can be, and I'm not blaming you—truly I'm not—but I have to . . . make a fresh start. With representation I hire myself."

"I see."

"I—I need to make sure that my opinion is the only one that counts."

"Ironic." Laura gave a dry laugh. "Yes. Yes, I understand. Let me know as soon as you've hired a new agent. I'll . . . try to make the transition as smooth as I can. Good luck, Georgie."

Laura hung up. No begging. No hard sell. Georgie felt sick. She dropped her forehead to the desk. "That was so unfair. Dad established the rules, and I went along. Now she's paying the price."

Bram took the phone from her and set it back on the cradle. "Laura knew it wasn't working. It was her job to do something about it."

"Still . . ." She pressed her face into the crook of her elbow.

"Stop it." He curled his fingers around her shoulders and drew her into a sitting position. "Don't second-guess yourself."

"Easy for you to say. You get off on being ruthless." She pushed herself out of the chair.

"I like Laura a lot," he said, "and she could probably have been a decent agent for you. But not as long as she served two masters."

"My father will never speak to me again."

"You aren't that lucky." He planted his hip on the edge of her desk. "So what brought about Georgie York's nuclear winter?"

"Dad wanted to play cards. And he splashed me in the pool." She kicked the wastebasket, which accomplished nothing except hurting her big toe and sending trash flying across the carpet. "Damn it." She dropped to her knees to clean up the mess. "Help me with this before Chaz sees."

He nudged a wad of paper toward her with the toe of his shoe. "Out of curiosity . . . Has your life always been a train wreck, or did I just happen to stumble on the scene during a particularly eventful time?"

She pitched a banana peel in the trash. "You could help, you know."

"And I will. I'm going to help you drown your troubles in some mind-blowing sex."

Considering the fragile state of her marriage, mind-blowing sex was probably a good idea. "I get to dominate. I'm sick of submission."

"I'm all yours."

A wedge of golden lamplight cut across Bram's naked body from shoulder to hip blade. He fell back into the pillows, spent and struggling for breath. He was a beautiful, debauched angel, drunk on sex and sin. "You're going to . . . fall in love with me," he said. "I know it."

She shoved her hair out of her eyes and gazed down at his sweat-slicked chest. The aftershocks of her last orgasm had left her soft and defenseless. She tried to pull herself back together. "You're delusional."

He gripped her thighs, which were still straddling his hips. "I know you. You'll fall in love with me and screw up everything."

She winced and pulled herself off him. "Why would I fall in love with *you*?"

He ran his hand over her bottom. "Because you have crappy taste in men, that's why."

She collapsed next to him. "Not that crappy!"

"You say that now. But before long, you'll be leaving threatening messages on my voice mail and stalking my new girlfriends."

"Only to warn them about you." His side pressed warm against her skin, and the earthy scent of their bodies mingled with the crisp smell of fresh sheets. The sex had been incredible as usual, and later she would blame her pleasure-fuzzed brain for what came next. Or maybe it was simply her day for burning all her bridges. "The only thing I might . . . *might* want from you is . . ." She threw her arm over her eyes and blurted it out. "Possibly . . . a baby."

He laughed.

"I'm serious." She lifted her arm from her eyes and made herself face him.

"I know. That's why I'm laughing."

"It isn't like it'd cost you anything." She sat up, all her lovemaking-lax muscles constricting. "No boring visitations. No child support. All you have to do is give me the goods and fade away before the main event."

"Not going to happen. Not in a trillion years."

"I wouldn't even bring it up—"

"Now *that* you're good at."

"—if you weren't so good-looking. Your faults are all character flaws, and since I wouldn't let you anywhere near my offspring except for an occasional public photo op, that's not a problem. Granted, by employing your DNA, I'm risking a few damaged chromosomes from your years of excess. But it's a risk I'm willing to take because, with that one exception, you pretty much represent the male genetic jackpot."

"I'm weirdly flattered. But . . . No. Never."

She dropped back into the pillows. "I knew you'd be too selfish to discuss this. It's so like you."

"It isn't as if you're asking me to lend you twenty bucks."

"A good thing, because I'd only have to pay myself back!"

He bent over her and nibbled at her bottom lip. "Would you mind using that gorgeous mouth for something other than idle chitchat?"

"Stop making fun of my mouth. What's the big deal? Tell me."

"The big deal is, I don't want a kid."

"Exactly." She bounced back up. "You won't have one either."

"Do you really think it'd be that easy?"

No. It would be messy and unbelievably complicated, but the idea of mixing their genes had been growing more enticing by the day. His looks and—she hated to admit it—his intellect, combined with her own temperament and discipline would produce the most amazing child, a child she yearned to bear. "It'll be easier than easy," she said. "It's a no-brainer."

"No-brain is right. Fortunately, the rest of your body makes up for your empty head."

"Save your energy. I'm out of the mood."

"I'm sorrier about that than you can imagine." He rolled on top of her and wedged her legs open with his thighs.

"What are you doing?"

"Reasserting my masculine supremacy." He captured her wrists and held them over her head. "Sorry, Scoot, but it has to be done."

He began to push inside her.

"I'm not using birth control!"

"Good try." He nibbled at her breast. "But futile."

She didn't press the point. First, it was a lie. Second, she'd turned into a sex maniac. And third . . .

She forgot about the third and wrapped her legs around him.

Bram couldn't believe it. A baby! Did she really think he'd go along with that harebrained idea. He'd always known he'd never get married, let alone have kids. Men like him weren't cut out for anything involving self-sacrifice, cooperation, or high-mindedness. What small amounts of those qualities he could muster up had to go into his work. Georgie was the weirdest combination of common sense and wacko bullshit he'd ever known, and she was starting to drive him more than a little crazy.

He waited until after his meeting with Vortex the next afternoon before he called Caitlin with the news. "Brace yourself, sweetheart. *Tree House* has a green light at Vortex. Rory Keene took the deal."

"I don't believe you."

"And here I thought you'd be happy for me."

"You son of a bitch! That option only had two weeks left."

"Fifteen days. And look at it this way. Now you can fall asleep at night knowing I won't let anybody turn your mother's book into a piece of crap. I'm sure that'll be a huge comfort."

"Go screw yourself." She slammed down the phone. He glanced toward the second floor. "Excellent idea."

Between a sinus headache, a demoralizing meeting with her superiors at Starlight Management, and a speeding ticket on the way to Santa Monica, Laura was having the mother of bad days. She punched the doorbell of Paul York's two-story Mediterranean town house, which was just four blocks from the Pier, although she couldn't imagine him ever going there. The deep V-neck of her new sleeveless silk print Escada dress gave her some added ventilation, but she was still hot, and ringlets had begun to form along her hairline. She began each day looking neat and orderly, but it didn't take long before she started to unravel—a fleck of mascara under one eye, a bra strap slipping off the other shoulder. She'd scuff a shoe, tear a seam, and no matter how expensive the salon cut, her baby-fine hair always lost its shape as the day went on.

She heard Steely Dan playing inside the house, so she knew someone was home, but he wasn't answering the bell, just as he hadn't been answering his phone. She'd been trying to reach him since Georgie had fired her two weeks ago, the day the quarantine had been lifted.

She banged on the door, and when that didn't work, banged on it again. The tabloids had gone into a frenzy searching out details of the quarantine, but the disclosure of Rory's presence and the news that Vortex had taken on *Tree House* had cast doubt on the more hysterical accounts of screaming catfights and hedonistic orgies.

The lock finally clicked, and there he stood, glowering at her. "What the hell do you want?"

His normally immaculate steel gray hair had misplaced its part, he was barefoot, and he looked as though he hadn't shaved in a week. Wrinkled shorts and a faded T-shirt had replaced his normal Hugo Boss. She'd never seen him like this, and something unwelcome stirred inside her.

She pushed hard on the door. "You look like Richard Gere's corpse." He automatically stepped back, and she slipped past him into the cool interior, which was dominated by bamboo floors, high ceilings, and bright skylights. "We need to talk."

"No, we don't."

"Just a few minutes," she said.

"Since we don't have any more business together, there's no point."

"Stop being such a big baby."

He stared at her, and she realized that even in his faded T-shirt and rumpled shorts he looked more together than she did in her Escada dress and strappy red Taryn Rose pumps. Again that inconvenient stirring . . . She gave him a grim smile. "I don't have to kiss your ass anymore. It's the only bright side of having my career ruined."

"Yeah, well, sorry about that." He walked away from her into his living room, a pleasantly decorated space, but without much personality. Comfortable furniture, beige carpet, and white plantation shutters. Apparently he hadn't let any of the sophisticates he'd dated over the years put her mark on the place.

She located his sound system and turned off the music. "I'll bet you haven't talked to her once since this all fell apart."

"You don't know that."

"Really? I've been watching you operate for years. If Georgie doesn't do what Daddy wants, Daddy punishes her by freezing her out."

"I've never done that. You do love to paint me as the villain, don't you."

"It doesn't take much paint."

"Go away, Laura. We can take care of leftover business by e-mail. We don't have anything more to say to each other."

"That's not quite true." She dipped in her tote and shoved a script into his hands. "I want you to audition for Howie. You won't get it, but we need to start somewhere."

"Audition? What are you talking about?"

"I've decided to represent you. You're a coldhearted prick in your personal life, but you're also a talented actor, and it's long past time you got out of Georgie's hair and focused on a career of your own."

"Forget it. I did that once, and it didn't go anywhere."

"You're a different person now. I know you're a little rusty, so I've scheduled a couple of sessions with Leah Caldwell, Georgie's old acting coach."

"You're crazy."

"Your first class is at ten tomorrow. Leah's going to put you through your paces, so get a good night's sleep." She withdrew a set of papers from her tote. "This is my standard agency contract. Look it over while I make some phone calls." She pulled out her cell. "Oh, and let's be clear from the start. Your job is to act. My job is to manage your career. You do your work, I'll do mine, and we'll see what happens."

He tossed the script on the coffee table. "I'm not auditioning for anything."

"Too busy counting up all those Kodak moments with your daughter?"

"You go to hell." Strong words, but delivered without much emphasis. He dropped into a muted plaid easy chair. "Do you really think I'm a coldhearted prick?"

"I can only judge by what I've observed. If you're not, you're a damn good actor."

That stopped her. He was a good actor. She'd been knocked out by his reading of the father in *Tree House*. She couldn't remember the last time a performance had excited her so much. And wasn't it one of life's great jokes that this performance had come from Paul York?

He'd always seemed so invincible, and watching him with his defenses down threw her off balance. "What's up with you anyway?"

He stared off at nothing. "It's funny how life never turns out like you expect."

"What exactly did you expect?"

He extended the contract toward her. "I'll read the script and think about it. Then we'll talk about a contract."

"No deal. Without a contract, the script and I are leaving together."

"You think I'm going to sign just like that?"

"Yes. And you know why? Because I'm the only one who's interested in you."

"Who says I care?" He slapped the contract on top of the script. "If I wanted to go back into acting, I'd represent myself."

"The actor who represents himself has a fool for a client."

"I think that's 'lawyer.'"

"The sentiment's the same. No actor can effectively sing his own praises without looking like an ass."

She was right, and he knew it, but he wasn't quite ready to concede. "You've got an answer for everything."

"That's because good agents know what they're doing, and I intend to be a much better agent for you than I ever was for Georgie."

He rubbed a thumb over his knuckles. "You should have spoken up."

"I did—more than once—but then you'd frown at me and—presto, chango!—I'd remember my mortgage, and there went my courage."

"People should fight for what they believe in."

"You're absolutely right." She jabbed her finger toward the contract. "So what's it going to be, Paul? Are you going to sit around feeling sorry for yourself, or do you have the guts to jump into a brand-new game?"

"I haven't acted in nearly thirty years. I haven't even thought about it."

"Hollywood loves talented fresh faces."

"Not so fresh."

"Trust me. Your wrinkles are in all the right places." She gave him her tough-girl look so he didn't take her comment as the blathering of a menopausal female who hadn't been on a real date in longer than she could remember. "It's hard for me to believe an actor with your talent has never thought about getting back to work."

"Georgie's career had to come first."

She felt a stab of sympathy for him. What had it been like to possess so much talent and do nothing with it? "Georgie doesn't need you now," she said more gently. "At least not for career advice."

He snatched the contract out of her hands. "Go make your phone calls, damn it. I'll look it over."

"Good idea." She stepped out onto the sundeck. Shady and sheltered, it was a great space for entertaining, but it held only a pair of unmatched metal chairs. She found it odd that someone so polished didn't have more of a social life. She flipped open her phone and checked her office voice mail, then had a lengthy conversation with her father, who'd retired in Phoenix. As they spoke, she forced herself not to spy on Paul through the windows. Next, she called her sister in Milwaukee, but her six-year-old niece answered the phone and launched into a story about a new kitten.

Paul came out onto the sundeck, and Laura broke into her niece's monologue. "He's an amazing actor. Hardly anyone knows that he trained at Juilliard Drama. He also did some really interesting off-Broadway work before he put his career on hold to raise Georgie."

"Who's Julie Yard, Aunt Laura?"

Laura tugged on her hair. "You have no idea how hard I've worked to convince him that he needs to start focusing on himself. As soon as you hear him read, you'll understand why I'm so excited about representing him."

"You're acting weird," the small voice replied. "I'm calling Mom. *Mom!*"

"Great. I'll give you a ring next week." Laura flipped her phone closed. "That went better than I expected." A drop of perspiration slithered between her breasts.

"Bullshit. You were talking to your voice mail."

"Or my niece in Milwaukee," she said, cocky as could be. "Or Brian Glazer's office. How I do my job isn't your business. Only the results I get."

He waved the contract in front of her. "Just because I signed this damned thing doesn't mean I'm going to auditions. It only means I'll read the script."

Had she really convinced him? She could hardly believe it. "It means you'll go where I tell you." She snatched up the contract and headed back inside, hoping he was following her. "This isn't going to be easy, so you'd better start giving yourself one of those lectures you used to give Georgie about how rejection is part of the business and not to take it personally. It'll be interesting to see if you're as tough as she is."

"You're enjoying this, aren't you?"

"More than you can imagine." She picked up her things. "Call me as soon as you finish the script. Oh, and I intend to advance your career by trading on Georgie's good name."

He flushed, angry. "You can't do that."

"Sure I can. She fired us, remember?" As she reached the front door, she stopped and turned back to him. "If I were you, I'd give her a call today instead of freezing her out."

"Yeah. Because your ideas have worked so well in the past."

"Just a suggestion." She let herself out and headed for her car. She wanted to kick up her heels with excitement. She'd crossed her first hurdle, and now all she needed to do was find him work.

As she backed out of his driveway, she reminded herself that getting Paul a job wasn't the only difficult task she faced. She also had to put her condo on the market, trade in her Benz for something cheaper, cancel her vacation in Maui, and stay out of Barneys. All potentially very depressing.

But for right now . . . She turned up the radio, bobbed her head, and sang her heart out.

Chapter 21

Georgie lifted her head from the pillows as Bram came out of the bathroom from his morning shower. Two and a half weeks ago, the night after the quarantine had lifted, she'd been faced with the dilemma of whether to move back into the guest room or stay where she was. She'd ended up telling Bram that her old room had so many leftover cooties from Lance and Jade that she couldn't go back. He'd agreed that some cooties were too contagious to risk.

She took a moment admiring him. The jet-black towel draped around his hips turned his lavender eyes to indigo. His hair was damp, and he hadn't shaved for the past few days, giving him a rugged, virile elegance. Her imaginary baby stirred in her womb. She blinked herself back to reality. "When did you say you and Hank Peters were going to start auditioning actors?"

"The Tuesday after our wedding party, as you very well know."

"Really? Only a week and a half away . . ." They'd gone into preproduction immediately because Hank Peters had a commitment to direct another film in November, and they didn't want to lose him. She let the sheet slip below one breast, a wasted effort as it turned out, since he was already heading into his closet for the jeans and T-shirt that had become his producer's work uniform. "And I'm still first up, right?"

"Will you relax? I promised you the first audition, and you'll get it. But I swear to God, if you pin your hopes on this . . ."

"Hard to do with you telling me how unworthy I am."

He popped his head out. "Don't exaggerate. You're a terrific actress and a gifted comic, and you know it."

"But not gifted enough to play Helene?" She experimented with a smirk. "Remember this moment, Bramwell Shepard, because I'm going to make you eat those words."

She wished she could be as confident as she sounded. She'd read the script twice more and begun creating a character log filled with ideas about Helene's backstory and physical mannerisms. But she only had ten days before the audition, and this would be the most complex character she'd ever taken on. She had a lot more work to do before she'd be ready, and she kept losing her focus.

His gaze dipped to her breast. She'd had to force herself not to give in to the urge to shop for the sexiest nighties she could find. Instead, she'd stuck with her normal sleepwear, but her plain white cami and black boxers printed with pirate skulls now lay crumpled on the floor by the bed. She deliberately pulled the sheet up to her chin. "Don't forget we have our last meeting with Poppy at nine."

He groaned and headed back into the closet. "No way am I sitting through any more meetings about floral arrangements and Jordan almonds stamped with the family crest. What the hell is a Jordan almond anyway?"

"An almond that tastes like soap." The general uneasiness that had been plaguing her since she realized that Bram now had everything he wanted propelled her out of bed. "The Skip and Scooter wedding extravaganza was your idea, and it's only eight days away. You're not dodging that meeting."

"I'll give you a hundred bucks and another back rub if you let me skip it."

"I don't need a hundred bucks. As for your back rubs . . . Study an anatomy book, pal, because what you've been rubbing isn't my back."

"And aren't you glad?"

She had to admit she was.

He ended up staying for the meeting.

Poppy Patterson's heavy perfume, exaggerated speech, and clattering charm bracelets drove them both crazy, but she was an imaginative and efficient party planner. She understood that the paparazzi's helicopters would make it impossible to hold an outdoor celebration, and she'd come up with the perfect indoor venue—the magnificent 1920s Eldridge Mansion built in the same English manor house style as the Scofield mansion. With its luxuriously appointed ballroom, it could comfortably hold their two hundred guests, all of whom had been instructed to wear a costume inspired by the show.

Aaron and Chaz joined in as they sat around Bram's dining room table to go over the final arrangements. They started with the decorations and ended with the food. Everything on the menu played a part in an episode of *Skip and Scooter,* beginning with the hors d'oeuvres: mini deep-dish pizzas; tiny, heart-shaped peanut butter sandwiches; and bite-size Chicago hot dogs—no ketchup.

The meal was more formal, and Chaz began reading the menu aloud. "Rocket and Parmesan salad, episode forty-one, 'Scooter Meets the Mayor.' Rum-glazed lobster tails with mango, episode two, 'Nice Horsey.' Black pepper–seared beef tenderloin, episode sixty-three, 'Skip's Lost Weekend.'"

"Rocket?" Bram yawned. "Sounds flammable."

"It's arugula," Chaz replied. "You like it." She eyed Poppy, who was dressed in a champagne knit St. John suit with goggle-size designer sunglasses pushed on top of her brunette socialite's bob. "I'm glad you got rid of that foie gras mousse crap."

From the beginning Poppy had let it be known she resented dealing with a currently purple-haired twenty-year-old who wasn't a rock star. "It was mentioned in episode twenty-eight, 'The Scofield Curse.'"

"When Scooter fed it to the *dog*."

Bram's eyes glazed over as the discussion went on. The past few weeks had been odd. Bram left for the studio early in the morning and didn't return until late. She missed him in a way she couldn't exactly define . . . just that life seemed flatter without their verbal sparring. Even their nightly sexual romps didn't quite compensate. Their lovemaking was fun and exciting, but something was missing.

Of course, something was missing. Trust. Respect. Love. A future.

Except . . . She'd developed a grudging respect for him. She didn't know another man who'd have taken

Chaz in, and she loved the way he'd find the homeliest woman in the crowd and eye-smolder her until she felt like a supermodel. He'd also acquired a surprisingly strong work ethic. But fundamentally, Bram had always been out for himself, and that would never change.

Eventually, Poppy packed up her python bag, releasing a great puff of perfume. "I have a small surprise planned for the evening," she announced. "Just so you know. One of the special touches I've made my trademark. You'll love it."

Bram snapped out of his preoccupation. "What kind of surprise?"

"Now, now. Spontaneity is everything."

"I'm not too crazy about spontaneity," Georgie said.

Poppy's charm bracelets clattered. "You hired me to arrange a spectacular party, and that's what I'm doing. You'll be over the moon. I promise."

Bram was impatient to get away, and he cut off Georgie's protest. "As long as I don't have to wear tights or drink lite beer, go ahead."

Poppy left soon after, and Bram headed off to the studio.

Georgie wanted to edit more film, and she needed to work on her character log for Helene, but first she called April. They'd been working together long-distance on Georgie's gown and accessories, and her last fitting was coming up. When their conversation ended, she jotted down some more thoughts about Helene, but her attention kept wandering, and she finally let herself go upstairs to look at the last footage she'd shot—a group of single mothers trying to make a living at a minimum-wage job. Hearing firsthand accounts of these working women's lives once again reminded her of how privileged she was.

Rory had helped her escape the paparazzi on her photographic excursions by offering one of her own garages as a place for Georgie to stash a car the paps wouldn't recognize. When Georgie wanted to leave the house without being followed, she slipped through the back gate and used Rory's driveway to drive off in the Toyota Corolla Aaron had leased for her. So far none of the paps was the wiser, and hauling around video equipment had provided her with a degree of anonymity she hadn't anticipated. Although the subjects she interviewed knew who she was, she found herself moving around with a small degree of freedom.

Several hours had passed when Chaz poked her head in. "Your old man's moving back into the guesthouse."

Georgie's head shot up from her monitor. "My dad?"

Chaz tugged on her fluorescent purple bangs. "He said they didn't get all the mold out of his house. Personally, I think he just wants to freeload off Bram."

Her father hadn't taken any of her calls since she'd fired him, so why had he suddenly shown up? She didn't need another lecture about her bad judgment and general incompetence, and she definitely didn't want to talk about Laura. Firing her might have been good business, but she couldn't feel completely right about it. She wished Bram were here.

Aaron wandered in from his errands, his arms full of packages. "Your father's downstairs."

"So I heard." She wanted to finish her film editing, not deal with the inevitable, and she stalked across the room to Chaz. "You listen to me . . . If there's even a tiny part of you that doesn't hate everything about me, would you keep him away from me, just for another hour? Please."

Chaz took her time thinking it over. "I will . . ." She smirked. "But only if you eat something first."

"Stop nagging."

Chaz responded with a megasmirk.

Thanks to Chaz's menus, Georgie had gained back the weight she'd lost, but that didn't ease her irritation. "Fine! But the hour doesn't start until I'm finished."

"I'll be back in ten minutes."

And she was, bearing two plates: one with a salmon-topped salad chock-full of fresh vegetable goodies, the other an enormous submarine sandwich stuffed with three different kinds of meat, cheese, and guacamole. Georgie and Aaron exchanged resigned looks as Chaz slammed the salad in front of him and the fat sub before Georgie.

"You need the calories," Chaz said when Georgie begged to trade. "Aaron doesn't."

Georgie grabbed the sandwich. "Now you're a big nutrition expert."

"Chaz is an expert at everything," Aaron said. "Just ask her."

Chaz folded her arms and looked smug. "I know Becky finally talked to you yesterday."

"She wants me to take a look at her computer, that's all," he said.

"You're such a moron. I don't know why I waste my time."

Georgie knew, but she wasn't stupid enough to point out that Chaz was a natural nurturer.

With lunch nearly over, Georgie made Chaz go back downstairs to watch out for her father. Aaron left to get the oil changed on her car, and Georgie returned to her editing. An hour ticked by.

"May I come in?"

Startled, she looked up to see her father standing in the doorway. He wore gray shorts, a light blue polo, and he needed a haircut. He nodded toward the computer. "What are you doing?"

He was certain to criticize, but she told him anyway. "New hobby. I've been shooting some film."

His answering silence unnerved her. She fiddled with the computer mouse. "Everybody deserves a hobby." She lifted her chin. "I bought editing equipment. Just for fun."

He rubbed his index finger with his thumb. "I can see."

"Is something wrong with that?"

"No. I'm just surprised."

He was surprised because the idea hadn't come from him.

A shrieking silence filled the room. She made herself sit straighter in her chair. "Dad, I know you don't approve of the way I've been doing things, but I'm not going to discuss it with you anymore."

He shifted his weight, nodded. "I . . . just wondered if you had any idea where the fuse box is located in the guesthouse. One of the circuits blew, and I didn't want to poke around without asking first."

"Fuse box?"

"Never mind. I'll check with Chaz." His footsteps faded down the hall.

She stared at the empty doorway. He'd been acting so strangely since the splashing incident in the pool.

She needed to talk to him—really talk—but hadn't she been trying to do that for years?

She glanced toward her monitor. He had a good eye. She wished she could show him some of the footage she'd shot, but she needed his support, not his criticism. If they could only . . . relax together.

A wisp of memory skidded through her.

A small, shabby room . . . an ugly gold carpet . . . books strewn everywhere . . . Her parents were fast dancing . . . and then they started tickling each other. Chasing around the room. Her father hopped over a chair. Her mother grabbed Georgie. "Now what are you going to do, big guy? I've got the kid."

All three of them falling on the floor, laughing.

Her father went out to dinner, so Georgie couldn't ask him whether her memory was real or not, although it probably wouldn't have done any good, since he had a habit of brushing aside her questions about the past. Georgie gave him credit for at least trying not to speak badly of her mother, even though it was obvious their marriage had been a mistake.

The next morning she woke up a jittery mess. The party was a week away. Her father had moved in. She had the most important audition of her career coming up for a part no one believed she could pull off. And . . . now that her fake husband had his film deal, he might decide he didn't need her fifty thousand a month and bail on her. The zit that broke out on her forehead was almost a relief. A small problem that wouldn't hang around for long.

She spent the rest of the morning having her hair highlighted and her brows shaped. By the time she got home, she felt like jumping out of her skin. She was too agitated to concentrate on prepping for her audition. Instead, she decided to pack up her camera equipment and drive outside the paparazzi zone, maybe Santee Alley to interview some of the women selling designer knockoffs.

She hadn't seen her father all morning, but he appeared just as she was coming downstairs with her equipment bag. He slipped his hand into the pocket of his khaki pants and jiggled his keys. "Do you want to go to a movie this afternoon?"

"You mean in a theater?"

"It'd be fun."

The word sounded strange on his lips. "I don't think so," she said.

"Then maybe lunch?"

She needed to get this over with, and she hitched her equipment bag higher on her shoulder. "You don't have to be so polite. It makes me nervous. Go ahead and say what you want to—that I'm a shitty, ungrateful daughter. That I don't understand the business. That—"

"You're not shitty or ungrateful, and I don't have anything more to say. I just thought you might want to go out for a while." He pulled the keys from his pocket. "It's all right. I have some errands to run." He left through the front door.

She frowned at his uncharacteristic retreat and followed him outside.

She'd always loved the covered entry porch of Bram's house, with its blue-and-white-tiled floor and arcade of twisted stucco columns. A purple bougainvillea formed a shady screen at the far end, and Chaz had recently added a few more terra-cotta pots along with a heavily carved Mexican bench and matching wooden chair.

"Dad, wait." Without thinking about it, she reached inside the bag.

His expression shifted from quizzical to suspicious as she pulled out her camera and set the bag aside. "I had this dream," she said. "Not really a dream. A memory . . ." The camera was her shield, her protection. She raised it to her eye and turned it on. "A memory of you and my mother dancing and teasing each other. You jumped over a chair. We were all laughing and . . . happy." She moved in closer. "These memories I sometimes get . . . I've made all of them up, haven't I?"

"Put that camera away."

She winced as she bumped into the sharp bench corner, but she didn't stop shooting. "I've made them up to cover the truth I don't want to face."

"Georgie, really . . ."

"I can count." She sidestepped the bench and pinned him with her lens. "I know that you only married her because she was pregnant with me. You did the honorable thing. And you hated every minute of it."

"You're overdramatizing."

"Tell me the truth." She'd started to perspire. "Just once, and then I won't ever bring it up again. I'm not going to blame you. You could have run out on her, but you didn't. You could have run out on me, and you didn't do that, either."

He sighed and stepped back up on the porch, as if this were a tedious meeting he needed to suffer through. "It wasn't like that."

She circled him, moving backward, putting herself between him and the steps, so he couldn't get away. "I've seen the pictures of her. She was so pretty. I know she loved having a good time."

"Georgie, put that camera down. I've told you that your mother loved you. I don't know what more you—"

"You also told me she was a scatterbrain. But you were only trying to be diplomatic." Her voice grew unsteady. "I don't care if she was nothing more than a party girl. A one-night stand that backfired. I just—"

"That's enough!" He thrust his finger toward the camera. A vein throbbed at his temple. "Turn that camera off right now."

"She was my mother. I need to know. If she was just another bimbo, at least tell me that."

"She wasn't! Don't you ever say that again." He snatched the camera from her hands and flung it to the tiles, where it shattered. "You don't understand anything!"

"Then tell me!"

"She was the love of my life!"

His words hung in the air.

A tremor passed through her. She locked her eyes with his. Anguish twisted his features. She felt dizzy, wobbly. "I don't believe you."

He pulled off his glasses and sagged onto the carved bench. "Your mother was . . . enchanted," he said in a husky rasp. "Enchanting . . . Laughter came as naturally to her as breathing. She was smart—smarter than I could ever be—and she was funny. She refused to see the bad in anyone." His hand shook as he set his glasses next to him. "She didn't die in a car accident, Georgie. She saw a pregnant girl being slapped around by her boyfriend and tried to help her. He shot your mother in the head."

"No," she said in a soft whimper.

He rested his elbows on his knees and hung his head. "The pain I felt when I lost her was more than I could handle. You didn't understand where she'd gone, and you cried all the time. I couldn't comfort you. I could barely find the energy to feed you. She loved you so much, and she would have hated that." He rubbed his face in his palms. "I stopped going to auditions. It wasn't possible. Acting takes an openness I didn't have anymore." His fingers tunneled into his hair. "I couldn't live through that kind of pain again. I promised myself I'd never love another person the way I loved her."

Her chest constricted, ached. "And you kept that promise," she whispered.

He looked up at her, and she saw tears brimming in his eyes. "No, I didn't. I didn't keep it, and look where it's taken us."

It took her a moment to understand. "Me? You love me like that?"

He gave a rueful laugh. "Shocking, isn't it?"

"I . . . It's hard to believe."

He dipped his head and nudged the broken camera aside with his shoe. "I guess I'm a better actor than I thought."

"But . . . why? You've been so cold. So . . ."

"Because I had to plow on," he said fiercely. "For us. I couldn't fall apart again."

"All these years? She died so long ago."

"Detachment got to be a habit. A safe place to exist." He rose from the bench. For the first time in her memory, he looked older than his years. "Sometimes you're so much like her. Your laughter. Your kindness. But you're more practical than she was, and not as naïve."

"Like you."

"In the end, you're yourself, and that's what I love. What I've always loved."

"I've never felt . . . very loved."

"I know, and I didn't—I couldn't figure out how to change that, so I tried to compensate by being scrupulous about your career. I needed to convince myself I was doing my best for you, but all the time I knew it wasn't good enough. Not even close."

Pity welled inside her, along with sadness for what she'd missed, and a certainty that her mother, the woman he'd described, would have hated seeing him like this.

He picked up his glasses. Rubbed the bridge of his nose. "Watching you after Lance left, seeing how you were suffering and not being able to comfort you. I wanted to kill him. And then your marriage to Bram.

I can't forget the past, but I know you love him, and I'm trying."

A protest sprang to her lips. She bit it back. "Dad, I understand I hurt you by telling you I need to run my own career, but I just . . . want you to be my father."

"You've made that clear." He took the bench across from her, looking more troubled than offended. "Here's my problem. I know this town too well. Maybe it's ego on my part, or maybe overprotection, but I don't trust anybody else to put your interests first."

Something he'd always done, she realized, even if she hadn't always agreed with the results. "You're going to have to trust me," she said gently. "I'll ask for your opinion, but the final decisions—right or wrong—are going to be mine."

He gave a slow, unsteady nod. "I suppose it's time." He bent down and picked up what used to be her camera. "Sorry about this. I'll buy you another."

"It's okay. I have a spare."

Silence fell between them. Awkward, but they stuck it out.

"Georgie . . . I'm not exactly sure how it happened, but it seems . . ." He toyed with the empty camera body. "There's a remote possibility—very remote— that I might . . . have my own career to concentrate on."

He told her about Laura's visit, her insistence on taking him on as her client, and the acting classes he'd begun attending. He seemed both embarrassed and a little bewildered. "I'd forgotten how much I love it. I feel like I'm finally doing what I should have been doing all along. As though I've . . . come home."

"I don't know what to say. It's wonderful. I'm shocked. Thrilled." She touched his hand. "You were brilliant that night we read *Tree House,* and I never told you. I guess you're not the only one who's been holding back. When do you audition? Tell me more."

He did, summarizing the script and the character, telling her about his first class. As she witnessed his animation, she felt as though she were watching a man beginning to free himself from an emotional prison.

The conversation shifted to Laura. "I can't blame her for hating me." Georgie's guilt reemerged. "Maybe I shouldn't have done it, but I wanted a clean start, and I didn't see any other way."

"You're going to have a hard time believing this, but Laura seems to be okay with what you did. Don't ask me to understand it. You've thrown a major monkey wrench into her income, but instead of being depressed, she's—I don't know—excited—energized—I'm not sure what to call it. She's an unusual woman, a lot gutsier than I gave her credit for. She's . . . interesting."

Georgie looked at him sharply. He rose from the bench. Another awkward silence fell. He rested his hand on the side of a column. "Where do we go from here, Georgie? I'd like to be the father you want, but it seems a little late in the game. I don't have a clue how to go about it."

"Don't look at me. I'm emotionally traumatized from all those beatings you gave me." Once a smart aleck, always a smart aleck, but she couldn't think of anything else to say except that she wanted him to hug her, just put his arms around her. She crossed her arms over her chest. "Unless you want to start off with some kind of lame hug."

To her surprise, his eyes closed in pain. "I—don't think I remember how."

His total helplessness touched her. "Maybe you could give it a try."

"Oh, Georgie . . ." His arms shot out. He pulled her against him and squeezed her so hard her ribs ached. "I love you so much." He tucked her head against his jaw and started rocking her as if she were a child. It was clumsy, uncomfortable, and wonderful.

She burrowed into his shirt collar. This wasn't easy for him or for her. She'd have to lead the way, but now that she understood where his heart lay, she didn't mind at all.

Chapter 22

The gray stone Eldridge Mansion had served as the setting for a dozen movies and television shows, but no one had ever seen the portico with two canopied entryways. The larger and more ornate, a pristine white canopy marked THE SCOFIELDS, led to the main entrance. A smaller green canopy positioned off to the side was marked SERVANTS ONLY.

The guests laughed as they emerged from their limos, Bentleys, and Porsches. In the spirit of the party, those garbed in gowns and tuxedos, tennis whites or Chanel suits, stuck their noses in the air and headed for the main entrance, but Jack Patriot was no dummy. The legendary rock star, wearing his most comfortable jeans and a work shirt, with a pair of gardening gloves and some seed packets tucked in his belt, cheerfully made his way to the servants' entrance, his wife at his side. April's simple black housekeeper's dress would have been plain if she hadn't modified it for the occasion with a boned bodice and plunging neckline. A pair of skeleton keys dangling from a black silk cord nestled into her cleavage, and she'd pulled her long blond hair into a soft and very sexy bun.

Rory Keene, in a modest version of a French maid's costume, joined Jack and April at the servants' entrance along with Rory's date for the evening, a debonair venture capitalist attired in a butler's uniform. He was Rory's customary companion for special occasions, a friend but not a lover.

Meg's parents used the main entrance. Actor-playwright Jake Koranda wore a garden-party white suit that accented his swarthy skin, and his wife, the glorious Fleur Savagar Koranda, modeled a swirly floral chiffon frock. Meg, who was dressed as Scooter's hippie best friend, Zoey, elected to go through the servants' entrance with her date for the evening, an unemployed musician who was a ringer for John Lennon, circa 1970.

Chaz stood just inside the ballroom, wondering why she'd let Georgie choose her costume. Now here she was, dressed like a frigging *angel,* in a glittery silver gown with a *halo* attached to a big orange wig. If she lifted her eyes, she could even see a few orange curls dripping over her eyebrows. The inspiration had come from episode thirteen, "Skip Has a Dream." When Chaz had bitched to Georgie about the costume, Georgie had given her this weird smile and said Chaz was an angel in disguise. What the hell did that mean?

She was supposed to be helping Poopy the Party Planner make sure everything was running smoothly, but she'd mainly been gaping at all the stars who'd showed up. According to Poopy, this was the most important party of the summer, and a bunch of celebrities that Bram and Georgie didn't even know had begged for invitations. Georgie kept telling Poopy, "No purse designers," which Chaz hadn't understood until Georgie explained it, and then Chaz had to agree.

The ballroom's polished walnut moldings and paneled wooden ceiling gleamed in the light of the crystal chandeliers. Lavender-and-blue-plaid taffeta overskirts topped the round, custard-yellow tablecloths. Blue moptop hydrangeas inspired by the show's opening credits served as centerpieces, the bouquets spilling from bright yellow teapots. A spun sugar model of the Scofield mansion rested at each place setting, along with a silver picture frame holding an engraved menu bearing both the Scofield family crest and a small paw print of Butterscotch, Scooter's cat. Four large television screens set up around the room silently ran episodes of the show.

Chaz saw Aaron coming toward her with a cute, but kind of nerdy-looking, brunette who could only be Becky. Aaron wouldn't have had the guts to ask her out if Chaz hadn't hounded him. Thanks to Chaz, he'd never looked better. "All you have to do is wear a really good suit," she'd said when she'd talked him into coming as the Scofields' lawyer. "One that fits. And make Georgie pay for it." One thing about Georgie. She wasn't cheap. She'd even sent Aaron to her dad's tailor.

With his good haircut, contact lenses, body that was getting thinner every day, and real clothes instead of those geeky T-shirts with video game crap all over them, he was like a different person.

"Chaz, this is Becky."

Becky was a little plump, with shiny dark hair, a round face, and a shy, friendly smile. Chaz liked how hard she was trying not to stare at all the famous people in the crowd. "Hi, Chaz. I love your costume."

"It's kind of lame. But thanks."

"Becky works in the H.R. department for a health care company," Aaron said, as if Chaz didn't already know that, just like she knew that Becky's parents came from Vietnam, but Becky had been born in Long Beach.

She took in Becky's V-neck white blouse, short black skirt, dark tights, and four-inch black stilettos. "You make a great chauffeur."

"Aaron suggested it."

In fact, Chaz was the one who'd suggested to Aaron that Becky come as Lulu, the Scofield lawyer's sexy chauffeur. She'd figured Becky would be super-nervous about tonight, and wearing something simple would be one less thing for her to worry about.

"It was sort of Chaz's idea," Aaron said, even though Chaz wouldn't have busted him if he'd pretended it was his.

"Thanks," Becky said. "The truth is, I've been kind of nervous about tonight."

"Pretty great first date, right?"

"Incredible. I still can't believe Aaron asked me." Becky looked up at him and gave him this big smile like he was super-hot, which he wasn't, even though he looked a lot better than he used to. When Aaron smiled back at her the same way, Chaz felt a stab of jealousy. Not because she wanted Aaron for a boyfriend, but because she'd gotten used to taking care of him. She liked talking to him, too. She'd even told him about all the crap that had happened to her. But if he and Becky got serious, he might only want to talk to her. Maybe Chaz also felt a little jealous because she'd like to have some really, really, really nice guy who wasn't a sleazeball look at her the way Aaron was looking at Becky. Not now, but someday.

"That's Sasha Holiday," Aaron said, pointing toward a tall, thin woman with long dark hair. Half glasses dangling from a chain rested on the bodice of her sophisticated black sheath. She was just like Mrs. Scofield's social secretary, except a lot sexier. "Sasha's one of Georgie's best friends," Aaron told Becky.

"I recognize her from the Holiday Healthy Eating ads," Becky said. "She's gorgeous. And even thinner than her pictures."

Chaz thought she looked too thin and sort of tense around her eyes, but she didn't say anything.

She and Aaron and Becky stood there, trying not to stare at the stars who were showing up—Jake Koranda and Jack Patriot, all the actors from *Skip and Scooter,* plus a bunch of Georgie's costars from her movies. Meg waved at her from across the room, and Chaz waved back. Meg's date looked like a loser, and Chaz thought she could do a lot better. From the look on Meg's dad's face, he thought so, too.

Chaz was surprised to see Laura Moody, Georgie's old agent, come in, but not as surprised as Poopy, who looked like she was going to have a heart attack. Laura had been invited before Georgie fired her, and no one expected her to show up.

"Where are Miss York or Mr. Shepard?" Becky whispered to Aaron.

It sounded weird hearing somebody call them that. Aaron glanced at his watch. "They're going to make a big entrance. Poopy's idea." He turned red. "I mean *Poppy.*" He frowned at Chaz. "Stop laughing. You're being infantile . . . and unprofessional." But then he laughed and explained to Becky that the party planner had serious attitude, and he and Chaz basically hated her.

As they sampled the hors d'oeuvres, Rory Keene came over to talk to them, which was super cool, because it made everybody in the room think they were VIPs. Laura came over, too. She didn't act like she was embarrassed being here, even though everybody knew Georgie had fired her and even though she didn't seem to have a date.

Poopy and the waiters began steering all the guests toward the grand foyer for the bride and groom's entrance. Chaz started to get nervous. Georgie was used to being onstage, but tonight was different, and Chaz didn't want her to trip or do something equally embarrassing in front of all these people. The musicians began playing an overture by Mozart or somebody. Bram came into the foyer from a door on the first floor. This was the first time Chaz had seen him in a tuxedo, but he acted like he wore one every day—like James Bond, or George Clooney, or Patrick Dempsey, but with lighter hair. He looked rich and famous, and Chaz felt a swell of pride that she was the one who took care of him.

He moved to the bottom of the grand staircase and gazed up. The music swelled. And then Georgie appeared, and Chaz felt that same rush of pride. Georgie was glowing and healthy instead of starved and sunken-eyed. Chaz had made sure of that. She glanced at Bram and saw that he thought she was beautiful, too.

Georgie had insisted they travel to the party separately, so Bram was seeing her for the first time. He'd half expected her to appear in Scooter's skunk costume, as she'd threatened. He should have known better.

Georgie looked as though she'd run naked through a crystal chandelier. The gown formed a slim column of sparkling ice that molded beautifully to her tall, slender body until it reached her knees, where it flared gently to the floor. A fine clasp of crystal lace caught the fabric at one shoulder, leaving the other bare, and a delicate lace panel cut a diagonal swatch across her body—offering the faintest and most ladylike glimpse of flesh.

This was what audiences had waited eight seasons to see—the vision they'd been cheated of by his destructive behavior—Scooter Brown's transformation from homeless orphan to an elegant woman with a generous spirit and lively openness that no Scofield had ever possessed. He was shaken. He could trifle with Scooter, but this intelligent, sophisticated creature felt almost . . . dangerous.

Her hair was perfect. Dark, soft curls pinned back, with a few left free to dip around her face in a stylish tousle. For all Georgie's insistence that she relied on April for everything, she had a strong sense of what worked for her, and she hadn't made the mistake of letting anyone get near her naturally pale skin with a tanning airbrush. Nor had she decked herself with too many jewels. A pair of spectacular diamond chandelier earrings dangled from her earlobes, but she'd left her slender neck bare to make its own statement.

Paul stood at her side, her hand resting lightly on the sleeve of his tuxedo. Having her father escort her down the staircase wasn't part of the plan, and the expression on their faces as they smiled at each other disconcerted him. He knew Paul had been hanging around a lot lately, but Bram had been working such long hours that he had no idea what had happened to improve their relationship.

Paul and Georgie began descending the staircase. Bram couldn't take his eyes off her. She wasn't considered beautiful by Hollywood standards, but the problem lay with the standards, not with her. She was something far more interesting than a Botoxed, lipo-sucked, trout-mouth, silicon-enhanced California Frankenbeauty.

As she paused at the landing, he belatedly remembered he was supposed to have climbed the steps to meet her. But she was used to him missing his cues, and she didn't wait for long. He unglued his feet and climbed the stairs, stopping three steps below her. He turned one-quarter profile to the crowd and extended his hand, palm up. Corny, but she deserved the most romantic picture possible. Paul kissed Georgie on the cheek, nodded at Bram, then yielded the stage to the bride and groom. Georgie's hand slipped warmly into his own. The guests broke out in applause as she descended the three steps to his side.

They faced a ballroom brimming with smiles and good cheer, although half the guests were undoubtedly placing bets on how long the marriage would last. Georgie gazed up at him, her eyes tender. He lifted her fingers to his lips and kissed them gently. He could play fricking Prince Charming every bit as well as Lance the Loser.

But he had to work hard at being cynical. Tonight might be nothing more than another Hollywood fairy tale, but the illusion felt real.

Georgie wanted it to be real. This night. The magical sparkling dress. Her friends around her, and the soft expression on her father's face. Only the man standing at her side was wrong. But he didn't feel as wrong as he should. They mingled with their guests, who were dressed in everything from jeans and tennis skirts to dinner jackets and schoolgirl outfits. Trev and Sasha had volunteered to give the toasts, but after everyone was seated, Paul rose unexpectedly and raised his glass. "Tonight we celebrate the commitment these two amazing people have made to each other." He gazed at Georgie. "One of these people . . . I love very much." His voice broke, and Georgie's eyes filled with tears. Paul cleared his throat. "The other is . . . growing on me."

Everyone laughed, including Bram. The past week with her father had been strange and wonderful. Knowing how much he loved her—how much he'd loved her mother—meant everything. But as Paul began expressing hope for the bride and groom's future, Georgie worked to keep a smile on her face. Telling her father the truth instead of trying to hide her mistakes for fear of disappointing him was the next step in her journey of becoming her own woman.

Paul had waited until this morning to tell her he'd invited her ex-agent as his date. She was glad he'd thought of it, no matter how awkward greeting Laura had been. "It's a nice thing to do for her," he'd said. "This way everyone can see that you still consider her part of your inner circle."

Georgie had tried to make a joke out of it. "It's also the perfect way to start letting people know you're returning to acting, and that Laura is representing you."

His face had fallen. "Georgie, that's not why—"

"I know it's not," she'd said quickly. "I didn't mean it that way." They were navigating a new relationship, with both of them trying to find their footing. She'd poked him in the ribs to make him laugh.

The other toasts followed—Trev's irreverent, Sasha's warm, both of them funny. As the meal began, she and Bram were subjected to frequent interruptions from guests tapping their water goblets. Their public kisses no longer felt so phony. She'd never known a man who enjoyed kissing as much as Bram Shepard . . . or one who did it so well. She'd never known a man she enjoyed kissing more.

At the next table, Laura toyed with a bite of lobster and surreptitiously pushed up her bra strap. She'd planned to wear a garden-party dress tonight, like so many of the other female guests, but at the last minute, she'd changed her mind. This was a business occasion, and she couldn't afford to be tugging on a bodice that would inevitably show too much cleavage or worrying about bare arms that weren't as toned as they should be. Instead, she'd opted for a simple beige business suit, a draped-neck camisole, and pearls—the sort of outfit Mrs. Scofield had worn. Other than her perpetual problem with bra straps, she'd done fairly well keeping herself neat.

Paul's invitation had been a shock. She'd called to break the news that he'd struck out on his first audition, but that the casting agent wanted to see him about another part. Just as she'd launched into her standard ego-repairing pep talk, he'd cut her off. "I wasn't right for the part, but the audition was good practice." And then he'd invited her to the party.

She would have been foolish to refuse. Being seen here tonight would help put a little of the luster back on her professional reputation, as Paul very well knew. But she couldn't help being wary. Paul's icy personality had always been the perfect antidote to his good looks and other male assets, but his new vulnerability made it tempting to view him in a more unsettling way.

Fortunately, she understood the perils of female rescue fantasies. She was clear about what she wanted from her life, and she wouldn't screw that up just because Paul York was both more interesting and complicated than she'd ever imagined. So what if she was sometimes lonely? Her days of letting a man distract her from her real goals were long behind her. Paul was a client, and being seen at this party was good business.

He'd been attentive all evening, a perfect gentleman, but she was too nervous to eat much. While the others at the table were engaged in private conversations, she leaned closer. "Thanks for inviting me. I owe you."

"You have to admit tonight hasn't been as awkward as you thought it would be."

"Only because your daughter is a class act."

"Quit defending her. She fired you."

"She needed to fire me. And the two of you haven't been able to stop smiling at each other all evening, so don't bother playing the tough guy."

"We talked. That's all." He pointed to the corner of his mouth, indicating she had something on her face. Embarrassed, she snatched up her napkin, but she didn't get the right spot, and he ended up dabbing at her with his own.

She grabbed her water glass when he was done. "It must have been a great talk."

"It was. Remind me to tell you about it the next time I'm drunk."

"I can't imagine you ever getting drunk. You're too self-disciplined."

"It's been known to happen."

"When?"

She expected him to brush her off, but he didn't. "When my wife died. Every night after Georgie fell asleep."

This was a Paul York she'd only just begun to know. She gazed at him for a long moment. "What was your wife like? You don't have to answer if you don't want to."

He set down his fork. "She was amazing. Brilliant. Funny. Sweet. I didn't deserve her."

"She must have thought differently, or she wouldn't have married you."

He looked slightly taken aback, as if he'd gotten so used to regarding himself as a second-class citizen in his marriage that he couldn't comprehend it any other way. "She was barely twenty-five when she died," he said. "A kid."

She rolled her pearls between her fingers. "And you're still in love with her."

"Not in the way you mean." He toyed with the spun sugar miniature of the Scofield mansion resting above his plate. "I guess the twenty-five-year-old inside me always will be, but that was a long time ago. She lived in her head a lot. I was as likely to find the car keys in the refrigerator as in her purse. She didn't care anything about her appearance. It drove me crazy. She was always losing buttons or ripping things . . ."

Gooseflesh crept along the base of her spine. "It's hard to imagine you with anyone like that. The women you date are all so elegant."

He shrugged. "Life is messy. I look for order wherever I can find it."

She pleated her napkin in her lap. "But you haven't fallen in love with any of them."

"How do you know? Maybe I fell in love and got rejected."

"Unlikely. You're the grand prize in the ex-wives sweepstakes. Stable, intelligent, and great-looking."

"I was too busy managing Georgie's career to remarry."

She heard his leftover self-rebuke. "You did a good job with her for a lot of years," she said. "I've heard the stories. As a kid, Georgie couldn't resist either a microphone or a pair of dancing shoes. Stop beating yourself up about it."

"She loved to perform. She'd climb up on tables to dance if I wasn't watching." His expression clouded over again. "But still, I should never have pushed her so much. Her mother would have hated that."

"Hey, it's easy to criticize when you're standing on the celestial sidelines watching somebody else do the heavy lifting."

She'd had the audacity to make light of his sainted wife, and his expression grew still and cold. In the old days, she'd have fallen all over herself trying to make up for it, but she didn't feel the urge, even as his frown grew more pronounced. Instead, she leaned closer and whispered, "Get over it."

His head snapped up, and his killer glare turned his eyes into bullets.

She met his gaze straight on. "It's time."

Withdrawal was Paul York's weapon of choice, and she waited for him to turn away, but he didn't. The ice melted from his eyes. "Interesting. Georgie said the same thing."

He retrieved the napkin Laura had dropped and gave her a long look that melted her bones.

Chapter 23

At first Chaz noticed the waiter because he was really cute and he didn't look like an actor. Too short, but with a nice body and a dark, burr haircut. As he passed the hors d'oeuvres trays, he kept stealing glances at everybody, a little sneaky, but she was doing the same thing, so she didn't think much about it. Then she noticed the awkward way he kept turning his body.

When she finally figured out what he was doing, she was totally pissed. She waited until the meal was nearly done before she excused herself and slipped into the service hallway, where she found him arranging dishes on a metal cart. As she came up next to him, he took in her halo with a cocky grin. "Hey, angel. What can I do for you?"

She glanced at his name tag. "You can hand over your camera, Marcus."

His cockiness faded. "I don't know what you're talking about."

"You have a hidden camera."

"You're crazy."

She tried to remember where television investigative reporters hid their cameras.

"I know who you are," the waiter said. "You work for Bram and Georgie. How much do they pay you?"

"More than you're getting." Marcus wasn't tall, but he looked like he worked out, and it belatedly occurred to her that maybe she should have gotten someone from security to handle this. But there were people around, and it seemed better to keep it quiet. "You can either give me the camera, Marcus, or I'll have somebody take it off you."

She must have sounded like she meant it because he looked uneasy. The fact that she could intimidate him, even a little, made her feel good.

"It's no skin off your nose," he said.

"You're only trying to make a living. Yeah, I understand. And once you hand it over, I'll forget about it."

"Don't be a bitch."

She moved quickly, reaching for the top button on his vest, the one that didn't quite match the others. The button came off in her hand, and as she pulled it free, she met resistance from a thin piece of cable.

"Hey!"

With a jerk, she yanked it free. "No cameras allowed. Didn't you get the message?"

"What do you care? You got any idea what the photo agencies pay for shit like this?"

"Not enough."

He'd turned red, but he couldn't wrestle the camera from her without everyone seeing. She started to walk away only to have him come up behind her. "You could sell your story, you know. About working for them. I'll bet you could get at least a hundred grand. Give me my camera back, and I'll put you in touch with this guy. He'll handle the whole thing for you."

A hundred thousand dollars . . .

"You wouldn't even have to say anything bad about them."

She didn't answer. She just walked away.

A hundred thousand dollars . . .

A funny video montage of *Skip and Scooter* clips played after dinner. Shortly before the cake-cutting ceremony, Dirk Duke appeared with a microphone. He was the most popular DJ in town—real name Adam Levenstein—and Poppy had hired him to spin music for dancing, which wasn't scheduled to begin for another half hour. Dirk was short, with a bullet-shaped head, tattooed neck, and Ivy League education he did his best to hide. Tonight he wore a badly fitted tuxedo instead of his customary jeans. "Yo, everybody! This is a great party! Let's give it up for Georgie and Bram."

The audience dutifully gave it up.

"All you *Skip and Scooter* fans. Seeing Bram and Georgie married is great, right?"

Applause and a couple of whistles, one of them from Meg.

"We're here to celebrate a marriage that happened two months ago. A marriage none of us was important enough to be invited to."

Laughter.

"And tonight . . . We're going to do something about that . . ."

Four waiters appeared bearing an arched bridal bower draped in white tulle caught up with blue hydrangeas. Poppy trailed behind in a floor-length black dress, her face smug with anticipation.

Georgie poked Bram with her elbow. "I think Poppy's just unveiled her surprise. The one you told her to go ahead with."

Bram grimaced. "You should have hit me over the head. I don't like this."

Georgie liked it even less as she watched the waiters position the bower at the front of the ballroom. Bram swore under his breath. "That woman is officially fired."

"As an ordained minister in the Universal Life Church"—Dirk paused for dramatic effect—"it is my honor"—another pause—"to ask our bride and groom to step forward and"—raised voice—"repeat their vows in front of all of us!"

The guests were eating this up. Even her father. Poppy's glossy, inflated lips formed a triumphant smile. A muscle ticked in the corner of Bram's jaw. Poppy had no right to stage something this personal without consulting them.

Bram clenched his teeth and rose. "Put on your game face."

Georgie told herself it didn't mater. What was one more public performance after so many? Her crystal gown rustled as she stood.

Dirk elongated his vowels like a game-show host. "Dad. Come up and join them. Mr. Paul York, everybody! Bram, choose your best man."

"He chooses me." Trev shot up, and the guests laughed.

Georgie felt as though she were suffocating.

"Georgie, who's your maid of honor going to be?"

She looked at Sasha, at Meg and April, and thought how lucky she was to have these wonderful women as her best friends. Then she cocked her head. "Laura."

Laura's face registered shock, and she nearly tipped over her chair as she got up.

They assembled at the bridal bower. Her father, Trev, Laura, and the reluctant bride and groom.

Dirk thoughtfully turned his back to the room so that Bram and Georgie were facing their guests, then he cupped his hand over the microphone. "Is everybody ready?"

She and Bram gazed at each other, and a moment of perfect, unspoken communication passed between them. He lifted an eyebrow. She told him with her eyes exactly what she thought. He smiled, squeezed her hand, and pulled the microphone away from Dirk.

"A priest, a rabbi, and a minister walked into a bar . . ." Everyone laughed. Bram grinned and brought the mike closer. "Thank you all for your good wishes. Georgie and I appreciate them more than we can say."

Off to the side, Poppy started chewing on her bottom lip. Bram's speech wasn't on her program, and she obviously didn't like pesky clients interfering with her agenda.

Bram released Georgie's hand and gestured toward the bower. "As you can probably tell, this ceremony is a surprise. But the truth is, while we both understand the allure of watching Skip and Scooter get married, Georgie and I aren't those characters, and this doesn't feel right to either one of us."

Georgie slipped her hand into the crook of his elbow and smiled for the nice people.

He covered her fingers with his own. "I'm tempted to say some very sentimental things about Georgie right now. How warmhearted she is. Sweet and funny. How she's my best friend. But I don't want to embarrass her . . ."

"It's okay." She leaned into the microphone. "Embarrass me."

He laughed, and so did the crowd. They exchanged another of their kisses followed by a long loving glance while Bram surreptitiously felt her up and she pinched him on the ass.

And then, out of nowhere, her knees started to shake. Really shake. Earthquake shake. But this earthquake was happening inside her.

She'd fallen in love with him.

All the blood rushed from her head. She absorbed the awful truth. Despite everything she knew, she had fallen in love with Bram Shepard, the self-absorbed, self-destructive bad boy who'd stolen her virginity, wrecked a television show, and nearly destroyed himself.

Bram glittered beneath the chandeliers, his burnished beauty and masculine elegance designed for the silver screen. She could barely breathe. Just as she was finally learning to be her own person, she'd sabotaged herself by falling in love with a man she couldn't trust, a man she was paying to stay by her side. The breadth of the calamity made her dizzy.

He finished his speech, and they wheeled out the wedding cake, a multitiered wonder of icing lace and confectionary hydrangeas topped by a pair of Skip and Scooter dolls dressed in wedding finery. Bram fed her the first piece, getting only a dab of frosting on her lips, which he kissed away. She somehow managed to return the favor. The cake tasted like heartache.

Afterward, April drew her aside to change out of her magical crystal gown into the modified cameo-blue flapper dress they'd chosen for dancing. Georgie moved through the rest of the night in a flurry of perpetual motion, dancing and laughing, her hips moving, her hair stinging her cheeks.

She danced with Bram, who told her she looked beautiful and that he couldn't wait to get her in bed. She danced with Trev and her girlfriends, with Jake Koranda, Aaron, and her father. She danced with her costars and Jack Patriot. She even danced with Dirk

Duke. As long as her feet were moving, she didn't have to think about how she would save herself.

Bram loomed over her as they stood in his foyer a little after two in the morning. His black bow tie hung loose at his neck, his shirt collar open. "What the hell do you mean, you're sleeping in the guesthouse?"

Georgie was still a little drunk, but not so drunk that she didn't know exactly what she had to do. She wanted to cry . . . or scream, but there'd be plenty of time for both later. "I have to audition for you on Tuesday afternoon, remember? Sleeping with you three nights before gives me an unfair advantage over the other actresses."

"That's the lamest thing I've ever heard."

Somehow she managed to conjure up the sass of the old Georgie, the Georgie who'd once again fallen so stupidly in love. "Sorry, Skipper. I believe in fair play. It'd be on my conscience."

"Fuck your conscience." He pushed her against the wall at the base of the stairs and started kissing her. Deep, invasive kisses with a stubborn edge. Her toes curled in her shoes. He shoved his hand under the hem of her little blue flapper dress and nipped at the upper slope of her breast as it curved above the bodice. "You make me crazy," he murmured against her damp skin.

She was dizzy with champagne, desire, and despair. He slipped his fingers inside panties so tiny and fragile they hardly counted as a garment. *Stop. Don't stop.* The words bounced in her head as his kisses grew more insistent and his touch so intimate she couldn't bear it.

"Enough," he said, and he swept her up in his arms.

The theme music swelled. Strains of *Dr. Zhivago* and *Titanic, An Affair to Remember* and *Out of Africa* enfolded them as he carried her up the stairs in the most romantic gesture ever, except it was two in the morning, and he banged his elbow against the door as he crossed the threshold.

But it took him only a moment to recover. He set her on the edge of the bed, tugged at her clothes, and it was like the first time on the boat all over again. Her naked hips at the edge of the mattress. Her dress pushed up to her waist. His clothing scattered. And herself stupidly in love with a man who didn't love her back.

It was like the first time . . . and it wasn't. After the initial breathless assault, he slowed down—loving her with his touch, his mouth, his sex, with everything but his heart. And she let herself love him back. Just this one last time.

Something faintly inquisitive flickered in his eyes as he gazed into her own. He sensed a change in her but couldn't figure out what it was. Their pleasure surged, the music rose to a crescendo in her head, and the camera pulled back. She closed her eyes and rode with him into oblivion.

As she lay curled against his shoulder, her despair resurfaced. This self-destruction had to stop. "So when did you fall in love with me?" she said.

"The instant I set eyes on you," he replied drowsily. "No, wait . . . That was me. The first time I looked in a mirror."

"No, really."

He yawned and kissed her forehead. "Go to sleep."

She lumbered on. "I've been getting this feeling . . ."

"What feeling?"

He was wide-awake now and suspicious, but she needed to know for sure exactly where she stood. This was too important for them to suffer some kind of sitcom misunderstanding that could be set straight with a few words. "A feeling that you're in love with me."

He sat up, dumping her unceremoniously. "Of all the stupid—you know exactly how I feel about you."

"Not really. You're more sensitive than you pretend to be, and you hide a lot."

"I'm not one bit sensitive." He glared down at her. "You want to rub it in, don't you? What I said at the party."

She couldn't remember what he'd said at the party, so she curled her lip at him. "Of course I want to rub it in. So say it again."

He released an exasperated sigh and lay back in the pillows. "You're the best friend I've ever had. Go ahead and laugh. Believe me, I never expected it to work out that way."

His best friend . . . She swallowed. "I don't know why. I'm a very likable person."

"You're a nut bar. In a million years I'd never have imagined you'd be the person I trusted most."

And she didn't trust him at all. Except about this. He was telling the truth about his feelings for her. "What about Chaz? She'd take a bullet for you."

"Okay, you're the second most trustworthy person I know."

"That's better." She told herself to let it go, but she had to try. One more time. "It could really screw us up"—she sighed, as if this were all too tedious—"if you turned into an idiot and decided to fall in love—"

"Jesus, Georgie, will you give it a rest? Nobody's in love with anybody."

"If you're sure . . . ?"

"I'm sure."

"That's a relief. Now stop talking so I can go to sleep."

Her leg cramped, but she didn't dare move until she heard the deep, even sound of his breathing. Only then did she ease out of bed. She slipped into the first thing she touched, his abandoned tuxedo shirt, and crept downstairs. Her father had gone back to his condo, leaving the guesthouse empty once again. She padded along the cold stone path, tears trickling down her cheeks. If she kept making love with him, she'd have to pretend it was only sex. She'd have to perform for him, just as she performed for the cameras.

She couldn't do it. Not for him. Not for herself. Not ever again.

Chapter 24

Bram arrived late for Georgie's audition, and Hank Peters's cool nod indicated he wasn't happy about it. Bram knew they were all waiting for him to fall back into his old, unreliable habits, but he'd been legitimately delayed by a call from one of the partners at Endeavor. Still, he couldn't bring himself to explain—he'd spewed out too many bullshit excuses in the past—and he merely offered a short apology. "Sorry to keep you waiting."

Although no one said it to his face, they all thought having Georgie read for them today was a waste of time. But he owed her an audition, no matter how much he hated being part of something that, in the end, would devastate her.

"Let's get to work," Hank said.

The audition room had bilious green walls, stained brown carpet, some battered metal chairs, and a couple of folding tables. It was located on the top floor of an old building at the rear of the Vortex lot that housed Siracca Productions, Vortex's independent film subsidiary. Bram took the empty chair between Hank and the female casting director.

With his long face, thinning hair, and glasses, Hank looked more like an Ivy League professor than a Hollywood director, but he was enormously talented, and Bram still couldn't quite believe they were working together. The casting director nodded at her assistant, who left to escort Georgie in from wherever they'd stashed her.

He hadn't seen her since the night of the party. Paul had gotten sick afterward—some kind of stomach flu, according to Chaz—and Georgie had driven off to take care of him before Bram had woken up the next morning. Georgie didn't need the distraction of playing nursemaid right before a major audition, and Bram couldn't believe Paul hadn't managed to send her home. Bram had wanted one more chance to talk her out of this.

The casting assistant returned and held the door open. Georgie's self-confidence was a lot more fragile than she let on. She wouldn't be horrible, but she wouldn't be good, either, and he hated the idea of everybody picking over her performance.

A tall, dark-haired actress entered. An actress who wasn't Georgie. As the casting director asked her what she'd been doing since her last film, Bram leaned closer to Hank. "Where the hell is Georgie?"

Hank regarded him oddly. "You don't know?"

"We haven't had a chance to talk. Her father has the flu, and she's been taking care of him."

Hank pulled off his glasses and polished them on the hem of his shirt, almost as if he didn't want to make eye contact. "Georgie changed her mind. She decided the part wasn't right for her, and she's not auditioning for us."

Bram couldn't take it in. He sat through the audition without hearing a word of it, then excused himself and tried to reach her. But she wasn't picking up. Neither was Paul or Aaron, and Chaz didn't know anything more than what Georgie had originally told her. He finally called Laura. She said she'd spoken with Paul only a few hours earlier, and he hadn't mentioned being sick.

Something was very wrong. He set off for home.

Only three black SUVs were standing guard near the gates. Sunday's wedding celebration had played big on TMZ and the other online gossip sites, but the craziness of the first two months finally seemed to be fading. It wouldn't take much, however, to reignite the flames, and if word got out that Georgie had disappeared, all hell was going to break loose.

His cell rang as he pulled up to the garage. It was Aaron. "I have a message from Georgie. She's said to tell you she's taken off for some R and R."

"What the hell? Forget that!"

"I know. I don't understand it either."

"Where is she?"

There was a long pause. "I can't tell you."

"The hell you can't!"

But Aaron's first loyalty was to Georgie, and Bram's threats didn't break his resolve. Bram finally hung up on him, then sat in his car dumbfounded. Was she ashamed to face him because she'd gotten cold feet? But Georgie had never been afraid of an audition in her life. None of this made sense.

Their odd conversation from the night of the party replayed in his mind. Could she seriously believe he'd fallen in love with her? He thought about all the mixed signals he'd sent her and snatched up his cell again. She didn't answer, so he was forced to leave a message.

"Okay, Georgie, I get it. You were serious the other night. But I swear to God, I am not in love with you, so stop worrying. It's total crap. Think about it. Have you ever known me to care about anybody other than myself? Why would I start now? Especially with you. Damn it, if I'd known you were going to freak out like this, I'd have kept my mouth shut about the friendship thing. Friendship. That's all it is. I promise. So stop making up crap and call me back."

But she didn't call, and by the next morning, something more insidious had occurred to him. Georgie wanted a baby, and right now she couldn't have one without him. What if this was blackmail? Her way of manipulating him? The fact that she might even be thinking of doing something so odious made him furious. He called her voice mail and let her have it. Since he didn't mince words, he wasn't exactly surprised when she didn't return his call.

The white stucco private villa Georgie had rented sat high above the Sea of Cortez just outside Cabo San Lucas. It had two bedrooms, a scallop-shaped Jacuzzi, and a sliding glass wall opening onto a shady patio. Since Georgie couldn't fly commercial to Mexico, she'd used a private charter service.

Every morning for a week, she donned an oversize T-shirt and a pair of baggy capris, then slipped on big sunglasses and a wide straw hat to walk for miles unrecognized along the beach. In the afternoons, she edited film and tried to make peace with her sadness.

Bram was furious with her for disappearing, and his telephone messages had ripped out her heart.

I swear to God, I am not in love with you . . . Friendship. That's all it is. I promise.

As for his second message about blackmailing him to have a baby . . . She deleted that halfway through.

Her father knew where she was. She'd finally told him the truth about Las Vegas and a little bit about why she'd needed to get away. Naturally, he'd tried to blame Bram, but she wouldn't let him, and she made him promise not to contact him. "Just give me some time, Dad, okay?" He'd reluctantly agreed.

A day later her father had called with a piece of news that left her reeling. "I did some investigating. Bram hasn't touched a penny of the money you were supposed to be paying him. It turns out, he doesn't need it."

"Of course, he does. Everybody knows he blew through all his *Skip and Scooter* money."

" 'Blow' pretty much describes it. But when he finally got clean and sober, he downscaled his lifestyle and started investing his residuals. He's done shockingly well for himself. He even paid off the mortgage on his house."

It was ironic. The only thing Bram hadn't deceived her about was his feelings for her. Friendship. And there it stopped.

She found herself staring at nothing, or picking up a book and reading the same sentence over and over. But she didn't cry as she had with Lance. This time, her sadness ran too deep for tears. The only activity that interested her involved taking a camera down to one of the luxury resorts and interviewing the maids. Since she couldn't endure that kind of public exposure, she set up her camera on the shady white stone patio and interviewed herself.

"Tell me, Georgie. Have you always been a loser in love?"

"More or less. How about yourself?"

"More or less. And why do you think that is?"

"A pathetic need to be loved?"

"And you're blaming that on . . . what? Your childhood relationship with your father?"

"Let's."

"So it's ultimately your father's fault you fell in love with Bram Shepard?"

"No," she whispered. "It's my fault. I knew falling in love with him was impossible, but I had to go and do it anyway."

"You gave up your audition and a chance to play Helene."

"How about that. What a woman will do for love, right?"

"Stupid."

"What was I supposed to do? Work with him every day, then go home with him at night?"

"What you should do is make your career your first priority."

"I don't care about my career right now. I haven't even hired a new agent. I only care about . . ."

"Being miserable?"

"A few months and I'll be over him."

"Do you really believe that?"

No, she didn't believe it. She loved Bram in a clear-eyed way she'd never loved her ex-husband, no rose-colored glasses or mindless giddiness, no Cinderella fantasies or false certainty that he'd put her life in order. What she felt for Bram was messy, honest, and soul-deep. He felt like . . . part of her, the best and the worst. Like someone she wanted to struggle through life with; share triumphs and catastrophes; share holidays, birthdays, every days.

"Excellent," her interviewer said. "I've finally made you cry. Just like Barbara Walters."

Georgie turned off the camera and buried her face in her hands.

Georgie had been gone almost two weeks, and Aaron was Bram's only source of information. Georgie's P.A.

had taken it upon himself to leak a series of fictitious stories to the tabs. He'd detailed Georgie's decision to take a vacation while Bram worked and also served up long descriptions of romantic phone calls between the newlyweds. Aaron's fabrications kept the press at bay, so Bram didn't correct them.

Tree House continued to move forward without any major snarls, even though they still hadn't finished casting. He should have been on top of the world, but he mainly wanted to look up his old drug dealer. He buried himself in work instead, to keep the devils at bay.

Chaz was waiting for him on Monday night when he got home from the studio, a new supply of cookbooks spread out on the kitchen table instead of the GED workbooks she still hadn't opened. She jumped up as he appeared. "I'll make a sandwich for you. A good one, with whole grain bread, turkey, and guacamole. I'll bet all you've eaten today is junk."

"I don't want anything, and I told you not to wait up for me."

She bustled over to the refrigerator. "It isn't even midnight."

Long experience had taught him the futility of arguing with Chaz about food, so even though all he wanted to do was sleep, he hung around and pretended to sift through some mail on the counter while she pulled containers from the refrigerator and filled him in on her life. "Aaron's being a pain. He and Becky split up—they haven't even been together three weeks. He said they're too much alike. But that should be a good thing, right?"

"Not always." Bram gazed blindly at a party invitation, then tossed it in the trash. He and Georgie were more alike than they were different, although it had taken him a while to figure that out.

Chaz slapped a container on the counter so hard the lip popped off. "Aaron knows where Georgie is."

"Yeah, I know he does. So does her father."

"You should make them tell you."

"Why? I'm not running after her." Besides, Bram already knew she'd gone to Cabo, thanks to a phone conversation with Trev, who was in Australia shooting his new film. Bram had thought about flying to Mexico and dragging her back, but she'd stung his pride. Bottom line—she was the one who'd left, and it was up to her to come back and make things right.

Chaz put a loaf of bread on the cutting board and began slicing it, her knife coming down with hard *thwacks*. "I know why you guys got married."

He looked up.

She flipped the lid on a container of guacamole. "You should have been honest about what happened in Vegas and gotten the stupid marriage annulled or whatever. Like Britney Spears did that first time she got married."

"How do you know what happened?"

"I overheard you and Georgie talking about it."

"You overheard with your ear smashed against a keyhole. If you ever say anything to anybody . . ."

She slammed the cupboard door shut. "Is that what you think of me? That I'm some big asshole blabber-mouth?"

Now he had two pissed-off females in his life, but getting back in Chaz's good graces was relatively easy. "No, I don't think that. Sorry."

She chewed over his apology but eventually decided to accept it, as he'd known she would. He sat down in front of the food she'd put out. He didn't want to end his phony marriage yet. It held too many advantages—starting with sex, which was so great he couldn't imagine giving it up yet. Thanks to Georgie, he was back in the game, and he intended to stay there. He wanted *Tree House* to be the first in a string of great films, and somehow she'd become an intricate part of making that happen.

Chaz set his sandwich in front of him. "I still can't believe she didn't audition. She goes to all that work and then blows it off. You wouldn't believe the way she made Aaron run around to get her a special outfit.

Then she kept making me check out different hairstyles and makeup. She even made me tape her stupid audition. Then she turns chicken and runs away."

He set down his sandwich. "You taped her audition?"

"You know how she is. She tapes everything. I probably shouldn't say this, but if she ever made any sex tapes of you, I seriously think you should—"

"Is the tape still around?"

"I don't know. I guess. Probably in her office."

He started to get up, then sat back in his chair. Screw it. He knew exactly what he'd see.

But before he went to bed that night, his curiosity got the best of him, and he searched her office until he found what he was looking for.

They had their first tussle over the check. "Give it to me," Laura said, genuinely surprised to see Paul grab the check before she could reach for it. They'd dined together more times than she could count, and she always picked up the check. "This is a business dinner. The client never pays."

"It was a business dinner for the first hour," Paul said. "After that, I'm not so sure."

She fumbled for her napkin. It was true that tonight had been different. They'd never talked about their high school embarrassments before, or their mutual love of music and baseball. And he'd certainly never insisted on picking her up at her new condo. All evening, she'd been doing her best to keep things professional, but he kept sabotaging her. Something had happened. Something she needed to make un-happen as quickly as possible.

She held out her hand for the bill. "Paul, I insist. This is a well-deserved celebration. You've only been my client for six weeks, and you've landed a great part." He'd been cast in a quirky new HBO series about a group of Vietnam, Gulf, and Iraqi War veterans who spent their weekends as Civil War reenactors.

He set his palm over the leather folder that contained the check. "I'll give this to you. But only if next weekend's on me."

Had he just asked her out? She was too old for games. "Did you just ask me out?"

He tilted his head, a vaguely amused smile playing at the corner of his mouth. "Did I?"

"No, you didn't."

"And why's that?"

"Because I'm not thin."

"Ahh."

"Or blond, or elegant, or divorced from a former high-ranking studio executive. I have no time for a personal trainer, I don't wear clothes well, and getting my hair done bores the hell out of me." She crossed her legs. "But most of all, I'm your agent, and I'm planning to make a lot of money off your career."

"So will you go out with me next weekend anyway?"

"No!"

"Too bad." The waiter appeared, and Paul passed over his credit card. A director they both knew stopped at their table to chat, and by the time the valet had delivered Paul's car, Laura assumed the subject was behind them. Paul quickly proved her wrong.

"The L.A. Chamber Orchestra is playing at Royce Hall next weekend," he said as they drove off from the restaurant. "I think we should go. Unless you'd rather take in a Dodgers game."

Two of her favorite activities. "I don't get this. You're the consummate professional. You know I can't date a client, especially such an important client."

"I like that 'important' part."

"I mean it. You're going to have a great career, and I want to negotiate every phase of it."

He turned north onto Beverly Glen Boulevard. "If you weren't my agent, would you date me?"

In a New York minute. "Probably not. We're too different."

"Why do you keep saying that?"

"Because you're cool and logical. You like order. How long has it been since you've forgotten to pay your cable bill or splashed wine on your clothes?" She pointed toward the small red splotch on the skirt of her silk shift. At the same time she covered up a recent snag. She wanted to make her point without looking like a total slob.

"That's one of the things I like about you," he said. "You get so wrapped up in a conversation you forget to pay attention to what you're doing. You're a good listener, Laura."

And so was he. The intent way he'd locked in on her tonight made her feel like the most fascinating woman on earth. "I don't get this," she said. "Why the sudden interest?"

"Not all that sudden. You were my date for the wedding party, remember?"

"That was business."

"Was it?"

"I thought it was."

"You thought wrong," he said. "That day you cornered me, you shook me loose from my moorings. You made me open my eyes about Georgie, and nothing's been the same since." The hint of a smile tugged at the corner of his mouth. "In case you haven't noticed, I'm fairly tightly wound. You're a very relaxing woman, Laura Moody. You unwind me. Oh, and I also like your body."

Laura burst out laughing. Where had all this charm come from? Wasn't it enough that he was intelligent, great-looking, and much nicer than she'd ever imagined? "You're so full of it."

He grinned and turned onto a narrow side street that ran above the Stone Canyon Reservoir. "You gave me my daughter back. You gave me a new career. I'm almost afraid to say it, but for the first time in longer than I can remember, I'm happy."

The interior of his Lexus was suddenly too small. It grew even more intimate as he swung onto a dark, unpaved road, pulled the car into the scrub, and lowered the windows. She sat up straighter as he killed the engine. "Any reason you're stopping here?"

"I'm hoping we can make out."

"You've got to be kidding."

"Look at it from my viewpoint. I've been wanting to touch you all evening. I'd definitely prefer the comfort of a nice couch, but I can hardly expect you to invite me in if you won't even agree to a date. So I'm improvising."

"Paul, I'm your agent! Call me crazy, but I have a policy of not making out with my clients."

"I understand. If I were you, I'd have the same policy. Let's do it anyway. Just to see what happens."

She knew what would happen. Oh, God, did she ever. His sexual magnetism had become more difficult to ignore every time they were together, but she had no intention of screwing up her already screwed-up career. "Let's not."

The automatic headlights, which had been illuminating a swath of chaparral and scrub oak, switched off, cocooning them in the soft, warm darkness. "Here's the thing." He unsnapped his seat belt. "I've let logic rule my life for years, and frankly, it hasn't worked out that well. But I'm an actor now, which officially makes me a maniac, so I'm going to start doing what I want. And what I want"—he leaned into her and pressed his lips over hers—"what I want is this . . ."

All she had to do was turn away. Instead, she let herself enjoy his taste . . . his scent . . . The heady, intoxicating rush. She wanted more.

But her days of sacrificing her best interests for a quick thrill were long over. She sank her hands into his hair, kissed him deeply, thoroughly, then pulled away. "That was fun. Don't do it again."

Paul hadn't really expected anything else. But he'd hoped. He stroked her cheek with his knuckle. She wouldn't believe him if he told her he was falling in love with her, so he didn't intend to. He could hardly believe it himself. At the age of fifty-two, he was finally falling in love again, and with a woman he'd known for years. But even in the days she'd let him bully her, he'd been physically attracted.

He'd always liked women with rounded corners and soft edges. With fluffy hair and eyes the color of Armagnac. Smart, independent women who knew how to make their own way in the world, who enjoyed food, and were more interested in talking to the person in front of them than checking their cells. The fact that he hadn't let himself get close to anyone with those qualities only proved how determined he'd been to keep himself safe from all the messy emotions that had nearly destroyed him.

But even though he'd been physically attracted to Laura, he hadn't respected her, not until the day she'd stood up to him. As he'd witnessed her integrity, her caring, she'd gotten under his skin, and she'd sealed the deal when she'd finally made him remember he was an actor. She'd known what he needed before he knew it himself.

These past weeks he felt reborn, sometimes as wobbly legged as a newborn colt, other times filled with a sense of rightness. He couldn't believe he'd allowed himself to stay lost for so long. Only his concern for Georgie shadowed his perfect contentment. That and the nagging worry he wouldn't be able to get past the very sensible barriers Laura would insist on maintaining between them.

But he had a game plan, and tonight he'd made his first move by letting her know that more than business lay between them. He intended to take it slow from here so she had plenty of time to adjust to the idea that they belonged together. There'd be no sudden moves. No baring of the soul. Just a patient, deliberate pursuit.

Then her purse slipped from her lap, and as she bent over to retrieve it, she bumped her forehead against the glove compartment, and his plan dissolved. "Laura, I'm falling in love with you."

He was so stunned to hear himself say it aloud that her burst of laughter barely registered. "I know it's crazy," he said, "and I don't expect you to believe me, but it's the truth."

Her laughter grew brighter. "I never knew you were such a player. You don't really think I'm going to fall for a line like that." Still laughing, she rubbed her forehead and gazed into his eyes. She took her time, paying attention as she always did. Tilting her head. Taking him in. Gradually her laughter faded, and her lips parted ever so slightly. Then she did something that truly shocked him. She read his mind. "My God," she said. "You're serious."

He nodded, unable to speak. Long seconds ticked by. He gave her the time she needed. Her bra strap slipped off her shoulder. She blinked.

"I'm not in love with you," she said. "How could I be? I'm only getting to know you." She pinned him with those brandy eyes. "But ohmygod, am I ever in lust, and I swear to God, if this doesn't work out, and you even think about firing me"—she unsnapped her seat belt—"I will blackball you with every casting agent in town. Is that understood?"

"Understood," he said, just before she attacked.

It was glorious. She cupped his jaw in both her hands and let their mouths play. As she offered him the sweet tip of her tongue, a wash of tenderness made his arousal all the more powerful. He slid far enough out from beneath the steering wheel for her to slip a knee over his thigh. Her flyaway hair brushed his cheek. Their kiss grew more urgent. He had to touch her, feel her. He curled his palms around her sides. Beneath the thin silk of her dress, her flesh was a poem of sensuality.

"I love you," he whispered, no longer caring about his game plan.

"You're a lunatic."

"And you're a delight."

He hadn't done anything like this in a car since he was seventeen, and it was no more comfortable. He fumbled for her zipper and managed not to make a muddle of lowering it. His hands slid inside her dress. He touched her bra.

"This is insane." She groaned against his mouth as he peeled her bra down far enough to suckle her. Her fingers plowed through his hair, and her head fell back.

The car had become their enemy. She pulled at his shirt, scratching him with her ring. Somehow he lifted her far enough so he could slide beneath her into the passenger seat, but not before he caught an elbow in the jaw and her knee jabbed his side. Finally, she straddled him. With their mouths still joined, he reached under her skirt . . .

Their caresses grew hotter. Her hand, bawdy and wise . . . Clothes in the way. Another lush kiss, and then he was inside her. Loving her. Filling her. Pleasuring her. Claiming her as his own. The sounds of their groans, their breath, their melding bodies, rushed in his ears. She clutched him. Went rigid. They hung . . . suspended . . . flying . . . dissolving.

Afterward he stepped out of the car to decompress and surreptitiously eased a kink from his back. She joined him a moment later.

"That," she said matter-of-factly, "was crazy-ridiculous. Let's pretend it never happened."

He gazed up at the stars. "Perfect. Then we can look forward to our first time."

Her toughness slipped away, leaving concern be-hind. "You're really serious about this, aren't you?"

"Yep." He put his arm around her. "And I'm just as shocked as you."

"Amazing. You're an amazing man, Paul York. I'm looking forward to making your acquaintance."

He turned his lips into her soft hair. "Is it still only lust for you?"

She rested her cheek against his shoulder. "Give me a couple of months to get back to you on that."

Georgie couldn't find her moorings. She lay on a teak chaise as the late-afternoon sun slanted over the white stone patio. It was Tuesday afternoon, exactly sixteen days since she'd arrived in Mexico. She would force herself to go back to L.A. before the end of the week instead of staying here forever as she wanted to. Stay here until she figured out what new form her life should take. Unless she was in front of the computer she'd bought a few days ago, she couldn't concentrate on anything. She hurt too much.

A pair of geckos scurried into the shade. Boats bobbed in the distance, their windshields flashing like strobes in the sun. It was too hot for her to lie out any longer, but she didn't move. Last night she'd dreamed she was a bride. She'd stood by a window in her gown, wisps of white ribbon in her hair, and watched Bram approach through a gossamer lace curtain.

The gate creaked on its hinges. She looked up, and there he was, sauntering onto her patio as if she'd conjured him, but the romantic bridegroom of her dream now wore gunmetal gray aviators and a surly expression. She hated the way her stomach dipped. He was lean, tall, and healthy, the years of dissipation long behind him. Her self-absorbed, self-destructive bad boy had stopped being a bad boy years ago, only no one had noticed. The constriction in her throat made words impossible.

Through the lenses of his sunglasses, he took her in from her sweat-damp hair to her purple bikini bottom and then to her bare breasts. The patio was private and she hadn't expected a visitor, especially this visitor, so here she was, topless when she least wanted to be.

"Enjoying your vacation?" The soft rumble of his voice drifted over her skin like the leading edge of a storm.

She was an actress, the cameras had started to roll, and she found her voice. "Look around. What's not to love?"

He wandered toward her. "You should have talked to me before you ran out."

"We don't have that kind of marriage." Her arm felt rubbery as she reached for her yellow-and-purple-striped cover-up.

He snatched it from her hand and flicked it across the patio, where it landed on a small table. "Don't bother getting dressed."

"Smooth." She walked over to fetch it, counting slowly under her breath so she didn't rush, letting her hips sway in the tiny purple bikini bottom—maybe in a last-ditch effort to make him fall in love with her? But he wouldn't. Bram didn't fall in love, not because he was as self-centered as he believed, but because he didn't know how.

She slipped on the cover-up and shook out her hair. "This is a wasted trip. I'm going back to L.A. soon."

"So I hear from Trev." His fingers curled into fists at his sides. "I talked to him in Australia a couple of days ago, but I got the full story from the tabs. According to *Flash,* we're both moving into his house while he's on location so we can enjoy summer at the beach."

"My once-retiring P.A. has turned into quite the media mouthpiece."

"At least somebody's watching out for you. What's going on, Georgie?"

She tried to pull it together. "I'm moving into Trevor's house. You're not. It's a good solution."

"A solution to *what*?" He jerked off his sunglasses. "I don't understand that part—why this happened all of a sudden—so maybe you'd better explain it."

He was so cold, so angry. "Our future," she said. "The next phase. Don't you think it's time we get on with our lives? Everybody knows you're working, so it won't seem strange for me to spend the summer in Malibu. Aaron can keep planting his stories if that's what you want. You can even show up for a couple of very public beach walks. It'll be fine." It wouldn't be fine at all. Any contact she had with him from now on would only prolong the agony.

"This isn't how we decided we'd handle it." He jammed the stems of his sunglasses into the neck of his T-shirt. "We have an agreement. One year. I'm holding you to it, every second."

He'd insisted on six months, not a year, but she let that go. "You're not paying attention." Somehow she pulled off Scooter's innocent act. "You're working. I'm at the beach. A couple of public appearances. No one will suspect a thing."

"You need to be at the house. My house. And I seem to have missed your explanation about why you're not there."

"Because it's long past time I started setting a new course for my life. The beach will be a great place for me to take my first steps."

The shadows of an African tulip tree cut across his face as he moved closer. "Your present life course is just fine."

She played the mildly exasperated female even as her heart broke. "I knew you wouldn't understand. You men are all alike." She picked up her towel and clutched it to her chest like a child's lovey. "I'm going to take a shower while you cool down."

But just as she turned to walk back into the house, he stopped her cold.

"I saw your audition tape."

Bram watched Georgie's expression change from confusion to puzzled understanding. He wanted to hold her, shake her, make her tell him the truth.

Her fingers grew slack on the towel. "Are you talking about the tape Chaz recorded for me?"

"It was great," he said slowly. "You were great."

She stared at him with her big green eyes.

"You nailed it, just like you promised," he said. "People underestimate me as an actor. It never occurred to me that I was doing the same to you. We've all done it."

"I know."

Her straightforward response unnerved him. *He* hadn't known, and when he'd seen the tape, he'd felt as if he'd been punched in the stomach.

Last night he'd sat in his darkened bedroom and watched it. As he hit the play button, the blank wall in Georgie's office had come into focus, and he heard Chaz's voice off camera. "I've got things to do. I don't have time for this crap."

Georgie stepping into the frame. Her hair was severely parted, and she wore a minimum of makeup: light foundation, no mascara, the barest hint of eyebrow pencil, and a shockingly deep scarlet mouth that couldn't have been more wrong for Helene. The camera caught her from the waist up: an austere black suit jacket, a white shell, and a set of intricately twisted black beads.

"I mean it," Chaz said. "I need to start dinner."

Georgie pierced Chaz's bluster with Helene's icy imperiousness instead of her normal friendly puppy-dog manner. "You'll do as I say."

Chaz muttered something the mike didn't catch and stayed where she was. Georgie's breasts rose ever so slightly under the suit jacket, and then a smile—a fucking ice-pick smile—curled over the bottom of her face and made that scarlet mouth seem absolutely right.

You think you can embarrass me, Danny? I don't embarrass. Embarrassment is for losers. And a loser is what you are, not me. You're a zero. A nothing. We all knew it, even when you were a kid.

Her voice was low, deathly quiet, and completely composed. Unlike the other actresses they'd auditioned, she didn't emote. No teeth gnawing or scenery rattling. Everything underplayed.

You don't have a friend left in this town, but you still think you've gotten the best of me . . .

The words poured out of her, cold fury prowling behind her bloodred smile, perfectly capturing Helene's selfishness, her guile, her intelligence, and her utter conviction that she deserved whatever she could grab. He sat spellbound until finally, with that smile frozen like black ice on her lips, she came to the end.

Remember how you used to make fun of me when we were in school? How hard you laughed? Well, who's laughing now, funny man? Who's laughing now?

The camera stayed on her, but she didn't move. She simply waited, every cell of her body discharging quiet rage, intractable pride, and dogged determination. The camera wobbled, and he heard Chaz's voice. "Holy shit, Georgie, that was—"

The picture went dark.

He looked at Georgie now, standing across from him on the whitewashed patio, her hair caught up in a sweaty, unkempt knot, her face scrubbed free of makeup, a beach towel dangling at her side, and for a moment he thought he saw Helene's calculating eyes looking back at him—resolute, cynical, astute. He'd fix that. "I woke Hank up this morning and made him look at the tape before he even had coffee."

"Did you now?"

"He was blown away. Just like me. No other actress we've seen has delivered what you did—the complexity, that dark humor."

"I'm a comedian. It's what I do."

"Your performance was chilling."

"Thank you."

Her reserve was starting to unnerve him. He expected her to crow and say she'd told him so. When she didn't, he tried again. "You blasted Scooter Brown into oblivion."

"That was my intention."

She still didn't seem to have registered his message, so he spelled it out. "The part's yours."

Instead of throwing herself in his arms, she turned away. "I need to take a shower. Make yourself comfortable while I get dressed."

Chapter 25

She locked herself in the bathroom and let the water wash over her. She'd been vindicated, and it didn't mean anything. She'd known exactly how good she was. Ironic. The only person's approval she'd needed was her own. How was that for personal growth?

She pulled on the same white shorts and navy babydoll she'd worn that morning and ran a comb through her wet hair. It was time to face him with as much of the truth as she could bear to reveal, but she couldn't do it by herself. She needed help from her most faithful companion.

The cool, compact living area had whitewashed walls, a tile floor, and brown wicker basket chairs with cool blue cushions. Every morning, she opened the sliding glass wall so the patio became an extension of the interior, allowing an occasional gecko to get inside, but she didn't mind. She'd read that some of the species were parthenogenic, meaning the females could reproduce without a male. If only she could do that.

Bram had located the iced tea pitcher in the refrigerator, and he sat with his feet propped on the coffee table, a heavy-bottomed green tumbler balanced on his thigh. He heard her padding across the cool terracotta tiles, but he didn't look at her. "You don't seem as happy about your casting as I thought you'd be."

"Apparently I only had something to prove to myself," Georgie's faithful companion Scooter chirped. "Who'd have expected that?"

"This is the career break you've been waiting for."

"Yes, but . . ." When she hesitated, he swung around to look at her. She held up her hand. "I have something to tell you. You're not going to be happy—I'm not happy. You'll call me every name you can think of, and I won't argue with you."

He rose from the couch and approached her as carefully as if she were an abandoned piece of airport luggage. "You're not staying at Trev's. I mean it, Georgie. I've honored every word of this stupid marriage agreement, and you can damn well do the same."

"You haven't honored it out of nobility. You have your own selfish reasons."

"Doesn't matter," he said. "I've stuck with my end of the bargain, and you need to stick with yours, or you're not the woman I thought you were."

"Fine in principle, but . . ." Time to blurt it out like the bubblehead she wasn't. "Cards on the table, Skipper." She straightened a magazine on the end table. "I can feel myself starting to fall for you again."

"The hell you can."

He hadn't even blinked. She plunged on. "Ridiculous, isn't it. Humiliating. Embarrassing. Fortunately, it hasn't gone very far, but you know me— determined to shoot myself in the foot whenever I get the chance. Not this time, though. This time, I'm nipping this sucker right in the bud."

"You are *not* falling in love with me."

"I can hardly believe it myself. Thank God, I'm only on the fringe." She jabbed her finger toward him. "It's your body. Your face. That hair. You're a total hunk, and, sorry to say, I'm as susceptible as the next woman."

"I get it. This is all about sex. You're fundamentally an old-fashioned girl who needs to believe she's in love to enjoy sex."

"God, I think you're right."

He blinked and, a few seconds too late, realized she'd cornered him. "What I mean is . . ."

"You're definitely right," she said emphatically. "Thank you. No more sex."

"That's not what I meant!"

"The alternative is for me to move back into your house and fall completely in love with you. I'm sure we can both imagine how that would play out. Embarrassing scenes with me crying and begging. You feeling like crap. Knowing me, I'd secretly stop taking my birth control pills. Are you getting the picture?"

"I can't believe this." He shoved his hand through his hair. "You're not that stupid. This isn't love. It's sex. You know me way too well to really love me."

"You'd think so."

"You, of all people, know what a selfish, self-centered womanizing jerk I am."

"I hate myself. Really."

"Georgie, don't do this."

"What can I say? Of all the crazy jams I've gotten us into, this is the worst." When he didn't respond, she licked her lips. "Awkward, isn't it."

"It's not awkward at all. It's you being you. You're too damned emotional. Use your head. We both know that you deserve better than me."

"Finally, we agree on something."

She'd hoped to ease the tension, but his scowl grew more pronounced. "That stupid conversation about falling in love . . . You had me convinced you were worried about my feelings," he said, "but you were just feeling me out."

"Please don't bring that up. Surely you realize what it's costing me to swallow my pride like this and admit that I'm slipping back into that old trap."

"It's temporary. You were sex starved, and I'm a damn good lover."

"What if it's more than that?"

"It's not. Remember that I've been on my semibest behavior. Now I can see what a mistake that was. Pack your suitcase and forget about it. I guarantee it won't happen again."

"Sorry. I can't do it."

"Sure you can. You're making way too big a deal out of this."

"I wish. How do you think admitting something so degrading makes me feel? I'm only hanging on to my self-respect by a thread."

"That's because you're behaving like an idiot."

"And I'm determined to put a stop to it."

"We finally agree." He jammed his fingertips in his pocket. "Okay, I'll compromise. You can move into the guesthouse for a while. Until you get your brain back."

"Too awkward with Chaz and Aaron around. Moving to Malibu is a lot better."

"Chaz already knows about Vegas, and Aaron would do anything for you. The guesthouse is the perfect place for you to deal with your craziness. As for our working relationship . . . When you're on the set, you'll be your normal professional self, and I'll revert to being an arrogant pain in the ass. It won't take you long to come to your senses."

This would be the hardest part of all, and just when she needed her help the most, Scooter disappeared to spread her perkiness somewhere else. Georgie couldn't look at him, so she made her way outside to the stone patio wall. "Bram . . . I'm not taking the job. I'm not going to play Helene."

"What? Of course you are."

She stared down the steep hillside at the red tile rooftops below. "No, I'm really not."

She heard the angry thud of his footsteps coming up behind her. "That's the stupidest thing I've ever heard you say. This is the chance you've been waiting for. All your talk about reinventing your career . . . Was it bullshit?"

"Not at the time, but—"

"Damn it, I'm calling your father!" He loomed at her side. "You're a pro. You don't throw away the opportunity of a lifetime over something this stupid."

"You do when the opportunity of a lifetime could possibly screw you up for years."

"You're not serious."

"I can't risk working with you every day, not the way I'm feeling right now."

He dug in then. He paced the patio, delivering one argument after another. As he moved in and out of the shade, she saw him as he was, a creature of light and shadow, revealing only as much as he wanted. When he paused for breath, she shook her head. "I hear what you're saying, but I'm not changing my mind."

He finally understood she meant it. She watched him retreat into himself, like a sea creature disappearing into a chambered shell. "I'm sorry to hear that." Cold. Withdrawn. "At least Jade will be happy."

"Jade?"

"She's wanted that part ever since the reading at the house. Haven't you figured that out yet? We were ready to make her an offer when I saw your tape."

"You can't give Jade that part!"

"It's going to stir up a hornets' nest all right," he said without a flicker of emotion. "But that means publicity for the picture, and I'm not going to turn down free press."

A roar echoed through her head. She couldn't move, could barely speak. "I think you'd better go now."

"Good idea." He pulled the sunglasses from his shirt pocket with cold, businesslike detachment. "It's Tuesday. You have until the end of the week to change your mind or Jade gets the part. Think about that when you're lying in bed tonight." He slipped the sunglasses back on. "And while you're at it, think about whether you really want to fall in love with a guy who's getting ready to feed you to the wolves."

Two days after Bram got back from Mexico, he returned home from the studio to find Rory Keene standing barefoot in his kitchen, squeezing pink icing blobs onto waxed paper under the supervision of a scowling Chaz. He'd barely slept since he'd returned. He had a sore throat, a nagging headache, and a perpetual upset stomach. All he wanted to do was bury himself in work.

"They're supposed to be roses," Chaz complained. "Did you pay attention to anything I told you?"

He winced as Rory slapped down the icing tube. "If you'd go a little slower when you demonstrate, I might be able to do it right."

When would Chaz figure out she was supposed to suck up to important people? He made himself care. "You'll have to excuse my housekeeper. She was raised by wolves." He dragged himself closer to study the pink blobs. "Looks delicious."

Rory and Chaz both practically sneered at him. "That's not the point. They're ornamental," Rory said, as if he should have known. "I've always wanted to learn cake decorating, and Chaz is teaching me the basics."

"A special-ed class," Chaz muttered.

"I'm an executive," Rory retorted, "not a pastry chef."

"That's for sure."

"Beat it, Chaz." Being with Rory always put him on edge, and he didn't trust himself to deal with both of them now.

"We're right in the middle of—"

"Go!" He nudged her out the door.

Rory picked up the icing tube and pressed the tip to the waxed paper. They hadn't spoken since their initial meeting in her lavish suite of offices on the Vortex lot, but the icy blonde in the gray silk suit sitting at a burled wooden desk beneath an enormous Richard Diebenkorn abstract painting didn't bear much resemblance to this woman in blue jeans with bare feet, a ponytail, and pink smudges on her fingers. He rubbed his back and headed for the refrigerator. "Sorry about Chaz. You basically have to ignore her."

Rory concentrated on squeezing out a C-shaped squiggle. "What's going on with Georgie?"

"Georgie? Nothing." He took his time reaching for the iced tea pitcher.

She deposited another squiggle next to the first one. "I hear from Chaz she's disappeared."

"Chaz only thinks she knows everything." He wished he still smoked. It was easier to look cool with a cigarette than a tumbler of iced tea. "We've decided to spend the summer at Trev's beach house. His new one. He sold his old house last month. It'll be weekends only for me while I'm working, but she's there now." At least she was according to Aaron's latest insider tip to the entertainment press, which had also included a description of Bram and Georgie's nonexistent reunion, along with a mention of their plans to spend romantic summer weekends at the beach house. Aaron was getting good at lying.

Rory jabbed the icing tip toward her misshapen blob. "Damn it. This is a lot harder than it seems." She finally looked up. "You can either tell me the rest now or we can talk in my office, along with Lou Jansen and Jane Clemati from Siracca."

A meeting he wanted to avoid at all costs. "About?"

She focused on creating a new set of rose petals. She wasn't going anywhere, and he finally gave in. "You must have heard about the audition tape."

"I've seen it. She's brilliant, and you need her."

He went for Johnny Depp cool, but the best he could do without a cigarette was to lean against the counter with his iced tea glass and cross his ankles. "My wife has a mild case of cold feet, that's all. I'm dealing with it."

"And what brought on this sudden case of cold feet?"

The head of Vortex shouldn't be involved with casting decisions on a small-time Siracca film, and he was more than a little sick of Rory's self-appointed role as Georgie's protector. "Georgie's been through a lot these last few years. She doesn't feel like taking any more risks right now." He fought to control his temper. "I intend to change her mind, and I'd appreciate it if everybody would get off my back while I do that."

"Really?" The lift of her eyebrow showed she didn't believe a word. "Here's what I think happened. I think you screwed up. Again."

Depp wouldn't flinch, and neither did he. "I didn't."

"According to everyone I've talked to, including Chaz, Georgie wanted to do this picture right up to the day before the audition." She tossed down the icing bag. "Georgie's a pro, and I've never heard of her getting cold feet. That leads me to believe she bowed out because, for some reason, she doesn't want to work with you."

He unclenched his jaw muscles. "You're the one who doesn't like working with me, not Georgie."

"I went to bat for you, Bram. Not just because I love the script, and not just because you gave a great reading. I went to bat for you because Georgie believes in you. Or at least she used to." She snatched the dish towel from the countertop and wiped her hands. "Don't kid yourself. A lot of people expect you to screw up, and this is exactly the scenario they've been waiting for. If you don't want to end your career hosting game shows, I strongly suggest you sort out your problems with your wife and get her in front of the cameras where she belongs."

"Is that all?"

"Tell Chaz I'll be expecting another lesson soon."

She strode past him out the back door.

Bram shut his eyes and cupped the cold glass in his palms. Rory's unwelcome visit fed the guilt he'd been living with every day, even though the lie he'd told Georgie had been for her own good. Because of her, his dream was going to come true, and as soon as she worked through this drama she'd created, she'd be grateful he hadn't let her throw away her own golden opportunity.

But a lie was a lie, and he couldn't back away from his dishonesty regardless of how much he wanted to.

The next morning, he pulled on shorts and a T-shirt and headed for Malibu. This time, only two black SUVs followed. Despite a stormy forecast, the Friday-morning traffic was brutal, so he had more time than he wanted to think. As he pulled up at Trev's house, he waved at the paps before they peeled off to search for parking, something they'd have a hard time finding today.

Georgie didn't answer the door, so he used the key Trev had given him. The house was quiet, but the open doors to the deck revealed an abandoned yoga mat. Trev lived on one of Malibu's most exclusive beaches, but today the impending storm had thinned out the sun worshippers. He got rid of his shoes and walked out onto the sand. The star of a TV cop drama lounged next to his third wife while his kids dug a ditch. A container ship chugged against the horizon, and a flock of gulls cried overhead.

Georgie stood alone near the water's edge, the wind whipping her dark hair. The same purple bikini bottom she'd worn in Mexico clung to her bottom, and her skimpy white T-shirt ended well above her waist. When had she grown so beautiful? He wanted to drag her into the house, pull off that little purple bikini bottom, and bury himself inside her.

She spotted him, but she didn't exactly throw her arms around him as he came up next to her. He missed her oversize enthusiasm more than he could ever have imagined. "Is your heart leaping at the sight of me," he said, "or have you wised up?"

"Some mild skittering. Nothing I can't handle."

"Glad to hear it." But he wasn't glad. He wanted her to laugh and kiss him. "Let's go for a walk." He grabbed her hand before she could protest.

Famous faces were a dime a dozen on this stretch of sand, and no one did more than nod as they passed. One of the best parts of his relationship with Georgie was never feeling as if he needed to make conversation, but today that ease had disappeared. "Guess who's taking cake-decorating lessons?"

"No idea."

He told her about Chaz and Rory but didn't mention the real reason for Rory's visit. He stalled a little longer by going after a Frisbee that had gotten away from a couple of kids. When he returned, Georgie was sitting in the sand, her arms clasped around her knees.

He sank next to her and watched the whitecapped waves boom toward the shore. "It's going to storm. Let's head over to the Chart House for lunch."

She gripped her knees tighter. "I don't think I can stomach a cozy meal with the man who fed me to the wolves."

He dug his heels into the sand. "I'll take that as a positive sign that you've wised up about me, and this craziness is behind us."

She snagged a strand of her hair. "Unfortunately, what they say is true. There's a thin line between love and hate."

Something unpleasant twisted in the pit of his stomach. "You don't hate me, Scoot. You've just lost what little respect you'd started to develop." He braced an elbow on his knee and studied the dark clouds skidding across the sky. "We made small-screen magic when you couldn't stand me. No reason we can't transfer that to the big screen."

She tilted her head toward him, her funny green eyes somber. "The deadline's passed. Jade has Helene locked up now."

He picked up a beach stone and rubbed it between his fingers. "She's not doing it."

"Oh? And why's that?"

He couldn't postpone this any longer. "Because she was never under consideration."

Georgie sat up straighter. He pitched the stone into the waves. "I lied to you."

She curled her hands into fists.

He couldn't look at her. "I had all kinds of good reasons at the time."

Her mouth twisted bitterly. "You really are a bastard, aren't you?"

"Exactly! I told you I was!"

Flying sand stung his bare calves as she jumped up. He shot to his feet and went after her. "Think about it, Georgie. Now that I've shown my true colors, nothing is standing in your way. The part is yours, and after what I've done, you can take it without worrying about any messy emotional crap getting in your way. You should be glad I lied."

Even as he spoke, he didn't believe a word of it. And neither did she. "I'm going in." She picked up her stride.

He matched her steps. "I'm . . . pretty sure that guy over there has a camera. We need to make out first."

"Make out with yourself." Her heels kicked up pinwheels of sand. He slid his arm around her shoulder, forcing her to a slower pace.

He might as well have been hugging a cactus.

The picture would get made without her. They'd find another actress, maybe not as good, but adequate. Except everyone wanted Georgie, and his job as a producer was to make the impossible happen. He couldn't let any of them—Rory, Hank, the lowliest crew member—see that he wasn't up to that job.

They reached the house as a crack of lightning broke over the surf. He snagged her wrist, pulling her to a stop just as she was about to climb up to the deck. "Georgie . . ." He had trouble getting enough air into his lungs. "I'm not quite sure how to tell you this . . ."

The wind blew another lock of hair over her face. She pushed it back and cocked her head. He released her wrist. "I've . . . missed you these past few weeks. More than I ever thought." Acid churned in his stomach as she continued to stand there, patiently waiting. "Help me out here."

"I don't know what you're trying to say."

"That . . . I didn't realize how much I'd gotten used to being with you until you left. The two of us . . . I thought it was just a great friendship, but—I don't know how to say this." An awning cracked in the wind. "I might be . . . falling for you."

She stared at him.

"Ironic, isn't it. Just when you've gotten over me, now here I am . . . wishing you hadn't."

"I don't believe you."

"That lie about Jade. There was something a little desperate about it, right? I guess I didn't want to . . . admit what I was really feeling."

"What are you really feeling, Bram? You're going to have to spell it out because I'm not getting it."

"You know what I'm saying."

Apparently she'd had enough of his hedging because she turned away and headed up the short flight of stairs.

"It started right here, you know," he called after her. "Not fifteen or sixteen years ago during *Skip and*

Scooter, but right here on Trev's deck three months ago. You and me." She stopped at the top and gazed down at him. He took the steps two at a time to reach her. "Ever since we woke up in the Vegas hotel room, we've been on this crazy Ferris wheel ride." A gust of wind blew a newspaper across the deck. "I kept thinking you were the best friend I've ever had, but now I know it's more than friendship."

"It's sex."

He felt a flash of anger. "Sure, it's sex, but that's not all. We don't have to put on false faces for each other. We . . . understand each other." He rushed on, forcing out the next part even as he hated himself for what he was about to say. "I've even been thinking— Just thinking. Your idea about"—a giant fist squeezed his chest—"about having a baby." She made a soft, indecipherable sound. He plowed on. "I'm a long way from saying let's go for it. I'm just saying that . . . Just that I'm ready to at least talk about it."

She was swallowing his face with her eyes, and he wanted to yell at her, to tell her he was a liar and not to be so damned gullible. Instead, he set aside whatever shreds of honor he had left and went for the big fucking finish. "I'm . . . falling in love with you, Georgie. For real."

She pressed her fingertips to her lips. A boom of thunder shook the deck. "For real?" she whispered.

Pebble-sharp raindrops stung his face, and he nodded.

She didn't do anything. She simply stood there. And then she said his name. "Bram . . ." Opening her arms, she threw herself at him. She wrapped herself around his chest, slid her legs between his, and he wanted to howl at the harm he'd done . . . right until the moment she jerked up her knee and slammed him in the nuts. Through his agonizing wheeze of pain, he heard two words.

"You bastard."

The roar of the wind . . . The stomp of bare feet across the deck . . . The slam of the door as she disappeared inside . . . And the sound of his own wrenching gasps. He clutched the edge of a stone and tried not to pass out. The door opened again and his car keys flew by, over the deck rail and into the sand.

The storm broke.

Georgie stood inside the locked door, clutching herself to keep her insides from boiling through her skin. The rain slashed at the windows, slashed at her. Bram hadn't changed. He was a user, as manipulative as ever, pretending to offer what she most yearned for in order to get what he coveted for himself.

The storm raged outside; a fiercer storm raged inside.

Her sham of a marriage was over, and there'd be no friendly divorce. No Bruce and Demi. This public humiliation would be so much worse than the first time. And she didn't care. Her years of posing and posturing had ended. She'd never be spunky Scooter Brown, the girl who could bounce back from any adversity with a smile and a wisecrack. She was a real woman who'd been betrayed.

And this time she'd have her revenge.

Once Bram was able to move again, he staggered down to the sand and threw himself in the ocean. Oblivious to the angry waves and dark undertow, he prayed for the water to wash away his sins. He dove under a wave, came up, and dove under again. All his life he'd hustled and manipulated, but he'd never done anything as wicked as what he'd just tried to put over on the person who least deserved it.

He saw the wave right before it hit him, a looming tower of water. It crashed on top of him and flipped him over. He twisted, pitched, floated for an instant, then flipped again. Sand scraped his elbow, then something sharp bit into his leg. He lost his bearings. His lungs burned. The current caught him and pulled him—up, down, he didn't know—the selfish current, following its own course without sparing a thought for its victim.

He broke through the surface, glimpsed the shore, then got sucked beneath again by the undertow. She'd become his conscience, his mistress, his guardian angel, his best friend. She'd become his love.

His body shot toward the light—a shimmering glow visible only in his head. He gasped for air, went under, plunged to the bottom. He loved her.

The current caught him and tossed him again, a useless scrap of human flotsam whose life's mission had been to please only himself.

The image of her face came to him, swept him up, seized him, and dragged him until his feet touched bottom. His elbow was bleeding, his leg, his heart. He staggered to shore and collapsed in the sand.

Chapter 26

She'd locked the doors against him. He felt as if his skin had peeled off, the beautiful facade he'd hidden behind ripped away to reveal all the ugliness beneath. He stumbled back to the beach, pulling off his sodden T-shirt and pressing it to his bloody elbow. He located his car keys in the sand, but Trev's house key had been on a separate ring and was nowhere to be found. After a last futile attempt to get Georgie to answer the door, he gave up.

The paps had disappeared. Shivering and bleeding, he made his way to his car and started the long drive back home through the storm. He couldn't imagine how he'd be able to make her understand what had just happened. She'd never believe him. And why should she? He'd even turned her desire for a baby into a bargaining chip.

The full extent of this disaster he'd brought on himself made it hard to breathe. What the hell had he done, and how was he going to fix it? Not with another phone message, that was for sure.

But after he got home, he couldn't stop himself, and when her voice mail picked up, he let it all spill out. "Georgie, I love you. Not the way I said earlier, but really. I know it doesn't seem that way, but I didn't understand like I do now . . ." He rambled on, mixing up his words, his thoughts, trying to get it all out and failing miserably, knowing he'd only made everything worse.

Georgie listened to every syllable of his message, every lie. The words burned into her flesh, leaving bleeding tattoos behind. Her fury was boundless. She would make him pay. He'd taken away what she wanted most, and now she'd do the same to him.

That evening, after Bram was cleaned up and more clearheaded, he drove back to Malibu. The paps must have believed he was still at the beach because no SUVs loitered at the end of his driveway. He'd decided to break down the door if she wouldn't let him in the house, although he doubted that would soften her heart. Along the way, he bought her flowers, as if a couple dozen roses would make a difference, then stopped to pick up mangoes because he remembered she liked them. He also bought her a snow-white teddy bear holding a red heart in its paws, but as he left the store, he realized that was the kind of thing junior high kids did, and he stuffed it in the trash.

As it turned out, the house was dark and her car missing from the garage. He waited around for a while, hoping she'd come back, suspecting she wouldn't. Eventually he headed for Santa Monica, his car still full of flowers and mangoes.

When he arrived at Paul's town house, he futilely scanned the street for Georgie's car. The last person he wanted to face was his father-in-law, and he thought about turning around, but Paul was his best shot at getting to Georgie.

He hadn't seen him since the night of the wedding party, and the visible hostility on his face as he answered the door eradicated any hope Bram might have been harboring that Paul would help him out. Paul's lips thinned as he gave Bram the once-over. "The golden boy looks a little under the weather."

"Yeah, well, it's been a rainy day. A rainy month."

He waited for the door to slam in his face and was stunned when Paul let him in. "Want a drink?"

Bram wanted a drink too much, a sure sign that he couldn't risk having one. "You got any coffee?"

"I'll dig some up."

As Bram followed Paul into the kitchen, he couldn't figure out what to do with his hands. They felt too big for his body, as if they didn't belong to him. "Have you seen Georgie?" he finally managed.

"You're her husband. You're supposed to keep track of her."

"Yeah, well . . ."

Paul turned on the water faucet. "What are you doing here?"

"I'm guessing you already know."

"Tell me anyway."

And Bram did. While the coffee brewed, he began by telling Paul about Las Vegas, only to learn that Georgie had already filled him in.

"I also know Georgie went to Mexico because she thought she was getting too attached to you." Paul pulled a bright orange mug from the cupboard.

"Believe me," Bram said bitterly, "that's not a problem now. What else did she tell you?"

"I know about the audition tape, and I know she turned the part down."

"It's crazy, Paul. She was amazing." He rubbed his eyes. "We've all underestimated her. We fell into the same trap as the public, only wanting her to play variations of Scooter. I'll send you a copy of the tape so you can see for yourself."

"If Georgie wants me to see it, she'll let me know."

"It must be nice to have the luxury of being noble."

"You should try it sometime." Paul filled the mug and passed it over. "Tell me the rest."

Bram described his visit from Rory and everyone's reaction to Georgie's withdrawal. "They know I'm responsible, they want her in the film, and they expect me to fix this."

"Not a good position for a new producer to be in."

He couldn't contain himself. He began pacing the kitchen, making awkward ovals as he told Paul the rest—his trip to Mexico, the lie about Jade, and then the worst, what he'd said to her today. He let it spill out, omitting only the detail about the baby, not because he was trying to protect himself—he was long past that—but because Georgie's desire for a child was her own secret to reveal.

"So let me get this straight," Paul said, an ominous note in his voice. "You lied to my daughter about Jade. Then you tried to manipulate her by pretending you were in love with her. After she threw you out, you magically realized you really do love her, and now you want me to help you convince her of that."

Bram slumped onto a bar stool at the counter. "I'm so fucked."

"I'd say."

"Do you know where she is?"

"Yes, and I'm not telling you."

He hadn't really expected it. "Will you at least tell her . . .? Shit. Tell her I'm sorry. Tell her . . . Ask her to talk to me."

"I'm not asking her for a damn thing. You created this mess. You can damn well fix it."

But how? This wasn't a misunderstanding that could be patched up with roses, mangoes, or a diamond bracelet. It wasn't a simple lovers' quarrel that a few words of apology could repair. If he wanted his wife back, he'd have to do something much more convincing, and he didn't have a clue what that could be.

Georgie came downstairs as he drove away. She hadn't been able to stay in Malibu with Bram pounding at the door, so she'd driven here. "I heard every word." Her voice sounded strange even to herself, so cold, so detached.

"I'm sorry, kitten."

He hadn't called her that since she was a child, and as he put his arm around her, she buried her face in his chest. But her fury burned so strong she was afraid she'd scorch him, and she drew away.

"I think Bram just might be telling the truth," he said.

"He's not. *Tree House* means everything to him, and I'm making him look bad. He'll do anything to get my name on that contract."

"Not long ago, that was exactly what you wanted."

"Not now."

Her father looked so troubled, she squeezed his hand—only for a moment, long enough to reassure him but not to blister his skin. "I love you," she said. "I'm going to turn in now." She temporarily pushed aside her rage. "Go see Laura. I know you want to."

He'd called Georgie in Mexico to tell her he'd fallen for her old agent. She'd been stunned until she'd considered all the women he hadn't fallen in love with.

"Are you getting used to the idea of Laura and me?" he asked.

"I am, but how about her?"

"It's only been four days since I told her how I felt, and I'm making headway."

"I'm glad for you. Glad for Laura, too."

She waited until after he'd driven off before she called Mel Duffy. Jackals were nocturnal creatures, and Mel answered right away. "Duffy."

He sounded sleepy, but she'd wake him up fast. "Mel, it's Georgie York. I have a story for you."

"Georgie?"

"A big story. About Bram and me. If you're interested, meet me in Santa Monica in an hour. The Fourteenth Street entrance to the Woodland Cemetery."

"God, Georgie, don't do this to me! I'm in Italy! Positano. Diddy's got this big fuckin' party on his yacht." He started to cough, a cigarette hack. "I'll fly back. Christ, it's not even eight A.M. here, and there's another goddamn labor strike. Give me time to fly back to L.A. Promise me you won't talk to anybody else till I get there."

She could call a member of the legitimate press, but she wanted a jackal to have the story. She wanted to give it to Mel, who was gluttonous enough to exploit every bloody angle. "All right. Monday night. Midnight. If you're not there, I won't wait."

She hung up, her heart racing, her fury seething. Bram had taken away what she most wanted. Now she'd do the same to him. Her only regret was having to wait forty-eight hours to exact her revenge.

Bram couldn't sleep, he couldn't eat, and he was seriously going to kill Chaz if she didn't stop hovering. At the age of thirty-three, he'd acquired a twenty-year-old mother, and he didn't like it. But then he didn't like much of anything or anyone these days, especially himself. At the same time, a steady sense of resolve had taken hold of him.

"Georgie's not doing Helene," he told Hank Peters on Monday afternoon, two days after that ugly scene at Malibu. "I can't talk her into changing her mind. Make whatever you want of it."

He wasn't surprised when, less than half an hour later, he received a summons to meet with Rory Keene. He stalked past her fleet of alarmed assistants and entered her office without waiting to be announced. She sat behind her burled wood desk, beneath her Diebenkorn painting, and ruled the world.

He kicked aside a wire chair shaped like a backward S. "Georgie's not taking Helene. And you're right. I've screwed up my marriage. But I love my wife more than I've loved anyone, and even though she currently hates my guts, I'd like you to stay the hell out of this while I try to get her back. Got it?"

Several long seconds passed before Rory put down her pen. "I guess our meeting's over then."

"I'd say so." As Bram strode from her office, he knew some of what he had to do. He only wished he could figure out the rest.

Georgie parked her rented Corolla in front of a two-story apartment building just north of the Woodland Cemetery entrance, close enough so she could see Mel arrive, but far enough away to keep him from spotting her until she wanted him to. It was almost midnight, and the traffic on Fourteenth had thinned to a trickle. As she sat in the dark, she found herself remembering it all—from the moment Bram had overheard her proposing to Trev to the stormy afternoon on that same beach when Bram had declared his undying love.

The pain wouldn't relent. She was going to tell the jackal everything. The story of Bram's phony declaration of love would take over the tabs, then make its way to the legitimate press. The reputation he'd been working so hard to polish would be tarnished all over again. Let Bram try to play the hero after she was done with him. She'd hurt herself in the process, but she no longer cared. She was angrier than she'd ever been, but she was freer, too. Her days of letting tabloid headlines rule her existence were over. No more smiling for photographers when she was falling apart. No more posturing for the press to preserve her pride. No more letting her public image steal her soul.

A black SUV pulled up just past the cemetery entrance. She sat lower in her seat and watched in the side-view mirror as the headlights went off. Duffy got out, lit a cigarette, and looked around, but he didn't notice the Corolla. The lies were going to end now. She'd hurt Bram as badly as he'd hurt her. It was the perfect revenge.

The jackal lit a cigarette. She'd begun to perspire, and her stomach wasn't right. He started to pace. It was time. After tonight, there'd be no more subterfuge. She could live honestly, with her head high, knowing she'd fought back, that she hadn't let herself become another man's emotional victim. This was the woman she'd grown into. A woman who took control of her life and her revenge.

The jackal pitched his cigarette into the gutter and headed toward the cemetery entrance. She hadn't counted on that. She wanted to tell her story near the safety of streetlights. A jackal in a deserted cemetery was too dangerous, and she reached for the door handle before he could go any farther. But as her hand closed around the cold metal, something cracked open inside her. Right then, she saw that the jackal inside the car was more dangerous than the one approaching the cemetery gates.

The jackal inside the car was her. This vengeful, furious woman.

She clutched the handle. Bram had betrayed her, and he deserved to be punished. She needed to hurt him, to destroy him, to betray him as he'd betrayed her. But that kind of destruction wasn't in her nature.

She sagged back in her seat and looked at who she was—at who she'd become. The air inside the car grew heavy and stale. One of her feet fell asleep. But she stayed where she was, and slowly, she began to understand her own nature. With a furious new clarity, she knew she'd rather live with the weight of her anger, the burden of her grief, than turn herself into a creature of vengeance.

The jackal finally emerged from the maw of the cemetery, cell phone to his ear. He smoked another cigarette, gave a final look around, then climbed into his car and peeled away.

She drove aimlessly, feeling empty, still angry, not at peace, but clear about who she was. Eventually, she ended up on a seedy section of Santa Monica's Lincoln Boulevard populated by massage parlors and sex shops. She parked in front of a brake shop closed for the night, hoisted her camera bag from her trunk, and set off down the sidewalk. She'd never been alone in a dangerous neighborhood at night, but it didn't occur to her to be frightened.

Before long, she found what she was looking for, a teenage girl with bleached hair and burned-out eyes. She approached her carefully.

"My name's Georgie," she said softly. "I'm a filmmaker. Can I talk to you?"

Chaz appeared at the beach house two days later. Georgie had been sitting in front of her computer, looking at film all morning, and she hadn't even had a shower. As soon as Aaron answered the door, an argument broke out.

"You followed me!" she heard him exclaim. "You don't even like to drive to the grocery, and you followed me all the way to Malibu?"

"Let me in."

"No way," he said. "Go home."

"I'm not going anywhere till I talk to her."

"You'll have to get past me first."

"Oh, puh-leeze, like you can stop me." Chaz stormed past him and soon found the spare bedroom where Georgie had set up her equipment. She was dressed in avenger black right down to her flip-flops. "You know what your problem is?" she declared, advancing on Georgie without preamble. "You don't care about people."

Georgie had barely slept, and she was too drained to deal with this.

"Bram hasn't come home from the studio for the past two nights." Chaz continued her attack. "He's miserable, and it's all because of you. I wouldn't be surprised if he started doing drugs again." When Georgie didn't respond, some of Chaz's fire gave way to uncertainty. "I know you're in love with him. Isn't she, Aaron? Why don't you just go back to him? Then everything will be fine."

"Chaz, stop badgering her," Aaron said quietly as he came up behind her.

Georgie had never imagined Aaron would turn into such a determined watchdog. His weight loss seemed to have given him a new confidence. One Tuesday, when Mel Duffy's story about Georgie's phone call had surfaced, Aaron had gone on the attack and issued a vigorous public denial without even consulting her. She'd told him that Mel's account was true and she didn't care anymore, but he refused to listen.

It was easier to attack Chaz's weaknesses than think about her own. "Here's the thing about people who are always sticking their noses into other people's lives. It's generally because they don't want to deal with their own screwups."

Chaz immediately went on the defensive. "Everything's just fine in my life!"

"Then why aren't you in culinary school right now? As far as I know, you haven't even glanced at those GED workbooks."

"Chaz is too busy to study," Aaron said. "Just ask her."

"I think you're afraid if you step outside the security of what you have now, you'll somehow end up back on the streets." The words were no sooner out of Georgie's mouth than she realized she'd betrayed Chaz's confidence. She felt sick. "I'm sorry, I—"

Chaz scowled. "Oh, stop looking like that. Aaron knows."

He did? Georgie hadn't expected that.

"If Chaz doesn't study," Aaron said, "she won't have to worry about flunking. She's afraid."

"That's bull."

Georgie gave up. "I'm too tired to deal with this now. Go away."

Naturally, Chaz didn't move. Instead, she regarded Georgie with displeasure. "You look like you're losing weight again."

"Nothing tastes good right now."

"We'll see about that." Chaz stormed into the kitchen where she stomped around for a while, banging cupboard doors, opening and closing the refrigerator. Before long, she'd produced a crisp salad and a bowl of gooey mac and cheese. It was comfort food, but not as comforting as having Chaz fuss over her.

Georgie made this big fricking deal out of Chaz borrowing one of her swimsuits and going down to the beach. "Unless you're afraid of the water." Georgie had said it with a kind of sneer, like she was daring Chaz to put on a suit. She knew Chaz hated showing off her body, and she must have decided this was some kind of therapy. But since she'd basically dared her, Chaz had put on the suit, then rummaged around in Georgie's crap until she found a terry cloth cover-up to wear over it.

Aaron lay on a beach towel, reading some kind of lame video game magazine. When she'd first known him, he wouldn't get anywhere near the water. Now he wore new white swim trunks with navy trim. He still needed to lose a few more pounds, so he shouldn't have looked so semihot, but he'd started working out with weights, and it showed. He was also spending money for decent haircuts, plus his contact lenses.

She sat on the end of the towel, her back to him. The cover-up didn't even reach the middle of her thighs, and she kind of tucked her legs under her.

He put his magazine aside. "It's hot. Let's go for a swim."

"I don't feel like it."

"Why not? You told me you used to swim all the time."

"I just don't want to right now, that's all."

He sat up next to her. "I'm not going to jump you just because you're wearing a bathing suit."

"I know that."

"Chaz, you've got to get over what happened."

She poked at the sand with a stick. "Maybe I don't want to get over it. Maybe I need to make sure I never forget so I don't get caught up in anything like that again."

"You won't."

"How do you know?"

"Simple logic. Let's say you broke your arm again, or even your leg. Do you really think Bram would throw you out? Or that Georgie wouldn't step in, or that I wouldn't let you stay at my place? You've got friends now, although you'd never know it from the way you treat them."

"I made Georgie eat, didn't I? And you shouldn't have said that to her about how I was afraid of flunking."

"You're smart, Chaz. Everybody knows it but you."

She picked up a broken shell and ran the sharp point over her thumb. "I could have been smart, but I missed too much school."

"So what? That's what a GED is for. I told you I'd help you study."

"I don't need help." If he helped her, he'd figure out exactly how much she didn't know, and he'd stop respecting her.

But he seemed to understand what she was thinking. "If you hadn't helped me, I'd still be fat. People are good at different things. I was always good in school, and it's my turn to do you a favor. Trust me. I won't be nearly as mean about it as you were with me."

She had been mean to him. Georgie, too. She stretched out her legs. Her skin was pale as a vampire's, and she saw this one little place she'd missed when she'd shaved. "Sorry."

She must not have sounded like she meant it because he wouldn't let it go. "You've got to stop being so rude to people. You think it makes you look tough, but it only makes you seem sort of pitiful."

She launched herself off the towel. "Don't say that!"

He looked up at her. She glared back, her arms rigid at her sides and her hands fisted.

"Stop the bullshit, Chaz." He sounded tired, as if he'd gotten bored with her. "It's time for you to grow up and start acting like a decent human being." He rose slowly to his feet. "You and I are best friends, but half the time I'm ashamed of you. Like that bullshit with Georgie. Anybody with eyes can see how bad she's feeling. You didn't have to make it worse."

"Bram's feeling just as bad," she retorted.

"That doesn't justify the way you talked to her."

He looked like he was ready to give up on her. She wanted to cry, but she'd kill herself first, so she tore open the cover-up and threw it down in the sand. She felt naked, but Aaron only looked at her face. When she'd been on the streets, the men had hardly ever looked at her face. "Are you satisfied?" she cried.

"Are you?" he asked.

She wasn't satisfied with much of anything about herself, and she was sick of being afraid. Leaving the house made her nervous. She was scared to take her GED. Scared of so much. "If I'm nice to people, they'll start to take advantage of me," she cried.

"If they start taking advantage of you," he said quietly, "stop being nice to them."

Her skin prickled. Did it really have to be all or nothing? She thought of what he'd said earlier, that she had friends who'd watch out for her. She hated depending on other people, but maybe that was because she'd never been able to. Aaron was right. She did have friends now, but she still acted like she was alone in her fight against the world. She didn't like knowing he thought of her as a mean person. Being mean wouldn't save her from anything. She studied her feet. "Don't give up on me, okay?"

"I can't," he said. "I'm too curious to see how you're going to turn out when you grow up."

She looked back up at him and saw this funny expression on his face. He wasn't looking at her body or even taking his eyes off her, but she was aware of him in a way that made her feel . . . itchy or thirsty. Something. "Are you ready to swim yet?" she said. "Or do you want to stand here all day psychoanalyzing me?"

"Swim."

"That's what I thought."

She raced for the water, feeling almost free. Maybe it wouldn't last, but for now it felt good.

Georgie edited film during the day and wandered around the more squalid streets of Hollywood and West Hollywood at night, with only her camera and her famous face for protection. Most of the girls she approached recognized her and were more than willing to talk into her camera lens.

She discovered a mobile health clinic that served street kids. Again, her fame paid off, and the health care workers let her ride with them each night as they offered HIV and STD testing, crisis counseling, condoms, and disease prevention education. What she saw and heard during those nights left her heartsick. She kept imagining Chaz among these girls and thinking about where she'd be without Bram's intervention.

Two weeks slipped by, and he made no attempts to see her. She was exhausted to the point of numbness, but she couldn't sleep more than a few hours before she jerked awake, her pajamas damp with sweat, the sheets twisted around her. She desperately missed the man she'd believed Bram to be, the man who'd harbored a caring heart beneath his cynical exterior. Only her work and the knowledge that she'd done the right thing by not giving up her soul for the sake of revenge kept her from despair.

Since the paps weren't prone to lurk in the neighborhoods she visited, no photos of her popped up. Even though she'd ordered Aaron to stop feeding the tabloids his stories of marital bliss, he kept on doing it. She no longer cared. Let Bram deal with it.

On a Friday three weeks after her breakup with Bram, Aaron called and told her to log on to *Variety*. When she did, she saw the announcement:

Casting has been completed on *Tree House*, Bram Shepard's film adaptation of Sarah Carter's bestselling novel. In a surprise move, Anna Chalmers, a virtually unknown indie actress, has been signed for Helene, the demanding female lead.

Georgie gazed at the screen. It was over. Now Bram no longer had a need to convince her of his undying love, which explained why he hadn't tried to talk to her again. She forced on her sneakers and took a beach walk. Her defenses were down, and she was exhausted, or she wouldn't have let herself drift into a sitcom world where Bram would show up at her door, throw himself on his knees, and beg for her love and forgiveness.

Disgusted with herself, she headed back to the house.

The next morning her phone rang while she was at her computer. She dragged herself out of her stupor and squinted at the display on her cell. It was Aaron. He'd flown to Kansas for the weekend to celebrate his father's sixtieth birthday. She cleared the muzziness from her voice. "How's the family reunion?"

"Fine, but Chaz is sick. I just got off the phone, and she sounded really bad."

"What's wrong with her?"

"She wouldn't tell me, but she almost sounded like she was crying. I told her to find Bram, but she doesn't know where he is."

Not in Malibu, Georgie thought, trying to win me back.

"I'm worried about her," Aaron went on. "Do you think . . ."

"I'll drive over," she said.

As she pulled out onto the highway, the sitcom began to play again in her head. She saw herself walking into Bram's house and discovering balloons everywhere. Dozens of them floating at the ceiling with their ribbons drifting in the air. And she saw Bram standing in the middle of them, his expression soft, anxious, tender.

"*Surprise!*"

She punched the accelerator and pulled herself back to reality.

Not a single balloon floated in the empty, quiet house, and the man who'd betrayed her was nowhere in sight. With the paparazzi once again staking out the end of the drive, she'd left her car at Rory's and slipped through the back gate. She set down her purse and called Chaz's name. There was no response.

She made her way through the empty kitchen into the back hallway and up the stairs to Chaz's apartment above the garage. She wasn't surprised to find it simply decorated and scrupulously neat. "Chaz? Are you okay?"

A moan came from what seemed to be the only bedroom. She discovered Chaz lying on top of a crumpled gray quilt, her knees pulled to her chest, her face pale. She groaned as she saw Georgie. "Aaron called you."

Georgie hurried to the side of the bed. "What's wrong?"

She clutched her knees tighter. "I can't believe he called you."

"He was worried. He said you were sick, and obviously he was right."

"I have cramps."

"Cramps?"

"Cramps. That's all. I sometimes get 'em like this. Now go away."

"Did you take anything?"

"I ran out." Her words were nearly a wail. "Leave me alone." She turned her face into the pillow and said, more softly, "Please."

Please? Chaz must really be sick. Georgie fetched some Tylenol from Bram's kitchen, made a cup of tea, and carried it back to the apartment. On her way to the bedroom, she saw a GED workbook open on the coffee table along with a couple of used yellow pads and pencils. She smiled, her first one of the week.

"I can't believe Aaron called you," Chaz said again after she'd taken the pills. "You drove all the way from Malibu to give me some Tylenol?"

"Aaron was pretty upset." Georgie set the bottle on the bedside table. "And you'd have done the same for me."

That drew Chaz out of her misery. "He was upset?"

Georgie nodded and held out the hot, sugared tea. "I'll leave you alone now."

Chaz pulled herself up far enough to take the mug. "Thanks," she muttered. "I mean it."

"I know," Georgie said as she left the room.

She picked up a couple of things she'd left behind, being careful not to even glance in the bedroom. As she came back downstairs, a wash of golden afternoon light splashed through the windows. She'd loved this house. Its nooks and spaces. She'd loved the potted lemon trees and Tibetan throws, the Aztec stone fireplace mantel and warm wooden floors. She'd loved the bookshelf-lined dining room and brass wind-bells. How could the man who'd designed such a welcoming home have such an empty, hostile heart?

And that's when he walked in.

Chapter 27

Bram's shocked expression clearly announced she was the last person on earth he expected—or wanted—to see. Her own face was chalky from too many late nights, and her eyes shadowed, but he looked ready for a *GQ* shoot. He had a crisp new haircut, almost as short as he'd worn it during their *Skip and Scooter* days, and she could have sworn his fingernails looked professionally manicured.

She couldn't bear having him think she'd sought him out. "Chaz is sick," she said flatly. "I drove over to check on her, and now I'm leaving."

She set her shoulders and crossed the room toward the veranda, but he was at her side before she could touch the knob. "Don't take another step."

"No drama, Bram. I don't have the stomach for it."

"We're actors. We thrive on drama." He grabbed her by the shoulders and turned her to face him. "I haven't gone through all this, for you to walk out on me."

The fury she thought she'd conquered burst into flame. "Gone through all *what*? *What* have you gone through? Look at you! You're not even wrinkled. You've been having the time of your life!"

"Is that how you see it?"

"You're producing and starring in a great movie. All your dreams have come true."

"Not exactly. I screwed up with you, remember? The most important person in my life." He trapped her against the French doors. "And I'm trying to fix that."

She gave a dismissive snort. "How?"

He gazed down at her, his stormy eyes telegraphing an Actors Studio version of a tortured soul. "I love you, Georgie."

Fireworks flashed before her eyes. "And why is *that*?"

"Because I do. Because you're you."

"You sound sincere. You look sincere." She sneered and shoved his arm away. "But I'm not buying a word of it."

Someone less cynical might believe honest pain tightened the corner of his mouth. "What happened that day on the beach . . . ," he said. "I know exactly how ugly it was, but I also got the wake-up call I needed."

"Aww, that's swell."

"I knew you wouldn't believe me, and I can't even blame you." He jammed his hands into his pockets. "Just listen, Georgie. We've cast Helene. It's a done deal. What ulterior motive could I still have left?"

No more of the quiet suffering that had followed her breakup with Lance. She let it all spew out. "Let's start with your career. Three and a half months ago, I was the person willing to sacrifice everything to protect my image, but now it's you. Your unsavory past was blocking your future, and you used me to fix it."

"That doesn't—"

"*Tree House* isn't some once-in-a-lifetime project for you. It's the first part of a carefully planned strategy to establish yourself as a respectable actor and producer."

"There's nothing wrong with having ambition."

"There is when you still want to use me to prop up your image as Mr. Trustworthy."

"This is Hollywood, Georgie! The promised land of the divorced. Who the hell—other than Rory Keene—cares whether we stay married?"

"Rory Keene. Exactly!"

"You don't really think I want this marriage to last just so I don't lose Rory's good opinion?"

"Isn't that what you've been doing?"

"What I *was* doing. But that's over. I'm more than happy to stake my career on the quality of my work, not on my marriage."

Her heart had grown calluses, and she didn't believe a word of it. "You'll say anything to avoid a public rift, but I'm done with faking it just so people I don't know will believe I'm someone I'm not. I'm ordering Aaron to stop talking to the press. And this time, I'll make sure he does what I say."

"The hell you are." The transformation started in his eyes, where cold calculation shifted into mulish determination. And then he went a little nuts. He gave her a hard kiss then half pushed, half shoved her ahead of him toward the back hallway. "You're coming with me."

She tripped over her feet, but he had too tight a grip for her to fall. "Let go!"

"I'm taking you for a ride," he retorted.

"Like that's something new."

"Shut up." He pushed her ahead of him into the garage. He wasn't rough, but he wasn't exactly gentle either. "It's time you understand exactly how much I value my respectable reputation." He looked like the wild man of his past.

"I'm not going anywhere with you."

"We'll see about that. I'm stronger than you are, I'm meaner than you are, and I'm a hell of a lot more desperate."

Her fury burned hotter. "If you're so *desperate,* why didn't you try to talk to me as soon as you finished casting Helene? Why didn't you—"

"Because I had something I needed to do first!" He shoved her into the car, and the next thing she knew, they were shooting down the drive and out through the gates with two black SUVs peeling after them.

He turned the air conditioner on full blast, too cold for her bare legs and thin T-shirt, but she didn't ask him to turn it down. She didn't talk at all. He drove like a maniac, but she was too angry to care. He wanted to break her heart all over again.

They hit Robertson Boulevard, which was bustling with Saturday-afternoon shoppers. She leaned forward in her seat as he screeched to a stop at the valet station in front of The Ivy, the paparazzi's second home. "Why are you stopping here?"

"So we can make a promotional appearance."

"You're not serious." One of the paps spotted them and tried to photograph them through the windshield. She'd left the beach house without a stitch of makeup. Her hair was a mess, her T-shirt exactly the wrong shade of blue to go with her wrinkled turquoise shorts, and she'd pulled on her beach sneakers instead of sandals. "I'm not getting out dressed like this."

"You're the one who doesn't care about image, re-member?"

"There's a big difference between not caring about image and going to a decent restaurant in dirty shorts and grimy sneakers!"

Three more photographers pressed against the car, with others darting through the traffic to get to them from across the street.

"We're not eating," he said. "And I think you're beautiful." He jumped out of the car, transferred a wad of bills to the valet, and muscled his way through the shouting photographers to open the passenger door for her.

Mismatched T-shirt and wrinkled shorts. Bad hair, no makeup . . . and a husband who just might love her but probably didn't. With a sense of unreality, she got out.

Mayhem erupted. They hadn't been seen together in weeks, and all the paparazzi starting shouting at once.

"Bram! Georgie! Over here!"

"Where have you two been?"

"Georgie, is Mel Duffy lying about your meeting?"

"Are you pregnant?"

"Are you still together?"

"What's up with the outfit, Georgie?"

Bram wrapped an arm around her and pushed through the crowd toward the brick steps. "Give us some room, guys. You'll get your pictures. Just let us have some room."

Pedestrians gaped on the sidewalk, patio diners craned their necks, and a trio of perfectly dressed purse designers interrupted their conversation to stare. Georgie briefly considered asking to borrow a little lip gloss, but there was something wildly liberating about standing in front of the world looking her worst.

He put his mouth to her ear. "Who needs to call a press conference when we've got The Ivy?"

"Bram, I—"

"Listen up, everybody." He raised his arm.

Georgie felt dizzy, but she somehow managed to curl her mouth in a Scooter-grin. And then she stopped. No more pretense. She was angry, agitated, and sick to her stomach, and she didn't care who knew it. She let everything she felt show on her face.

A crowd blocked the sidewalk. As shutters clicked and video cameras recorded the scene, Bram spoke above the noise. "You all know that Georgie and I got married in Las Vegas three months ago. What you don't know . . ."

She had no idea how he'd spin this, and she didn't care. Whatever lies he told were his own to deal with.

". . . is that we were the victims of a couple of drug-spiked cocktails, and we basically hated each other's guts. We've been faking this marriage ever since."

Her head shot up. For a moment she thought she'd misheard. Bram was willing to stand on the front steps of The Ivy and expose it all?

As it turned out, he was. He told everything—a condensed version, but the facts were there, right through the ugly scene on the beach. She studied the determined set of his jaw and found herself thinking of the formidable movie heroes hanging on his office wall.

The paps had more experience with deception than truth, and they weren't buying a word of it. "You're punkin' us, right?"

"No punking," Bram said. "Georgie's got this new thing about living an honest life. Too much Oprah."

"Georgie, are you making Bram do this?"

"Have you two split?"

They attacked like the jackals they were, and Bram shouted them all down. "From now on, whatever we tell you is the truth, but don't count on us telling you anything we don't want to, even if we have a movie to promote and need the publicity. As for the future of this marriage . . . Georgie's ready to bail on me, but I love my wife, and I'm trying my damnedest to change her mind. That's all you're going to hear from either one of us right now. Got it?"

The paps turned rabid, pushing and shoving. Somehow Bram strong-armed the two of them back through the crowd, holding her so tightly that her feet left the ground and she lost a sneaker. The valets managed to wedge the car door open, and she got inside.

As Bram pulled away, he nearly took out the two photographers who'd draped themselves over the hood. "I don't want to hear another word about ulterior motives." His dark scowl and unsteady voice left no room for argument. "As a matter of fact, I don't want to talk at all right now."

That was fine with her because she couldn't think of one thing to say.

A circus train of SUVs followed them back to the house. Bram zoomed through the gates, pulled up to the front, and braked to a sudden stop before he turned off the ignition.

His labored breathing filled the suddenly quiet interior. He opened the console and took out a DVD. "This is why I couldn't come see you earlier. It wasn't done. I was planning to deliver it tonight." He set the DVD in her lap. "Watch it before you make any more big decisions about our future."

"I don't understand. What is this?"

"I guess you could say it's . . . my love letter to you."
He got out of the car.

"Love letter?" But he'd already disappeared around
the side of the house.

She glanced down at the DVD and took in its hand-
printed label.

SKIP AND SCOOTER
"Going Underground"

Skip and Scooter had ended after 108 episodes, but
the label marked this as EPISODE 109. Clutching the
DVD to her chest, she kicked off her remaining sneaker
and rushed barefoot into the house. She didn't have the
patience to fumble with the complicated equipment in
the screening room, so she carried his cinematic love
letter upstairs and slid it into the DVD player in his
bedroom. She sat in the middle of the bed, wrapped an
arm around her knees, and with pulse racing, hit the
play button.

Fade in on two sets of small feet walking across an
expanse of vivid green lawn. One set sported black
patent leather Mary Janes with ruffled white socks.
The other, shiny black boy's oxfords that brushed the
cuffs of black dress slacks. Both sets of feet stopped
walking and turned toward someone behind them.
The little girl whimpered, "Daddy?"

Georgie hugged herself.

The boy's response was fierce. "You said you weren't going to cry."

Another whimper from the little girl. "I'm not crying. I want Daddy."

A third set of shoes came into view. Black men's wing tips. "I'm here, sweetheart. I had to help *grand-mère*."

Georgie shivered as the camera panned up along sharply creased black slacks to a man's long-fingered, manicured hand bearing a platinum wedding band. The little girl's hand slipped through his.

A close-up of the child's face came into view. She was seven or eight years old, blond and angelic, wearing a black velvet dress and a delicate strand of pearls.

The camera pulled back. A solemn-faced boy of about the same age took the man's other hand.

Cut to a wider angle showing the tall, lean man and two small children from the rear as they walked across the manicured lawn. A shade tree appeared, a broader stretch of lawn, more trees. Some kind of stones. The angle expanded.

Not stones at all.

Georgie pressed her fingertips to her lips.

A cemetery?

Suddenly the man's face filled the screen. Skip Scofield. He was older, more distinguished, and perfectly groomed, as all the Scofields tended to be. Crisp,

short hair, tailored black suit, a respectable dark bur-
gundy tie knotted at the neck of a white dress shirt.
And deep lines of grief etching his handsome face.

Georgie shook her head in disbelief. He couldn't
possibly—

"I don't want to, Daddy," the girl said.

"I know, sweetheart." Skip picked her up. At the
same time, he wrapped his free arm around the boy's
thin shoulders.

Georgie wanted to scream. *It's a sitcom! It's supposed to be funny!*

Now the three stood at the side of an open grave
with black-clad mourners in the background. The boy
buried his face in his father's side, muffling his words.
"I miss Mommy so much already."

"So do I, son. She never understood how much I
loved her."

"You should have told her."

"I tried to, but she didn't believe me."

The minister began to speak off camera, his reso-
nant voice familiar. Georgie narrowed her eyes.

Cut to the end of the service. Close-up of the coffin
in the ground. A handful of dirt landed on the polished
lid followed by three puffy blue hydrangeas.

Cut to Skip and the minister—the minister who had
no place being a minister. "My condolences, son," the
minister said, patting Skip on the back.

Dissolve to Skip and his two weeping children standing alone by the grave. Skip went down on his knees and drew them close, his eyes squeezed shut with pain. "Thank God . . . ," he murmured. "Thank God, I have you."

The boy pulled away, looking smug, almost vindictive. "Except you don't."

The girl splayed her hands on her hips. "We're imaginary, remember?"

The boy sneered, "We're the kids you could have had if you hadn't been such a jerk."

Just like that, the children vanished, and the man stood alone at the graveside. Anguished. Tortured. He picked a hydrangea from one of the floral arrangements and lifted it to his lips. "I love you. With all my heart. This is forever, Georgie."

The screen went dark.

Georgie sat there stunned, then shot off the bed and stalked into the hallway. *Of all the . . .* She raced down the stairs, across the veranda, along the path, and out to the guesthouse. Through the French doors, she saw him sitting at his desk, staring at nothing. As she charged inside, he jumped to his feet.

"Love letter?" she cried.

He gave a jerky nod, his face pale.

She shoved her hands on her hips. "You *killed* me off!"

His throat worked as he swallowed. "You . . . uh . . . didn't think I'd kill *me* off, did you?"

"And my own father! My own *father* buried me!"

"He's a good actor. And a—a surprisingly decent father-in-law."

She gritted her teeth. "I spotted a couple of familiar faces in the crowd. Chaz and Laura?"

"They both seemed to"—he swallowed again—"enjoy the ceremony."

She threw up her hands. "I can't believe you killed off Scooter!"

"I didn't have a lot of time to work on the script. It was the best I could come up with, especially since I had to . . . shoot around you."

"I'll say!"

"It would have been done yesterday, but your angelic fake daughter turned out to be a diva. Total pain in the ass to work with, which doesn't bode well for *Tree House.* She's playing the kid."

"A great little actress, though," Georgie drawled, crossing her arms over her chest. "I know I had tears in my eyes."

"If we ever have a child who acts like that . . ."

"It'll be her father's fault."

That stopped him cold, but she wasn't ready to let him off the hook, even though little balloons of happiness had started to rise inside her. "Honest to God, Bram, that was the stupidest, sappiest, most maudlin piece of cinematic garbage . . ."

"I knew you'd like it." He couldn't seem to figure out what to do with his hands. "You did like it, didn't you? It was the only way I could think of to show you I understood exactly how much I hurt you that day on the beach. You understood that, right?"

"Oddly enough, yes."

His face twisted. "You're going to have to help me, Georgie. I've never loved anyone before."

"Not even yourself," she said quietly.

"Not much to love. Until you started loving me back." His hand slipped into his pocket. "I don't want to hurt you again. Ever. But I've already done it. I sacrificed what you wanted the most." His face twisted. "Helene is really gone, Georgie. The contract is signed. That role meant everything to you—I know it—and I screwed that up, but I couldn't think of anything else to do. Unless I signed another actress, I had no way to prove I need you for yourself."

"I get that." She thought of the painful things people did to themselves and to each other because of love, and she knew the time had come to tell him what she'd only recently figured out herself. "I'm glad."

"You don't understand. I can't fix this, sweetheart, and there's no way I can make that up to you."

"You don't have anything to make up." She said it aloud for the first time. "I'm a filmmaker, Bram. A documentary filmmaker. That's what I want to do with my life."

"What are you talking about? You love acting."

"I loved being Annie. I loved being Scooter. I needed the applause and the praise. But I don't need that anymore. I've grown up, and I want to tell other people's stories."

"That's fine, but— Your audition? That amazing performance?"

"Not a bit of it came from my heart. It was all technique." She chose her words carefully, pulling the pieces together as she spoke, trying to get it exactly right. "Preparing for that audition should have been the most exciting work I've ever done, but it was drudgery. I didn't like Helene, and I hated the dark place she took me to. All I wanted to do was escape with my camera."

He cocked an eyebrow, beginning to look more like himself. "Exactly when did you figure this out?"

"I guess I knew it at the time, but I thought I was reacting to how messy everything had gotten with you. I'd rehearse for a while, and when I couldn't stand it any longer, I'd pick up my camera and pester Chaz, or go interview a waitress. With all my talk about re-inventing my career, I didn't understand I'd already done it." She smiled. "Wait till you see the footage I've shot—Chaz's story, street kids, these amazing single mothers. It doesn't all fit in the same film, but figuring out what goes where is going to teach me so much."

He finally came around from behind his desk. "You're not just saying this so I don't feel guilty?"

"Are you kidding? I love you guilty. It makes it easier for me to wrap you around my finger."

"You've already done that," he said huskily. "Tighter than you can ever imagine."

He seemed to drink in her face. She'd never felt more cherished. They gazed into each other's eyes. Into each other's souls. And neither one offered up a single wisecrack.

He kissed her as if she were a virgin. The tenderest meeting of lips and heart. It was embarrassingly ro-mantic, but not as embarrassing as their damp cheeks. They held each other close, eyes shut, hearts hammer-ing, naked in a way they'd never been. They knew each other's flaws as well as they knew their own, and each other's strengths even better. That made the moment all the sweeter.

They talked for a long time. She wouldn't hide any-thing, and she told him about her call to Mel Duffy and what she'd almost done.

"I wouldn't have blamed you if you'd gone through with it," he said. "And remind me not to ever let you have a gun."

"I want to get married again," she whispered. "Really married."

He kissed her temple. "Do you now?"

"A private ceremony. Beautiful and intimate."

"All right." His hand wandered to her breast, and the lust that had been simmering between them erupted. It took all her effort to pull back. "You can't imagine how hard this is for me to say." She drew his hand to her lips and kissed his fingers. "But I want a wedding night."

He groaned. "Please don't let that mean what I think."

"Do you mind so much?"

He thought it over. "Yes."

"But you'll agree anyway, right?"

He cradled her face in his hands. "You're not going to give me any choice, are you?"

"I am. We're in this together."

He smiled and curled a hand around her bottom. "Poppy has exactly twenty-four hours to put together the wedding of your dreams. I'll take care of the honeymoon."

"Twenty-four hours? We can't—"

"Poppy can."

And Poppy did, although it took her forty-eight hours, and then they banned her from the ceremony, which she didn't like at all.

They were married at sunset on an isolated stretch of beach in a sandy cove. Only five guests stood with them: Chaz and Aaron, Paul and Laura, and Meg, who'd come alone because they wouldn't let her bring a date. Sasha and April couldn't make it back in time, and Bram refused to wait for them. Georgie wanted to invite Rory, but Bram said she made him too nervous, which caused Georgie to hoot with laughter, which in turn forced Bram to kiss her breathless.

They asked Paul to perform the ceremony. Georgie said it was the least he could do after burying her. When he pointed out that he wasn't ordained, they brushed him off. The legalities had been observed months ago. This wedding was a ceremony of the heart.

A Crayola box sunset framed the beach that night. Bouquets of larkspur, iris, and sweet pea spilled from simple galvanized pails tied with ribbons that floated in the warm breeze. Although Georgie had forbidden Poppy to erect a bridal bower or paint hearts in the sand, she'd neglected to mention building a sand castle, so a six-foot seashell-and-flower-bedecked replica of the Scofield mansion rose up near the bride and groom.

Georgie wore a simple yellow cotton dress with a spray of flowers in her dark hair. Bram went barefoot. The vows they'd written spoke of what they knew, what they'd learned, and what they promised. After the ceremony, they sat around a bonfire to feast on crab and Chaz's cream-filled chocolate cupcakes. Paul and Laura couldn't take their eyes off each other, and as the fire snapped, Laura briefly left Paul's side to approach Georgie. "Do you mind about your father and me? I know it's too fast. I know—"

"I couldn't be happier." Georgie hugged her as Chaz and Aaron wandered off, side by side, down the beach.

Bram watched his wife's beautiful face glow in the flames from the bonfire and realized that the panic that had been his silent companion for as long as he could remember had disappeared. If a woman as wise as Georgie could accept him, flaws and all, then it was long past time he accepted himself.

This exquisite, caring, smart, wonderful creature was his. Maybe he should be afraid of failing her, but he wasn't. In every way that counted, he would always be there for her.

As night settled in, Georgie finally noticed a dinghy approaching from a yacht anchored offshore. "What's that?"

"My surprise," he whispered against her hair. "I wanted our wedding night to be on a boat. To make up for the first time."

She smiled. "You did that long ago."

Their guests saw them off with a shower of organic brown rice Meg had brought along. As they rode out to the yacht, Bram held his wife tight. He wanted their wedding night to be perfect. Lance had given her a carriage with six white horses, and Bram couldn't stand the idea of falling short.

As soon as they were on board, he led her through the quiet ship to the largest stateroom. "Welcome to your honeymoon, my love."

"Oh, Bram . . ."

Everything was just as he'd arranged. White pillar candles nesting inside hurricane shades cast a shimmering light across the warm wooden paneling and luxurious carpets. "It's beautiful . . . ," she said in a way that convinced him she'd forgotten all about the carriage and horses. "I love it. I love you." Her gaze moved past him to the bed, and she burst out laughing. "Are those rose petals scattered on the sheets?"

He smiled against her skin. "Too much?"

"Way too much." She threw her arms around him. "I love it!"

He undressed her slowly, kissing all that he uncovered: the curve of her shoulder, the swell of her breast.

He went to his knees and kissed her belly, her thighs, knowing he was the luckiest man on earth. She undressed him just as slowly, and when he couldn't endure it any longer, he drew her to the bed, and the rose petal sheets.

Which had seemed like a good idea, but . . .

He pulled a petal from his mouth. "These suckers are everywhere."

"I'll say. Even here." She eased open her thighs. "Do something about it, will you?"

So maybe the rose petals weren't such a bad idea after all.

The boat rocked beneath them. They made love again and again, cocooned in their private, sensual world, vowing with their bodies everything they'd promised with their words.

The next morning, he awakened first and simply lay there, with his wife cradled in his arms, breathing in her scent, giving thanks . . . and thinking about Skip Scofield. *You're going to need to help me out, pal. I don't have as much practice being a sensitive guy as you do.*

You could start by losing the sarcasm, Skip replied.

Georgie wouldn't recognize me.

At least pick your moments.

That he could do. Georgie nestled closer, and he curled his hand over her hip. *I'm finally one up on you, Skipper. There you are, stuck forever with little Scooter Brown. And here I am . . .* He kissed his wife's soft hair. *Here I am with Georgie York.*

She finally stirred, but she wouldn't let him kiss her until she'd brushed her teeth. As she stepped naked out of the bathroom, he took in a withered rose petal clinging to her nipple and held out his hand. "Come here, wife," he said softly. "Let's get you pregnant."

She shocked him by waving him off. "Later."

He eased up against the pillows and eyed her warily as she pulled her video camera from one of the suitcases delivered to the yacht. "Chaz warned me about this," he said.

She smiled and positioned herself at the footboard of the bed so she was facing him. The morning sun sliding through the portholes buttered her dark hair. He leaned against the pillows and watched her raise the camera.

"Start at the beginning," she said. "Tell me everything you love about your wife."

He could see that she was teasing him, but he wasn't playing her game. Instead, he leaned back against the headboard, cradled her foot in his hand, and did exactly as she asked.

Epilogue

I ris York Shepard was as unhappy as a four-year-old could be. She stood in the middle of her backyard, with her arms crossed over her flat chest, her small foot tapping ominously in the grass, a scowl stretched across her adorable little lopsided face. Iris didn't like it when the attention shifted too far from herself, and even her adoring grandparents had moved away to talk to Uncle Trev.

Bram spotted his daughter from the veranda and grinned. He had a fairly good idea what was coming. So did Georgie, who'd noticed Iris's mutinous expression from the other side of the yard, where she was chasing their toddler son. "Do something," she called out over the heads of their guests.

He thought about it. He could sweep Iris up in his arms and tickle her, or swing her upside down from her heels, which she loved, or even have a little talk with her—something he was getting surprisingly good at—but he didn't. It was more fun to let events take their natural course.

Twenty-five of Bram and Georgie's closest friends had been invited to their annual backyard anniversary party, this one marking five years since their beach-front wedding. So much had happened in those years. *Tree House* had been a modest hit with audiences and a monster hit with critics, which had led to half a dozen juicy acting roles for him. Then, with Rory's back-ing, he'd produced his own screenplay. Audiences had loved it, and his career was set.

As for Georgie . . . She was still interpreting the world through her camera lens and doing a damned fine job of it. Each of her three documentaries was better than the last, and she was starting to pile up some major awards. But as much as they both loved their work, not even filmmaking gave them as much joy as their family.

Chaz began weaving her way through the crowd. As Bram took in her shiny dark bob, cherry red sun-dress, and silver sandals, he could barely remember the desperate girl he'd picked up outside that bar so many years ago. Even the angry young woman who used to rule his kitchen had mellowed. Not that Chaz had lost her sass—she and Georgie could still go at it—but they were all family now—he and Georgie and their kids; Chaz and Aaron; and, of course, Paul and Laura, who'd gotten married in this very backyard.

Their wedding had been Chaz's first job after culinary school. Instead of working at a high-end restaurant as she'd always planned, she'd surprised them by deciding to open a catering business. "I like being in people's homes" was how she'd explained it.

She stopped next to him. "Iris is getting ready to lose it. You'd better do something fast."

"Or I could just stand here and watch her drive Georgie crazy." He sampled a canapé and gestured toward the pool area, where Georgie's former P.A. was engaged in an earnest discussion with April and Jack Patriot. "When are you going to put Lover Boy out of his misery and marry him?"

"After he's made his second million."

"I hate to break the news, but I think he's already done that." Aaron had started his own video game company and hit it big with a game called Force Alpha Zebra. With his toned physique, air of command, and surprising emergence as something of a male fashionista, he'd changed even more than Chaz. Bram grabbed another canapé. "It took the two of you long enough to figure out you were in love."

"I had some growing up to do." Her eyes softened as she gazed at Aaron. "I'll marry him one of these days, but for now, I'm having too much fun keeping him on his toes."

Paul finally spotted his unhappy granddaughter and broke away from his wife, but he was too late. Iris had already chosen her table, a wrought-iron one located in the exact center of the crowded backyard, and begun to climb on top.

"Iris!" Georgie tried to move, but a swing set and their wriggling son kept her trapped. "Iris! Get down."

Iris pretended not to hear. Instead, she carefully stepped around someone's discarded drink, threw her arms wide, and addressed the crowd in a commanding voice far too big to come from such a small body. "Listen to me, everybody! I'm going to sing!"

Aaron put his fingers to his lips and whistled. "You go, Iris!"

Skirting the crowd, Bram made his way to Georgie's side and took their son from her just as Iris opened her tiny mouth and let the music rip. By the time she reached the first chorus of her vigorous and tuneful rendition of the opening number from *Annie*, neither Bram nor Georgie had the heart to pull her down.

"What are we going to do with her?" Georgie said on a sigh.

"I guess we'll eventually have to hand her over to Grandma Laura." He kissed his son's sweaty head. "You know Laura and Paul are dying to see how Iris will audition."

"We know how she'll audition. She'll be fabulous."

"She really is good, isn't she?"

"Not a bad note. She was born to perform. And we don't need another child star in the family."

Bram set their squirming toddler on the ground. "The good news is, she'll never feel as though she has to perform to earn anyone's love."

"True. There's more than enough love here to go around."

They were too wrapped up in smiling at each other to notice their son plop down on his bottom and begin clapping in perfect rhythm to his sister's song. Bram's voice grew husky, the way it so frequently did when he came face-to-face with his blessings. "Who could have imagined a guy like me would end up with a family like this?"

She leaned her head against his shoulder. "Skip couldn't have done any better." And then she winced. "Oh, dear . . . Here comes the tap dance."

"At least she's keeping her clothes on."

But he'd spoken too soon. A little floral sundress floated into the roses.

"She gets that from her mother," he whispered. "I never knew a woman so eager to take off her clothes."

"Not my fault. You're very persuasive."

"And you're irresistible."

Skip Scofield chose that moment to tap Bram on the shoulder. *Who'd have imagined it? You've turned into a family man after all.*

And what a family, Bram thought, gazing around him.

Iris bowed and moved on to her next number. His son rolled over in the grass. And his wife, his very own wife, rose on tiptoe and whispered in his ear. "This is the best reunion show ever."

He couldn't have agreed more.

Author's Note

All of my fictional characters exist in the same creative universe, so astute readers will have noticed the reappearance of some familiar people: April Robillard and Jack Patriot from *Natural Born Charmer;* Fleur, Jake, and Meg Koranda from *Glitter Baby.* I can't resist revisiting old friends and plan to keep on doing it.

Some very special people helped me as I wrote this book. Thank you to Joseph Phillips for sharing his knowledge of Southern California with this midwesterner; to Julie Wachowski for guiding me through the modern universe of filmmaking; to Jimmie Morel, whose insights always help me dig deeper; and to Dana Phillips, who has temporarily given up editing film to take care of the two most adorable children in the universe. Any mistakes are, unfortunately, all mine. (But feel free to blame them!)

More thank-yous to Carrie Feron, my longtime editor and dearest friend, as well as Steven Axelrod and Lori Antonson at the Axelrod Agency. My extraordinary assistant, Sharon Mitchell, is invaluable. Hugs to my family; my sister; to Dawn and the Chili Babes; to my walking buddies, Kathy and Suzanne; to Kristin Hannah and Jayne Ann Krentz; and to the Seppies on my Web site Message Board. Every writer should have so many great people cheering her on.

Finally, a great big curtain call to everyone at William Morrow and Avon Books, with a little extra applause for Lisa Gallagher. I never forget how lucky I am to be part of such an enthusiastic, talented publishing team.

Susan Elizabeth Phillips
www.susanelizabethphillips.com